A LAND
WITHOUT LAW
SAGA OF THE SIERRAS

A LAND WITHOUT LAW

SAGA OF THE SIERRAS

Three Bestselling Novels Complete in One Volume

Cannons of the Comstock

The Year of the Grizzly

Shooting Star

BROCK & BODIE THOENE

Inspirational Press
New York

First Inspirational Press edition published in 1999.

Inspirational Press
A division of BBS Publishing Corporation
386 Park Avenue South
New York, NY 10016

Inspirational Press is a registered trademark of
BBS Publishing Corporation.

Published by arrangement with Bethany House Publishers.

Library of Congress Catalog Card Number: 99-71880

ISBN: 0-88486-253-4

Printed in the United States of America.

CONTENTS

Cannons of the Comstock   1

The Year of the Grizzly   165

Shooting Star   311

CANNONS
OF THE
COMSTOCK

Everything is Jake!

1

THE CLATTER OF hooves on the rust-colored cobble-stones rang like musket fire down the lanes of Richmond, Virginia. As soon as one dispatch rider passed the bronze statue of George Washington, the staccato echo of another's approach could be heard in the distance.

Though they were official couriers charged with bearing military communiqués to the Confederate cabinet, the messengers could not help shouting their reports to the eager citizens who jammed the sidewalks. "The *Cumberland* has been rammed and is sinking!" cried one.

The crowds applauded and yelled their approval. "Hurrah for the *Virginia*! No Yankee blockade shall hold!"

Another rider cantered by.

"What news?" the mob demanded.

"Our iron-hulled alligator has blasted the *Congress* to kingdom come and is turning toward the *Minnesota*," the hoarse-voiced officer croaked.

Directly in front of Washington's statue, the rough, flushed face of Colonel James turned away from the excitement of the street to lock eyes with a small black child perched atop the eight-foot-high block of marble. "You, Mont! Nigger! Look sharp," he demanded. "Don't forget why you're up there, or I'll whup your worthless hide clean off!"

The boy's vantage point on the statue's pedestal lifted him above the heads of the crowd, but he paid no attention to their enthusiasm. The florid-cheeked colonel did not need to remind Mont of his assignment or the merciless temper behind the whip. The child was so intent that he did not even turn his head as yet another dispatch rider galloped past, bearing more news of the great naval battle taking place at Hampton Roads.

The sharp-eyed boy spotted the approaching carriage when it was still a full three blocks away. He could pick it out from all the other traffic on the Richmond street because of its unmatched team of horses. The near horse was a gray, while the off horse was deep chestnut. In an era when respectable gentlemen prided themselves on the perfection of their teams, the object of Mont's search stood out like the wispy beard of President Jefferson Davis.

"He's a comin' yonder," called out Mont in a high treble.

" 'Bout time," grunted Colonel James. "All right, shinney on down here right now."

Mont jumped down from his perch and took his position behind his master as the carriage came to a stop.

The young man who stepped from the carriage was clean shaven. He was not wearing a uniform as Mont had expected, but instead wore a brown suitcoat with a dark brown velveteen collar. The knot of his cravat was crooked, and his movements seemed anxious and hurried. He clutched a scuffed leather portfolio against his chest with both hands and peered nervously up and down the street.

Colonel James made his customary approach. "I'm James," he announced with a squinted eye, "and your name is Hastings."

"Avery Hastings," agreed the newcomer. He extended his right hand, but James ignored it, and Hastings awkwardly brushed it against the leather pouch. "How soon can you get me in to see him?" he asked abruptly.

"Depends," remarked James in a stone-cold voice. "President Davis is a very busy man." The two started to cross the street with Mont trailing along behind. "He don't have time to bother with every crackpot schemer that comes around." The distant patter of an approaching troop of cavalry could be heard from the far end of the avenue.

"Crackpot! Schemer!" bristled Hastings, stopping in his tracks and turning to face his accuser. "Colonel," he corrected in an intense whisper, "I'll have you know that it's in my power to deliver California and *all* its gold into the hands of the Confederacy!"

Colonel James remained unmoved and only returned a silent stare.

Hastings quickly yielded to the silence and asked, "Where is my valise?"

"Boy!" James bellowed at Mont. "Fetch the man's bag and be quick about it." He gave Mont a shove that sent the child sprawling on the cobblestones. "Run, blast you!"

Mont jumped up and dashed back across the road in a flurry of eagerness to please. His dark eyes were serious, and he bit his lower lip as his skinny arms strained to wrest the heavy carpetbag from the carriage.

James and Hastings had turned away from the street to enter an office building, but not before Mont caught an impatient glare that made him redouble his efforts. Raising himself on his tiptoes as he balanced on the carriage's running board, he mustered all his strength to hoist the case upward.

As this last effort freed the valise, Mont jumped backward into the middle of the boulevard without having paid any heed to the cavalry unit now bearing down on him less than fifty feet away. Mont suddenly felt the impending danger of the thunderous noise of hoofbeats penetrate his attention.

Transfixed at the sight of twenty-five riders racing toward him, Mont saw a solid wave of angry-eyed bay war horses that stretched from curb to curb. The ringing of their hooves vibrated through him from the crown of his tightly curled hair to the worn-out soles of his cheap shoes.

The front rank reached him, seemingly a single beast with twenty-four flailing limbs and twelve blasting nostrils. No individual sounds could be distinguished. All he heard was a continuous roll of hoofbeats, shouts and snorts. Mont could not even hear his own scream of terror as the foaming wave crested above him.

Mont awoke with the cry stuck in his throat as the vivid sight of the Confederate cavalry troop replayed once more in his memory. Above the narrow bunk he shared with Nathan Dawson, gingham curtains at the window tossed on a swirl of frosty January air. Sheets and down comforters were damp with the sweat brought on by Mont's recurring nightmare. His heart still drummed in his ears like the echoing hoofbeats of the horses that had borne down on him that long-ago hot afternoon in Richmond. *Was it only his heart he was hearing? Or was it something else?*

A distant rumble of galloping horses seemed to float past the curtains. He covered his face with his hands to shut out the sound and the memory. But the drumming did not diminish. He sat up in bed and stared, trembling, toward the half-open door. If only he could escape the horror of the room— away from the sound . . . away from the dream that would not leave him alone. But his shaking legs refused to move, just as they had stood like wooden posts when the wall of horses had thundered toward him.

He squeezed his eyes tight and forced himself to remember how the brown-suited man had suddenly appeared out of nowhere and propelled him to safety.

A split second more and they would have perished. There had been no attempt to pull back on the stampeding horses. In that frantic moment, Mont had dropped the valise. The bag and its contents had been trampled into unrecognizable scraps of leather and tiny fluttering bits of ragged cloth before those churning hooves disappeared around the corner. Mont had stared in disbelief at the wreckage. It might have been his own body in pieces on the street.

Mortified at Mont's stupidity, Colonel James had sworn to make the boy pay dearly for this public shame. He said it would have served Mont right if he had been trampled. The colonel had whipped the boy with a razor strop every day for several weeks after the incident. But Mont never dreamed about the sting of leather on his bare backside. He only re-lived the vision of those approaching horses.

Tonight he could not escape the nightmare. He was awake. At least he *thought* he was awake. This was California, not

Richmond. His brutal master was long since dead. Mont now lived at the ranch of the widow Dawson with her two sons, Jed and Nathan. Eight-year-old Nathan was snoring soundly beside him. Why, then, could he still hear the sound that carried his mind back to that violent Richmond street?

Another gust of wind off the Sierras carried the rattle of iron shoes on ice-hardened dirt lanes. *Still dreaming?*

He reached out a finger in the darkness and poked Nathan as yet another shudder of fear coursed through his thin body.

"Huh?" Nathan responded sleepily. "Wha . . . Mont?"

"I hears h-hawses," Mont stuttered.

"You're dreamin' agin," Nathan moaned unhappily.

The ghostly drumming rose and fell. This was *no dream*! Now Nathan heard it too and lay silently listening for a moment.

"Hear dat?" Mont whispered.

"Uh-huh." Now Nathan sat up beside Mont and scrambled to the window. Ducking beneath the curtain, he squinted out across the dark yard toward the barn. Mont squeezed in beside him, greatly comforted that the hoofbeats were not merely in his mind, and that his legs were working again.

The tiny orange flare of a match erupted behind the window of the lean-to where Nathan's uncle, Tom Dawson, lived beside the barn. Then the light became brighter as Tom lit the kerosene lamp.

"Uncle is up," Nathan said reassuringly. "Ain't no ghosts we're hearin', I guess."

From the lower bunk, Jed called out, "Go to sleep or I'm tellin' Ma . . ."

Mont did not take his eyes from the back-lit figure of Tom Dawson as the big man wrapped a blanket around his shoulders and stood beside the lamp to listen. Craggy, sunbrowned features displayed concern. Tom reached down to grasp his carbine and put it by the door. Then Mont could see him tug on his trousers and his boots. The sound of approaching horses grew louder.

"Comin' this way," Nathan muttered.

By now the increasing noise of hoofbeats had stirred Jed to a wakeful apprehension. "What is it?" He pulled his comforter tight around him and climbed up to join Mont and Nathan at the window. At the sight of his uncle emerging from the lean-to with rifle in hand, Jed added, "Call Ma!"

A gray swirl of morning fog hung at streetlamp height above the intersection of Montgomery and California streets. The bustling activity of San Francisco's business district had not yet begun. A solitary pedestrian paused in the shadows in the middle of the block, beyond the reach of the lamplight. In unhurried fashion, he extracted a cigar from his waistcoat pocket and lit it. Ducking his head toward the match cupped in his hands, he took the opportunity to scan the sidewalks. Satisfied that no one was following him, he walked briskly toward an even deeper gathering of darkness and plunged quickly into it.

One knock thumped on the alley doorway leading into the building of the Atlantic and European Express Company. After a pause, two knocks followed, then another pause and one more.

A gravelly voice from within demanded, "What is it?"

"An inquiry about shipping" was the short reply.

"Why so early?" The voice from the interior of the building sounded gruff and irritated.

"It is never too early for important business" was the precisely spoken response, every word distinct.

There was a rasping noise as a heavy bar was lifted inside, followed by the sound of two iron bolts being drawn.

"Come in slowly, friend," the whiskey-roughened voice instructed. "And don't do nothin' fancy."

The man with the cigar nudged the door open with his foot and slowly advanced into the spotlight of a bull's-eye lantern that shown directly into his face, blinding him. He carefully held both hands open in front of his expensively tailored coat. When he had moved to the center of the dingy room, he saw that the lantern hung from the bannister of a dilapidated wooden staircase leading upward. The door quickly closed behind him, and the bolts clanked back into place.

"Up the stairs," he was told.

Halfway up, it struck him that he had never seen the form, much less the face, of the doorkeeper. "Very impressive," he muttered to himself through teeth clenched around the smoldering cigar.

Emily Dawson's room was below the loft where Mont and her sons were sleeping. But it was not the noise of the approaching horsemen that awakened her—she had roused before first light to stir up the fire. The new day promised to be fair and clear-skied, but the feeble light of the winter dawn would be a long time warming the air.

The rocky battlement known as Shadow Ridge curled down among the foothills of the Sierra Nevadas into as pretty an oak-trimmed valley as existed anywhere in the world. Three thousand feet above the level of the Pacific Ocean which lay one hundred and fifty miles or so to the west, the Dawson ranch sat safely above the malarial fogs of the Great Central Valley, but lower than the redwood-studded backbone of the Sierras. The high passes were shrouded now with snow and would be uncrossable till spring, but in the watershed of the Poso, life went on.

Emily's husband Jesse had located well, and had made a good life of farming potatoes and breaking horses. The Union army had proved a ready customer for both.

At first The War between the States had been only a distant source of unhappy news, until a Confederate conspiracy reached California and engulfed the Dawson home. Jesse and his brother Tom had been close to uncovering the secrets of Shadow Ridge when Jesse was tragically murdered.

Listening to the hoofbeats, Emily paused as she ran a brush through her honey-blonde hair. Her fair complexion was smooth, but a deep sadness lingered in the depths of her blue eyes. Like Mont, she also noted when the approaching riders turned to cross the creek.

Drawing her dark blue dressing gown tightly around her, Emily looked for a shawl to throw over her shoulders. Best see that her brother-in-law Tom was awake.

Shadow Ridge was still thick with Southern sympathizers.

As battles raged in the East, tempers flared higher here in the West. Why would riders come to the ranch at this hour unless they meant to settle some old score?

2

AS HIS APPREHENSION mounted with the approaching riders, Tom Dawson levered a round into the fifteen-shot Henry rifle he carried. The cold of the brass receiver was enough to make his hand ache, but he took no notice. Five purposeful strides across the yard and he reached up to knock on the door of the house.

"Em!" he called. "Wake up, Emily. Riders coming!"

The door opened at the first knock and Emily stood regarding him, a worried frown printed across her delicate features. "I heard them too," she said worriedly. "What do you suppose it is?"

"More'n likely nothing fretful. But it's a sight too early and icy for this to be a social call. You and the boys stay inside with the door bolted till we see."

"Aren't you coming inside?" she asked, concerned.

"No, I'll be just across the way there." He jerked his thumb over his shoulder toward the corral. "Get Jed to watch the creek side of the place in case someone sneaks up that way, and you—"

"I'll be right here beside the window," she vowed coolly, pulling a twelve-gauge double-barrelled Thomas shotgun into view.

"Good girl," Tom said with a grin. "You just keep out of sight, and if need be," he paused to nudge her shotgun's barrel, "let 'buck' do the talking for you."

Taking his position, Tom stood in the angle formed by the corral fence and the wall of the barn. From there he had a clear field of fire without shooting toward the house, and a line of retreat into the barn if he needed one.

He went through the preparations for battle with a mechanical detachment, loading the Henry's tube magazine and checking the Colt Navy revolver. All the time his conscious mind was racing through a series of questions. Who could be coming? There were gangs of men calling themselves Southern sympathizers, but who really were only thieves and murderers of the lowest sort. There had been raids by Confederate regulars into New Mexico and Arizona as well as the threat that they would rush into California.

Tom's last gun battle with one such outlaw came swiftly to mind. The ache in Tom's right hand was a constant reminder of that fight. Byrd Guidett was buried, unmarked and unmourned, in the pauper's corner of Oak Grove Cemetery, but who knew the whereabouts of the other outlaws with whom he rode?

Tom crouched lower than the top rail and peered over the second whip-sawn two-by-twelve. Where he had placed himself gave him some advantage, but it wasn't perfect. Looking east as he was, the riders would be coming toward him out of the morning sun, which was just now climbing over Greenhorn Mountain.

Sounds like five or six riders coming, he thought. *Not good odds if they're hostile. 'Course*, he reassured himself, *this isn't exactly a sneak attack either.*

The approaching riders turned the last corner off the road and onto the lane leading up to the Dawson ranch. The jingle of harness rings now joined the rhythmically snorting breath of the horses. From the barn, Tom's own favorite mount, Duncan, bugled a warning.

They finally moved into his lane of sight, a moving mass of dark-garbed men on muscled bays. Puffs of vapor from the horses' nostrils streamed back along the trail, as if tracing the passage of a steam locomotive. Brass buttons glinted on the men's caps and shoulders. Sunlight flashed on carbines slung over shoulders. Military men, for certain—but, against the morning's glare, what color coats did they wear? Blue or gray?

A tall, broad-shouldered figure rode at the head of the column of twos. He was flanked by a much shorter man dressed in lighter-colored clothing than the rest. The smaller man seemed to be haranguing the larger, who ignored him.

They clattered into the yard. The horses milled about and called out to those in the barn.

"Hello the house," called out the leader of the troop in a resonant bass voice. A reedy echo from the smaller man repeated the phrase. The two sat their horses nearest the door and were ringed by a semi-circle of four others dressed in the dark blue uniforms of the United States Cavalry.

Tom blew a sigh of relief and eased his grip on the carbine. He stepped up on the bottom rail of the fence and casually swung the Henry across his arm. "Morning, Colonel," he called. "What brings you and Deputy Pettibone out here so early?"

The worn stairs in the warehouse of the Atlantic and European Express Company swayed under the weight of the cigar-smoking man. He passed two landings with branching walkways leading into dusty storerooms, then the rickety treads made an abrupt turn and zigged back the other direction.

He knew he was being watched. He could almost feel the eyes peering at him from the dark shadows. The man smiled to himself because anyone trying to observe him would be able to track only the glowing tip of his cigar on the darkness-shrouded stairway.

A faint illumination suddenly appeared above him at last. The rectangular outline of a curtained doorway loomed above him, showing a rim of lantern-light from a room beyond.

The man straightened his necktie and tile hat, then brushed a speck of ash from his coat lapel. Satisfied with his appearance, he pushed past the curtain and found himself in an anteroom confronting a pair of sliding oak doors. The solidly built doors were tightly shut, as if guarding the treasure room of some ancient king. *Or his tomb*, the man thought wryly.

He gave the same pattern of knocks as he had used to gain entrance to the building, but this time a voice from within inquired through a tiny wrought-iron grill, "Who comes here?"

"A knight" was his reply.

"A knight of what allegiance?" the voice demanded.

"A knight of the Golden Circle."

"And where are you bound, Sir Knight?"

"From darkness to light, from oppression to freedom; and on the glorious destruction of all tyrants."

"Enter, Brother Knight."

The room into which the new arrival ventured was grim and unappealing. The windowless walls were bare brick and the air was thick and oppressively dust-laden. He immediately felt as if he were choking.

A single lantern, reeking of rancid whale-oil, sat on a circular table. Around the circle were nine seated men and a single empty chair. No greeting was given as he entered. Instead, the men sat in silence, waiting for the meeting to begin.

At the touch of an unseen doorkeeper, the oak panels slid shut behind him. Directly opposite the entry sat a man whose face was masked. He was sitting rigidly upright in a throne-like chair. Its scroll-carved back rose higher than the others, and the cigar-smoker instinctively looked to its occupant for instruction.

But it was a man with a high forehead and a pointed beard seated on the left who spoke first. "Take your place, Brother Knight" was the order. An imperious wave sent the newcomer to the empty chair.

The bearded man continued, "The first meeting of the Knights of the Golden Circle for the year 1864 will come to order. The situation grows critical, and time is short, so we will dispense with formalities. Each of us has committed to finding and recruiting ten men of uncompromising convictions and unquestioning loyalty to the cause of the South. Each of those ten captains will be responsible for raising a company of soldiers under our command . . . twenty-five hundred men armed and ready to strike . . . within four months."

An outburst of noisy whispers erupted. Biding his time, the speaker grasped his beard thoughtfully, his head inclined toward a young, clean-shaven man seated on his left. The babble around the table concerned the timespan named; no one thought that four months were adequate time to recruit and train such a number for their purpose.

Eventually, the hurried consultations subsided and the speaker resumed his remarks. "There are many good reasons why we must strike soon. Last November, before the victory of that cursed fiend Grant at Chattanooga, we almost had the French and the British convinced to recognize the Confederacy. Gentlemen, we need California, and we need it *now*!"

He paused to allow his words to make their impact, then laid an approving palm on the back of the young man on his left. "We know how to obtain the necessary arms. Will you please tell us Bro . . . , ah, but no. Where are my manners? We should hear first from our new acquaintance. Brother Franklin, late of Washington, D.C."

The man with the cigar crushed it out under his bootheel, stood up and looked at each man seated around the circle, then cleared his throat. He explained how he had been privy to certain war department planning sessions and could speak with authority on Grant's plans for the Union's spring campaigns.

"He will attack Atlanta, that's certain, and Mobile after the fall of Shreveport. It will cut the South in two. We desperately need your aid, brothers. You must prevent the flow of gold and silver from reaching the blood-stained hands of the baboon king, Abe the First. That's why I was despatched here personally: to urge your immediate action and to carry back encouragement to our brave leaders by telling them of your progress."

As Franklin sat down, the leader in the mask nodded his appreciation of this message and spoke at last. "Atlanta and Mobile . . . truly terrifying and calamitous! It must be prevented at all costs. Exactly what our other source has indicated." His voice sounded muffled and sinister.

"What other source?" queried Franklin in consternation. "Only I was sent to bring you this secret and carry back your plans."

"Carry back our plans, eh? No doubt, no doubt. . . . Seize him!"

The two men seated on either side grasped Franklin's arms and pressed them firmly against the table top. A third attacker swung around and dropped a loop of rope over his body, securing it to the chair.

"What is this?" he sputtered. "This is an outrage!"

"Gentlemen," said the bearded man, "I give you not Franklin of the Golden Circle, but Sterling of the Pinkertons!"

The man now identified as Sterling continued to squirm against the rope and protest his innocence. "I am Franklin," he insisted.

"No," corrected the masked leader sternly. "We know that Franklin was killed. Obviously, your masters did not know that we already had gotten word of his death."

Sterling's eyes grew wide with fear, and he tossed and struggled furiously. "Wait!" he pleaded. "You're mistaken!"

The bearded man slowly shook his head, his pointed whiskers describing a short arc like a swinging dagger-blade. "Goodbye, Mr. Sterling," he said, then lifted a concealed pistol from his lap and shot the helpless Sterling through the heart.

The young, clean-shaven man jumped up in alarm. "Was that necessary?" he demanded. "What if you were wrong? What if this was the real Franklin? How can you be so cold-blooded?"

"Sit down, Brother Hastings," commanded the leader. The burlap sack that served as his mask swelled and shrank ominously as he puffed with anger at the disapproval. "I shall overlook your rash comments this once—only because of your youth and inexperience. But let me warn you: *Never* be critical of a decision of mine ever again, unless you wish to join the Yankee spy. Do you understand?"

Hastings turned ashen. In a stricken voice he muttered, "Of course, General. I forgot my place. Please pardon me." He sat down, tightly grasping his hands together in a vain attempt to stop them from shaking.

"By tomorrow, General, Sterling's body will be a crab's meal at the bottom of the bay," commented the bearded assassin. "And his hotel room is even right now having a mysterious and most destructive fire."

Smiles broke the lingering tension, and the Knights of the Golden Circle seemed genuinely pleased.

"Very good, Brother Perry," commented the masked leader. Ignoring the body slumped across the loop of hemp and the growing dark red stain pooling beneath the chair, he continued, "Now, gentlemen, on to business. Prudence dictates that we conclude these proceedings quickly and reconvene tomorrow night at our alternate location. Remember, from now on, we must be constantly on guard against spys."

3

THE FOUR TROOPERS ranged around the dining table looked awkward and slightly ill at ease. Colonel Mason had ordered them to remain outside because of their trail-worn and mud-spattered condition, but Emily Dawson had over-ruled him and insisted they come in from the cold.

The cavalrymen were not used to seeing their colonel coun-termanded, certainly never successfully. They nervously han-dled the china cups Emily had distributed to them, as if en-joying their coffee would call down the officer's wrath. Each man carried the conviction that dropping a cup could earn him a firing squad.

Deputy Pettibone felt no such reservations. He rattled his cup loudly on its saucer, sloshing the coffee over the sides, then helped himself to a refill and two more cookies from the tray. Colonel Mason frowned at the officious and self-impor-tant little man behind the enormous moustache, then contin-ued his conversation with Tom.

"As I was saying, Mr. Dawson, we now believe that the man known as Colonel James was linked to a secret California Confederate society that had a plan—"

"That's right," Pettibone broke in, his whiskers powdered with cookie crumbs. "James was supposed to deliver orders to the men who had been stealing the gold shipments, but he went and got hisself killed by Byrd Guidett sorta accidental-like over a cardgame 'cause Guidett didn't know who he was and—"

"Pettibone," snapped the colonel, "Dawson knows all that! He's the one who rescued the boy from Guidett after the shooting! Now, keep your mouth shut and let me get to the point."

A crestfallen Deputy Pettibone plunged his drooping mous-tache into his coffee, while the wary troopers exchanged amused glances. "We believe that the outlaw band here on Shadow Ridge was motivated by greed," Mason paused. "Nevertheless, we think the secret society is very real and still active."

"So what's the purpose of your early morning ride?" Tom wondered. "You didn't come all this way to talk about Guidett's gang. What help could I possibly be?" he continued. "I never saw Colonel James before his death."

"Not you," corrected the colonel. "We think that the colored child, Mont, may be able to tell us about others in the group whom James met."

"Colonel," said Emily, her eyes instantly flashing, "Mont is a nine-year-old who still has horrible nightmares from all he's been through. I'll not have him upset needlessly."

Now it was Mason's turn to fidget, picking idly at the crossed-saber insignia on the crown of his hat before replying. "Mrs. Dawson, I know the loss you have personally experi-enced and I am truly sorry," he said at last. "But if the Union loses California, the course of the war will be prolonged, at a cost of many thousands of additional lives. What's more to the point for your family is that unless we can stop this con-spiracy before it takes root, California may become a battle-ground as bloody as Shiloh or Gettysburg. If this can be pre-vented, is it not worth the attempt?"

The round faces of two boys, one pale and one dusky brown, peeked over the rail of their sleeping loft. "Miss Em-ily, I kin answer questions. It cain't hurt me none."

"All right, Mont," Emily agreed with a sigh. "You boys come on down here."

Colonel Mason attempted to take Mont backward through his memory. "All right," he said kindly, "we already know that you stayed at the home of Thomas Baker down in the valley. While you were there, did you see anyone you had met before, or hear any names mentioned?"

"No suh, I surely didn't," declared Mont.

Trying a different approach, Mason asked, "Well, then, how about before you got to the valley? Did you meet anyone in California that you had seen before in Missouri?"

Mont pondered this question with great intensity, frowning and wrinkling his forehead. Finally he shook his head. "No suh, not so's I recollects."

The colonel was about to give up on this idea, but he tried once more. "Do you remember the names of any other places that you stopped in California?"

Mont gave a wide smile and nodded vigorously. "We was in Frisco! We stopped at a powerful fine hotel too and—" He stopped abruptly as a sudden thought galloped visibly across his face.

Mason looked at Tom and Emily and raised his eyebrows. "What is it, Mont? What did you remember?"

"Well, suh, does you care just about folks I seed in Californy and Missouri?"

The colonel urged Mont to go ahead with whatever he could remember. Pettibone took the opportunity to exhale loudly and crossed his arms over his thin chest, declaring that all this was simply a waste of time.

"In Frisco I did see this man I seed befo', but not in Missouri."

"Where, then, Mont?" urged Emily gently.

"It was the same man what come to see Colonel James in Richmond."

"What?" burst out Colonel Mason. "Richmond, Virginia? Who was this man? What was the meeting about?"

"I don't rightly know, 'ceptin' . . ."

"Yes, go on."

"I heerd them say they was goin' to see Jeff Davis."

"Really!" exclaimed Mason, slapping his knee. "Now we're getting somewhere. Think, Mont, think. What was the man's name?"

Mont shook his head slowly. Even Pettibone sat motionless, waiting for Mont's answer. "I cain't recall no names, but I'd shor nuff know him agin to see him!"

Mason looked extremely pleased.

"Mr. Dawson," Colonel Mason said, "could you bring Mont to Fort Tejon in say, two days' time? I'd like Mont to remember all he can, and then I have something to discuss with you. I also have a prisoner there I want Mont to take a look at."

Avery Hastings stood silently with Jasper Perry on Telegraph Hill, looking down toward the Vallejo Street Wharf and a picturesque scene. Moored at the right of their view was the river steamer *Yosemite*. The side-wheeler's paddle housings reached almost to the level of the wheelhouse, four decks above the waterline. A thin trickle of smoke from the twin stacks showed that the boilers were fired and being kept ready for departure upriver.

But the men's attention was actually directed at two vessels moored one dock closer to their vantage point. One of them was the Pacific mail ship *Arizona*, newly arrived from Panama with letters, parcels and newspapers from "the states." The *Arizona* was a hybrid ship, carrying three masts for sail and a smokestack amidships as well.

The other occupant of the nearer wharf was the United States warship *Cyane*. She had also recently arrived from Panama after a voyage of fifty-one days.

"There is the hen and there the watch dog," said Perry, pointing first toward the mailship and then at the man-of-war.

"What is the turn-of-speed of the *Arizona*?" inquired Hastings.

"Inconsequential, compared to the *Cyane*. The warship is what we must be able to outrun, and then we'll have no difficulty overtaking our quarry."

"Have you a vessel in mind?"

"Come along and I'll show you," replied Perry as he turned and led the way to a waiting hack.

Montgomery Street was lined with pedestrians and cabs, and they all seemed to be flowing downhill toward the wharf at the end of Jackson Street. Avery raised his eyebrows in question at the seemingly single-minded crowd, but Perry only smiled knowingly and withheld his explanation until the Jackson docks came into view.

Moored there was a schooner bearing the name *Chapman*. It was being unloaded, the swinging cargo nets discharging piles of sacks labelled BEANS onto the dock that was bustling with activity.

"What is so special about this ship?" scoffed Hastings. "A little hundred-ton cargo ship entrusted with freighting beans? You must be joking."

Perry stroked his beard and studied the schooner without comment. A group of onlookers had gathered all around the wharf, and there was a low hum of conversation.

"What is so special about the *Chapman*?" demanded Hastings again. "Why are all these people interested in her?"

"Thirty-eight days from Valparaiso" was Perry's quiet comment.

Hastings was examining the crowd and seemed not to have heard. "That man in the naval uniform is Bissell, commander of the *Cyane*. I believe the man he's speaking with is Ralston of the . . . thirty-eight days from where?"

"Valparaiso," repeated Perry smugly. "If memory serves, it's on the coast of South America."

"But that's—"

"Exactly," Perry interrupted, finally condescending to elaborate. "That is thirteen days faster than it took the *Cyane* to go half as far!"

Suddenly, Hastings' former disdain was replaced with a curious enthusiasm. "And being schooner-rigged, she'll sail closer to the wind and be more maneuverable. She can also be handled by a smaller crew than the square-rigged ships require."

"And there is one more thing in the *Chapman*'s favor," Perry hinted.

"What more could there be? She already outsails one of the fastest warships. This sounds too good to be true."

Jasper Perry's smug look turned into a smirk. "She is for sale. The owners have asked $7500, but I believe we can get her for less."

The air was still and crystal clear as Tom and Mont rode across the toe of the Great Valley toward their meeting with Colonel Mason at Fort Tejon. The peaks they faced stood out in sharp relief, and the furrowed shoulders of the mountains were lightly dusted with powdery snow.

They rode up a treeless, mesquite-covered slope. By turning in his saddle on Duncan's back, Mont could see a hundred miles of the Sierra Nevada mountains sprawled out toward the east and equally as much of the coast range toward the west.

Tom was riding beside him on a young sorrel gelding. With a delighted grin, Mont asked, "Ain't it real plain, Mr. Tom?"

"Isn't what plain, Mont?"

"The smile on God's face when He sees what He done here?"

The two stopped riding to gaze around them in silent admiration. Directly ahead of them was a great cleft in the mountains, which looked as if a giant ax had split the rocks to open a passage.

Tom considered the child's remark and smiled in agreement. Mont's insight had long since ceased to surprise Tom. *The depth of the small boy's understanding must also please the Creator*, Tom thought.

After a few reflective moments, the two urged their mounts forward again, the young red horse dancing sideways at times in his eagerness. Duncan tramped along steadily with the thickly muscled arch of his neck and shoulders leaning into the grade. Duncan had the appearance of a plodding draft animal, but his constantly flicking ears betrayed his alertness.

The wedge-shaped canyon looming ahead had been the subject of old Spanish legends. It was reputed to have been formed when a demon caballero burst out of his underground lair for a diabolical midnight ride.

Tom decided not to share this story with Mont, or the fact that they had recently passed the place where, a few months earlier, Tom and a squad of soldiers had come upon a wrecked stagecoach and another of Byrd Guidett's murder victims. Young Mont was reveling in the grandeur of the scene; why disrupt it with unpleasant reminders of evil and human misery and destruction?

But for Tom himself, it was too late to push back the thoughts and feelings. Forcing its way into his mind was the additional memory that on the day of the stagecoach holdup, his brother Jesse had still been alive.

4

THE DUSTY BROWN adobe walls of Fort Tejon's barracks were just barely visible through the screening branches of the leafless cottonwoods and willows along the creek. Once across the rocky ford, the grassy field of the parade ground began and fanned up the hill for three hundred yards.

Tom exchanged greetings with several soldiers he knew from his horse-trading activities. "Hey, Dawson," yelled a stork-thin corporal with a prominent beak to match, "no horses this time?"

Mont received some curious looks. The sight of several whispered conversations told even a nine-year-old mind that his story was being shared with the new recruits.

A pot-bellied man with a bald head and ferocious side whiskers taunted, "What now? Gone to sellin' nig—" His question stopped abruptly with an exhaled gasp as the bony elbow of the corporal slammed into his gut.

"Dawson!" boomed the colonel from the wooden steps of his office. "Thank you for coming. Come in, come in." Turning to his left he said, "Corporal, have Flannery there see to Mr. Dawson's horses."

The two men and the small boy climbed the wooden stairs to Mason's office. "There are more secessionists in this country than the Easterners believe," Colonel Mason remarked to Tom and Mont. The colonel seated himself in a revolving chair next to his roll-top desk. He gestured out the faintly frosted window of his second-story office toward the stretch of valley spreading northward. "Perhaps as many as a third of California's population are from the south or, like yourself, from the border states."

"That doesn't make them secesh," corrected Tom. "Many, like myself, came West to get away from the war."

"True enough," agreed the colonel, "but the outspoken secessionists are not the real problem. The danger lies with those who are outwardly loyal but secretly traitors."

"What do you think this secret society can really accomplish? I keep hearing it claimed they can pull California out of the Union. How, exactly?"

The colonel shook his head. "That's what we need to find out. We know that as lone gunmen or in small bands they are capable of assassination and robbery, but whether they can actually organize an armed insurrection . . ."

Mont was sitting wide-eyed at being included in such a grown-up conversation. Tom gestured toward the boy and asked Colonel Mason, "What do you expect to accomplish by having Mont look at your prisoner?"

"If Mont recognizes him and can tell us where he saw him before, we hope to trace the man's associations in order to get inside the ruling circle of the society. We have some isolated names of those we suspect, but the links between them are missing," replied the colonel.

"Has anything happened to make this more urgent than it was last fall?"

Mason looked at his hands, then up at his saber suspended by a tasselled cord over his desk. With embarrassment in his voice he replied, "Mr Dawson, I am a soldier, plain and simple. I never wanted to be anything else. But there is . . ." He spoke the next phrase with as much visible distaste as if he had just received a dose of cod liver oil. "There is a *political* issue which cannot be ignored. There is a substantial and growing Northern peace movement. If this spring goes badly for the Union, then Mr. Lincoln's reelection will fail. The new president may sue for peace, even at the cost of letting the seceding states depart."

Tom hunched over in his chair and rubbed his palms together beside a small cast-iron stove. "If that would stop the bloodshed, I'm not so sure it's a bad thing," he commented.

Mason stiffened visibly, but his voice was even and soft when he spoke. "I won't press you with emotional arguments about the sacrifice of those who have already died," he said. "But one fact cannot have escaped your notice: Do you want to see the continued existence of a system that would keep Mont here and millions of others as slaves?"

With the slightest of motions of his hand, Tom beckoned toward the small boy who quietly listened to their conversation. Mont, who had been perched on the edge of the chair, jumped off and ran to stand at Tom's side. "No," Tom said with finality. "No, I do not. Never again."

The fort's jail was housed in a low-roofed adobe building across the frost-browned parade ground. Mason stopped in front of a barred door and indicated it to Mont.

"Take a good look, Mont." The colonel boosted the boy up to peer through the bars of the guard house. A sullen-faced man with a tan complexion and dark brown hair sat on a rough wooden bench in leg irons even though the cell door was bolted securely.

Tom glanced in while Mont was studying the prisoner. "Shackles inside the cell?" he asked the colonel.

"You of all people know better than to underestimate the ruthlessness of the conspirators. This man killed two of my men before we captured him. Yesterday he clubbed the guard bringing his supper and almost escaped. I'm taking no chances. Seen enough, Mont?"

Mont nodded and Colonel Mason set him down. "Have you seen him anywhere before?"

"No suh, I surely don't think so."

"Think hard," Mason urged. "The man's name is Wilson, or at least that's what he goes by part of the time. Does that help at all?"

Mont asked to be lifted once more, but still shook his head after studying the prisoner a second time. "I never seed him befo'," Mont said. "I'se powerful sorry. They is one thing though . . ."

"Yes, what is it?" urged Mason.

"Well," the boy began, then stopped, looking uncertainly at Tom. "That man in there, he put me in mind of Mistuh Tom."

A few moments later the trio were back in the colonel's office. "Mont's sharp eyes confirmed what I had already noticed," observed Mason. "You bear a remarkable resemblance to our prisoner."

Tom studied the officer warily. "So? What are you driving at?"

"It means, Mr. Dawson, that if you are willing, you may be our method of gaining entrance to the secret society known as the Golden Circle."

"You want me to pretend to be this man Wilson?" asked Tom incredulously. "How do you expect me to carry it off? Isn't he known to the others in the group?"

"No, he isn't. He was imprisoned in the East for activities as a spy. When he escaped, we had word that he would sail for California to join a conspiracy group. Sure enough, we apprehended him when his vessel from Panama put in at Santa Barbara. But no one outside this command knows that, and all the Southern sympathizers have is Wilson's history and general description. That much we coaxed out of him.

"We believe you will be able to infiltrate the Southern sympathizers as well as give Mont an opportunity to keep an eye out for someone he recognizes."

The thump of the iron against the ironing board sounded angry. Tom sat quietly at the kitchen table and waited for Emily to tell him in words what she was indicating every time she clanked the iron onto the hot stove and then tested the temperature of the second iron with the hiss of a drop of water.

"So you're leaving." Her tone was flat when she finally spoke. She set the crease on a flannel shirt sleeve and thumped the hot iron down hard against it.

Tom sipped his coffee and did not reply. Her words were not a question, they were an accusation. She knew that he was leaving her and Nate and Jed for a while. What else could he do?

"For how long?" she asked, not looking up at him.

"I don't right know for sure, Emily, but—"

"What about the ranch? What about . . ." Her voice trailed away. "What about Jed and Nate?" Had she also been wondering what she would do without him?

"This is the best time of year . . . the only time really that I could go. Leave the ranch. Another month there'll be calving to tend to."

"You'll be back in a month, then?" She looked up sharply.

He shrugged his uncertainty. How could he say? "If I'm not . . . well, I already talked to Pastor Swift. He'll lend a hand. And Deputy Pettibone, of course, if there should be any trouble."

"They know what the Union army has put you up to?"

"Not the details, of course. Not all. Pettibone says not, but Mason believes that what began here with Jesse's dyin' isn't over for us yet. Nobody's fooled about this, Emily. There's still plenty of men out there actively working to push California into the Confederacy." He was trying hard to justify leaving the ranch and the boys . . . and her. She would have none of it.

"And I suppose you're the only one who can put a stop to it?" She raised her chin in a mocking gesture. Occasionally, Tom had seen her look that way at Jesse when there had been a disagreement. Now she challenged him.

"There are hundreds of other men who could go," he replied softly. "But there's only one little Mont to go with them and point out just who a leader of the secesh movement is here in California. The boy *saw him*, Emily, in Richmond! He overheard it all because no one bothered to think that a slave child had the brains to remember all their big talk." He leaned back in his chair and eyed her as she smoothed out the red material of his shirt with a slight touch of gentleness now. "And I don't aim to let anyone else take that poor boy on such a dangerous job. I've kinda grown fond of him, you see?"

She nodded. Her expression was one of misery and some shame that she had not seen it clearly without such a discussion.

"You and your brother . . ." Her voice was laden with emotion. "Before Jesse was . . . before he left . . . we had the same kind of talk. A man has to do what is right. I know that. But, *will* you come back?"

"Of course." He tried to sound light, even though his heart was heavy with the thought of leaving her. And the ranch, of course.

"Jesse *said* he would come back." She put her hand over her mouth and closed her eyes. Tears she thought she had used up squeezed out from between the lids. Jesse had not come back, and Tom alone shared her pain and carried the family responsibilities.

Tom stood and put his hands gently on her shoulders. She did not look at him, for fear of what her eyes might say to him. He kissed her lightly on the forehead—a brotherly kiss, but his voice was thick with emotion. "Emily. Emily. I could walk out the door this morning to mend a fence and if it was my time, well, then, I wouldn't come back. My life and yours are in the hands of the Lord, Emily. I learned that on a long, hard road." He pulled her close against him and she laid her cheek easily against his chest. "So I'll tell you this . . . if it's what the Lord wants for me, I'll be back in time for the calving. And if it's what the Lord wants for *us*, you'll be here when I return."

5

THE BUCKBOARD RATTLED noisily down the snaking turns of White River Canyon and past the mining town of Tailholt. In some years, crossing the log bridge over White River in January was hazardous because the storm-swollen creek raged through the narrow rocky arroyo. This year the passage was easy and the stream a modest trickle flowing quietly. Despite the early snows in the high country, not much had fallen since, nor had much rain come to the valley. It looked as if last year's drought would continue.

The climb out of the gorge wound around steep-sided buttes of decomposed granite. Dirty white boulders littered the landscape like the discarded toys of a giant's game of marbles.

To help pass the time, Tom told Mont stories from old Indian lore. "See that funnel-shaped rock? The one that looks like an Indian gathering basket? The Yokuts say that it was once an Indian girl who was turned to stone right on that very spot."

"How come?" Mont worried aloud.

"For looking back toward some evil her family was running from. You know, sort of like Lot's wife in the Bible."

"Jest granite, 'stead of salt," Mont observed.

Mont was still looking back at the upside-down cone of the boulder when the buckboard crested the rise out of the canyon. Spread out before them, yet still a thousand feet lower, lay the great fertile valley—only . . .

"Hey!" Mont exclaimed, spinning around on the spring seat. "Where'd all the valley go? How'd all them clouds get down yonder?"

Tom chuckled, and Duncan's ears flicked back and stayed pointed at the humans as if he too were interested in the explanation. "Tule fog," Tom said. "When it warms up on winter days with no wind, the next night all that marshy land gives off a vapor. It goes on getting thicker and thicker till daybreak, then the sun goes to work burning it off. Sometimes it gets so thick it'll stay like that for weeks till some wind comes to blow it away."

"It look like big, dark water," commented Mont.

Tom agreed. The solid mass of dingy gray fog that stretched across the valley did indeed resemble a stormy sea lapping at the foothills of the Sierras. Here and there a taller knob of rock elevated itself through the mist like an island rising from the waves.

Wispy vines of fog drifted between the branches of the oaks, and soon the rest of the trees were obscured by the floating streamers of mist. A sudden dip in the road plunged the travelers into the dark sea of clammy vapor, and the cheerful yellow sun disappeared. Even the steady clip-clop of Duncan's hooves seemed muffled.

In the dim obscurity, it was easier than ever to conjure up bears out of boulders and lurking Indians from fallen limbs. Mont hoped they would all stay frozen in place until he was past.

Tom also felt oppressed by the grayness. As the fog drew a curtain between them and the ones they loved, his thoughts drifted off into a melancholic study of the trip he and Mont were making, and how long it would pull them away from home.

"Mother, come quick!" Nate's voice rang through the frosty air like the sound an ax makes biting into a cedar tree in the high country. Emily heard the edge of terror in his shout.

Fresh-baked loaves of bread just coming out of the oven spun off toward the corners of the kitchen and the pan dropped unheeded on the floor. Emily grabbed the shotgun from the corner of the front room and raced out the door.

What could it be? Her frantic mind conjured up a hundred calamities: a rattlesnake? a mountain lion? the barn was on fire? Jed had hurt himself with the hatchet while chopping kindling?

Nate shouted again from inside the barn, still anxious but more controlled. She was relieved to see Jed sprint around the side of the barn from the woodpile—one less possibility to fret about. Jed warned his mother to be wary in case a wild animal should burst out, but Emily paid no heed and ran headlong into the barn, calling for Nate.

In the same moment that the two charged in, Nate's yell came again, "Mother!" He was inside the box stall of the young red horse. It lay prostrate on the straw, breathing in shuddering gasps. The fine sleek body was seized by a convulsion that started at its neck and rippled down through its whole frame. Every muscle became rigid and taut until it seemed that the flesh would tear apart the overstretched skin. Even the horse's lips curled back from his teeth in a horrid parody of a grin.

Just as suddenly, the grip of the seizure relaxed. The gelding was instantly gasping for breath as if he had been held under water and almost drowned. He began to thrash his limbs in all directions, frantically pawing and snorting. He threw his head backward and forward, trying to escape the grasp of pain that had clutched his whole body. It was too great to be borne.

"Nathan!" Emily screamed. "Get out of there!"

Before Nate could make a move, he was bowled over by a fling of the sorrel's head. Thrown against the partition of the stall, he landed with a thud that left him dazed in the dirt. "Get up!" his mother cried. Jed vaulted the boards of the stall and scooped up his little brother like a sack of potatoes.

By the time Jed boosted Nate over the stall into his mother's waiting arms, he was able to speak again and pleaded, "Help him! Help him!"

"He's colicked," said Emily firmly. "I'll do what I can, but . . ." At the mute entreaty in Nate's eyes, she stopped and left the sentence unfinished. "Are you all right, Nate? Able to help?"

Stifling a great shuddering sob, Nate controlled himself and pulled himself erect. "Yes, Mother," he agreed. "What can I do?"

"Run into the house and bring me the jug of molasses. Get an unopened crock of sausage out of the pantry. Pour the teakettle into the bucket and fill the bucket with cool water, then bring everything out to me. Quick as you can, now."

Before the final instructions had even left her mouth, the boy was out of the barn and dashing toward the house. She called after him, "Mind the kettle! Don't burn yourself." To Jed she said, "All right, Jed, we've got to try to get him up. Quickly now, before another seizure takes him."

Even as she spoke the horse became rigid once more. In the extremity of the convulsion, he ceased to breathe and his eyes took on a fixed, glassy stare. The color of his exposed gums turned a deadly white. "We're losing him," Emily shouted, and just as unmindful of her own safety as she had been worried about Nate's, she rushed into the pen. She threw her weight on the sorrel's rib cage, forcing him to breathe.

After a few seconds that seemed like an eternity, the horse came out of the spasm. This time he was so weak that he could not even swing his head, let alone thrash his legs.

"Help me roll him upright," Emily said to Jed. It took all their combined strength just to move the horse off his side and onto his stomach. "Grab those feed sacks," she ordered, "and stuff them along here next to the wall. We have to keep him from getting down flat again."

By this time Nathan had returned with a double-arm load of the things Emily had requested. Tears were streaming down his cheeks, but he was all business when he set the water bucket down and lined up the molasses and the sausage crock for his mother's inspection. "Now what?" he asked manfully.

"Now pray," she instructed. Into the warm water she poured a half-gallon of cottonseed oil that had been covering the sausages as a preservative. To this she added a pint of molasses. "Get the funnel with the longest spout you can find," she told Jed.

When he had returned, Emily had Jed pull the horse's tongue out the side of his mouth and hold it there. With his other hand he directed the spout of the funnel down the animal's throat. "Pray hard," Emily said again to both the boys. "If he seizes while we're pouring this down him, he'll strangle for sure."

"Wait!" demanded Nate. With his eyes screwed tight shut, he made a fervent request with moving but soundless lips. "All right," he said at last. "Do it now."

Emily poured the funnel full, then massaged the gelding's neck until swallowing motions appeared and the liquid in the funnel went down. She paused to look for signs of another convulsion, and when none appeared, began to pour again. This process was repeated and repeated until every drop of two gallons of fluid had been drained into the animal.

"Now," Emily said, "let's see if we can get him up." The warm mixture and all the human attention seemed to ease the horse's panic. He appeared to understand what was wanted even if he could not oblige. "Rock him," she said, and the boys sprang to obey.

After several heaves and shoves and coaxing pulls on his mane, the red horse rose unsteadily to his feet. Emily put the loop of a lead rope loosely around his neck, and motioned for Jed to open the stall gate. Twenty paces down to the end of the barn, a short pivot, and twenty paces back. "Keep him moving," she instructed Jed, who took over from her after ten turns around the barn. "We'll need to do this turnabout all day and through the night, till whatever bad he got into works its way out. I'll go heat more water so we can dose him again in a bit. Mind," she said looking at Nate intently, "if he goes to take another fit, keep clear of him."

"Yes'm," agreed Nate. "We'll walk him good. Won't we, Jed?" The two brothers started off on the first of hundreds of little circuits inside the barn.

Emily looked out the window toward the barn for the tenth time in an hour. She watched the flickering lantern light shining through the half-open door until the shadows of boys and horse passed, then she returned to her sewing.

At least she tried to concentrate on the never-ending pile of mending. Even when not fretting about the boys, she was worrying about Tom and Mont. She wished now that she had objected more to their going. She thought about how difficult life on the ranch was even when they were here. There were always problems with the stock, or some machinery broken down, or something on the house, barn or corrals that needed to be fixed. She sighed. Why compound all those things by going hundreds of miles away on business that properly belonged to the Union army?

The truth was, she and her little brood had grown very comfortable, despite the constant stresses of ranch life, and she hated to see that comfort disturbed. Having Tom around made her feel secure, almost like having her husband again.

She stopped and shook her head. That direction of thinking was no good at all. Best to not dwell on it.

Emily roused herself to look at the time: past midnight already. She decided to go out and check on the boys, even though their turn was not up for another hour.

At the stable she found a weary and leaden-eyed Jed tramping in smaller and smaller circles, leading a droopy looking red horse. At first she could not see Nathan at all, then spotted him, curled up like a cat, asleep on the feed sacks.

"Jed, I'll take over now. You get your brother and go on in and get some sleep. I'll come for you when I need you."

"Huh?" was all the reply he could manage.

Shaking the slumbering Nate, and putting his hand in Jed's, she led them to the door and pointed them toward the house. Then she resumed the circuits of the barn.

The air inside the barn was growing colder until it penetrated the coat Emily was wearing. She paused in her pacing to look around for something to throw over her shoulders.

Her eyes lit on the empty feed sack Nathan had been curled up with, and she shook it out.

A scrap of paper fluttered free. Emily wondered if it had fallen out of Nate's jacket. She retrieved it, and carried it till the next pass under the lantern gave her light enough to read.

In scrawled pencil marks the unsigned note read: DAW-SON—THIS COULD HAPEN TO ALL YER STOCK. KEEP CLEER OF ARE BIZNES.

6

VISALIA WAS THE county seat of Tulare County in the Great Valley of California and was two days' travel down from Shadow Ridge. It stood on a plain noted by the old Spanish explorers for its grove of magnificent oaks. The confluence of the rivers draining the Sierras made the location a natural way point for hunters and prospectors as well as those who would sell to them and buy from them.

It was also home to a large population of people whose sympathies clearly lay with the Confederacy. The local newspaper, the *Equal Rights Expositor*, had an outspoken editor who saw every issue as an opportunity to brand the Union army as invaders, Lincoln as a tyrant, and Yankees as fools, generally. He was something of a local hero but had earned himself some enemies as well.

The paper's third issue of 1864 was especially strong. Half the columns were devoted to editorials deploring the brutality of Northern aggression. Garrison, the editor, took particular aim at the establishment of Camp Babbitt, near Visalia.

The ranchers and farmers in the valley had always been nervous about Indian raids sweeping in from the eastern reaches of the Sierras. When the regular army forces had been withdrawn from the valley to carry out patrol assignments in the deserts of the Southwest, the ranchers' concern increased even further. A volunteer force had been raised to fill in for the reassigned regulars. Camp Babbitt was the headquarters for a portion of the Second Cavalry, California Volunteers.

Lieutenant Colonel William Hardy commanded the detachment of horse soldiers at Babbitt. He and his patrol had just returned from two weeks in the high lonesome, chasing Indians who seemed little more substantial than the rapidly melting snowflakes.

Sparse snow had not meant sparse cold, however. Hardy and his troopers had gone to bed with icy winds howling through the passes and into their tent flaps. They had been treated to the experience of watching their breath solidify into ice crystals inside their tents. There had been no escaping the bone-chilling cold.

As if this were not bad luck enough, Hardy had received the additional indignity of coming down with the worst fever of his life. It was fortunate it came near the end of the ride. Now he was huddled in the eight-by-eight cabin that served him as both quarters and office. A shawl was drawn around his shoulders, and his feet soaked in a pan of steaming water to which half a bottle of turpentine had been added.

There was a timid knock at his door. "What is it?" he croaked angrily.

The door opened a fraction and a wisp of fog drifted in, followed by a cautious Corporal Brant. "Sorry to disturb you, sir," the corporal began.

"Get on with it!" exploded the colonel. The last word was punctuated by a particularly violent sneeze.

"Yes, sir, sorry, sir. The Visalia telegrapher reports the line is down, sir."

"Indeed? And since when is that army business? Tell him to attend to it himself. That's what he . . . he . . . *achoo!*"

The corporal waited patiently until Hardy finished sneezing and concluded his sentence, ". . . what he gets paid for!"

"Yes, sir. But he found that the line had been cut, sir. In twelve places, sir."

"What!?" Hardy demanded, standing upright and almost tripping over the pan. "Blasted secesh!" The colonel swore, sneezed again and bit his tongue, which made him swear even louder. "Get Captain Warner. Tell him to take . . . what now, Corporal?"

Corporal Brant backed up a step before replying, which put his shoulders squarely against the cabin door. "Captain

Warner is not in camp, sir. You sent him and Lieutenant Miller to Fort Tejon."

Hardy angrily dismissed the rest of the explanation with an irritated gesture. "I remember, Corporal. All right, sound assembly. Company A ready in fifteen minutes. That will be all, Corporal."

Brant fumbled with the door to make his exit. By the time he got it open, another monstrous sneeze and another violent burst of profanity propelled him out into the fog.

A handbill nailed to the trunk of a large oak caught Mont's attention. "What do it say?" he asked.

"Go on, you can make it out," Tom urged.

"Tonight," the child read, "Perfesser William Brewer will speech—"

"Speak," Tom corrected.

"Speak on the . . . what did the rest say?" Mont asked since the buggy had by this time rolled past the announcement.

"It says that Brewer will speak on the drought in California." Tom added, "I've heard of Brewer. He's part of a group making a survey . . . you know, maps and such . . . of California's mountains."

"Kin we go?"

"I don't see why not. We're staying the night in Visalia, and we can find a place to camp close by the lecture hall."

Across the street from the newspaper office of the *Equal Rights Expositor* was the Oddfellows Hall. The hall was a two-story affair with whitewashed board-and-bat siding. Downstairs it contained two small offices, one for a doctor and the other for an attorney. Only the physician's space was occupied for the time being; the lawyer had gotten himself killed in a stage holdup only a week earlier.

The lodge room upstairs was often used for community gatherings, town meetings, and the like, as well as serving as the temporary home of the Cumberland Presbyterian Church. The single large room that filled the second floor had a raised platform at the end opposite the door. The backless wooden benches could seat close to a hundred if closely packed, and half-a-hundred more could be accommodated with standing room.

There were nowhere near that number present for William Brewer's lecture. When Tom and Mont climbed the outside wooden stairs that led to a balcony outside the meeting hall, only thirty or so had come out on the foggy night to listen to the professor of agricultural chemistry.

The tall man with the stooped shoulders was already speaking: "And just how severe is the present drought? The year 1862 produced over twenty-four inches of rain in San Francisco, while in 1863 the same area received only three inches. What is worse, no rainstorm of any consequence has struck the southern half of the state since last January—twelve months ago."

Standing in the doorway listening was a short, skinny man with a disorderly ring of white hair around his otherwise bald knob of a head. In between nodding at what Brewer was saying, the small man cast an occasional look over his shoulder at the newspaper office. He gave no evidence of intending to step aside from blocking the entrance to the room, but continued to brace himself between the doorposts like a miniature Samson in training for the destruction of the Oddfellows temple.

Tom cleared his throat by way of asking for permission to pass, and the short figure did in fact whirl around at the sound. But instead of moving out of the way, he stretched out a bony finger down toward the street and broke into a cackle of laughter that Mont thought would have done credit to the black speckled hen at the Dawson farm.

Turning to see what the source of amusement was, they spotted a bedraggled troop of horsemen riding wearily into town. The men's heads drooped, and so did the heads of their mounts.

"Who are they?" Tom questioned cautiously.

The man stopped in the middle of his cackling and turned to stare at Tom. "Who are *you* is the question." But before waiting for an answer, he swung back to the scene below and said, "Them's farmers playin' at being soldiers," and went into another gale of raucous laughter.

"What's the matter, toy soldiers?" he shouted down at them. "Can't find no Injuns to play with? Can't find no Rebs neither? Best you go back to your plows, boys, if you can still find them!" He laughed uproariously at his own jokes, and everyone at Brewer's lecture turned around to view the commotion.

A trooper muttered something and another nodded tersely. A third made a little louder grumble and stopped his horse's shambling walk.

Usually Colonel Hardy was a stickler for discipline and would not have tolerated speaking in ranks, but he was feeling too rotten to care. Besides, the little man's comments stung.

The self-appointed tormentor spoke again. "It's no wonder the blue dogs of the Baboon King are gettin' whipped. They can't any of 'em fight any better than you!"

Hardy's Troop A from Camp Babbitt had covered thirty miles out and back. They had repaired a dozen places where the telegraph line had been cut. But when they came to a thirteenth break, they found that it was not repairable. It was not just cut, the line itself was nowhere in sight. For the space of four telegraph poles, the wire had been stripped completely and carried away.

Colonel Hardy had been alternately sneezing and coughing as the unit rode back into town. The vandals had left plenty of tracks to follow—tracks that ended beside Pronghorn Slough where the last telegraph pole perched next to a stagnant sheet of green, slimy ooze. But the slough ran for miles in both directions, giving the rebels plenty of maneuvering room to hide their trail.

Something in Hardy snapped. The fever and chills, the agonizing ride and the salty remarks rubbed into open wounds had pushed him over the edge. In a voice that sounded like a coffee grinder he ordered, "Seize that secesh and his treasonous paper!"

It was then that Tom realized the little man was Garrison, the infamous editor of the secesh newspaper. Not to be deterred, the head man of the *Equal Rights Expositor* rushed down the stairs toward his business shouting, "Ned! Seth! Get the guns!"

Six troopers moved to carry out Hardy's order to seize the paper, and Corporal Brant went after Garrison. The banty rooster of a man lowered his shoulder and plunged straight into the surprised corporal, bowling him completely over. But two more soldiers had greater success, tackling Garrison and tying him up.

The two employees of the *Expositor* looked up from their printing duties to see half-a-dozen soldiers burst into the one-room building. Seth, the printer's devil, threw himself toward a cupboard beside the press and flung it open.

The one named Ned rushed toward the counter across the front of the room, reaching it just as a trooper named Stillwell vaulted over it. Ned's sweeping right fist caught Stillwell on the point of chin at the exact moment that the man's toes touched the floor. The impact lifted him so forcefully that it appeared he jumped backward up onto the counter like a puppet suddenly jerked upward on its strings.

Brandishing a pistol, Seth spun from the cupboard, but a soldier on each side of him caught his arms at the same moment. There was a resounding roar as the Remington forty-four exploded, but the shot went into the ceiling.

Ned turned from cold-cocking Stillwell to help his friend, but two more troopers jumped him from behind and wrestled him to the ground. The three men rolled over and over, crashing into the compositing bench. Slugs of type rattled and bounced, flying through the air like spent bullets.

Jerking free of his attackers, Ned grabbed up the plate of text he had been completing. He swung it sideways into a soldier's face, smashing the man backward into a wall and leaving the word TYRANNY neatly incised across his cheekbone. An instant later, the butt of a carbine struck Ned behind the ear and he collapsed in a heap.

Two more cavalrymen ran into the *Expositor* office carrying a long coil of rope. As Tom and Mont watched from their balcony perch across the street, the end of the rope was soon brought back outside and made fast to Corporal Brant's saddlehorn, while the bound Garrison screeched a protest.

At a nod from Hardy, Brant applied the spurs to his bay, which responded with a sudden spurt forward. There was a thunderous crash, and Garrison's printing press erupted through the wood of the counter and tore apart the doorway and one porch support before landing in the road.

Garrison raged and cursed, savaging all within sight and sound with a blistering string of foul oaths. The porch roof of the newspaper office tilted crazily and an ominous screeching suggested that the entire building might collapse.

As Tom looked on with mounting horror, Brant returned, fashioning a noose in the rope he had retrieved. The corporal looked expectantly toward Hardy, who gave a grim nod, then Brant tossed the coil over a nearby oak limb and tied it off so that the loop dangled eight feet off the ground.

Another trooper brought his horse alongside Garrison, who was roughly boosted into the saddle. The spindly editor was led toward the waiting noose.

"No!" shouted Tom, almost involuntarily. "Don't!" To Mont he said, "Stay up here. Whatever happens, stay up here!"

Tom vaulted over the railing, landing cat-like on his feet. He ran full force into the man holding the horse. The violence of the impact rolled the man completely over backward. The horse spooked and reared, tumbling Garrison off on the ground.

Grabbing the young rancher from behind, Brant roughly pinned Tom's arms to his sides. The man Tom had knocked down rose and drew back his fist, aiming a blow at Tom's chin.

Tom twisted Brant sideways, and the hapless corporal caught the blow intended for Tom on his right ear. Howling in pain, Brant released his hold, and Tom added an elbow smash to Brant's face.

Snatching up his fallen rifle, the other soldier levelled a two-foot-long bayonet at Tom's throat. Stopping perfectly still, but without flinching, Tom called out loudly, "Colonel! Don't do this! Enough!"

Colonel Hardy turned his flushed face toward Tom. The officer's red-rimmed eyes had difficulty focusing on the man who stood before him. Hardy's breath was ragged and a shiver worked its way down his spine and out to the ends of his fingers. He looked the part of a madman.

"Colonel," Tom repeated, "don't do this. Think what you are doing. Think of the women and children." Tom slowly gestured toward the crowd of people huddled on the balcony of the Lodge Hall where all thought of Brewer's talk on the drought was forgotten.

Hardy turned his feverish gaze upward to take in the on-lookers, then at the oak where the noose was dangling. Despite the chill, beads of sweat broke out on the colonel's fore-head and ran down into his eyes. He brought a gloved hand up to clear them. When he took it down again, new clarity had replaced the glazed stare of a moment before. He looked at Tom and the group of soldiers preparing to lynch the editor, as if seeing them for the first time. "You there! You men, stop that! Hold that horse, Brant!"

There was grumbling from some of the cavalrymen, but most moved sheepishly to comply, glad that some force had stopped them short of the hanging. "Brant," Hardy croaked at the corporal, "the others are to be released. Mr. Garrison is under arrest. Bring him along."

With no word of acknowledgement to Tom or the others viewing the scene, Troop A gathered themselves and moved off toward Camp Babbitt. Ned and Seth were left to nurse their wounds and collect ink bottles and overturned chairs.

Ned walked unsteadily outside, ducking to pass under the sagging porch roof. He rubbed a huge lump behind his ear and groaned. Stumbling toward Tom, he extended his hand. "Thanks, mister. I figured old Garrison for a goner, and maybe me an' Seth for after. If there's anything you ever need . . . what's your name, anyways?"

Tom looked down at a tug on his coat sleeve to find Mont trying to get his attention about something. . . . "It's Wilson," Tom said. "My name is Wilson."

"Are you just passing through, Mr. Wilson?"

"We're on our way to Frisco. I've been told we'll find friends there who think like Garrison."

"Frisco." Ned rubbed his aching head thoughtfully, as if making a careful assessment before saying any more. "Well, Mr. Wilson, I can steer you to a mighty good place to stay. Look for the Tehama House Hotel. You'll find the company to your liking there. And before you leave, let me send a message with you. You just give it to the person at the desk. He'll take care of the rest."

7

THE THREATENING NOTE fluttered in the hand of Deputy Pettibone. He squinted at the words and then looked at the weary sorrel gelding still being led slowly around the barn by Jed in the morning light.

"You're mighty lucky you ain't callin' a crew to haul a dead horse out of that barn this mornin'. How'd you save him?" he asked Emily.

"I didn't think of poison. It looked like a bad case of colic, so first thing we did was pray; then we dosed him with cotton-seed oil and . . . well, we've been walking him all night."

"And you all by yourself, too. A woman alone faced with such a thing." He clucked his tongue sympathetically. "That brother-in-law of yours done run off already, has he?"

"Not run off." Emily did not like his tone, even though there had been times through the ordeal when she, herself, had angry thoughts toward Tom. "But he and Mont are gone on their business."

"Well, now," Deputy Pettibone suddenly seemed real interested. He looked at the note again. "Well, well. And you and these here boys saved the horse. And what about the rest of your stock, Widow Dawson? Says right here . . ."

Emily put a hand to her aching forehead. How could she keep an eye on every animal on the ranch? How could she prevent anyone from carrying out a threat to poison the Dawson livestock? And whom could she trust?

"Tom said you would help if we had any trouble."

"Don't know how even the Union army could stand guard against something like this." He folded the note and slipped it into his coat pocket. "Where's Tom headed?"

She paused before answering. Hadn't Tom told even Petti-bone where he was going? "San Francisco."

"Well, then. Well, well, Widow Dawson. I'll tell you what I can do for you. I'm headed up to Fort Tejon, and then on to Los Angeles myself. I'll stop at the fort and inform the captain what's happened here. Tell 'im he oughtta get word to that brother-in-law of yours. In the meantime, since the Union has borrowed your man, they oughtta send a few blue-bellies this-away to help you out, I figger."

Emily nodded with relief. How grateful she was that Petti-bone had stopped to check on her and the boys this morning. If Tom had not talked to the deputy, she felt it could be no accident that he had arrived just in the hour of her greatest desperation. "Will you stop and ask Parson Swift to come out before you leave, Deputy? I'm in need of comforting after last night. I surely am."

"We must have a suitable captain," demanded Jasper Perry. "An experienced man, someone who knows these waters . . . a man with sand, who will stop at nothing."

Hastings looked crestfallen. "Is my appointment to mean nothing, then? My commission in the Confederate States Navy names me as captain."

Hastily hiding a mocking smile behind his hand, Perry said soothingly, "Avery, I mean no offense! You will have the command of the vessel, of course. But you agree to the wisdom of having a sailing master, do you not?"

Avery gave in to the soundness of this suggestion. "Do you have someone in mind?"

"By the stroke of good fortune, I do!" Perry explained that the man he intended to recruit for the conspiracy had once been an officer on the Pacific mail steamship *Oregon*. "He knows the routes of the mail ships and the thinking of their owners and officers. Come on, I think I know where to find him."

Perry led Hastings toward a shabby waterfront saloon. The name stenciled on the filthy smoked glass window had been "Devil May Care," but when one pane had been broken in a brawl, half the sign was destroyed and never replaced. What remained in a quarter arc of dingy suggestiveness read "Devil May."

Inside the dimly lit saloon were a handful of customers drinking toasts to midmorning forgetfulness. As Avery stood in the doorway, he saw a wrinkled crone leap back from riffling a rummy's pockets as he lay sleeping across a table. When the hag saw that neither newcomer was the law, she brazenly returned to exploring the man's coat.

A nudge in Hastings' ribs startled him out of his disgusted stare. "Keep one hand on your watch and the other on your wallet," Perry hissed, but he was smiling as he said it. Jasper Perry did not seem out of his element at all.

At a corner table that could barely be seen in the artificial gloom sat a lone man with a squat body and a dark, leathery face. His broad features included a nose that was little more than a shapeless lump of red-veined gristle. Sagging jowls mirrored the corners of his downturned mouth.

The man was dressed in the dark blue denim of a sailor, so his form faded into the black shadowy recess. His face and one bandaged hand seemed to float above the greasy table like apparitions in a spiritualist's show.

Perry approached the figure without hesitation, although Hastings hung back a pace. "Captain Law?" Perry asked tentatively.

For a long moment there was no reply. Avery wondered if they had made a mistake, or if perhaps the man was deaf, or in a drunken stupor. Perry was on the point of repeating himself when the sailor held up his bandaged left hand.

"I am not captain no more, they say. I am a cripple and cannot command, they say. The infernal deep take them all, I say! I have more to captain with in these stumps than they in all their whole worthless carcasses!"

"How did it happen?" Avery burst out. He was instantly sorry that he had spoken, for Captain Law's upturned eyes engaged his in a murderous stare. The pale blue, watery orbs bulged slightly from their sockets and reminded Hastings of the staring eyes of a drowned man he had once seen fished out of a river. *Dead lights*, he thought.

"Was a thieving kanaka, what done it. Caught him at the ship's stores. Would not take his medicine like a man. Fought me, he did. Me! His lawful captain!"

"You lost your fingers protecting ship's property and then the ungrateful owners discharged you?" said Perry in a voice surprisingly full of sympathetic indignation.

"Claimed I need not have killed him, they did," continued Law. He leaned back from the table to display a sheath knife with a folding marlin-spike in its handle. "Had a right tussle, too."

"Of course," blurted Avery. "He cut off your fingers in the fight—surely the owners can see that it was self-defense."

"Not so, neither," corrected Law. "'Twas not in the fight I lost 'em. When I went to put the noose around his scrawny neck to haul him to the maintop he bit one of 'em clean off, but the rest the doctor chopped. Gangrene from the stinkin' dog."

Perry looked at Hastings significantly, then said to Law, "Captain, we have a business proposition to discuss with you."

Avery Hastings hoped that he did not look as green as he felt.

The Market Street scene unrolling in front of Mont's view overwhelmed his nine year's worth of experience in a way he had never felt before. San Francisco was so amazing that despite this being his second visit, he was goggle-eyed. Three-and-four and even five-story buildings loomed all around, and hundreds of curious people walked or rode into his attention.

A covey of Chinamen in quilted cotton pajama-suits shuffled by, chattering to one another in singsong cadence. Their pigtails and round cloth caps were bobbing in time, and they were oblivious to Mont's stare.

From the other direction, three men in suits and bowler hats were riding two-wheeled contraptions with pedals on the front axles. Tom said that the machines were called velocipedes. Mont wanted to know if they were somehow related to the many-legged critters he had seen up in the mountains.

A horse-drawn streetcar made its appearance, announced by the plodding clop of hooves and the musical ringing of the bells for fares and crossings. Pursuing the streetcar were two nondescript mutts of indifferent breeding. The dogs were not actually running after the vehicle, but kept a steady trot close behind. At the corner stop closest to where Tom and Mont were standing, an impressive figure in military garb stepped from the coach. In his epauletted uniform and plumed top hat, he plunged through the crowd directly toward them, followed closely by the two dogs.

Several passersby tipped their hats to the portly, bearded man with the brass-headed cane and his canine attendants. Mont overheard him addressed as "Your Excellency," "Your Honor," "Your Highness," and even "Your Magnificence."

With single-minded purpose in his step, this high potentate, whoever he was, walked straight over to the two of them as if their meeting were prearranged. Stopping right in front of Tom, the man rapped the tip of his cane on the ground three times, as if calling a courtroom to attention.

"We note from your apparel that you are from the interior reaches of our domain," said the individual in the gold-braided dress coat. "We would inquire as to the state of our affairs in the hinterlands."

Mont wondered who the "we" was—decided that it must mean the dogs who were now seated politely one pace behind.

If Mont was confused about the plural form of address, Tom was just as baffled by the questions. "Well, I—" he began, then stopped.

"Come, come, man, speak up. Is aught amiss with your home province? Is our attendance required to redress error and quell rebellion?"

Fortunately, Tom was spared further interrogation by the aid of a helpful newsboy who had been listening to the exchange with amusement. "Scuse me, Emperor, your Highness. Jim Daly at your service. These here vis'ters don't speak any English. They are just arrived from . . ." Here the boy pivoted quickly to slip Tom a broad wink, "from Egypt."

"Splendid!" exclaimed the emperor, his ostrich plume waving with delight. "Welcome to our country! Quick, lad," he said to the newsboy, "proclaim us properly, Master Daly."

"Yes, sir, your Majesty. This here is Emperor Norton the First of America."

"And?" prompted the emperor.

"Oh, I almost fergot. Protector of Mexico."

"Quite right. Well done. Well, we must be off. We are late for luncheon with the cabinet. Matters of state. Master Daly, direct the ambassador to come round and present his credentials when he has the proper formal attire, and render him every assistance." He snapped the ferrule of his cane alongside his hat in a kingly gesture.

"Bow," hissed Jim. "Bow, 'fore he gets mad." Tom and Mont obediently bent their necks.

Emperor Norton smiled pleasantly and clicked his fingers. "Come Bummer, Come Lazarus. To luncheon." The emperor continued his stately progress down Market Street, accompanied by his bulldog and terrier comrades. Tom, Mont, and the newsboy watched him until he paused before a sign that read: Golden Nuggett Saloon—Free Lunch. Emperor Norton pivoted with military precision and entered the saloon at the head of his happily wagging cabinet officers.

"Who was that?" burst out Tom with a suddenly exhaled breath and laugh.

Jim grinned. "Emperor Norton? He's just a poor crazy man what lost a fortune—and then lost his mind. Thinks he's royalty."

"Why isn't he locked up?"

Shocked and angry, the newsboy shot back, "He don't hurt nothin'. Everybody here is a little crazy . . . him a mite more'n most . . . but we like him thataway!"

"No offense, son," soothed Tom. "Thanks for explaining. Maybe you can help us with something else. We just left off our rig at the livery stable here, and now we need to get to the Tehama House."

"Tehama? Sure enough. Corner of California and San-some." Jim proceeded to give directions, concluding with which stop to leave the streetcar. "You can see it from there," he said.

"Much obliged," said Tom, reaching in his pocket.

"Naw," said the newsboy, looking down the street toward the Golden Nuggett. "Wouldn't be right. It was a—what ya say, royal command."

"Then consider this a token presented by the ambassador of Egypt," Tom laughed and handed over a dime.

"Leave off tellin' me how sure of success you be, and splice me the cable of your plan instead," demanded Captain Law. The room on the third floor of the Tehama Hotel was occu-pied by Law, Perry, and Avery Hastings.

"Do you swear to be true to—" Hastings began.

"You can leave off unfurling any of your oaths, too," snorted Law. "I give you my word to say naught of your scheme. . . . That will have to serve, for I'll not promise more without the full chart of the voyage." His pale blue eyes flashed in defiance that clearly read: "You need me more than I need you."

Perry and Hastings withdrew to a corner of the room for a hasty consultation. Law meanwhile wandered over to the win-dow looking out on Sansome Street. He studied the forms of several passing women, squinting first one eye and then the other against the glare of the sun. His attention briefly touched on a tall, well built man who walked up Sansome with a small black child at his side. Hastings called Law back to the table.

"All right, Captain," said Avery reluctantly. "We will trust you with our entire plan, and then you can make up your mind."

Inclining his bulldog face in approval, and carefully laying his injured left hand on the tabletop, Law prepared to listen.

"We intend to purchase the *Chapman* and outfit her with enough arms and men to seize a Pacific mail steamship," Avery explained.

"Hold fast there a minute," objected Law. "And what of the *Cyane*? You might stop one mail ship, but they'll have an escort after that. Your puny schooner may outrun 'em, but it can't outfight a warship."

Jasper Perry took over the narration, his brooding eyes growing more animated with his enthusiastic portrayal of the conspiracy. "We mean to use the steamer to transport men to seize the arsenal at Benecia and the warships at Mare Island. Next, we'll sail down and capture or destroy the *Cyane* and occupy Fort Point."

"Lay off the point instead," remarked Law, shaking his head. "Where will this army come from?"

"We have trusted lieutenants who are even now recruiting loyal sons of the South from the gold fields between here and the Comstock. When the time comes, they'll be ready. But we must do our work as well, to be able to furnish transport to the attack on Benecia and what follows."

Law appeared to be considering this proposition. He stared hard at the stumps of his damaged hand, maybe contemplating the fingers that were no longer there. Hastings felt uneasy around the sea captain and wished that they could hurry and conclude their business. He was glad that he was leaving for the Comstock and would not have to deal with Law.

At last Law said, "And you want me to be master aboard *Chapman*, is that it? To command a pirate ship on a pirate's mission?"

"Privateer," Avery protested. "Duly authorized—"

"Bah!" Law snorted again, like the sound of a signal cannon firing. "Does a man's neck stretch any less if he be called 'privateer,' when those that catches him decides to hang him? And you?" he added, sneering into Avery's face. "Mind you, it's all one to me. There's some as would say that pirate is a step up from the days when I was captain aboard a slaver on the New Orleans run. . . . All right, here stand my terms: *Chapman* is mine when the job is done and . . ." He paused to wave his bandaged hand under Avery's nose. "I want one thousand dollars, gold, afore we start. Do you have it?"

Hastings and Perry exchanged looks and decided to tell Law the truth. "No," Avery reported. "We only had enough for earnest money for the *Chapman.* We don't yet have the funds to complete the purchase or outfit her, or pay you what you ask."

"And what will you do about it?"

"That is not your concern," retorted Perry. "We will have the additional amount soon. In fact, we want you to make out a list of equipment needed aboard the *Chapman*, and we will order it for delivery in two weeks. Our agent will have secured the money by then."

8

WITH ITS GREEN steep gabled roof and white clapboard siding, Mount Carmel Presbyterian Church was a jewel among the surrounding buildings of Greenville in the valley below Shadow Ridge. The bell in its steeple had rung out to announce the election of Lincoln, and some months later, the beginning of the war between North and South. For a time, discussion of politics had been off-limits within its sanctuary. But the death of Emily Dawson's husband by the treachery of a member of the congregation had split the church. It had caused Emily herself to support the Northern cause with renewed dedication.

This morning several pews were empty as the congregation rose to sing the *Battle Hymn of the Republic.* Even empty pews did not dim the fervor of those who sang and then prayed for the restoration of the Union. Those who supported the Southern cause met in a newly framed plainer building just across the street. Their voices bellowed the tune of *Onward Christian Soldiers* in an attempt to drown out their Yankee neighbors. In Greenville, only the dusty road separated North and South, but the gulf between neighbors and onetime friends was as wide as an ocean.

Pastor Swift preached a mighty sermon from the thirty-seventh Psalm. *"Fret not thyself because of evildoers. . . ."* He pounded the plain wooden pulpit and his gray-streaked beard trembled with righteous indignation as he gestured out the window toward the congregation that had seceded from the union of his church.

"For evil men will be cut off," he shouted, striking the pulpit again with energy that would have rivaled old John

Knox himself! "A little while, and the wicked will be no more!" He waved his arm toward the Southern Baptist building. "Though you look for them, they will not be found!"

Nate grimaced at these words. Jed rubbed his cheek thoughtfully. Both boys had told their mother they would rather have their old school friends back in the pews with them instead of having swords pierce their hearts as Pastor Swift said. The majority of their classmates cheered the victories of Jefferson Davis and openly cursed Lincoln's army. Would they ever be friends again?

Emily squeezed the hands of her sons when they leaned forward to whisper such thoughts to each other. Even a church, it seemed, was not the proper place to preach political peace and reconciliation.

"The Lord loves the just and will not forsake His faithful ones," Pastor Swift preached on. "They will be protected forever, but the offspring of the wicked will be cut off."

So much for the children of Southern sympathizers. Well, if the war didn't get over soon, a whole lot of offspring would be missing from school.

Nate and Jed did not want the whole Baptist building to disappear. But they did think it would be just fine, however, if the Lord would cut off the fellows who had poisoned the sorrel gelding and keep them from poisoning the rest of the stock. Such thoughts flew between them as Parson Swift delivered an ear-shattering message that certainly could be heard by the Baptists.

The boys were relieved when the sermon finally ended and they sang the doxology. Standing at the door to greet his parishioners, Parson Swift extended his gnarled hand to Emily as she passed by.

"I was expecting the whole of the Union Army to be in church with you today, Sister Dawson. Have you left them back at the ranch then?"

"They have not come yet," Emily answered quietly.

"Not come?" He seemed astounded by the news that Emily and the boys had remained alone at the ranch this past week without the protection Pettibone had promised to send. "How have you managed, woman?"

"We take turns through the night." She lay a hand on Jed's shoulder. He stood a little taller. "We each keep a two-hour watch. Most of the stock has been brought in to the near corrals. We've hung lanterns on the fence posts and lit the barn as well."

The parson looked grieved at the news. "Sister Dawson! I do declare! You've managed the week without calling for assistance. Well, well, like the builders of the wall of Jerusalem, we must stand watch and pray! The days are evil. The nights a heap more so. Sister Dawson, you are most welcome to stay here at the parsonage until the soldiers arrive at your place." He placed his hand on Nate's shoulder. "Well, boy, would you like to move to town for a while?"

An instant of excitement passed over the faces of both boys, and then Nate replied quietly, "No, sir. Tom told us we was the men on the place till he and Mont come home again. We ain't leavin'."

Pastor Swift looked surprised and then amused. "Well now." He thumped Nate on the back. "A manly attitude, I'll say. And one your father would be right proud of. But your uncle had not foreseen what happened out your way with the horse and the threat to you. Otherwise he would have made arrangements for you to come to town and stay."

"We are managing fine," Emily said proudly. "Thank you for your concern, but you needn't to worry yourself. I have not slept away from the ranch even one night since Jesse brought me here. And I will not be chased out of my home now. Besides, Deputy Pettibone was sure that soldiers would be sent. Perhaps they've arrived while we've been at church."

The muffled cry that reached Tom's ears from across Sansome was a high squeak, abruptly cut off. Tom looked up and down the wooden-planked street in order to find the source. No one was in sight in either direction on the still January night. The theater crowds had all dispersed, gone home before the thin sliver of moon hung its pale crescent overhead.

Tom had felt like a caged animal in the hotel room where Mont lay sleeping. After several uneventful days in San Francisco, what was supposed to happen next? It seemed as though even staying in a haven for Southern sympathizers like the Tehama House and the message he'd given to the desk clerk were no guarantee that Mont would ever chance across some conspirator whom he'd recognize. The people staying at the Tehama were more likely to sing the praises of Jeb Stuart and Bob Lee than Sherman or Grant, but so what? They were still only pursuing ordinary lives. There had been no knocks on the door, no one hanging around that looked sinister, and no one offering to buy military secrets. Perhaps the escaped spy named *Wilson* was not as hot a commodity as the army had thought?

So Tom had come outside to think. How long would they have to remain on this fruitless quest? Two weeks? Three? What if the "plot" turned out to be no more than the ravings of a few lunatics like the harmless Emperor Norton? The thought made Tom grin wryly to himself in the darkness.

A scuffling sound and another anguished protest froze the smile on his face. It sent Tom's hand to his side where the Colt, now on the bureau upstairs, would have hung. Slapping his palm against his leg in frustration, Tom charged across the street anyway, toward a blackened alley beside the American Theater.

Two dark-clad forms and one in lighter colors twisted and spun in the shadows. As Tom approached, the dimly seen forms resolved themselves into rough, drunken men and a panicked, desperate woman.

One man held the woman around the waist with one arm while his other hand was clamped across her mouth. The second attacker, smaller in height than the first, tried to catch the woman's legs. The men struggled to carry her a few steps farther into the darkness of the alley. Lunging and kicking, the woman partially freed herself and the threesome spun and clattered again in a blur of rustling petticoats and coarse oaths.

Charging straight into the group, Tom tackled the smaller man in a headlong rush that drove both past a stage door and into a brick wall that stood across the middle of the passage. The man's head connected with the masonry with a satisfying crack, and Tom dropped him and whirled around.

The second assailant flung the girl aside. From beneath his dark blue coat he drew a knife with a blade that seemed to be a foot long. "You better go, mister," the man breathed hoarsely. "You hadn't ought to butt into Grove Kinnock's business, unless you's fixin' to meet your Maker."

Tom circled warily, palms open. He kept his eyes on the knife-hand of his opponent.

Tom feinted toward Kinnock, hoping to draw a rush that would give the woman an opportunity to flee. But the knife-wielder was too wary for that, and he stayed an arm's length from the woman, brandishing the tapering blade drunkenly toward Tom's face.

"Cut you good, I aim to," sneered Kinnock. Behind Tom, the smaller man groaned and stirred.

Now the struggle was reaching a critical stage. No doubt the second attacker also had a knife, and from the sounds, he would soon be awake enough to use it. Tom would be caught between the two, still without a means to free the girl.

His boot brushed over a hard, lumpy object—a loose cobblestone or broken chunk of brick. Tom stooped quickly to retrieve it; anything to even the odds.

Tom's fingers had just touched the stone when Kinnock attacked. Shouting "Grab him, Rafe" to his still prostrate accomplice, he lunged toward Tom with a vicious swipe of the dirk.

The point of the blade caught the sleeve of Tom's denim jacket and slit it up to the elbow as he flung himself backward. A second slash of steel followed as a backhand arc at eye level passed within an inch of Tom's face.

Seizing the chance while Kinnock's guard was open, Tom swung the chunk of rock into the side of the man's head. Now it was Grove Kinnock's turn to jump awkwardly aside, but not before the brick had grazed his temple, splitting the scalp and leaving blood dripping from his hair.

"Run!" Tom shouted at the woman, who was still in a tumbled heap of petticoats on the slimy stones. "Run!" he commanded urgently.

With the blow, Kinnock's rage was up. For the moment, he forgot the girl. What he wanted was the chance to drive his blade into Tom's belly; to leave this foolish, interfering stranger gasping out the ebbing of his life.

His alcoholic clumsiness burned away by his anger, Kinnock curled into a fighting crouch. He advanced on Tom with the lightly balanced tread of a man used to the rolling deck of a ship.

"I'm gonna slit you from jib to mizzen," he hissed. "An' when I'm through, I'm gonna feed you to the fish piece by piece."

Tom was silent, standing a pace out from the wall and throwing a quick glance toward Rafe, who was on his knees, struggling to stand. *Why doesn't the girl run? Is she hurt or knocked unconscious?*

The moment for pondering flashed by as Kinnock's stalking approach brought him again within striking range. Though he was enraged, Kinnock was wary of the stone club Tom held aloft in his right hand. He had already suffered a stinging blow, and now moved toward his prey cautiously.

Kinnock lunged with the point of his knife held straight ahead, like a sword thrust. As Tom jumped aside, the sailor turned the movement into a sickle's sweep, expecting to catch Tom in the side.

Tom chopped downward with the improvised club. Using the stone like the primitive ax of an ancient tribesman, Tom snapped his elbow taut, speeding the impact of the jagged edge against Kinnock's forearm.

There was an audible crunch as Kinnock's arm shattered. A howl of pain and a clatter followed as the dirk fell from his nerveless fingers.

Bending swiftly to try and retrieve the knife, Tom caught an upraised knee on the point of his chin. Hundreds more stars than could actually be seen in Frisco's foggy skies exploded in front of his sight. He staggered back, shaking his head to try and clear his vision, but only setting off more cascades of meteors.

Tom could hear Kinnock cursing and scrabbling in the debris with his uninjured arm. The sailor stood slowly, holding the knife again, his broken arm cradled against his chest.

"I can stick you just as easy . . . with my . . . other hand," he panted. "Rafe," he called, "catch hold of this fella for me. I'm gonna gut him like a sea bass."

The smaller man was up now and staggering forward. Tom still held the stone club, but there was little he could do with it against two. Kinnock blocked the exit and Rafe was closing in.

There was one chance. Rafe still looked unsteady on his feet and Kinnock favored his injured arm. If Tom could maneuver himself behind Rafe, keep the smaller man between him and Kinnock's knife thrusts—

When Kinnock sprang again, Tom flung himself toward Rafe instead. The smaller man did not expect to be attacked and gave ground suddenly. The force of Kinnock's wild slash spun him around out of position.

Tom pressed his rush toward Rafe and had the man by the coat lapels. Swinging him around, Tom prepared to throw him into Kinnock when . . . Tom's feet slipped on the damp pavement and he and Rafe tumbled down together.

Over and over they rolled, thrashing in the alley. They fetched up against the brick wall again.

Kinnock moved into position like a victorious spider, towering overhead. He held the long-bladed knife, point downward, like an ice pick.

"Good," he growled. "Hold him there, Rafe. I'm gonna poke his eyes out, and *then* gut him!" The knife was drawn back to end the battle when—

The explosion of a pistol shot in the narrow confines of the brick canyon sounded like mortar fire. The thunderous roar deafened Tom to all but the reverberating beat of the echoes dying away.

Kinnock was flung back against the wall as if a giant wind-storm had thrown him there. Like garments blown from a Telegraph Hill clothesline, he stood propped against the wall, motionless and stiff. An instant later, as a dying breeze releases its stolen prizes, he slumped into a heap.

"Grove? Grove!" shouted Rafe, kicking himself free of Tom. The depth of his concern for his friend evaporated, and he ran out of the alley and down California Street. The tromp of his footsteps on the plank roadway echoed hollowly. The slowly diminishing sounds of his headlong retreat showed that he was still running after blocks and blocks.

The woman came to stand beside Tom. "Did you do that?" he asked, gesturing toward the lifeless Kinnock.

"Yes," she said simply, "with this," and she handed Tom a two-shot derringer, still warm from the explosion of its first charge.

"Ma'am, I . . ." he began, but she took his arm and pulled him toward the street.

"Someone will have heard the shot and the police will come to investigate," she said. "It will be much simpler for us to leave now. Please," she begged, "I promise I'll explain. My hotel is just across the street."

By the lobby light that spilled out on the street as the woman entered, Tom could see that she was startlingly beautiful. Dark ringlets of hair fell in disarray over the shoulders of the evening cloak she wore.

She was tall and her disheveled clothes did not conceal her feminine figure silhouetted against the interior light. Tom allowed her to enter first, alone, as she had requested.

Shortly after, Tom also entered the Tehama House lobby. He wondered if all their caution was necessary. No one had come to investigate the gunshot, and the night clerk was dozing behind the counter.

Her room was 2-B, up one flight and immediately next to the stairs. The door opened quickly at Tom's quiet tap, and she drew him into the room with a nervous glance down the empty corridor.

"Ma'am, I only came to see that you were all right," Tom began awkwardly. "I'll go on now—"

"Please wait," she insisted. "I want to thank you for coming to help me. It was a very brave thing you did."

Tom shuffled his feet and stared down at the roses woven into the carpet. He was trying to avoid looking at the expanse of creamy throat that appeared above the opening of her silk dressing gown. "It seems to me that I should be thanking you," he mumbled.

"Nonsense," she laughed. A slight tremor in her voice betrayed that she was not as entirely in control as she wanted to appear. "Those brutes! I dropped my pistol in the struggle before you appeared. If you had not arrived when you did, they would have . . ."

Tom cleared his throat and again acted as if leaving as soon as possible would please him.

"Please sit," she insisted, and she seated herself on a mahogany divan whose needlepoint cushions matched the carpet. Tom obliged her by perching stiffly in a straight-backed chair near the door. The air seemed filled with an exotic aroma—the scent of a flower garden blooming in the dead of winter.

"My name is Belle Boyd," she said, pausing as if Tom should recognize it immediately. When he made no comment, she continued. "I'm an actress. I stayed late in the theater tonight, studying lines for a new role. Since the theater is just across the street, I wasn't worried about coming out alone. But those two men! They were right outside the stage door and grabbed me when I stepped out!"

"Why didn't you want the police, ma'am? You could have described the second man. Perhaps they could have caught him."

"That's why I felt I had to explain," she said. "You know that those two men were sailors—*Yankee Navy sailors*," she spat, as if repeating especially harsh and distasteful swear words. "My sympathies are well-known and clearly with the Confederacy—I would not have received justice. Not after having killed one of *them*. No, it's better this way."

9

THE MORNING AFTER his first encounter with Belle Boyd, Tom and Mont sat in the dining room of the Tehama House having breakfast. Looking out the window toward the street, the two took in the porticoed veranda and wrought-iron scrollwork by which the builder conveyed an air of Southern gentility.

A lilting voice at their elbows made them turn abruptly. "This view always puts me in mind of Atlanta. Don't you think so, Mr. Wilson?"

Both males jumped to their feet. "Ah, um, Miss Boyd . . . I'm sure the resemblance is exact, if you say so," stammered Tom.

The Cupid's bow of a mouth parted into a smile that included Mont. "What an adorable boy. What is his name, Mr. Wilson?"

Mont took an instant dislike to the dark-haired woman, beautiful and friendly though she was. Miss Emily had never spoken *about* him as if he were not present. And besides, what right did this person have to be so familiar with Tom? They had only met the night before.

"This is Mont, Miss Boyd. Mont, make your manners to Miss Boyd," Tom directed.

Mont bowed stiffly from the waist and said in a too quiet, brittle-sounding voice, "Pleased to meet you, ma'am."

"Delightful!" Belle enthused. "So well trained. Have you had him long?"

At least this was a question Tom and Mont had rehearsed. "Oh yes," Tom replied, "and his family before him."

"How nice," Belle responded, but it was plain from her tone and the gaze which she fixed on Tom that her interest in Mont had evaporated, if any had really ever existed. "May I join you?"

"Please," agreed Tom, signaling to a white-coated waiter passing by with a silver coffee pot.

When both adults were seated, Mont, who was still standing, said in a voice that was over-loud this time, "Marse Wilson, shall I go up an' check on your laundry?"

Puzzled by the abrupt departure, Tom agreed rather than asking in front of Belle for an explanation of this contrivance. After Mont was gone and the waiter had poured two fresh cups of coffee, Belle launched into another lengthy thank you for Tom's role in the events of the night before.

"It isn't necessary to thank me," said Tom, looking into the dark brown eyes that held his from across the table. "I could not have done anything else."

"But I am *so* grateful," purred Belle. "Besides, I sense a real kinship of spirit with you. You *are* the Wilson who rescued that dear little editor from those criminal soldiers?"

Tom acknowledged the event with a nod. "Nothing to brag about. I could not let the good man be lynched, even though he acted the part of a fool. There are more effective methods of dealing with Yankees than deriding them in public. But tell me, how do you know that story?"

Belle's chin tilted toward the dining room ceiling as a peal of bell-like laughter bubbled from her throat. "Why Mr. Wilson," she said with mock sternness, "I'm surprised at you! A gentleman never asks a lady to reveal her sources!

"But since you are *that* Wilson, I don't mind telling you," she continued in a conspiratorial tone. She extended her gloved hand across the table toward Tom's coffee cup and wrapped her long, slender fingers around his sturdy, tanned fist. She pulled his hand toward her side of the table with a surprisingly strong grip, and Tom leaned in until their heads almost touched.

"There are still a few true sons of the South in this state," she murmured, "but not nearly enough that a gallant hero like yourself can go unnoticed or unremarked."

A whiff of the same exotic perfume Tom had noticed in Belle's room hit his senses. For an instant the clatter of crockery and the bustle of the waiters disappeared. It felt as if he and Belle were alone together. The two were eye to eye, only a breath apart.

The reverie was interrupted when a dark-suited man walked over to their table and stood alongside. Tom first noticed the pointed toes on the black leather shoes, then scanned upward to the pointed beard and the brooding eyes below the heavy dark brows.

Unhurriedly, Belle leaned back in her chair and said in a completely conversational tone, "As I was saying, Mr. Wilson, your actions have not gone unreported. The fact of the matter is that Mr. Perry here would also like to congratulate you."

Once again, Tom stood and the two men shook hands. Perry had still not said anything. His eyes seemed to try and penetrate Tom's, and his expression was sharp, even harsh. He squeezed Tom's hand with a grip far stronger than courtesy suggested.

If that's how you want it, thought Tom, *I'll play along*, and he returned the crush of the handshake, pound for pound. Belle watched the contest of strength with undisguised amusement.

The first indication that either man was faltering occurred when Perry unlocked his stare and glanced down at his hand. The tips of his fingers had turned white up to the second joints. An involuntary grunt escaped his tightly clenched jaws.

Tom immediately relaxed his grip and gestured with his free hand toward Mont's empty chair. "Please have a seat, Mr. Perry."

"Sturdy handshake," Perry remarked gruffly. Then, as if remembering Belle's introduction, he continued in a friendlier tone, "It's fortunate that a man of your strength was around to come to my fiance's assistance."

Tom's glance at Belle saw her momentarily flustered, but she recovered her composure quickly. A faint pink tinge lingered as evidence of her discomfort.

Perry draped his arm possessively across the back of Belle's chair. "The Yankee tyrant Lincoln, with his army of invaders, thinks that he can tread on the rights of sovereign states with impunity. Thankfully, courageous men like Garrison still stand up and spit in his eye! But the wheels of oppression are grinding harder and harder. Brave men are fighting and dying for want of assistance. We dare not stand idly by."

Tom's thought ran from how much like a prepared speech this sounded to how ironic it was for a cause that endorsed slavery to speak of being oppressed.

"I have heard similar sentiments expressed before," commented Tom with an air of cautious approval.

"Stronger, Mr. Wilson, stronger! You may speak your mind freely here—you're among friends! You were already vouched for, but your recent actions not only underline your character, but place me personally in your debt. How may I improve your stay in San Francisco?"

Tom's look around the room paused briefly on nearby diners, judging whether the conversation had been overheard. His prolonged stare at a bald-headed man seated alone at a corner table caused both Perry and Belle to follow his gaze.

As if satisfied at last that he could proceed safely, Tom replied to Jasper Perry's offer. "I have been sent," he said with a note of mystery, "to offer myself to an extremely important effort to aid a glorious cause—at any cost." These words were part of a formula explained to Tom by Colonel Mason.

Perry's expression did not change. In an off-hand way he said to Belle, "I'm sorry you have to leave, my dear. Thank you for your kind introduction." Perry stood and helped the actress up from her chair.

Belle looked nonplussed at the abrupt dismissal, but offered no argument. "I'm sure I won't miss anything but boring man talk and speech making," she said with a flutter of her eyelashes. Then to Tom she said, "Don't believe *everything* he says, Mr. Wilson. Mr. Perry is prone to exaggeration." After this small act of defiance, Belle took her leave. It was clear from the way she bestowed smiles and hellos around the tables that Belle understood the power of her charms.

Both men followed her out of the room with their eyes. At last Perry spoke. "Your arrival could not be more fortunate. We need to move quickly and decisively."

"You are the leader of the castle, of course," observed Tom. "I knew it immediately."

Perry shook his head with a self-deprecating shrug. "No, not me. I am only a messenger—a foot soldier, if you will. But I'd like you to accompany me to meet our general."

"When?"

"Tonight."

In a carriage with drawn shades, Tom was taken on a roundabout drive through San Francisco. When the ride was over, he was hustled into a warehouse.

"Greetings, Brother Wilson," said a breathy and muffled voice from someone in a throne-like chair with a mask over his face. Tom took his seat in a circle of four men.

"As you see," Jasper Perry explained in rather unctuous tones, "we are small in number, but not in courage. Many have abandoned our cause because of cowardice or personal greed, but those who remain are undoubted. You have shown yourself to be worthy of our trust."

Perry continued, "We need your help on an important matter. We want you to join forces with some brothers in Virginia City, Nevada Territory. Will you go?"

"What am I to do there?" Tom asked.

"That will be explained at the proper time," Perry responded. "All you must do for now is take a room at the Tahoe Hotel. You will be contacted there. Will you go?"

"Yes, of course," Tom responded, not really certain if he meant to go or not. "But I have business to take care of tomorrow. I can leave the next day."

"Very well," intoned the leader, concluding the discussion. "We appreciate your willingness, Brother Wilson. The others in Virginia City are expecting us to send assistance. When you get to the hotel and register, all you need to do is put this word—CHAPMAN—after your name. You'll be contacted. Now, if you'll wait in the next room for just a minute. . . ."

After Tom had left the room, the tone turned less formal. "Do Ingram and Hastings really need his help?" one man asked.

"Ingram has grit; he will stick. But Hastings is young and sometimes soft. He may need to be replaced."

"But what do we really know about this man?"

"We have the description of what he looks like and the report of his escape. We know that he is brave and has shown himself able and willing to stand up to the Yankees. Besides, let me add that Miss Boyd will also be going to the Comstock shortly after. She will keep an eye on him as well. If need be, she can do more than charm him."

The side-wheeler *Yosemite* was just easing into the docks when Tom and Mont approached the wharf. The tall black smokestack towered over the paddlewheels and the walking-beam amidships, dwarfing the pilot house. But the flag of the United States waving bravely at the stern stood out plainly above the gleaming white ship.

"Isn't that a grand sight, Mont?" Tom asked.

" 'Deed it is," agreed Mont. "Mighty proud!"

"You know," Tom added, "if we go to the Comstock like Perry and the secesh want, that boat, or one like it, is how we'll travel up river."

Mont's eyes grew as big as saucers. "You means we'd go 'cross the bay on it?" he asked. The *Yosemite* seemed to sense his enthusiasm and responded by announcing its arrival with a great blast of its steam whistles.

"Not just across the bay, but clear to Sacramento. From there the stage company runs to Virginia City, Nevada Territory." In an afterthought he added, "Of course, from Sacramento you could catch a stage back home, too. Yes sir, just two days from where we're standing and we'd be home." He sounded as if he wished that were the journey being planned, instead of one going farther away.

"Is we goin' to Virginia City for shore?"

"I don't know. I want to ask some advice from the two military men Colonel Mason mentioned to me. I'm afraid if I don't agree to go, then it will look suspicious to Perry and his group. But if I do go, I'm worried about taking you along. The Comstock is plenty rough at the best of times."

Mont started to protest that he'd be just fine, but Tom continued, "You know, if I had any good place to leave you, I'd have you stay here till I got back. I just don't know who with."

Mont's mouth closed with a snap. He'd already decided that the sooner this subject got changed, the better.

They spotted the man Tom had come to see outside an office near the South Beach Ship Yard. Commander Fry was an imposing figure, as tall as Tom and nearly as muscular, despite his sixty years of age. He had a shock of white hair and impressive white burnsides.

His uniform, all brass and braids, included a sword. Mont thought the commander looked a lot like woodcuts he had seen of Andrew Jackson.

"Commander Fry?" Tom confirmed. "My name is Wilson. I believe Colonel Mason may have mentioned my name to you."

"Wilson, of course. Come in," Fry said tersely. Then to a man dressed in greasy coveralls who had been receiving rapid-fire instructions, he concluded, "I want them here to-morrow. Tomorrow, understand? Not one day later or by thunder I'll have a new foreman."

"Yes sir, Admiral," said the worker in an Irish brogue. "Come sunup tomorrow, they'll be here. It'll be a grand sight, to be sure." The man pulled on his forelock and backed away.

Fry drew Tom and Mont into a small office that contained only one chair and a desk overflowing with plans and blue-prints. He did not seat himself, so all three stood in the tiny space. "Wilson," he said again, "heard from Mason. Think it's poppycock. This conspiracy. Anyway, no time to play games. Too busy already."

"Well, sir," said Tom with rising indignation. "Colonel Mason has reason to think there is truth to it and I have already met—"

"Some secesh die-hards? Rubbish," Fry said abruptly. "Good luck to you, Mr. Wilson. What we're about here is more important than chasing fairies. Now if you'll excuse me," and he ushered them out and shut his door.

"Come on, Mont," Tom said, thrusting his hands into his pockets and walking with such angry strides that Mont had to run to keep up. "Let's go see if the Army treats us any better. If nobody wants to give us the time of day, maybe we'll just go home."

10

THE PATH LEADING down the hill toward Fort Point took Tom and Mont past the commander's house. They knocked, but no one answered.

The commander of Fort Point's garrison of two hundred men lived in a small frame house, freshly painted white and trimmed in forest green. It stood on a knoll just above the brick fortress. From the yard beside the home, the soldiers on guard duty atop the walls of the fort could be seen patrolling their posts.

A northwest wind funnelled past the Marin headland and made the flag waving over the casements snap on its halyard. It was a pleasant day for an outing to view the Golden Gate, the entrance to the greatest natural harbor in the world.

But if the scene from the knobby hill was inspiring and enjoyable, descending the wooden staircase to stand in the shadow of the three-story-high citadel brought back the reality of war. Soldiers were drilling on the cleared area in front of the fort's single entrance. They marched and counter-marched under the critical eye of a red-bearded sergeant-major. He gave them the benefit of his opinion at every opportunity, expressed in a voice that resounded from the brick walls and rocky cliffside with such volume that Tom thought it must be heard in Sausalito across the bay.

Tom and Mont heard him question a soldier's intellect, morals, upbringing and ancestry when the man had failed to execute "order arms" properly. When the sergeant-major saw Tom and Mont approaching, he must have decided that another opportunity for a lesson had presented itself. He pointed to three soldiers and waved them forward.

"Kirby, Seldon, Morris—you three are the guard detail. Kirby is acting corporal. Let me see you make a proper challenge and report."

"Halt! Who goes there?" demanded the one named Seldon, pointing a bayonet at Tom's midsection.

"Corporal 'the guard! Post number one!" shouted Morris.

"Escort the uh, the uh—" Kirby stumbled, uncertain if these were prisoners or visitors. The glare he received from Sergeant-Major Donovan would have melted one of the antique bronze cannons that flanked the entrance.

Under Donovan's withering stare, Kirby swallowed hard and reported. "Corporal 'the guard, Sergeant-Major. Post number one is escorting two unknown persons."

Donovan puffed out his whiskers like a surfacing sea lion and advanced past where Kirby stood quivering at attention.

"Sergeant-Major Donovan," he announced to Tom. "What is your name and purpose?"

"My name is Wilson," said Tom, "and this is Mont. We are here to see Captain Tompkins."

"Regrettably, sir, Captain Tompkins is ill and in the hospital. Lieutenant Reynolds is in command."

"I see," said Tom with some consternation. "Would you please ask the lieutenant if he will see me? My business here was suggested by Colonel Mason of Fort Tejon."

"Of course. If you will wait here, please."

In a brief space of time, Donovan was back and now offered to escort Tom and Mont to Reynold's office himself. As they passed into the interior of the fort, the high walls shut out the sunlight and sound with the finality of a prison cell door.

Lieutenant Reynolds was a plump, soft-looking young man, about Tom's age. He had a receding chin but a prominent nose that he was fond of looking down, as though sighting a cannon. He affected the dress uniform of the artillery, including a red sash and black ostrich-plumed hat.

After introductions, Tom proceeded to explain his real identity and his reason for being in San Francisco with Mont. "So you see," he summarized, "Colonel Mason believed that the plot was real enough to bear investigation and that Mont might recognize one of the principals."

"And has he?" Reynolds inquired, aiming his nose at Mont.

"No," Tom said, "but *I* may have stumbled on to something." He went on to describe Jasper Perry and the mysterious meeting that called for him to make a trip to the Comstock.

When he had finished, Reynolds leaned back in his chair and laced his pudgy fingers together. "There may be some real importance to what you have uncovered, and I want you to know I take it seriously. But we must proceed slowly and carefully. It would not do to spook one bird and let the covey escape. Are you agreeable to going to Virginia City to see if you can discover the others in the plot?"

"Yes, except that I dislike dragging Mont all over the countryside. Besides, it could be dangerous for him. But I think the gang will be suspicious if I don't go."

"Acting reluctant at this point would certainly raise some questions," Reynolds agreed. "How about this: Mont can stay with me while you make a rapid trip there to see what you can discover, then return on some pretext, and we'll round up all of them you can identify."

"Leave Mont with you?" Tom said a little dubiously.

"Would you rather that we arrest this actress—what's her name, Boyd, for questioning? See what information we can get from her?"

"No, no," said Tom hastily. "You're right that we should know more first. We don't want to tip off the others."

"Splendid," said Reynolds. "You can leave Mont with me now and send his things back. Will you be leaving tonight?"

Tom looked over at Mont and thought he saw a tear forming in the corner of the boy's eye. "No," he said quickly, "we have some important business tonight, Mont and I. Why don't you come and pick him up at our hotel, Tehama House, tomorrow at ten, if that's all right. I'll leave on the noon steamer."

"Excellent," agreed Reynolds. "Now come and let me show you around the fort. Mont, you will see that it will be fun to stay here." To Tom he added, "And you will see how foolish it is to think of any Confederate attempt to seize this position. By the way, I think it's best if you say nothing to anyone else about the plot. You can't tell who might be secesh in this town."

Their footsteps echoed hollowly as he led the way up dark staircases. They emerged on the highest level of the fort. Walking over to a row of cannons, Reynolds patted one affectionately, as if it were a prize horse in a show ring. "Sixty-eight pounder," he said proudly. "Columbiad with a rifled barrel. This weapon can propel a shot two miles or more. The one hundred and twenty of these command more than a half circle on the entrance to the bay."

"What's this?" asked Mont, pointing at a brick and cast-iron contraption with a chimney.

"Furnace," observed Reynolds, "for heating shells red-hot."

"This is all very impressive," commented Tom. "But what if the garrison were surprised and the guns seized? After all, these guns all face the water."

"True enough," agreed Reynolds, "but we have field pieces and mortars to defend the landward side, and two full companies of troops."

Tom and Mont prepared to take their leave then, after thanking Reynolds for showing them around. "Not at all, not at all," he concluded. "I'll see you both tomorrow."

He and Tom conversed quietly for a few more minutes, then Mont and the rancher from Shadow Ridge left the fort.

Halfway up the hill again, the man and the boy turned to view the harbor channel one more time. A Pacific mail steamer was bustling into the Gate, churning a streaming wake of white foam and a double trail of black smoke. She passed an outbound square-rigged sailing ship and the two exchanged salutes—steam whistle screaming a reply to the sharp report of a swivel cannon.

Both ships dipped pennants by way of respect to the American flag flying over the fort. A thirty-two pounder roared a reply. It seemed also to be a reminder of how strong and solid the Union defenses of the bay really were.

Tom stood with his hand on Mont's shoulder and both took in the panorama of the scene. "I can't understand how Perry and the others can be so confident," Tom said, half to himself. "Maybe they *are* crazy."

"I 'spect they see somethin' we doesn't see," Mont suggested.

In the glow of the lantern light, Jed looked older than his eleven years. He perched in the hayloft with his father's old Greener shotgun across his lap. At Emily's footstep on the threshold of the barn, he challenged, "Who's that there?"

"Ma," she answered, struck by the manliness of his young voice. "I've brought you another blanket. Some milk and bread with butter and sugar." She stood at the bottom of the ladder as he peered over and then climbed down to retrieve the tin lunch bucket. "You let me know if you get too tired and I'll take the watch," she offered.

He replied with an indignant snort. "I ain't little no more like Nate. I can take his watch and yours as well, if I need to. Nobody's gonna get past that barn door unless I give 'em permission."

She did not ask him if he was ever frightened. To do so would have been an insult. Nor did she admit that a dozen times throughout her own watch she had felt the chill of fear at the rustling sounds in the night. An owl hooting in the oak tree, the restless stirring of the horses in the corral at the side of the barn, had tightened her grip on the stock of the gun and turned calm prayers into a torrent of frightened entreaties to the Almighty for protection.

No doubt Jed had felt the same. Little Nate had fled into the house and now could not stand his watch alone anymore. Jed simply slept beside him in the hay throughout Nate's watch. A dozen times Nate woke him with a shake and the frantic question, *You hear that?* After his watch, Nate would stumble into the house and Jed would shake himself awake to sit alone for another two hours.

"You're doing fine, son," Emily said with genuine admiration. "Just remember when you're tired, the Lord never sleeps nor slumbers. He is keeping watch over us in ways we cannot see."

Jed nodded and sipped his milk. "I just wish He'd send us some soldiers to help out. I mean blue-coated soldiers that I could see." A wry smile crossed his lips. A smile so much like his father's.

"They're bound to come." She looked at the animals in the stalls and wondered if perhaps the Union soldiers did in fact consider guarding the Dawson ranch a trivial matter. Too unimportant to deal with. She did not express her doubt to Jed, however. "In the meantime, it's just us. And no doubt great armies of angels all around us. Enough for now or there would be others here as well."

He nodded and glanced up toward the loft. One hand on the ladder and then he froze.

Far away in the darkness the sound of hoofbeats echoed on the rock-hard roadbed. Jed shoved the bucket into his mother's arms and scrambled up the ladder to retrieve the shotgun. "Get to the house," he instructed her in manly tones. "They're still aways off. Get the rifles and the revolver."

Emily ran to the house, wishing that there were soldiers of the blue-coated sort right now to help them! The hoofbeats came nearer, turning onto the lane that led to the ranch house. She took the Winchester from the gun rack and wrested the Colt revolver from its holster. Asleep on the sofa, Nate stirred, groaned, and rolled over to settle into a deeper sleep. It was good that he was unaware of her own sense of fear, Emily thought. Then a renewed anger flooded her as she thought of Tom Dawson off chasing shadows when there was such a real and terrible threat right here at home! When were those soldiers coming? And when would Tom be back? She would give him a piece of her mind when he showed up!

She carried the kerosene lantern outside with her and put it on the tree stump beside the hitching rail. Then she stepped back in the shadows to wait as the riders came near. The Dawson family had rehearsed this plan several times.

"I'm here, Jed," she called loudly. "I've got the guns!" She hoped the riders would hear the threat in her voice and turn around. They did not.

"We got 'em covered, Ma," Jed called bravely. No doubt he too hoped to discourage whoever was coming.

It was then that a familiar voice rang out from the darkness of the lane. "Sister Dawson! Young Jed! Do not shoot! It is Parson Swift here! I've brought my sons along to stand watch with you tonight!"

11

AWAKE AND LOOKING out the window, Mont watched the misty fingers of fog just beginning to relinquish their grip on the street lamps. Today Mont would go to stay with the lieutenant at Fort Point, but right now he was waiting in the room at the Tehama Hotel.

Tom had left long before daylight. After checking steamer sailings from Frisco and stage connections from Sacramento to Virginia City, Tom had decided on the early departure. "I can save a whole day's wait in Sacramento this way," he explained to Mont. "Don't worry. I'll be back soon and Lieutenant Reynolds will look after you."

The lieutenant had wanted Mont to stay at the fort last night, but Tom had insisted that he and Mont have dinner together and take in a show at the Melodeon Theater. Besides, Tom had suggested to Reynolds that Mont could point out secesh conspirators around the hotel. Reynolds had agreed. He would come in civilian clothes in the morning to pick up Mont. His Army uniform would certainly frighten the rebels, and it could be disastrous if a Union officer were seen talking with Tom and Mont.

Even without the lieutenant's red sash and ostrich-plumed hat, Mont now spotted the officer coming up the street. Reynolds paused to strike a match on a lamppost and lit his cigar. He was wearing a plain, dark blue cape and a cloth cap.

Mont was already dressed and bounced out of the room to the stairwell in anticipation of Reynolds' arrival. In the silence of the still early morning, Mont could hear the clump of the heavy boots coming up the stairs. Ten steps to the landing and ten more to the second floor, Mont counted. The climbing tread stopped. *That's funny*, Mont thought, *guess he forgot we wuz on three.* Mont leaned over the railing to call down to Reynolds to come up one more flight.

Stretching out above the stairwell, Mont caught a glimpse of a dark blue back and shoulder one floor below. As he watched, a fist rose and fell on the door nearest the steps in two quick knocks; followed by two more.

The door to Miss Boyd's room was opened by Jasper Perry. Reynolds stepped hastily through and the panel was quickly closed behind him.

Something was wrong, very wrong. Why was the Union army officer going to meet with the conspirators? It did not look like he was there to arrest them. Mont had to find out.

He tiptoed quietly down the steps, then looked all around to see if anyone was nearby before placing his ear close to the keyhole. The volume of voices coming from Belle's room was loud enough that Mont did not have to strain to hear:

"What do you mean, he's not one of us!" shouted the voice of Jasper Perry.

"Calm down and lower your voice," demanded Reynolds. "There is no harm done. We'll take care of him the same way we did the other imposter."

"But he's already gone to the Comstock," murmured Belle.

Now it was Reynolds' turn to be surprised. "What?" his voice squeaked. "He wasn't due to leave till noon."

"I saw him off early this morning," said Belle, "on his way to the steamer."

"All right," said Reynolds, back in control. "Belle, you are leaving for the Comstock at once. I won't trust this message to the wire, what with Pinkerton men everywhere. You must see Ingram. Tell him to hire someone outside the circle, but do it quickly!"

"But, General, what about the nigger brat?" Perry wanted to know.

"We'll hang on to him as a hostage till we know the job is done," Reynolds concluded.

"Ho there, you boy," boomed a voice down the hall behind Mont. "What are you sneakin' 'round that door for?" The conversation in the room stopped abruptly and running steps came toward the door.

Mont's headlong flight took him down the stairs three steps at a time. At the bottom he did a neat swing around a wrought-iron bannister and came off the last six steps airborne, flying feet first.

His boots collided with the stomach of a well-dressed, portly, recently fed gentleman. The collision produced an "oof," followed by a groan. The large man revolved slowly like a ship capsizing and sank down on the bottom step, holding his paunch. His girth blocked the stairs and when Mont's pursuers reached the ground floor, they could not get by.

Reynolds made one polite, encouraging noise, asking the man to move. When Perry saw Mont race past the doorman, he tried to leap over the roadblock . . . unsuccessfully, as it turned out.

The large man had tried to oblige Reynolds by clearing the stairs, and so stood up just as Jasper Perry hurdled over. A kick behind the ear dropped the poor man to the floor again and sent Perry sprawling onto the marble tiles. He partly caught himself on his hands, but not soon enough to keep his forehead from smacking the pavement. He got up looking dazed, and wandered toward the desk clerk.

Running past the jumbled heap of bodies, Reynolds dashed out the front door. He spotted Mont a half block away, running north on Sansome.

At the same time, a policeman turned the corner of Sacramento Street, right in Mont's path. Behind him, Reynolds yelled, "Stop him, he's a pickpocket!" The nine-year-old did not think of trying to explain his side of the story. All he saw was another pair of arms outstretched to grab him. Mont ducked his head one way and threw his body the other. The policeman's arms closed around only empty air.

A bell began to clang behind him in furious alarm. Mont accelerated his pace, terrified at the size of the alarm that was being raised—all of San Francisco must be after him!

The clanging bell was getting closer. It seemed to be chasing him up the street. Everyone on the sidewalks had stopped to watch the pursuit. A pair of ladies in long-skirted dresses and high collars formed a barrier with their folded umbrellas. Mont jumped between them, barely clearing the spiked tips.

He caromed into a man wearing baggy trousers and holding a basket of oranges. The fruit the man had been displaying for sale to passersby spun up in the air and all over the sidewalk. A second later an orange flew past Mont's head, and a stream of angry foreign words like "cochito prieta" and "serpeinto" also pursued his flight.

Now the sounds of a whole cavalry troop chased Mont. His short legs were beginning to tire, but he forced himself to keep them churning, struggling to stay ahead of the army that must be pursuing.

A trio of boys a little older than Mont watched him run toward them. They made no move to step aside, but kept staring back the way he had come as if they could not believe the strength of the chase either!

Mont lowered his head and plowed straight into them. Cries of "Hey, watch out!" and "What'er you tryin' to do!" erupted. Mont was showered with fists and boots, but he kicked free and made a dash to cross Clay Street. The terrible clanging alarm bell and the thundering hooves were right behind. Mont took off from the curb in a jump that would have landed him in the middle of the street—and was tackled from behind by all three boys yelling, "Look out! You're gonna get killed!" as the hook-and-ladder wagon of Engine Company Number Five rattled, pounded, and rumbled around the corner.

The rear of the elongated vehicle careened around the turn, brushing the lamppost that hung over the boys' heads. The iron-shod hooves of the coal-black horses and the iron-rimmed wheels pounded past them only inches away.

"You better watch where you're runnin'!" yelled a tow-headed boy in a cloth cap.

"Yeah," agreed another, "them firemen don't stop for nothin'!"

"What was you runnin' so hard for anyway?" questioned the third, an olive-skinned street urchin with bare feet.

"I was . . ." Mont began, looking fearfully down the street. He spotted Reynolds, puffing and wheezing but still pursuing, two blocks behind. "I gotta go," Mont shouted, jumping up. "Thanks!" And off he went, sprinting around the corner on Clay, following the rapidly disappearing fire wagon with its load of men, ladders and axes.

Setting his sights on a large brick and granite building ahead of him kept Mont from accidentally turning back toward his pursuers. He jogged left, then two rights, and then left again. What he was in search of, he could not have said, except to be far enough ahead to have a chance to hide.

The opportunity just did not present itself. His landmark, when he passed it, turned out to be a bustling collection of businesses with offices of the Alta California newspaper and the Bank Exchange Saloon. The people there were all well-dressed men in business suits, top hats, and frock coats. Mont thought about asking one of them for help. Then he remembered that Jasper Perry was wearing a top hat and a frock coat, so he ran on, turning again toward the west.

When he reached Washington Street, two things changed: the most enormous hill yet reared up in front of him and the nature of the pedestrians altered. As if by magic, the sidewalks were suddenly filled with hundreds of small pigtailed men dressed in dark blue tunic-shirts. Their shirt-tails hung below their waists and the over-long sleeves concealed their hands.

An elderly Chinese man was coming slowly toward Mont. He wore the same flapping shirt and baggy trousers as the rest, but he had a black silk skullcap on his head. He was followed by two lean, angry-looking men who walked five steps behind. They were dressed completely in black, and their eyes were constantly moving from side to side as they scanned alleys, balconies and doorways.

The rising slope of the approach to Nob Hill was too much for Mont's short, tired legs. His scamper slowed to a trot, then to a walk. He was even considering turning around and heading downhill, when he spotted Reynolds, still chasing, behind him again. Mont tried to speed up again, but found he could not. His legs felt like lead.

Reynolds, too, was exhausted. His puffing and wheezing had made it impossible for him to call out for help to any of the passersby. He had tried to shout, "Stop, thief!" and wave his hat in the hopes that some citizen would tackle a supposed pickpocket, but the sound of the fire wagon's passing had eclipsed his strangled yell. After that, he just had not had the breath.

When the lieutenant realized that Mont was leading him up Nob Hill, he knew it was over unless . . . Bending down to a cross-draw holster that hung inside his cape, Reynolds drew an octagonal-barrelled Colt and leaned against a lamppost to steady his aim.

The two bodyguards of the elderly Chinese man saw Reynolds draw his gun. They had no idea why this man would want to kill their boss, but their job was to protect him, no matter what.

From the deep pockets of their black tunics, both men drew short-barrelled Allen pepperboxes and began firing. The range was long and the guns inaccurate even at much closer distance, but their shots made Reynolds throw himself to the ground and hug the base of the post.

As soon as they had fired, the bodyguards dragged their employer into a shop that sold ginseng roots and disappeared with him through its back door. Mont also managed to disappear at the sound of the first shot: he ducked into an alleyway so narrow that two men could not walk side by side.

There was a hole in the pavement of the alleyway. Ten running steps down the passage, the rungs of a wooden ladder protruded two feet above the surface.

Mont grasped the topmost rung and looked into the shadowy darkness below. Then making up his mind as he gathered his courage, Mont dropped quickly off the face of San Francisco and into the depths of Chinatown.

12

THE FIRST THING Mont noticed when he descended into the man-made underground grotto was the incredible variety of smells. Not the dark, or the dirt, although there were plenty of both. It was the strange, almost touchable swirl of aromas assaulting his nose that gave Mont the sense of having dropped into another world.

At first he couldn't quite identify the odors, but somehow they stirred up memories. Sharp but pleasant smells that brought to mind Emily's kitchen: tea. Steamy, starchy air full of reminders of iron kettles in slave quarters: boiling rice. Pepper, oranges, fish—dark smells, bright smells, clean smells, moldy smells, all jumbled in a stew of airborne concoction. Floating through the mix was a too sweet, too heavy aroma of decay . . . the odor of wilted flowers heaped on a grave.

Mont crept along the passageway toward a dimly flickering lantern. Beneath it, the corridor came to an intersection. Three underground roads led off in different directions.

The tunnel that went straight ahead had no features to distinguish it from the other two, but Mont chose it in order to find his way back to the ladder and the outside air. Another lantern in the distance provided a new goal as the tiny square of sunlight dwindled and finally disappeared.

A room opened beside the next lantern. It was a low-ceilinged cavern packed with narrow, wooden bunks like the crews' quarters on ships. These bunks were only five feet long and were stacked five deep, with little more than one foot of space between them. At first Mont thought the room was empty, but his ears told him otherwise: some of the bunks were occupied with gently snoring sleepers.

A soft padding sound like that a cat makes walking on a hardwood floor caused Mont to turn around quickly. Mont faced a pair of pajama-coated Chinese, whom he had not even heard till they were three feet behind him.

When they spotted Mont lurking in the doorway, both men burst into excited questions and accusations. Though Mont could understand no word of their talk, the meaning was plain: "What are you doing here?" "You don't belong here!" "Go away at once!"

Mont dashed off again, deeper into the darkness. Erupting from a lighted side passage ahead, a blast of steam shot into the corridor as if an Oriental dragon's lair shared the tunnel.

The chatter of voices slowed Mont's travel. He listened, trying to sort out the meaning of the repeated rubbing, thumping, and splashing noises. Slowly he went up to the doorway and peered in. It was an underground laundry. Pig-tailed workers stripped to the waist amid clouds of steam and the vapors of soap, starch, and bluing were boiling copper cauldrons full of clothes, which they stirred with long wooden paddles. Near a wooden staircase leading up stood a thin man with sharp angles to his face. He was dressed all in black and he kept apart from the workers' conversations.

The staircase looked promising. To be able to pop back out of this rabbit warren a different way than he entered seemed like a good plan. But would the Chinese notice him? Would they let him pass?

The question was answered as soon as Mont appeared in-side the room. None of the workers saw him, but the man in black certainly did. Raising a yell that could not mean any-thing other than "Get him!" Mont again found himself pur-sued, this time by a half-dozen Orientals. *How can everybody be in on trying to catch me?* he wondered. *Two hours ago, nobody was after me.*

Mont turned to flee the laundry, but met with a greater problem. His desire to get out of the underground world was blocked by the approach of more shouting Chinese voices, so he had no choice but to plunge still deeper into the maze.

And maze it had become. At the next intersection Mont took the path toward the right and almost immediately came to another branching choice. This time the fork was not a straight line at all, but a sinuous, winding curve. Several times it came to dead ends or blind corners that required hasty backtracking. Twice he had to duck under a low doorway and twice more he had to jump up and climb over a brick partition.

It was as if someone had built that passageway to be deliberately difficult to follow. The sounds of his pursuers dropped further and further back and presently died away altogether.

Mont glimpsed a light up ahead. He prayed that it would be a way out, but still he approached it with caution.

The light came through a doorway blocked by a wrought-iron grate. Mont could see a room beyond the grate, but could not tell if it was occupied. The boy stifled a cough as the sticky, sweet decayed flower aroma that pervaded the whole underground suddenly increased a hundred times.

Creeping up to the grate, Mont peered through. It was a dimly lit room with walls painted in dark red. Near the center of the room burned a small coal fire on a short round stand.

Shifting behind the grate, Mont changed his angle to see as much of the room as he could. Built against the wall opposite was a series of bunks, much like the ones Mont had seen earlier, only these were covered in black lacquer and had curtains that could be drawn across the openings.

Mont jerked back into the shadows as a moving form appeared in the room. A wizened man, whose sallow face sagged with the weight of his years, padded noiselessly into the room. His pigtail was yellowed with age, and his wispy yellow chin-whiskers divided into two long strands that hung down on his green silk brocade robe.

The figure bent over a clay jar that was emblazoned with intertwined red and gold dragons. From it he extracted a tiny quantity of something on the tip of a long blackened fingernail. He rolled the substance between forefinger and thumb, then inserted it deftly into the tiny bowl of a short brass-bowled pipe from a rack near the fire.

A glowing splinter of wood grasped in one clawed hand and the brass pipe clutched in the other, the ancient man shuffled toward the curtained alcove. "Mista Sims," he called softly. "You likee mo' black smoke?"

From behind the curtain, a croaking groan emerged, followed by, "What . . . what time is it?"

The old man gave a low wheezing chuckle. "Is no time here, Mista Sims. In plenty black smoke is only dreams."

"Blast your eyes!" the croaking voice reviled. "What is the time?"

In a hurt tone, the withered stick of a man responded, "If you no wantee mo' pipe, I take away," and he turned half around from the bunk.

"Wait!" the addict demanded. His hand tore open the curtain and grabbed the old man roughly by the shoulder. "Give me that pipe!"

"All light, Mista Sims. Takee pipe . . . Here fire . . . good, good. . . ." The man named Sims seized the offered opium pipe and puffed it eagerly, then drew the pipe inside the bunk space and shut the curtain with a long contented sigh.

The old Chinaman returned to squat by the fire. He rubbed his hands together over the coals, then appeared to recall some necessary errand. Slowly straightening to a crooked comma shape, he shuffled toward an unseen exit at the far end of the room and disappeared.

Wincing at the creaking of the rusty iron hinges, Mont pushed on the lattice grate. A thin shriek of protest came from the little-used frame, then it swung open into the room. Mont breathed a sigh of relief: he had been afraid it would be locked.

His head felt funny from the opium smoke that floated around the underground chamber. Mont listened carefully for any sounds of movement, but heard nothing. Even the addict in the bunk had fallen completely silent now. When a chunk of coal collapsed on the brazier into a pile of ash, Mont started nervously. He was ready to dash back into the tunnel, but he controlled the urge, telling himself that the way out of this underground maze lay forward, not back.

At the far end of the room was a doorway, partly concealed by a silk hanging. A stray breath of fresh air somehow found its way down into the opium den, stirring the thin cloth. *Hurry*, it seemed to urge, *get out quickly*.

Mont's headlong rush into the silk curtain made a pair of streamers that flew from his shoulders as he raced through. Like a Chinese kite trailing twin tails as it soars upward, Mont sailed up the incline at top speed. And just as a kite's ascent is halted abruptly when it reaches the end of the string, Mont's progress suddenly stopped as a clawed fist seized him by the arm and demanded, "Where you go, little black child?"

As Mont kicked and flailed his arms trying to free himself, a second ghastly set of fingernails closed around his neck. "You be still," the ancient Chinaman ordered, "or pletty soon I tear throat out!" When Mont complied and stopped struggling, the old man observed, "You no thinkee Wo Sing hear you breathe in tunnel? What you do here?"

He released just enough pressure from the nail points against Mont's windpipe to allow a reply. "Please, sir," Mont begged. "I was just running from some bad men and I come down here to hide. Can you help me?"

The wiry little man gathered both strands of wispy beard in the claw he took off Mont's neck and stroked downward. "Helpee you? Sure, sure. You come with Wo Sing."

The two walked quietly along another twisting passage with the appearance of friendliness, but a threatening hand rested lightly on Mont's shoulder all the time. Presently, they turned a corner to face an alcove watched over by two black-suited guards.

Some discussion in Chinese passed back and forth before the opium den attendant was permitted to take Mont through the doorway. The room beyond the door looked like the descriptions Mont had heard of the throne rooms of kings. The walls were covered with red silk hangings, embroidered with Chinese characters worked in gold. A thick carpet lay under-

foot and overhead were round hanging lamps made of pale
green glass with brass fittings.

Against one wall sat a group of musicians who seemed to
be tuning their strange instruments. When the discordant
sounds continued without pause, Mont decided that this was
what passed for music among the Chinese. A closer look revealed that Mont could not recognize any of the instruments
anyway—no wonder it sounded strange to his ear!

Just as Mont was beginning to enjoy inspecting the alien
surroundings, he was shoved hard from behind. "Is not time
for gawking," said Wo Sing harshly. Mont was propelled
toward a raised platform at the far end of the room.

On the platform sat a Chinese man of indeterminate age.
He wore a long cream-colored robe, which Mont thought
looked like a night shirt, a dark blue vest trimmed in red, and
a pair of round spectacles.

He was smoking a long-stemmed ivory pipe, resting the
bowl on his knee as he drew leisurely puffs. Four men sat at a
low table just below and to the side of the "throne." They had
been eating and talking, but stopped to watch Wo Sing bring
Mont forward.

About halfway to the platform, Mont again received a
shove from behind, this time throwing him to his knees. Wo
Sing got down beside him and hissed, "Knock head! Knock
head! Do all same me." Wo Sing proceeded to prostrate himself on the floor, while helping Mont by grabbing a handful of
the little boy's tightly curled hair.

Wo Sing then crawled over to the edge of the platform,
dragging Mont along with him. Every few feet, he paused to
knock Mont's head against the carpet.

The man on the high seat gestured for Wo Sing to speak. A
conversation took place in which Mont must have been central, because Wo Sing plucked the boy's sleeve several times
and butted his head down to the floor twice more.

When the speaking was finished, Wo Sing again stretched
himself on the floor, then began crawling backward toward
the door, leaving Mont behind.

"Hey!" Mont called, raising up and looking around. "Where you goin'? Do I get out of here now?"

Never pausing in his backward slither, Wo Sing merely shook his head and replied, "This great master of Sum Yop Tong, Fujing Toy. You belong him, now."

Mont jumped up exclaiming, "Belong? I doesn't *belong* to nobody no more!"

From the shadows at the sides of the room, two more blackshirts rushed forward. They seized Mont and carried him suspended by the arms out of the room through a door behind the platform. Once in another dim passage, they opened a heavy oak door and threw him in.

Reynolds had given up the pursuit and returned to Jasper Perry. "It doesn't matter," he said. "He can't harm us anyway. And if he turns up again, we'll—"

Captain Law burst into the room. His normally wary pale eyes were unusually animated as he waved his bandaged hand wildly. "It's the *Camanche*, I tell you! We've got to move now —now, or it's hopeless."

"Start again, man," Perry urged. "Slowly and from the beginning."

"Whiskey," Law demanded and Perry complied. After swallowing half a water glass full in one gulp, Law visibly took control of his nervousness and tried again to explain. "I was down on the docks, a sizin' up wharf rats for crew, just as ye said. Outside the South Beach Ship Yard I sees a line of men a waitin' at a guard shack . . . hundreds of men, maybe. I like to keep a weather eye on how blows the news, so I sharpen my course toward a likely knot of greasy-lookin' customers. 'Well mates,' I sez, friendly-like, 'what's the scuttlebutt? Are ye shippin' out for China or to go fight the Rebs?' An uncommon hairy one riz up on my port beam an' throws in with, 'We ain't no swabbies, we be mechanics.' "

"So what?" interrupted Reynolds in an exasperated tone. "The boat works has some rich man's yacht to float, no doubt. Probably ten or twelve underpaid jobs."

Law's eyes now snapped with anger as he shook his shock of white hair from side to side in denial. "Put a reef in your mouth and unfurl your ears," he snorted. "The hairy one sez they's hirin' close on *one hundred* men—*iron workers!*"

"Iron workers?" responded Perry incredulously. "What do they think . . ." His voice trailed off uncertainly as an unpleasant thought crossed his mind.

Law nodded vigorously and the white stubble of his three-day-old beard waved in agreement. "Now you catch my drift *and* you can smell the storm on the breeze. Why *does* a ship-yard need iron workers? And why hire up such a mob all at once?"

"Because," Perry said soberly, sitting down abruptly on his bed, "because they are finishing an ironclad—a monitor—right here in San Francisco Bay."

"Dead on! And in a terrible hurry, too. Word is the Navy Department wants this new Ericsson-boat to protect the coastwise shipping against rebel attacks."

"No!" exclaimed Reynolds, a look of horror and betrayal on his face. "How can they know? Where is the traitor?" He shot a murderous look at the sea captain as if he suspected Law of having personally given away their plans for piracy.

"Steady on," Law demanded, helping himself to another glassful of whiskey. "If they knew, they'd be a hirin' police, not mechanics. This be a *pre*-caution, I thinks, and a way to put fear into would-be rebels. How is the temper of *your* metal, anyway?"

Reynolds considered what Law had said and began to regain his composure. "An ironclad here! Soon! This certainly changes things. We will have to move quicker than ever, *and* we will need to capture or destroy that ship, or all our plans will come to nothing. What did you say they call it?"

"*Camanche,*" Law replied grimly.

Mont pounded on the cell door, but the dull thuds made by his small fists barely even echoed within the cell. Slowly his eyes adjusted to the darkness until the light from the corridor that outlined the crack around the oak barrier spread into a thin glow by which Mont could examine his prison.

His gaze froze when he discovered he was not alone. In the back corner of the tiny chamber stood a man. Or was he sitting? The figure's head almost touched the ceiling, but the bony projections drawn up in front of him had to be knees. *Impossible!*

"Who are you?" Mont breathed, backing up till his own head brushed the rough timbers of the door.

"Han" was the brief reply.

"Han," Mont repeated. "Is that your name? I is Mont, Mont James. Why is you in here?"

The gaunt-faced man responded slowly, unsure of his words, "I ran from Fujing Toy."

"You mean you was trying to escape? Me, too," said Mont, eager for an ally in this strangely mysterious world.

Han stretched out his knees and his legs extended half the length of the cell.

"Say," Mont marvelled, "how tall is you?"

"Umm, seven feet," the man responded.

"Wow!" Mont exclaimed. "I never seed a Chinaman big as you. Fact is, I thought they was all short fellers. Is you Chinese?"

Han nodded wearily. "Mountain people in China. I brought here as slave for Tong lord Fujing Toy."

"You is big enough to wallop four of them blackshirts," Mont observed. "Next time you'll make it to freedom."

Shaking his head Han replied, "They not feed me . . . I too weak to fight boo-how-doys, blackshirts."

13

EACH EVENING A different family from Mount Carmel Presbyterian Church arrived at the door of the Dawson ranch. While the men took turns sitting up throughout the night to guard the livestock against unseen threat, the women sewed and the children played upstairs in the loft until bedding down for the night.

What Colonel Mason and the Union army had not done to protect the Dawsons, the church family had managed nicely. Ranchers who could fervently belt out a hymn or recite a scripture passage by heart now sat with scatter-guns across their laps as they gazed down at dark shadows from the loft in the barn.

Pastor Swift preached that vengeance indeed belonged to the Lord, and the Lord would just as well use a shotgun as a bolt of lightning if any varmint tried to harm the widow Dawson and her young'ins or their stock!

Each morning, men chopped firewood while their women and children fixed breakfast in the Dawson kitchen. With the light of day, the watching ended. Except that Emily continued to watch the road for the return of Tom and Mont, or for the coming of the blue-coated army that Deputy Pettibone had pledged to send.

The next morning (at least Mont supposed it was morning), two small bowls of rice and a jug of water were thrust into the cell. A terse instruction delivered in Chinese was translated for Mont by Han. "We are wanted. We must be ready soon."

"Wanted for what?" Mont asked.

"Fujing Toy is master of Sum Yop Tong. Chinese war lord. When he meet other Tongs, he must impress them with his power and wealth."

"Meaning you and me go on display?"

"Yes," Han agreed. "If other Tong lords see plenty wealth, then maybe they settle fight with talk-talk."

The giant took his bowl of rice. The cup disappeared within his massive hand. One swallow and all the rice disappeared.

"Is that all they feeds you?" Mont asked.

"Fujing Toy keep me weak so I cannot escape."

Mont looked at his own bowl of rice, then at the huge man. "Whyn't you take this away from me?"

"No," Han replied, "we are brother prisoners. It not right."

Mont picked up Han's empty bowl. After a moment's thought, he scooped half of his rice into it and handed it to Han.

"Why you do?" the man asked.

"I'm smaller than half of you," Mont replied. "Reckon you need a lot more'n me."

At the far end of the reception hall, Mont could see Han standing stiffly at attention beside the door. Han's arms folded across his chest were at the height of the other men's heads, while his head was on a level with the lanterns hanging from the ceiling. He was dressed in finely embroidered silk to match the wall hangings, and he might have been mistaken for a carved pillar or oversized statue.

Mont's own place was beside Fujing Toy's throne. Mont was wearing a long coat that hung below his knees and a pair of pointed-toed slippers. Around his head a cloth was wound, and then a long cane pole topped with a fan of peacock tail feathers was placed in his hand. He was instructed to wave the fan gently toward Fujing Toy, but under no circumstances to move from his place unless told to do so.

An audience was in progress. Several Chinese merchants had come to complain that boo-how-doys from rival Tongs had vandalized their businesses and injured their employees. Mont gathered this from watching the gestures and exclamations of the merchants, and from seeing the bandaged clerks holding broken merchandise. That the subjects were impressed with the wealth of Fujing Toy's palace was also apparent from the expressions on their faces.

More than once the Tong lord had gestured toward Mont as part of the furniture and fixtures, but the merchants were even more impressed with Han. With his long face, high cheekbones exaggerated by the hollows beneath them, and his implacable features, Han looked to Mont like a Chinese angel of death.

More important from Mont's point of view was the fact that Han drew all the attention to the opposite end of the room. The little boy was then able to pick up pieces of dried fish from a serving cart and fill his pockets. Later, Mont saved one small piece for himself and gave the rest to Han.

Tom's first glimpses of Virginia City were not inspiring, to say the least. After the awesome scenery of the High Sierras and the majesty of Lake Tahoe, the descent to Carson and the barren hills of the Washoe Valley reminded Tom of the Hebrews turning back to the desert after glimpsing the Promised Land.

Clouds of acrid dust churned up from the wheels of the Pioneer Line coach as if a perpetual sandstorm accompanied the stage. The fine gray powder settled on everything. *In everything*, Tom thought as he futilely tried to clean out his grit-caked eyes and ears.

Glancing at the other passengers with their sour expressions and comical appearances, Tom imagined ruefully how silly he must look. Shirts became a uniform shade of dun, as did beards, hats, hair, boots, coats and trousers. The only exceptions made matters worse: where weary travelers wiped their faces, a lighter shade of grayish-pink contrasted with the surrounding darkness till everyone resembled either piebald horses or war-painted Indians.

The coach rattled onto C Street past brick buildings, timbered sheds, and canvas awnings. The principal decorations seemed to be handbills. Silently acknowledging the barrenness of the surroundings, the advertisements covered every available wall, post, and boulder. Each strove to outdo the others with bright colors, flamboyant claims, and lurid drawings. *Buy Dr. Fry's Liver Tonic*, shouted one. It posed a consumptive, bald man with a sunken chest next to a robust fellow with a full head of hair. Another ordered, *Look Here! Square Meals at the Howling Wilderness Saloon!*

Mounds of pale dirt and dark ore were piled around every curve and beside each level stretch of road. The dumps from the mines formed conical heaps like the frenzied work of giant, demented ants.

Over the entire scene hung a pall of white steam compounded with black smoke and mixed liberally with noise. An incessant battering from the hundreds of stamps in the mills crushed quartz rock into rubble, and rubble into gravel, and gravel into sand, with a pounding as if the mountain's heart beat just beneath the surface.

The stagecoach pulled up in front of the Pioneer Company office. Near at hand was a bar called the Fancy Free and a billiard parlor of doubtful reputation known as the Boys' Retreat. Nearby was the Tahoe Hotel and the much advertised Howling Wilderness Saloon.

The storm of dirt that accompanied the travelers roiled up and over the coach, and for a time Virginia City disappeared behind a curtain of dust. All nine passengers inside the coach gave way to fits of coughing. Eyes streaming tears, Tom stumbled out of the stage, vaguely wondering if the six passengers riding on top had fared better or worse than he.

When the air cleared to the point of being breathable, the buildings of C Street reappeared. Tom retrieved his carpetbag and crossed the busy road toward the Tahoe Hotel. The ground underfoot was formed of a curious pavement-mixture known as "mining camp macadam": dirt, broken boards, cast off boots, battered tin cups and ragged playing cards, all stuck together with tobacco juice.

"Tom! Tom Dawson!"

The familiar, friendly sounding voice with the funny drawl-
ing whine at the end of the words floated over the passing
rumble of an eight-ox team hauling a high-sided ore wagon.
Oh no! thought Tom. *Someone who knows me has spotted
me. This is sure to give me away.* He scanned the streets, sidewalks and storefronts, but could not locate the source of the
greeting till the voice called out again, "Hey, Tom, up here!"

Behind him and on the balcony of the Stage Company office was Sam Clemens. Sam and Tom had known each other
in Missouri, and both had left about the same time with similar desires to get away from that war-torn area. Sam was . . .
a writer and something in politics. Tom had gotten a letter.
He could not remember exactly what, only that Sam's
brother, Orion, had been an official of the territory and had
planned to get Sam a post.

"Hey, Sam," Tom waved. "Good to see you!"

"Stay right there," Clemens ordered. "I'm coming down."

In a few seconds the skinny young man with the wavy dark
brown hair and the drooping moustache appeared in the
street beside Tom. His black frock coat, plaid vest and baggy
trousers spoke of money and quality, but were wrinkled and
creased. *Sam always did have a rumpled look*, Tom thought.

Sam grasped Tom's hand and pumped it vigorously in genuine pleasure at the reunion. "It is so good to see you," he
drawled. "Now things can get lively again around here." As
he spoke, a pair of brawling miners crashed through the doors
of the Fancy Free Saloon and wound up wrestling in the dust
twenty feet from where the two friends stood. No one in
Virginia City, least of all Sam Clemens, paid any attention.

"Where you staying? International Hotel, of course," Sam
both asked and answered.

"No," corrected Tom. "The Tahoe."

"That dump?" questioned Clemens. "No, no. It'll burn
down most any day. Why, the way the wind blows right
through its walls, the management has taken to advertising
'scenic views' from the mountains of sand that pile up in the
corners!"

"Come with me, Sam," suggested Tom. "I promise I'll explain, if you'll just wait till we're in the room and don't question anything you hear me say."

Clemens narrowed his bushy brows and his eyes twinkled with mischievous delight. "I love mysteries," he said. "We haven't had a mystery in Virginia since some unknown scoundrel substituted a woodcut of a skunk for the profile of the publisher on the masthead of—"

Tom never got to hear the conclusion of that story, because right then a runaway horse and buckboard came plunging and careening down C Street directly toward the two men. The snorting and bucking chestnut draft animal was racing as if his life depended on getting away from the wagon chasing him.

Tom grabbed Sam and threw both of them aside and to the ground, rolling under the belly of a parked ore wagon. There was a terrific crash as the runaway horse pivoted away at the last second, spilling the buckboard broadside into the ore wagon. The buckboard's rear axle broke with the force of the impact, sending a spinning wheel flying under the ore wagon. It narrowly missed Tom's head, bounced off the boardwalk and rebounded to land on top of the two friends.

Clemens opened one eye and peered around cautiously. "I think it's done," he said in a shaky sort of voice. As they crawled out from under the ore wagon and dusted each other off, he regained his sense of humor and added, "Greetings from the Comstock! That's what I call a real Washoe welcome —almost crushed and decapitated at the same time—show me another town that can arrange that!"

The buckboard's owner, a short Irishman with flame-red hair came running up. "For the love of . . . What could uv did it? I had me rig's brake set."

"Ah," demanded Clemens sternly, "but did you have the horse's brake set as well?"

Nighttime at the Tahoe Hotel. The shabby, makeshift furniture and the thin, bare walls and floor contrasted hugely with the remembered beauty of the hotel's namesake. Tom prepared for bed by hanging his clothes over the foot of the cobbled-together bed frame and his hat on the nail that protruded from the door. He placed the Colt Navy near at hand on the wobbly table that served as nightstand, desk, and makeshift dresser, and blew out the oil lamp.

When he lay down on the straw-stuffed mattress, more grayish dust puffed upward. As tired as he was, Tom did not expect to get to sleep soon. Even if the hurdy-gurdy music from downstairs had not come up in full volume through the floor, the hammered piano tunes from the saloon next door or the jangling banjo from the dance hall across the street would have served to keep him conscious.

Taking stock of his situation, Tom was not impressed with his prospects of accomplishing anything useful on the Comstock. As he had explained to Sam that afternoon, he did not know who was to contact him, did not know what he would be asked to do, and in any case, did not have Mont with him to identify a supposed conspirator as part of any real threat.

Clemens had agreed. "There's fifteen—maybe twenty—thousand folks living on the lead between Virginia, Gold Hill and Silver City—more if you include every canyon round about. Every one of them is crazy all right—but about speculating in silver, not about the war."

Ownership of the Comstock mines was by the *foot*, measured along the lead. Stock in the Ophir mine was being sold at over two thousand dollars per foot; that of the Gould and Curry at just under four thousand. These proven producers were mining such rich ore that any rock assayed at less than fifty dollars of silver per ton was discarded as being not worth the trouble.

But according to Sam, the speculation was wildly inflated and dangerously fraudulent: "No more than twenty out of hundreds of mines have ever paid expenses, let alone showed a profit, but that doesn't stop the speculators, no sir. Let a man turn one shovelful of dirt and pretty soon he's printed fancy stock certificates and listed on the Frisco Change as a 'promising prospect.' Next he buys new clothes, a fancy rig and dinners for his friends, and pays for it all with *feet*! And *everybody* accepts it!"

The fantasy outstripped the reality, but even so, Sam reported that the mines were producing and shipping close to a *ton* of bullion a *day*. That information would be attractive to anyone outside the law, whether rebel operative or common thief.

The loud music from downstairs took on a frantic tone as the accompanying din of loud voices swelled to include the sounds of smashing furniture and shattering glass. That a brawl was breaking out was neither a surprise to Tom nor did it interest him.

He got out of bed and stood at the window in his night shirt. His mind was far from the Comstock mines, the rebels, and the war. He stared out his south-facing window and cast his thoughts across the intervening three hundred or so miles between Virginia City and Greenville . . . and Emily.

He missed her—missed having her to talk to—missed her gentle, forthright counsel. Too bland, that thought—he missed her warm smile and the way she lit up a room: he thought about her honey-blonde hair and the way she looked dressed in blue calico. The vagrant image of Belle Boyd entered his mind—saucy curls, white throat and exotic perfume. Tom shook his head as if to banish the distraction: he wanted to think about Emily and nothing else.

Trying to return to thoughts of Emily was not possible, even when the ghost of Belle had vanished into the dusty Comstock air. A volley of gunshots broke out downstairs as the ruckus escalated one more notch. A musical crash came as a hurdy-gurdy player dove for cover. The sounds of many booted feet running toward the exits added to the impression of a stampede or a cavalry charge. More shots were fired and there was the sound of smashing glass as someone jumped through a window.

Tom was still facing the street when three loud rapping sounds spun him around. He could not see, but he could smell a new cloud of dust floating about the room. Edging around the wall to the nightstand, Tom relit the oil lamp.

The blanket that covered the straw-filled mattress had three new holes in it that Tom did not recall. Grasping the corner of the bed frame and giving a downward yank that flipped it toward him, Tom pulled it over on its side. Sure enough, in the planks of the wooden floor, grouped directly beneath the center of where the bed had stood, were three bullet holes. A hand's breadth would have covered the spread.

14

"**H**AN," MONT ASKED after they were locked in for the night. "You could be the greatest warrior Fujing has. Why don't you join his boo-how-doys for real? Then they'd feed you real good and not keep you in this cage."

The giant looked distressed that Mont would suggest such a thing. "Oh no," he said. "They are bad men who kill with guns and hatchets. If I join, then this is what I will have to do also . . . and for what? So Fujing Toy can rule over three more streets of frightened shopkeepers? It is better this way."

"But if you was free, couldn't you defend them shopkeepers? Help 'em out?"

Han seemed thoughtful. "Back in my mountain home, this is what a man once said to me. He told me that God wanted me to use my great size to help others. When I asked him which god wanted this, he named one I did not know—Christos."

Clapping his hands in surprise and delight, Mont exclaimed, "He meant Jesus Christ. Han, that man was a Christian."

The giant agreed. "So, I found out later. But I was taken away as a slave and heard him speak no more. Perhaps you can tell me about him, the one called strong and gentle?"

" 'Deed I can," said Mont. " 'Deed I can!"

The small amount of sleep Tom caught the rest of that night came while sitting cross-legged on the floor and leaning back in a corner of the room. Just before dawn there was a furtive tap at the door, then the lockless knob turned, and the panel was pushed inward.

Tom made no sound. He slowly elevated the muzzle of the Colt until a .36 caliber slug was ready to greet an unwanted visitor. The door continued to swing open, but no one came in. From the shadows of the hallway, Tom heard a muttered exclamation and then the whispered comment, "Something's wrong. He's not in there!"

Two vaguely seen forms advanced into the room. When both were clearly inside the doorway and their dark shapes plainly outlined against the paler walls, Tom cocked the Navy. The double ratchet and locking click had an air of authority in the tiny room. Both figures stopped dead still, one with a foot upraised in mid-step.

At last a nervous voice spoke. "Mister, whoever you are . . . we are not armed."

"*I am*," commented Tom, "and if you don't want further proof, you'd better walk to the far end of the room and lean your palms up against the wall." The two men complied.

Rising from the floor at last, Tom struck a match against the thumbnail of his left hand and touched it to the lamp's wick. Eyes and gun barrel never left their target.

By the warm glow of the oil lamp, Tom could see that the two were well dressed. Both men were shorter than he, one with light brown, wavy hair, the other with slicked back, dark hair. "Turn around slow," he ordered, "and keep your hands out where I can see them."

"Are you Wilson?" asked the dark-haired one when he had turned.

Tom offered no confirmation and only waited to see what would follow. The lighter-haired man, younger than the other, slowly lowered his hands.

"If you are Wilson," he said, "then there is no need for that gun. I am Hastings and this is Ingram. The word is Chapman."

"Why so nervous, Wilson?" asked the one referred to as Ingram. "Are you always this cautious, or have you been followed?"

"I generally get like this when somebody tries to plug me when I'm sleeping." Tom gestured with the gun barrel toward the overturned bed. "See for yourselves."

Hastings looked at the splintered trio of bullet holes and gave a low whistle. "Who is trying to kill you?" he asked.

"I thought you fellas might be able to answer that question," Tom replied. "Where were the two of you last night?"

"Listen, Wilson," said Ingram, "if that's really your name. Accidental shootings are five for a quarter around this town. Sure, you got cause to be upset, but coming up through the floor like that . . . if someone had meant to kill you, he did a mighty poor job of it."

Tom frowned at the thought that maybe it had been a mindless act by some drunk after all. He lowered the hammer of the Colt to the half-cock safety.

Ingram continued in a less belligerent tone. "Besides, if Hastings or me *had* fired those shots, would we come around here this morning? 'Howdy do, Mr. Innkeeper. Find any fresh corpses this morning? Mind if we lay claim to one?' "

"Why *are* you here before sunup?" Tom asked.

Ingram refused to answer any questions. He said Tom had to prove his identity as a member of the conspiracy. After being satisfied that Tom had been sent by Jasper Perry, he explained the early morning visit. "We don't think we should be seen in public together. Hastings and I even came here by different routes. Too much depends on pulling this off for us to take a tumble now."

"What is the delay?" Tom asked. "Perry seemed to think you'd have the money by now."

Ingram looked angry as Hastings answered in a chagrinned tone. "It's the boom . . . bonanza . . . flush times. Call it what you will, the Comstock is *too* successful. All the men we thought we could count on are either mining or speculating. All those traitorous souls who pledged an oath to our Glorious Cause have renounced their vows for the sake of silver. But to arm the *Chapman* and seize a steamer, we must act soon."

Tom turned the bed back upright and gestured for his visitors to be seated. Finally he was getting close to the plan. He did keep the Colt in his folded arms while he remained standing with his back to the corner. "So what's to be done? We three are not enough to take an Express wagon by force."

"Working on it," said Ingram gruffly. "We'll have help when the time comes. We've got one superintendent who may still honor his oath."

"And what do you want me to do?" Tom inquired.

"We need better information on shipments. Any way you could get close to a mine official or an assayer? Someone who might hear news of a useful nature?"

Tom appeared to be thinking for a time before he answered, even though his mind had jumped immediately to what he thought was a perfect strategy. "Well," he said slowly, "I do know a reporter for the *Enterprise*."

Sam was agreeable to participating in the ruse. "Sure, I can pretend to take you in, show you around, that sort of thing. But these fellas aren't too bright, else they'd know that nobody *ever* tells a reporter the truth!"

Tom grinned. "I didn't know you had made such a name for yourself, *Mark Twain*," he quipped, leaning heavily on the writer's pseudonym.

"A passing fancy," said Sam, airily waving an unlit Eureka cigar. "There's no fame and glory in writing satire. But what about your safety? And mine, I might add. What if these characters are dangerous, even if they aren't smart? Why not turn them in now?"

"I thought of that," Tom replied, "but there's still a bigger group out there, including this mine official, whoever he is. I don't want to alarm the rest if we can identify them all."

"All right, let's start poking around today, and day after tomorrow I'll take you down in a mine. I always get a good reception. Royal treatment. Just the fact that a reporter is looking raises the price of the 'feet' by a hundred dollars or so.

"By the way," he added, picking up his flat-crowned, rolled brim hat, "I wouldn't worry too much about the shots from below. Friend of mine was sitting on his bed taking off his boots. He was just straightening up when a celebratory bullet came up through the floor, right between his feet. Carried away an eyebrow and a lock of his hair."

"What did he do?" asked Tom.

"Same as you're fixing to do . . . changed hotels."

Mont was awakened by the noise of Han exercising. Uncurling himself from the single blanket and the pile of straw on which he lay, Mont opened one eye and peered around.

In a corner of the room was Han. His legs were braced against the floor and the upper half of his body strained against the brick wall as if he were trying to push it over. *Like Samson*, Mont thought.

Mont waited until the exercise was complete, then asked in a low voice, "Han, why didn't you try to escape again before you lost your strength?"

Regarding Mont as if deciding whether to tell him or not, Han at last said, "If Han escape once more, Fujing say boo-how-doy put out my eyes."

"But you can't live like this," Mont said angrily. "They can't keep you between starvin' and blind."

"Ah, my little friend, but they can," Han said.

" 'Pears to me," Mont concluded, "what we really need is a permanent escape."

The next day was Sunday, but from the window of the International Hotel where Tom now had a room, the tramp of men toward the seven o'clock shift changes looked like any other morning. Four dollars a day was the going wage for a hard-rock mine. A man could take Sunday off if he elected to, but, of course, he went unpaid.

Giving up one seventh of your income was more than most would do. Living on the Comstock was not cheap. With two-dollar rooms and fifty-cent meals, four dollars did not stretch very far—not far enough to cover a whole day lost.

Tom turned around at a knock on his door, laying his hand on the Colt. He relaxed when he heard Sam's cheery greeting, and Clemens entered the room. "Watching the parade of honest miners?" he asked.

A steady stream of denim-clad men flowed past. Almost to a man, each was bearded, hatted, and booted. Then Tom noticed one figure that stood out. He did wear denim and boots, but his white hair was uncovered and the face clean-shaven. What was more, the man seemed too frail and stoop-shouldered to be a miner.

"Who's that?" Tom asked, pointing.

"That's my good friend, the Reverend Bollin, on his way to conduct services," Sam replied. "Looks like a broken-down prospector from the days of '49, doesn't he? But he's a lot tougher than he looks. Been here since the beginning practically."

"Where does he preach?"

Sam's eyes twinkled as he said, "Right in the teeth of Satan . . . a little district called Devil's Gate. Has a regular church there, too. When he holds forth with one of his two-fisted, sin-killing, devil-chasing sermons, the monte dealers head for the city limits. He gets up early to catch the men coming off shift, and he'll preach three times today."

"Is he as old as he looks?"

"Older, maybe. His son David is running a mission church in Hawaii that the father founded back in the '20s."

"Can I meet him? He sounds like someone who knows what's happening around here."

"Sure," agreed Sam, surprised at the sudden interest in the preacher. "I'll fix it for tonight."

Just as Tom and the good reverend had settled down in the parson's cottage for a cup of coffee, there was the sound of running feet and urgent pounding on the door.

Pastor Bollin opened it to find a raggedly dressed boy of ten or eleven years bent over on the front step, trying to catch his breath. "What is it, son? What's wrong?"

The boy fluttered a hand across his chest to signal his inability to talk. The pastor called for Tom to bring a glass of water while he patted the child's heaving back. Presently, the spasmodic shuddering of the boy's shoulders eased and the single-knotted suspender holding up his overalls stopped bunching up and down.

"Come . . . quick," the child gasped, "Miss Eva . . . hurt bad . . . Miss Sally sent me."

"I'll just be a moment," said the pastor. "Let me get my coat." He emerged with a coat and Bible. To Tom he apologized, "I'm sorry. We can have our visit another time."

"No apology needed, Pastor. Mind if I come with you? Maybe I can be of help."

The preacher sized up Tom's six-foot-plus frame and remarked, "Maybe you can at that. The house where Miss Eva lives is below D Street. It can be a very rough area."

The hike from the pastor's home on the hillside above A Street went straight down the incredibly steep slope to which Virginia City clung. On the way, the small messenger gasped out his story.

"Miss Eva has a steady caller name of Stone. He a powerful mean secesh. Tonight he catch her with a Yankee feller. The men, they go to tusslin' and Miss Eva, she try to stop 'em."

"Yes, boy, and what happened?"

The boy gulped as if even retelling the next part frightened him. "Miss Eva, she got stabbed! The Yankee, he run off. Miss Sally hear the screamin' and try to help, but Stone won't even let her in. He drunk and he says Miss Eva got what's comin' to her. Miss Sally send me for you."

The row of shabby clapboard one-room houses that formed the Maiden Lane of Virginia City soon came into sight. In front of one stood a woman screaming at a man who fended her off by waving a Bowie knife in her face. His other hand held a large pistol.

"All right, son," said the pastor, "I understand now. You run along home."

Tom drew his Colt and checked the loads, but Pastor Bollin laid a cautionary hand on his arm. "Let's see what we can do

without more bloodshed first," he said. "Stone is a genuine
killer who will shoot us both and, no doubt, some other innocent bystanders, if we crowd him."

Tom replaced the weapon in its holster and dropped a few
paces behind the preacher. Bollin went directly up to the
hysterical woman and drew her back from the doorway.
"Keep her away," slurred Stone. "Else I'll give her some of
what the other tramp got! Serve her right," he muttered,
"taking up with Yankees."

"Help her, preacher," sobbed the woman. "She's dying in
there. . . . I heard her scream! Won't somebody *do* something?"

Pastor Bollin passed the woman to Tom, asking him to stay
by her, then he confronted Stone from two arms length away.
"Lijah," he said, "it's not like you to pick on women. Let me
see to Miss Eva. Quickly, man!"

"No!" thundered the cutthroat. "I ain't never put no
woman in my private cemetery a'fore this, but this'n deserves
it! Ain't no business for a Bible-thumper, any road."

"You aren't thinking straight, Stone," argued Pastor Bollin.
"This town won't stand for it. There'll be a posse after you
with a rope if she dies. For your own good, then, let me help
her." As if adding her agreement, an anguished groan came
from the wounded woman inside the house.

It was more than Sally could stand. She squirmed in Tom's
grasp on her shoulders, twisting to reach the Colt Navy. "I
won't let her die!" she yelled, drawing the pistol and wrestling
with Tom.

Stone saw the struggle and raised his own pistol. Before he
could aim, the preacher had stepped inside his guard and
knocked the gun hand aside. Stone's pistol discharged into
the ground with an explosion that caused the growing crowd
of curious onlookers to dive for cover. He gave a bellow like
an angry bull and aimed a knife-thrust at the preacher's chest.

Pastor Bollin parried the jab with his large black leather-
bound Bible. The sharp tooth of the Bowie penetrated cover
and pages, but was caught and swept aside. Bollin followed
this move with an overhand right that arced down on Stone's

eye with a crunch that drove him to his knees. Without even waiting for any further outcome, the preacher jumped past the outlaw and crashed open the door.

Stone started to rise. His pistol was aimed at the preacher's back, and he was thumbing back the hammer when Tom leapt on him from behind. The gun flew from his grasp and slid into the house. It came to rest beside Pastor Bollin where he knelt next to a woman lying on the floor in a pool of blood.

Tom and Lijah Stone rolled over and over on the muddy slope of Virginia City. Tom was the stronger of the two, but he held off the knife with difficulty since the outlaw outweighed him by forty pounds.

A savage chop downward thrust the Bowie into the hillside, just missing Tom's left ear. As he concentrated on keeping the knife-hand tied up, Stone unleashed a roundhouse left that hit Tom over the other ear.

Tom threw his weight into pulling around on Stone's captive right arm. As they rolled over yet again, Tom thrust his forearm up across Stone's throat as hard as he could. The larger man's eyes bulged and the knife flipped from his fingers as they clawed at the earth. Tom threw the forearm yet again, his elbow this time smashing into the side of Stone's head. The big man sagged, gasping for air.

Tom retrieved the Bowie and thrust it into his own belt, then entered the cabin. Pastor Bollin was tearing a bed sheet into bandages and using them to bind up Eva's wounds. At his side was a softly crying Sally who kept repeating, "Will she live? Will she live?"

Completing his work before he responded, the preacher at last replied, "You must pray now. We have done all that can be done till Doc Warner arrives. The knife wounds on her face and arms aren't deep. The worst one, the one in her chest, turned on a rib and is not as bad as I feared. But she has lost a lot of blood and won't be out of danger for some time."

Tom picked up Pastor Bollin's Bible. A jagged tear penetrated over halfway through, but stopped with the tip resting on Psalm 91. "Thy truth will be my shield" the verse read.

15

TOM WAS PULLING a pair of canvas overalls on over his Levis and flannel shirt. The borrowed work outfit was discolored with brown dirt and streaked with the traces of black and yellow ores. It was sweat-stained, and the shoulders were spotted with drops of candle wax.

He paused before adding the floppy felt hat with the dented crown that completed the mining costume. "If I'd come to Virginia City dressed like this," he said, laughing at Sam who was similarly 'fitted out,' "you'd never have recognized me."

Sam nodded his agreement but added, "That's because you stood out like the thirty-five foot flag waving on top of Sun Mountain. Now you look like one of the boys."

Sam took his turn to laugh at Tom's grimace before he continued, "You know, the boys figger you for real brave, standing up to Lijah Stone like that."

"Oh?" Tom replied blandly. "You can't call it bravery if there isn't any choice. I'd say the real courage was shown by Pastor Bollin."

"No dispute there, but I hear tell that you had your hand in it, too. The boys think you should have killed Stone while you had the chance. How soon does your stage leave?"

"You know I'm not through here yet," Tom replied. "Do 'the boys' figger me to run away?"

Sam looked genuinely concerned for his friend. "You don't understand," he said seriously. "Lijah Stone chews railroad spikes for amusement, but that's not how he got those notches on his pistol grips. You shamed him and he'll be on the shoot for you till he cleans his reputation."

"Why isn't Stone arrested for attempted murder? Isn't there any law and order in this town?"

"Course there is, or at least there's plenty of law—every third rock's got a lawyer under it. But 'order'—now, that's altogether different. Judge Turner swore out a warrant for Stone's arrest, but he can't get anybody to serve it!"

Tom snorted with disgust. "That's enough about the quaint customs in Washoe," he said. "Let's go look at a mine."

The two friends fell in with a file of miners walking toward the shafts of the Gould and Curry Mine. "There are three ways into the diggings," Sam instructed. "We can walk in through a long tunnel in the side of the hill, we can climb down a thousand feet of ladders, or we can ride the lift. What'll you have?"

"Seems to me the lift would be the easiest," Tom observed. "Let's go that route."

"Everybody says that," replied Sam with a grin. "Just remember, I *did* give you a choice."

The hoist operator greeted Sam like an old friend. When Tom was introduced, the man respectfully removed his hat and shook his hand with reverence. Tom was puzzled until the man glanced around, then announced, "It's about time someone stood up to Stone. Nice to have you visit us. When you're ready to come up, give me three rings, then three more."

The lift platform was only four feet square and made of oak planks, reminding Tom of the door to the hay loft back home. The lift was suspended from the four corners and the center by ropes that met in an iron ring hanging from a cable ten feet over their heads.

Both men stepped onto the platform and reached for the center rope. "You may want to use both hands," Sam observed when Tom grasped it with only one.

"Why?" Tom started to ask, "How fast does this thing. . . ?" when suddenly the tiny section of wooden floor dropped toward the center of the earth!

"How . . . does . . . it . . . stop?" shouted Tom as the square patch of daylight dwindled overhead and the lift shot into the mountain's heart.

"Clutches," the reply was bellowed back. "If the operator doesn't misjudge or the cables snap!"

"What happens then?" Tom's words whirled up the shaft.

Tom thought he heard the words "An inquest," and just then the platform slowed and the stretching and contracting cables bounced the lift to a halt.

At the top of the shaft, the lift operator hummed contentedly to himself. He was pleased to have shaken the hand of the man who bested Lijah Stone in a fight. *"Do you remember sweet Betsy from Pike?"* he sang in an off-key tenor.

From behind a pile of cable spools stepped a man whose battered face bore the marks of a recent battle. The butt of the Colt in his hand had a string of notches filed into it. He stepped almost casually up to the lift operator and stuck the barrel of the Colt in the man's ear.

"What the . . . ?" the operator stammered, then stopped abruptly and his eyes grew wide with fear.

The hoarse, rasping voice of Lijah Stone demanded, "Was you sayin' you were glad someone stood up to me, Clay? How was that again?"

The operator stuttered, "Mister Stone . . . I didn't mean . . . that is, you . . ."

The gun's muzzle twisted into Clay's ear. "Now suppose you just shut your mouth and listen so's I don't have to clean your ears with this here forty-four. You know, I always wanted to know how to run a hoise, and you're gonna show me."

Pushing aside two swinging half doors, Sam and Tom stepped into a rock-walled chamber that opened to a tunnel running across in front of them. Miners, all dressed exactly as Tom, passed in front of them. Some were carrying picks or shovels and a few transported heavy-looking wooden crates marked "danger—explosives."

But the first thing that caught Tom's eyes was the timbering. Huge square posts, eighteen inches thick, supported a framework of similar shoring all across the ceiling. By the flickering oil lamps hanging at intervals along the tunnel, Tom could see the cells made of beams marching into the far distance.

"Deidesheimer square sets," Sam explained in response to Tom's look. "The hard-headed Dutchman wouldn't believe it when people said you couldn't mine this deep without cave-ins. Said he got his inspiration from looking at honeycombs. Whole forests of trees have been replanted down here."

"So this here lever runs the cage up and down, is that it?" questioned Lijah Stone.

Clay, the lift operator, nodded slowly, grimacing at the feel of the gun barrel in his ear and the harsh grating of Stone's voice.

"And this little red knob speeds the whole shebang up or slows it down?"

Again, a single nervous nod.

"My, my," chuckled Stone hoarsely. "Ain't we learnin' fast?"

Stone removed the muzzle of the Colt from Clay's ear and negligently waved it around the little room that contained the hoist controls. "And when someone wants brought up or down, that there bell rings?" he asked, pointing with the Colt.

"Yes sir, Mr. Stone, it surely does."

"And the signals tells you what direction and how far, even who it is doin' the ringin'?"

"Yes sir," Clay agreed, trying to sound obliging. "It's kinda like a private telegraph, don'cha see and . . ." He stopped abruptly, afraid that he'd been too agreeable.

"So when the scribbler and his tin-horn friend want to get all the way back up here, it'll ring three times and then three more, and won't nobody else ring that ring. Well, well."

The two friends walked down one of the seemingly endless corridors. "Try not to think about the thousand feet of solid rock that these tiny tree stumps are holding over your head," Sam said with malicious glee. "Actually," he continued, "the biggest problem down here is water, not rock. You get . . . well, here, see for yourself."

At intervals along the gallery, drifts opened on either side, and in these men were working. As the vein of silver ore slanted downward into the great mountain, the ant-like efforts of humans followed.

The ringing of picks and the clatter of shovels echoed noisily out of the right-hand chamber. As Tom and Sam stepped to look, a yellow-bearded man with enormous shoulders pushed an ore car up out of the blackness along a narrow set of rails. "Step aside, please, gents," he said as he muscled past with a quarter ton of bluish-black rock. Tom pressed himself back against the tunnel wall to avoid being run over by the cart; only the thickness of the timber sets gave room to stand.

"Say, friend," Sam called to the miner, "are they pumping on this level?"

The miner shook his head, waving the candle mounted in the reflector on his hat. "Down one more," he said.

The rattle of tin lunch pails and the stomping of boots alerted Stone to the approach of a group of men. He stepped back behind the stack of cable spools. "Now, Clay," he advised the lift operator, "you just do your job nice and easy like. I like you, but this here Colt ain't so sure . . . and it has a nasty habit of blowin' big holes in things it don't like."

The group of miners tramped onto the lift platform and waved at Clay. "Goin' down to three," one of them hollered.

As Clay moved the lever and pulled the red knob, the great spool unwound and lowered the men into the shaft. If Clay acted any differently than usual, the miners never indicated any notice.

In the next chamber on the left, the ore had already been removed. All that remained in its place was a dark hole from which a ladder protruded. A rhythmic chugging noise came up from the hole. "How far down is it to the next level?" Tom asked.

Sam shrugged. "Hard to say. That little black hole may be twenty feet deep or may be eighty. Two days ago a miner slipped and fell in one like it. Dropped over a hundred feet. His funeral is today."

Tom was extra cautious in the placement of his feet on the rungs and his grip on the ladder as they descended. When they reached the bottom, they discovered a steam engine was the source of the chugging sound. It was struggling to operate a pump to drain a sulphury-smelling pool of steaming water.

The two men stood for a while in the stench and the noise, but exited to a quieter drift before speaking. "There you see the real difficulty facing the Comstock," Sam pointed out. "Sometimes just the swing of a pick will bust through a place and water will come pouring in faster than it can be pumped out."

"And hot, smelly water at that," Tom observed.

Sam nodded. "Scalding sometimes. More than one miner has died from burns. After the cave-in that hit the Ophir mine, one entire gallery flooded in the space of two hours."

"I thought you said the square-set timbering prevented cave-ins."

The light from the candle flickered on the merriment in Sam's eyes and his teasing grin. "I did not say 'eliminated.' "

"What would happen if you was drunk on the job?" asked Stone. "Couldn't you drop some folks clean to the bottom and squash 'em like eggs?"

"No," maintained Clay stoutly. "This rig has got a governor and a . . . ." The sound of what he was about to say rattled through his head, mimicking the chatter of his teeth.

"A what?" Stone demanded.

"A dead man set," Clay finished with a gulp. "It keeps the hoist from runnin' too fast or past the bottom gallery, or from flyin' out of the shaft comin' up."

"Hmm," Stone pondered out loud. "Then the only thing can go wrong real bad like is if that cable or them ropes should bust."

"So what is the answer to the problem with the flooding?" Tom asked as he and Sam returned to the hoist.

Sam shook his head. Little drops of candle wax ran off the sides of the candle holder and dripped from the brim of the felt hat onto the shoulders of his coveralls. "I don't know for certain. A man named Sutro claims he can tunnel clear up from the valley and hit the two thousand foot level here; drain the whole mountain."

"Do you think it'll work?"

"Some experts say it will. Others say it'll cost too blame much. It's eight miles down to the outlet from here. That's millions of dollars spent before one pound of ore much below where we're standing ever gets mined. Well, what do you think? Have you seen enough?"

At Tom's nod of agreement, Sam flicked the switch of the telegraph three times, a short pause, then three more.

Stone's face lit up with a broad smile that showed his missing front teeth when he heard the signal bell. He held his breath, and when it rang three more times, said exultantly to Clay, "Go on, Clay, send it to 'em. Don't be makin' 'em wait, now."

The lift dropped away empty into the blackness. Stone watched the great spool of cable unwind and lower downward till it slowed and finally stopped.

Over Clay's shoulder he asked, "How do you know when they're ready to come up?" Without Clay needing to reply, the signal bell gave one long continuous peal. "That's just fine," he remarked casually. Without warning he slammed the gun barrel into the side of Clay's head, and as the operator slumped to the floor, Stone yanked back on the lever.

"The boys say the Comstock is the richest silver lode in the world," Sam commented as the lift started up the shaft.

"What exactly does that mean?" Tom asked. The hoist pulled even with another gallery, then continued upward between barren rock walls. The momentary glimpse of miners' candles looked like fireflies darting about in the cavern's gloom.

"It means that Virginia City and the other mining towns of the Comstock will ship somewhere between twenty and thirty *million* dollars of bullion *this year*."

The hoist was accelerating now, speeding upward past three galleries in quick succession. A brief swirl of cooler air blew on the two men as the mouth of each tunnel yawned and closed. "That makes this territory a real prize for . . . say, are we stopping?"

The platform slowed and halted with a jerking, bouncing motion and hung suspended. "Maybe somebody else is ready to . . . no, that can't be; we're between galleries." It was true: the flickering glow cast by the candlestubs burning in their hat-top holders showed four rough walls of granite with streaks of shiny quartz, but no opening.

"Confound that Clay," spouted Sam. "What's he playing at, anyway?"

At that moment, the platform started upward again with a bump. Sam just had time to remark "about time," when the cage stopped, then dropped suddenly. Beneath the candle's feeble light, Tom could see Sam's bushy eyebrows knit together in consternation.

"I bet that scoundrel Higbie is behind this," he said. "I wonder how much he paid Clay to give us a rough ride."

This descent did not end with a gently rocking bump. Instead, the cable stretched downward with a complaining creak. The lift rebounded sharply, as if someone had shifted from downward to upward without slowing the machinery.

Up charged the platform, gaining speed. Just as abruptly the hoist paused once more. The oak floor continued on a few feet by its own momentum, floating up the shaft before falling freely.

Before it could hit bottom, the winch was unwinding again, speeding the descending lift downward. Overhead the ropes securing the platform to the iron ring began to sing with an ominous twang and the platform yo-yoed up and down.

"Sam!" Tom called sharply as the hoist topped out another rapid ascent and again fell freely before hitting the end of the restraining cable. "Sam, this is no joke! Someone's trying to bust the platform loose!"

"What'll we do?" shouted Sam over the creaking, grinding sounds.

"Get ready to jump for the next tunnel mouth as we pass."

The next upward swoosh and downward plunge extinguished both candles. Now in pitch blackness, suspended hundreds of feet above a crushing impact, neither man could even see the other, much less the momentary shadow that meant a lead to safety. Far overhead, a tiny scrap of daylight winked mockingly.

"Now what?" Sam yelled.

"We'll have to jump one at a time. On the next drop, I'll drag my boot along the shaft," ordered Tom. "When I yell, jump!"

Sam tried to position himself to make the leap for his life. When the next stomach-wrenching swoop occurred, the hobnails of Tom's bootsole cast tiny sparks as the heads grated on the wall. Feeling the gap, Tom screamed.

With a fragment of a cry, Sam disappeared! One second he was on the platform and the next he flung himself outward through space. Tom was alone on the lift.

The platform hit the bottom of its fall. With the twangs of bowstrings and the sharp cracks of pistol shots, two of the suspending ropes parted. The lift tipped toward the unsupported edge and began to drag along the rock walls, canted at a crazy angle. Tom clung desperately to the center support. His feet dangled over a gaping crack that would either drop him to oblivion, or catch him and crush him against the granite shaft.

Like a giant hand trying to shake off an obstinate drip of water, the platform rose and fell, almost jerking Tom's grip loose from the cord. His boots drummed a running clatter on the oak planks as he struggled to push back upward.

The lift rose and halted, then dropped again, slapping at Tom as if the platform were a threatening palm trying to swat him like a fly. He heard a shout from the blackness, "Tom!" it shouted. "Up here!"

Sam's voice, just above his head. Only one second to de-cide, an instant to make a choice which might be no choice at all, but a farewell.

Tom jumped for the unseen lip of the tunnel mouth; pushed off hard with his feet. One boot tangled in the center rope and spun him half around. His leap was not clean and only one hand caught the ledge of the passage. The other hand scrabbled for purchase, only to scrape bare rock.

His right arm and shoulder screamed with the pain of his weight hanging from his clawed hand. He heard the motion of the lift reverse and knew it would knock loose his fragile handhold, dropping him into the pit.

A dangling rope brushed his face—one of the broken sup-port cables dragged over his shoulder. Another fraction of an instant to decide, then his wildly flailing left hand grabbed the rope. His body instantly jerked upward.

The handhold gone, Tom swung wildly, blindly, toward the tunnel mouth. He felt the rush of the lift at his feet when something wrapped around his knees, pulling him toward the darkness.

"I've got you," Sam yelled, and the two tumbled down to-gether onto the rocky floor of the mine tunnel.

16

THE PLACE INGRAM selected was near the top of a grade on the climb out of the Tahoe Basin. Cedars and tall Ponderosa Pines surrounded the looping roadway so that only tiny glimpses of sky could be seen through the overhanging trees.

Snow had collected to a depth of eight feet all along this stretch of highway. Avery had heard the Pioneer Stage Company driver talk about the years before the drought when the snow had reached twenty or thirty-foot depths along the same route. He could scarcely credit such a story; believed it to be a whopper, until Ingram confirmed it as fact.

In years like those, the stage and express companies suspended their operations for the duration of the first big storm. Then they brought out special coaches built on sled runners that were able to glide over the icy surface. But this year and last, it had not been necessary. Several teams of mules drawing iron-bladed buck scrapers were kept in constant employment keeping the roadway clear.

The coaches operated in an eight-foot-deep canyon of hard packed snow, but their wheels stayed in well-worn ruts, and commerce over the Sierras continued unchecked. The cleared passageway was just barely wide enough for two teams to pass each other, and heaven help the teamster who swung too wide on a blind curve.

Two hundred yards below the summit, the road made a sharp turn to the left coming out of a canyon. Next, a sharp switchback to the right for fifty yards elevated the coach almost to the peak, when another abrupt turn to the left reversed the direction of travel once more. Given the steepness of the grade and the icy conditions, drivers favored breaking into a gallop as soon as they came out of the canyon. They were trying to keep the momentum up all the way to the peak.

The highway plunged down again immediately after reaching the summit. There was no more than a five-hundred-foot-long level spot at the top of the ridge.

The most logical place for a holdup was just after the third switchback, when the horses were laboring on the steepest stretch. Their energy would be spent on the galloping climb and the coach would be starting to slow.

The straining bodies of the six-up team rippled with the demands of the load and the mountain. The salty-acrid odor of their effort drifted back to the driver on the wagon box.

Floyd was a careful driver; careful of his teams, if not always so cautious with the comfort of the passengers. He knew better than to push the horses till they sweated, and he kept the pace one notch less than enough to lather them, knowing that the thirty-five-degree air of the eight-thousand-foot pass would kill a sweaty horse the same as a man.

Passengers with their complaints about the ride and the temperature in the coach had always rubbed Floyd the wrong way. After all, he was completely out in the open all the time, right? What business did a puny, thin-skinned fare-payer have of voicing anything other than gratitude?

Floyd was grateful that he no longer had to cope with the foibles of passengers. Since leaving the Pioneer Stage Company to take on the Wells, Fargo express wagons, Floyd was much happier. He was still driving a six-in-hand over the same magnificent Alpine scenery, but now there were no whining passengers to bother him.

Glancing over his shoulder at the shotgun-toting guard in the wagon bed, Floyd wondered if he had any complaints. The difference was, guards were employees and Floyd was their boss as long as the wheels rolled—he could tell them to stow it. Not that this one made any complaints, or any small talk either. He was huddled down inside a fleece-lined jacket as if trying to disappear completely. Ordinarily, there were two guards on the box, but one had not appeared at departure time. "Drunk, more'n likely," Floyd had remarked to the station agent.

The two outriders were within call, but the one ahead appeared and vanished with each curve of the road. Floyd had not seen the one behind since they began the ascent of the Truckee.

The heavy iron ice shoes rang with every step up the grade, but the enforced slow pace made it a dismal sound, like the tolling of church bells for a funeral. Floyd noted the slack in the middle line of the three thick leather straps moving through the fingers of his left hand. He gave it a quick flip and called to the near-side bay of the swing team, "Get up there, Candy. Quit yer loafin'."

The guard in the box stirred and stretched, trying to ease the cramp of his leg muscles. Seeing the driver's glance, the man remarked, "It's almighty cold today, Floyd."

Letting rip a string of profanity, Floyd promised to make things real hot, real quick, if he had any more complaints. The nerve! All the guard had to do to earn his pay was sit tight and hold on to a twelve gauge. How would he like it if he had to sense every change of gait, every curve of the road, every different surface and—

A sudden shout from ahead brought Floyd out of his indignant reverie. He jerked his hand up and called to the guard, "Look sharp. May be trouble."

From around the bend of the road just ahead came Clive, the point rider. His hat was tied down over his ears with a bandanna or otherwise it would have flown off. He waved his arm and shouted, skidding his chestnut gelding to a stop beside the wagon.

"Floyd," Clive panted, "there's been an accident up ahead!"

"Bad one?"

"Powerful bad! Wagon turned over, two men down, blood all over!"

"Could you help any of 'em?"

Clive looked startled. "I come straight back here to tell you. I didn't think—"

"You sure enough didn't! Now get outta the way!" Shaking the lines with a sudden snap, Floyd called to the leader, "Get up, Abel! Rattle your hocks, Ben!"

The express lurched into motion. "Fire a shot, Jerry," Floyd ordered the guard in the wagon bed. This was the signal for the drag rider to come up pronto. "And keep low. If this is some sort of trick, you be ready to go to blastin'."

The scene on the top of the rise was a grisly one, indeed. A Murphy wagon was upside down off the side of the road. One man was pinned beneath it. Only his floppy black hat covering his head and shoulders was visible. Another body lay flung like a rag doll on the snow on the other side of the road. Dark crimson blood streaked his face and clothes and was splashed on the snow bank all around.

Floyd stopped the express wagon as soon as the accident was in view. He gestured curtly to the guard, "Don't just sit there gawkin'! Get on up and see if you can help!"

Floyd regretted the missing guard. Talking aloud to himself he said, "You be watchin' the back-trail and the woods either side. Yup, that's the ticket."

Clive stepped off his horse, tying it to the wreck, and the box guard, Jerry, joined him beside the overturned wagon. Clive whistled a sharp note and shook his head. "There ain't nothin' to do for this one, Jerry. The box pert near cut him in two—musta throwed him off, then rolled acrost him."

Fingering the shotgun nervously and glancing around at the snow-covered trees, Jerry stayed far back. He was young and scared—Jerry was the Virginia City Station agent's nephew and he owed his job to that relationship. Right at the moment, he was wishing he had stayed in Ohio; but his ma had sent him west to save him from the war, and here he was.

Clive crossed the icy expanse of roadway toward the blood-spattered second body. Jerking his attention away from the flattened figure, Jerry ran after the point rider.

In his haste to catch up, Jerry failed to account for his slick-soled boots and the skating-rink quality of the highway. Three running strides and he lost his balance, three awkwardly bouncing hops to try to regain it, and a backward sprawl in which both feet flew up in the air.

It cost him his pride and a sharp rap on the head, but it saved his life—at least for the moment. Clive was just bending over to examine the corpse when the body on the ground grinned through its mask of chicken blood and raised a sawn-off double-barrel from beneath a fold of oilcloth duster.

The load of double-shot at a distance of three feet almost cut Clive in half. Echoes of the shotgun's explosion bounced from rocky ledge to snow covered meadow and down the mountain slope, till the continuous roll sounded like thunder in the high peaks and clumps of snow fell from the trees.

Floyd saw the blast that killed Clive and whipped up his team. He drove with one hand, his calloused right fist closing around the double-barrelled scatter-gun he carried beside him and thumbing back the hammers.

"Keep down," he yelled to Jerry. The advice was unnecessary because the young guard had also seen Clive's death. Jerry crouched below the margin of snow bank that bordered the road. A second barrel of buckshot tore into the frozen crystals right in front of him, pelting him with icy fragments. He touched off a blast of his own shotgun without ever lifting his head from where he had it buried in the crook of his arm.

Behind him, the man under the faked wreck was having trouble struggling free. The set-up was almost too realistic, and for a moment he really was pinned. He fired two more shots at Jerry, but the depression of the roadbed coupled with his own prone position made the bullets pass harmlessly overhead.

The hooves of the six-up team clattered and skidded on the frozen lane. The express wagon lurched forward with Floyd standing upright on the driver's platform, holding his shotgun pressed tightly against his side. He fired a round at the robber who had just succeeded in crawling from beneath the wagon. The boom of the twelve gauge was like the climax of a conjuring trick: the bushwhacker dove head first back under the overturned wagon and disappeared.

Clive's horse reared against the reins by which it was tied to the tongue of the Murphy wagon. The second time the animal reared, plunging and kicking, the leather leads snapped and the horse bolted across the road.

Jerry heard the pounding hoofbeats, and in a move that would have done credit to an Oglala buffalo hunter, sprang up and grabbed the horse's neck. Using the animal's momentum to his own advantage, Jerry swung aboard the saddle. He discovered, to his amazement, that he still had the shotgun in his hands.

But the magic could not continue. Floyd could not reload as quickly as Clive's murderer could fling aside the sawed-off weapon and produce a Colt.

Three shots in quick succession hit Floyd high in the chest and toppled him from the wagon seat. He stood up tall as if to urge the team for one last burst of speed, then pitched headlong off the side.

The sudden yank to the left as Floyd fell, followed by the slack in the line, confused the six-up team. The leaders jerked the others off the road into deep snow. They continued to pull a short distance, floundering, then stopped.

Jerry saw Floyd shot off his perch, knew he was dead. Two shots from the Colt whipped past him, but he was already far enough away to spoil the aim. He never slackened his pace away from the scene, just rode as fast as he could for help.

Ingram wiped the chicken blood from his face on the sleeve of his duster and hurried over to the overturned wagon. "Get on out," he called sarcastically to Avery, who was still hiding under the wreck. "Fat lot of help you turned out to be. Whyn't you shoot?"

Trembling all over like an Aspen leaf in a high wind, Avery crawled out of his hiding place. "So bloody," he said.

"Yeah, so what? Now shake yourself and lead that express wagon over to the trees where we got our rig. Hurry, you worthless lump! We ain't got forever."

Avery did as instructed, but he kept repeating over and over, "So bloody, so bloody."

17

MAGUIRE'S OPERA HOUSE had been playing to packed houses ever since it opened in Virginia City some months earlier. Anticipation was running high for the coming attraction *Mazeppa*. Lurid handbills depicted scantily-clad actress Adah Isaacs Menken bound to the back of a fiercely snorting runaway stallion. It caught the boys' attention. Each one imagined himself as her rescuer, a modern-day knight-errant, dispatching villains with six-gun instead of sword.

The boys liked drinking and gambling as recreations, but they liked variety, too. A pretty actress and an opening night provided just the different kind of excitement they craved. Even though Belle Boyd did not have the reputation or the promotion of "The Menken," her soft-spoken, helpless femininity inspired the boys to chivalrous thoughts. This was especially true since the advertised production was *Fortune's Handmaid*, a riches-to-rags-to-riches story with despicable, thieving relations and a much-abused, pure-hearted heroine.

Maguire's was filled to capacity. From the orchestra pit to the billiard tables in the foyer, it was crowded with mine superintendents wearing diamond stickpins and miners wearing their only clean shirts.

Lijah Stone was holding court in one of the red-velvet-lined boxes in the second tier of private rooms. Without giving specifics, he was bragging about having evened a score. Stone was secure in the belief that even when the double murder came to light and people began to speculate, old Clay would be too terrified to ever act as a witness against him. The proof of the accuracy of his belief was the fact that while the town had already heard of the wreck on the previous day of the

Gould and Curry lift, it was being referred to as an accident. Stone figured that the bodies had not yet been found and that Clay was keeping quiet.

The opening notes from the orchestra hurried the late arrivals into their seats and urged the last-minute drinkers to leave the ivory-inlaid mahogany bar. Lijah Stone and his cronies settled back in the gilt chairs as the houselights reflected in the crystal chandeliers began to dim.

A spotlight aimed from the catwalk overhead was directed toward the center of the still-closed curtain. It illuminated a beautiful painted backdrop of sparkling Lake Tahoe surrounded by an evergreen forest.

There was only a moment to admire the painting, then the curtain was raised. The opening scene showed the interior of a mansion's great hall and a beautiful woman caring for an invalid father.

There was a disturbance at the front of the theater. A latecomer made his way down the aisle of the theater. He probably would not have attracted Lijah's attention except for the fact that he came all the way down front. The front row of seats was reserved for the drama critics and other reporters of the *Enterprise* and the *Union* and the *Gold Hill News.* This tardy playgoer walked into the ranks of newspapermen, and singled one out for a greeting. That man stood and started up the aisle in a hurry. His characteristic shuffle was gone, but there was no mistaking his face.

Stone leaned over the railing and stared. It could not be, but it was! Somehow Sam Clemens had escaped from the mine shaft. And if *he* had, then perhaps . . . Stone half rose from his chair and turned to find himself staring into the barrel of Tom Dawson's Navy Thirty-Six.

"Stone," Tom said softly, "some folks want to talk to you about a little mining accident." He gestured over his shoulder toward three grim-faced Gould and Curry security guards.

"Why me?" blustered Stone. Heads in the audience swivelled to look up at the box. Then Stone saw the bandaged head and fiercely cold eyes of Clay, the hoist operator.

"Attacking a woman one day and a mining operation the next," said Tom, shaking his head. "Seems to me you managed to get everybody in the Comstock down on you this time."

Stone started to protest, then noticed all his former friends melting away and disappearing through the curtained exit behind the guards. "Here now," he said, extending his hands in front of him. "I'll come peaceable."

Everyone was so eager to see that Stone kept his hands empty and in plain sight that no one paid any attention to his feet. With the toe of one boot underneath the velvet-cushioned chair, Stone smacked it sharply upward, flipping the chair into Tom's face.

Tom fought to knock the chair aside without accidentally firing his Colt, for fear of hitting a bystander. Stone had no such compunction. As soon as the furniture was airborne, he went for his gun.

The first shot hit an oaken chair leg, which deflected it just enough to make the bullet miss hitting Tom in the chest and smash a brass lamp instead. The guards scattered and several women in the audience screamed.

Firing again, Stone jumped toward the painted wooden railing that marked the front edge of the theater box. This second shot was not aimed at all and crashed harmlessly into the ceiling, but it made half the theatergoers hug the legs of their chairs, while the other half drew weapons of their own.

The drop to the Opera House floor was fifteen feet, but Stone vaulted the rail without a moment's thought. He smashed, boots first, into a recently vacated chair, splintering it into myriads of pieces and sending another wave of screams through the audience.

On stage, the invalid father experienced a remarkable healing, jumped up from his sickbed and ran with his daughter into the wings. As they were running out of the spotlight, producer Maguire ran into it. With both arms raised, he pleaded for calm. "Please, please!" he begged. "No more shooting! Settle your differences somewhere else!"

Stone came up from the floor with the seat of the broken chair tangled around one leg, but with his pistol still in his hand. He knocked aside a fiddle player, then hoisted himself up onto the stage. "Give it up!" Tom yelled over the hubbub of shouts and cries. "You can't get away."

The only reply Stone made was to fire another awkwardly off-balance shot toward Tom. This third slug clipped a crystal chandelier and sent it plummeting toward the crowd, who clawed all over one another to escape its crushing impact. For an instant, everyone's attention was distracted and Stone ran offstage into the wings where Belle had taken refuge.

"Not that way," she hissed, as Stone made for the stage door. "Up to the catwalk and out on the roof."

The audience on the floor of the theater could not see where Stone had gone. They guessed that he would exit by the stage door and a large crowd of men brandishing guns surged out the rear of the auditorium along with the guards who had been with Tom.

From Tom's position up in the box, he could see Stone pause halfway up the ladder to thrust his pistol into his waistband. Glancing upward toward the catwalk, Tom spotted Stone's goal: large windows set into the ceiling above the narrow iron ledge that provided ventilation for the hot lights. If Stone reached them, he could escape onto the roof of the Opera House and, in the darkness of the surrounding shops and stores, make good his escape.

"He's headed for the catwalk," Tom shouted. "After him! He's trying for the roof!" But no one heard him amid all the other noise and confusion, and Tom's warning went unheeded.

The unarmed spotlight operator saw Stone coming up the ladder and ran for his life. The man pushed open one of the large windows and took himself out of harm's way.

There was one chance for Tom to head off Lijah Stone. Along the corridor of the second story boxes were French doors that opened out onto a balcony. Tom threw open the closest one and jumped through to stand on the overhang. A drainpipe provided a means of ascent to the roof and the row of rooftop windows through which Stone would be coming.

Tom pulled himself onto the roof not an instant too soon. The dark mass of a man's body appeared, framed in the open window as Stone stood on the iron railing of the catwalk. "Hold it right there, Stone," Tom demanded.

In response, a surprised Lijah Stone drew his pistol at the same moment that his boot heel slipped on the slick iron rail of the catwalk. His hand flew up and the pistol struck the window and was knocked from his grasp. It spun away from him and dropped to the theater floor.

"Come on out, Stone," Tom instructed, gesturing with his Navy.

"Come in and get me," Stone retorted, then jumped from the railing back down to the catwalk's iron grate. He turned to run back toward the ladder.

Diving in the window right after him, Tom landed on Stone's back and knocked him down on the narrow hanging ledge. The two men grappled on the walkway, each struggling for control of Tom's pistol. Tom tried to turn the muzzle toward Stone to call a halt to the battle, but Stone smashed Tom's hand down again and again on the sharp metal lip of the catwalk's floor.

Feeling his grip weakening as his hand numbed, Tom pounded Stone in the kidneys with his left. In return he caught a headbutt that opened a gash above his left eye. Fearing that Stone might get the pistol, Tom deliberately let it fly from his hand and off the catwalk the next time his wrist was pounded on the metal.

Stone gave an angry, frustrated bellow. He locked his hands together and brought them down hard toward Tom's face. Tom jerked aside and the blow thudded into the iron grate.

Sitting upright to give himself more force, Stone tried again to land a piledriver on Tom's head. It was a blow intended to crush his opponent's skull like an eggshell.

Using the force of Lijah Stone's downward swing to aid him, Tom kicked up hard in an attempt to roll Stone over his head. Stone tried to keep from being thrown off by stopping the swing of his arms and flattening out his body as Tom pushed him over. Instead of rolling off Tom onto the catwalk, Lijah Stone sailed through the opening between the narrow iron rails and plummeted forty feet to the Opera House floor.

There were a few people who remained in the auditorium. They heard the noise overhead and watched the fight on the catwalk, dodging the falling pistols. A collective intake of breath went up when Stone jackknifed through the bars. When he landed with a dull thud in one of the aisles, there was a momentary silence, followed by a clamor of exclamations and questions.

His face streaming blood, Tom held a bandanna pressed over the wound for a moment before tying it around his head. He walked unsteadily to the ladder that led down to the stage and slowly descended it. Partway down he had to stop and squeeze his eyes shut till a wave of dizziness passed.

A few moments later, Tom stood over the crumpled form of Lijah Stone. He was not dead, but nearly so. "Get a doctor," Tom called to the people who stood milling around. "Get a doctor!" he said again with exasperation.

"No . . . time," groaned Lijah Stone. "Get preacher, 'stead. Quick!" He bit off the words in a spasm of agony. "Get Bollin . . . nobody else!"

Tom looked to see that someone was going to get the pastor, then sat down and stared at the wreck of a man. A wasted life, now in terror of his soul's unreadiness. One of Stone's eyes darted toward Tom, took in his presence. The other already seemed fixed and vacant.

"Want to tell you, Dawson—" Stone began.

Tom started. Stone had used Tom's real name. *His identity was known!*

"They are on to you . . . hired me to kill you . . ."

Tom nodded his understanding. "Then you're the one who fired through the floor of the hotel and caused the wagon accident?"

Stone's face contorted in a mixture of agony and confusion. "No," he said with difficulty. "Don't know what you mean. . . . They came to me after our fight . . ."

"Who?" Tom asked. "Who came to you?"

"Don't know names," Stone's head lolled to one side when he tried to shake it, then it would not straighten up again. "Get . . . get preacher!" he said with urgency.

"All right, Stone, lie quiet. I'm sure he's on the way."

"Good." Stone's word came with a long, drawn-out sigh, then his body arched again in a spasm of pain. "Dawson!" he almost shouted. "Girl . . . the actress . . . She's one of 'em."

"I know," said Tom quietly.

Pastor Bollin was hustled through the doors of the Opera House. He came and knelt beside Stone. The killer's eye flickered on Bollin's features and one corner of his mouth twitched in a smile. "Knew you'd . . . come. Best man I . . . ever saw. Don't mind losing . . . to better men." Stone's breath was shallow and a pink froth appeared on his lips. "Help me, preacher . . . Ah God, I'm so scared."

Tom stood, and moving all the curious onlookers before him with the force of an expression that accepted no argument, cleared the great hall. At the last he looked over his shoulder to see Pastor Bollin bent to speak in Lijah Stone's ear and the dying man's attempt to nod.

Sam met Tom on the steps outside Maguire's. "You all right?" he asked, looking with concern at the clotted blood drying on Tom's face and the gory bandanna.

"Stone's dead," Tom said. "He tried to escape and fell from the catwalk. Where'd you go, anyway?"

"Message came right before things heated up at the Opera House. Bullion shipment was robbed 'tween here and Tahoe. Only one guard escaped alive."

"That's it, then," concluded Tom. "I'm sure of it. They put Stone up to finishing me off while they went after the silver. How much did they get?"

"Twenty or thirty thousand. Oh, and there's more. Soon as the word came in, a reporter tried to meet the mine superintendent, a man named Baldwin. Seems he lit a shuck out of here earlier today. What do you make of that?"

"Same as you. He must have had a hand in the robbery. Posse out after him?"

"And the Army," Sam amended. "Some reporter for the *Enterprise* tipped off the soldiers that this was a secesh plot." Sam looked very pleased with himself.

"Well, round up some more men," Tom instructed.

"What for? Who's left to arrest?"

"Belle Boyd."

"The actress?" Sam asked with surprise. "What's she got to do with this?"

"She's in it up to her pretty neck," said Tom grimly. "But on my word, she's about to get helpful."

18

REYNOLDS, PERRY, HASTINGS, Ingram, and Law gathered aboard the *Chapman*. The recently stolen silver shipment had already been exchanged for weapons through a Mexican arms dealer who asked no questions.

"Five cases of powder," Perry read from a list. "One hundred fifty revolvers, thirty rifles, one hundred fifty pounds of bullets, two hundred cannon shells and," he paused impressively, "two brass twelve pounders, brought aboard in crates labelled 'machinery.' "

"Well done," complimented Reynolds, "and again to you, Ingram and Hastings."

"I still want to know when the thousand-man army will show up," growled Law.

"Hold your tongue," snapped Perry. "Just let us seize one Pacific mail steamer and the take won't be thirty thousand dollars, it'll be three hundred thousand or even three million. Men will flock to our recruiting."

"Maybe," said Law without enthusiasm. "One passage at a time I says. Where's my next payment?"

Reynolds handed it over grudgingly. "See that you earn that," he demanded.

"Aye," agreed Law. "Reckon I will day after tomorrow."

"Are you certain, Ingram, that Dawson is disposed of?" Perry asked.

"Nothing easier," said Ingram. "Stone told us that the spy and a newspaper snoop were both at the bottom of a thousand-foot shaft."

Tom shook hands with Sam and prepared to board the Pioneer Stage for what he hoped would be the fastest possible trip back to Frisco. He had stepped one foot up on the coach when Belle Boyd was led out of the Express Line office in handcuffs. "Just a minute," he called to the driver, and he moved in front of the procession leading Belle to jail.

"You can only have a minute, Mr. Dawson," said the Express Lines guard in charge. "We've lost two good men and thirty thousand in bullion. This little she-devil don't even try to act innocent. She's been spoutin' venom about Abe Lincoln and everybody else since we caught her. The big bosses want her locked up pronto an' us to hit the trail after Superintendent Baldwin."

"I won't tell you anything, Mr. Wilson or Dawson—whatever your name is," Belle spat at Tom.

"Belle," Tom said reasonably, "the game is up. You're already an accessory in two murders. Tell me what you know before your gang gets you involved in more."

Belle smiled a malicious smile. "Here's all I'll tell you: You won't see that little black brat ever again!"

The audience chamber was especially tense. Two ranks of boo-how-doys stood attentively in front of Fujing Toy's throne. Each carried a hatchet at shoulder arms and appeared ready to use it.

The reason for the special precaution was the arrival of an emissary of the most powerful rival tong, the Sue Yops. It was not impossible to think that this ambassador might have orders to assassinate Fujing. The show of force was to impress on the visitor how immediate and horrible would be the vengeance if any such attack were attempted.

The emissary announced that he had come bearing a gift from the Sue Yop leader to Fujing Toy. Before he approached any closer, two blackshirts stepped forward, and at his permission, the ambassador allowed himself to be searched. He was in his best formal attire, wrapped in yards of silk that rustled continuously. The ambassador advanced on his knees with the parcel, also wrapped in rustling silk, and placed it at Fujing's feet.

A snap of the fingers summoned Mont. He placed his peacock fan in a brass holder and crept forward on his stomach as he had been taught.

Loops of bright yellow ribbon tied up the lid of the box. Mont carefully untied the bands, then looked to see if Fujing wished him to open the present further. A frown of the impassive face told him that Mont should only pass the box up to the Tong lord's lap.

Mont was still kneeling at Fujing's feet when with a final rattle and rustle of the silk wrapping, the Sum Yop master thrust his hand into the box. A terrible scream erupted from his mouth, and he flung himself backward and the box away. The rattlesnake that had been coiled inside the gift had attached itself to Fujing's forearm by its fangs.

The ambassador-assassin grabbed the fallen box and from inside the thickly padded interior drew a pistol. Fujing was still screaming and shaking his arm frantically, trying to dislodge the snake. Its fangs had pierced the brocade of his sleeve as well as his flesh and it continued to hang there.

Two of the blackshirts went down in quick succession to shots from the emissary's pistol, then there was a crash against the entry door and armed men burst in. These were also dressed in black, but they wore yellow armbands and carried two-pronged pitchforks instead of hatchets.

Fujing had finally succeeded in shaking the snake loose. It fell across Mont's back where he cowered at the foot of the throne. The rattlesnake slithered onto the floor of the platform and quickly retreated under the throne where it coiled and struck out at the air.

Reacting swiftly to the invading Sue Yops, Han picked up a solid oak table that was almost eight feet long. He turned it into a combination shield and battering ram, carrying the front rank of the enemy soldiers back through the door.

Suddenly he stopped and flung down the piece of furniture. Ripping a leg the size of a fencepost off the table, he set out across the throne room, scattering startled musicians, fearful guests, and confused bodyguards in all directions.

When a blackshirt sized him up as a traitor and took a swing with a hatchet, Han parried the chop with the improvised quarter-staff. He then spun the end around so that it caught the man under the chin and lifted him completely off the floor with its impact.

The assassin had killed two more of Fujing's men before their hatchets had silenced him, and now several waves of yellow armbands flooded through the doorway. Every boo-how-doy was engaged in fighting for his life, and no one had any time to regard Han, except when he grabbed two opposing bodyguards and smashed both their heads together before leaping over them.

The dread master of the Sum Yop Tong had fallen off of his throne. He had fainted and his unconscious form lay on top of Mont.

Picking up his recent owner as if he were a fragment of lint to be brushed away, Han flicked Fujing against the wall. Then gathering up Mont by a handful of robe, Han made a hasty exit up the passage behind the throne.

"You all right?" he asked Mont when he had ceased swinging the boy like a dinner pail and brought him up head high.

"Yes," Mont coughed. "Just a little shook up is all. Does you know your way out of here?"

The giant man shook his head.

Mont thought for a moment. "Can you get us back to the main corridor?"

"Yes," Han replied. "This I do."

"All right, then," Mont concluded. "I'll show us the way out."

"Oh no," worried Mont as he and Han stood in front of the iron gate that covered the passageway behind the opium den. "It's locked!"

Han rattled the grill with one hand. "So it is," he said.

The fleeing pair had traveled fast, but the news of the great battle raging between the rival tongs seemed to have traveled even faster. All the usual traffic in the underground tunnels had suddenly disappeared. The normal commerce of the common Chinese folk would resume as soon as it was safe, and it mattered little to them which master won.

Han and Mont had needed to hide only once on their flight to the iron gate. But as soon as the group of yellow armbands raced by, the two continued their escape and now stood before the locked gate.

"So it is," Han said again, giving the gate another shake. He set Mont down a few paces behind him and off to the side. "Wait," he said simply.

Curling his fingers around the latticework, Han bent his back like an ox leaning into a heavy load. There was a moment of immobility, and then a rending sound as chunks of bricks and mortar fell from the gate's anchor bolts. The entire gate and its frame pulled free of the wall, and Han threw it aside with a crash.

When they at last emerged into the alley off Washington, it was late at night. "Good thing," Mont observed, looking down at his own fanciful robes and up at the imposing height of his friend. "We two is gonna stand out like . . . like I don't know what!"

"Where we go now, little friend?"

"Well, now, we . . . that is I . . ." Mont paused and considered. "I don't rightly know. We can't go back to the hotel 'count a dem bad fellers might still be there, an' I don't know if Tom is back."

"If we seek your home?" Han asked.

"Greenville? It's a powerful far piece from here. I think de best thing to do is to put some miles 'tween us an' Frisco. How 'bout we cross the bay by steamer and figger the rest out tomorrow?"

Han agreed and the two were soon slipping through alleys on their way to the wharfs. They had just turned the last corner before the waterfront when they heard the voices of several men approaching.

By much folding of knees and tucking in of elbows, it was just barely possible for Han to conceal himself behind a packing crate. Mont peeped around to examine the passersby who stood together in a little huddled cluster beneath a street lamp. "It's them!" Mont exclaimed in a stifled whisper. "The pointy bearded one and the Army man! And with 'em is . . . the one I saw in Richmond!"

"It a blessing, then, that we see first," Han said. "Come, we slip back quickly."

"No, wait," Mont insisted. "I got's to see where they go. This is what I come all this way for."

The men walked toward a small sailing ship docked at the wharf. They all descended below-decks on the schooner, leaving a hatch cover half-open, from which a lantern light glowed. "Come on," urged Mont. "Let's get closer. I gotta hear what they says."

Without waiting for Han's approval, Mont darted across the intervening space and crept up on the deck. Han followed and plucked at Mont's sleeve with huge but gentle fingers, wanting the boy to come away. Instead, Mont put a warning finger to his lips and bent his ear to the hatch cover.

"Is everything on board?" a voice asked.

"Loaded and stowed," answered another. "The twelve pounders can be rigged out in five minutes."

"When do the recruits get here?"

"First light. Then we can get underway. Where are Ingram and Law?"

"Coming," a younger voice replied. "Should be here any minute now."

Mont shot a worried look at Han and they started to creep back toward the gangplank. The sound of heavy footsteps clumping along the dock sent them scurrying aft. Han had to lie down flat on the deck to fit behind the boom and furled sail of the mizzenmast.

Reynolds greeted Ingram on the deck. "All the officers are here except Law," Mont heard him say. "I'm going back before I'm missed. Get underway as soon as you can after the crew arrives."

19

WAKING WITH A start, Tom had a moment's difficulty in placing his whereabouts. Dimmed lanterns casting a glow over tufted velvet cushions and a steady drumming sound served as reminders that he was in the forward passenger salon of the steamer *Yosemite*. Thirty-six hours of churning stage and steamer travel had given him plenty of time to ponder questions but produced few answers.

Had Belle been telling the truth about Mont? Were the secesh holding him as a hostage, or had something worse happened to his little friend? Tom not only did not know the answer, he could not figure out how to easily determine it. As far as the gang knew, Tom reasoned, only two people in San Francisco knew that Wilson was really Dawson: the gruff, unhelpful Commander Fry and the obliging Lieutenant Reynolds.

Suddenly, Tom realized one of the two had to be a traitor. Either would be in a position to assist the Confederacy in a scheme that involved piracy and seizing of forts and arsenals. Perhaps both men were conspiring against the Union? How was he to tell? If Reynolds was a traitor, then Tom had delivered Mont right into the gang's hands. Then again, maybe Mont was really safe at Fort Point—but now he must find out without revealing himself, or risking Mont's life.

One other troubling question remained: What about the other attempts on Tom's life? Was there an unknown member of the conspiracy who had been stalking Tom? But how could the others not already know?

Tom went outside to stand all alone on the fog-shrouded foredeck. He listened to the mournful sound of the fog whistles and hoped that the chill swirling air would clear his head.

Mont and Han stayed concealed behind the sail, hoping for a chance to somehow get off the *Chapman*. Each time they made a move toward the gangplank, another small group of men would arrive out of the darkness and send them scuttling back to their hiding place.

Toward dawn, Mont had actually fallen asleep in a fold of the furled sails while Han kept watch. A sharp poke in the boy's ribs with a twice-normal length finger woke him. "What is it?" he asked sleepily.

"Shh," Han cautioned. "Men talk louder now."

It was true. The quiet rocking of the ship and the gentle lapping of the waves against the side were disturbed by the sound of voices arguing. "He's not coming, I tell you! He's sold us out!" worried one.

"Then let's sail right now," said another.

"We can't none of us navigate. We'll sink for sure!"

"Do you want to rot in a Federal prison instead?"

The clamor rose even louder, with some voices calling to cast off at once while others argued that the enterprise should be abandoned altogether. The somewhat shrill voice of Jasper Perry climbed above the rest, from the steps of the companionway, "Nobody is going anywhere! This Colt and I will see to that. We'll stay here, quiet," he underlined with his tone, "till full light. If Law hasn't shown by then, we'll sail without him. You all know too much to leave now! Is that clear?"

A grumbling murmur of assent answered him, but Mont and Han had not stayed to hear it. Fearful that the crew were coming up on deck, they slipped down a small aft hatch that led down into the evil-smelling darkness of the ship's bilge.

There they waited and prayed.

Yosemite's forward flagstaff carried the sky-blue triangular pennant of the California Steam Navigation Company. Tom glanced up at it, then back to the gray water streaming past the broad prow of the ship. He shivered slightly in the chill and wished he'd put on his jacket before coming on deck. *How much longer?* he wondered. *Can't this thing go any faster?*

Tom put his hand up to lean against the flagstaff, when a furtive tread behind him made him turn. As he did, a gun barrel slammed into the side of his head and a boot in his back tried to shove him into the bay.

Spinning half around on the pole, Tom crouched on the deck and found himself staring into the business end of a forty-four Remington. Raising his eyes upward from the gun, he took in a form bundled in a thick blanket coat with the collar turned up. Next he saw an enormous moustache, and behind it the cold, intent face of Michael Pettibone. "Pettibone! So, it was you all along!"

"Keep your voice down, Tom," the deputy ordered. "I didn't aim to shoot you, but if you yell I won't have a choice."

"But you were going to toss me in the bay. Why, Mike?"

Pettibone shrugged. "The Golden Circle paid me to keep quiet about some holdups, that's all. And everything was quiet, too, till you decided to stir things up again. I kept hoping I could scare you into giving up and going home. But it's too late for that now and—"

"And now you've got to kill me, is that it?"

" 'Fraid so, Tom," Pettibone agreed, gesturing with the pistol for Tom to stand. Tom studied the distance to the deputy, knowing that he'd have to spring into the blast of the gun. Pettibone's finger tightened on the trigger. *That's it,* Tom thought. *He's waiting for the next time the fog whistle blows.*

Tom sprang, and at that exact second the whistle sounded. Not the hooting noise of the fog signal, but the long, drawn-out scream of the collision alarm. *Yosemite* swung sharply to starboard and heeled over with the momentum of the turn. Tom's lunge connected with the pistol just as it fired, the bullet striking the deck between his feet.

A shuddering crash made the steamer tremble all over like a wet dog shaking himself dry. The unexpected impact threw

Tom and the deputy spinning toward the rail and over it into the icy waters below.

Striking the surface flung the two men apart. Pettibone floundered in the heavy coat he wore, struggling frantically, before slipping beneath the waves. The current carried Tom along the side of the steamer. He fought to keep his head above water, gasping for air, unable to call out for help and alarmed at the numbness already overtaking his arms and legs.

A round tower loomed out of the fog, like a giant floating tin can. *I must be dying*, Tom thought. *I'm seeing things.*

His hands struck hard metal and scrabbled at a deck that looked like an iron-plated raft. The next instant, strong arms were lifting him out of the water. Two bearded sailors snapped to attention as an officer strode up and demanded, "What's the damage? This cursed fog and *Camanche*'s profile so low in the water, too. I . . . Dawson, is that you?"

Through chattering teeth, Tom assured Commander Fry that it was indeed. "But what is this?" he asked as he was wrapped in a blanket and helped below.

"This," Fry announced proudly, "is our new iron-clad, *Camanche*. She's out for sea trials today under cover of darkness, but I suppose our secret's out now. Gordon," he called to one of the sailors, "what's the damage?"

"None to us, sir," was the report, "and minor to *Yosemite*. She's steaming away right enough. Glancing blow only. She struck us."

"Good thing it wasn't the other way round," Fry harrumphed. "Our ram would have ripped her belly out."

"Commander," Tom said urgently, "the secesh plotters have seized a bullion shipment and are arming a ship—perhaps have already done so. What's more, I think Lieutenant Reynolds at Fort Point may be one of them."

"Old news, that," commented Fry. "Reynolds was arrested last night. Seems Captain Tompkins wasn't just ill; he was poisoned, but lived. What's this about a ship?"

"The *Chapman*, sir. The plot is to outfit her as a privateer."

"*Chapman*, eh? I know where she's berthed. We'll steam over there now and take a look."

"One more thing," asked Tom, looking back at the departing bulk of the *Yosemite* and the receding line of foaming water where Pettibone sank. "Has anyone seen the black child, Mont James?"

20

"**H**EY, HAN," MONT whispered. "What are all those noises?" The *Chapman*'s hold had been as quiet as a tomb. Now the sound of running feet could be heard along with shouted commands and a creaking, sighing commentary from the ship herself.

"Very bad," observed Han, holding Mont close. "Ship making sail—leaving dock."

"Come on, then," Mont exclaimed, struggling free. "We've got to get off!"

Mont started up the ladder when an arm as long as he was tall reached out a hand to grasp his ankle and draw him back. "I will go first," Han said. He picked Mont up and set him on a cold coil of rusty anchor chain.

"There's the *Chapman* now," said Fry, pointing, "and she's already underway. Helmsman," he ordered, "steer to cross her bow." *Camanche* turned to intercept the schooner, whose sails were hoisted and filling with the rising morning breeze.

At a distance of three hundred yards, there was a flash from the *Chapman*, a splash nearby *Camanche*, and then the report of a cannon. "Shelling us, by thunder," commented Fry. "Foolish move. No doubt of their intentions now."

"Why don't we fire back?" asked Tom.

"Can't," answered the officer, indicating the empty gun carriages inside the revolving turret over their heads, where *Camanche*'s cannons would go. "She's not armed yet. This was only supposed to be a sea trial, not a combat patrol."

Another flash aboard *Chapman*, and a shell smashed into the ironclad's deck. There was a loud clanging noise and some exclamations of alarm from below deck, but no damage done.

"More speed," Fry ordered. "If she gets the wind of us, she can outrun us."

Camanche's vibrations increased as more steam pressure was applied to turn the propeller, but the *Chapman* was still pulling away. "She's making to round Alcatraz on this leg, then turn downwind for the run down the channel," Fry observed.

"We can't let them get away," Tom said anxiously. "Can't we stop her?"

"Not without a miracle," Fry replied. "She's got her speed up now. There's no way we can catch her."

The hatch cover slid back noiselessly. *Chapman*'s deck stretched forward of the small opening, with the men on deck grouped around the twelve-pound cannons, or tensely holding rifles. They were arguing and pointing, angry and afraid.

Han slipped up the ladder. The closest sailor was the helmsman, who was alternately looking up at the sails, out toward the approaching *Camanche*, and ahead to the dim outline of the rock of Alcatraz.

For Han, the distance to the helm station was only two strides. There was not even a startled exclamation from the sailor when two fists the size of melons struck him on both sides of his head at once. The man fell in a crumpled heap, and Han peered anxiously around for a small boat in which he and Mont could escape.

The helm, untended, spun lazily off course. The sails flapped and *Chapman* began to lose speed. The men on deck did not seem to notice as they clumsily loaded and fired the cannon, with Jasper Perry maintaining order at the point of a gun.

"We're gaining," Tom observed.

"Yes," agreed Commander Fry as bullets began to rattle and ricochet off *Camanche*'s iron hide. "We're inside small arms range now. Helmsman," he ordered, "I'll have that ship rammed, if you please." To a knot of sailors gathered below, he said, "Mr. O'Toole, have the men prepared to board that vessel and seize it."

"Helmsman!" shouted Perry, finally noticing *Chapman*'s decreasing speed and wandering course. "You at the wheel, where are you steering? Who is that?" he yelled, catching sight of Han's looming figure.

"Rush him, whoever he is!" shouted Ingram. "Shoot him down."

Han seized a fire ax and in one swing chopped the main sheet in two, dropping the sail, and spoiling the aim of the confused mass of men up forward. He then severed the line that restrained the boom of the mizzenmast. With a huge shove, he swept the boom up the length of the schooner, catching the knot of men who were advancing on him, carrying eight men over the side, and crushing the others against the rail and into one another.

"Brace yourself," Fry called below. "Prepare to ram!"

Camanche's broad iron wedge plunged into the *Chapman* amidships. With a splintering roar as if a thousand trees were felled at once, *Camanche*'s ram ripped into the schooner, tumbling the secesh sailors about the deck like marbles.

"Stand to the guns!" Perry roared as men began raising their hands in surrender.

"Stand and fight!" yelled Ingram as he leveled his pistol at Tom and the sailors swarming out of *Camanche*'s hold.

From the rear deck of the *Chapman*, a hundred pounds of chain came whirling through the air like a runaway saw blade. It struck Perry and Ingram as they stood beside the cannon and wrapped completely around them both, binding them together in an iron embrace. There was just time for each to vent a horrified scream directly into the other's face, before the weight of the chain carried them over the side and out of sight into the depths of San Francisco Bay. All the others threw down their weapons, and begged to surrender.

Tom vaulted over from the deck of the ironclad to the steeply listing *Chapman*. Out of the fearful, clamoring men on board, he selected Avery Hastings and demanded, "Where is Mont James? Where is the black child? Talk quick or I'll throw you in after your friends."

"I swear I don't know," pleaded Avery. "Don't kill me, and call off your Chinese giant. He's a madman!" He looked nervously at Han, who loomed overhead with a menace.

"My giant?" asked Tom.

"Hey!" said a small voice from the stern hatch. "I wants out of here!"

Han leaned over the opening and reached his arm in like a cargo crane lowering its hook. Out of the hold and into the brightening sunshine rode a laughing and smiling Mont James.

The front room at the Dawson home was buzzing with eager questions for Mont and Tom from Emily, Nathan, Jed and Colonel Mason. "You mean that Pettibone poisoned our horse and then came back here the next day?" Emily shuddered.

"Yes," Tom agreed, "but only because he didn't know that Mont and I had already left. He was trying to frighten us out of going."

"It certainly frightened *us*," Emily said.

"Twice more in Virginia City he tried again, each time a little more murderously," Tom added, without going into detail. "The funny thing is, none of the *Chapman* conspirators knew him to give away his guilty secrets, so he was really running from shadows."

Emily nodded. "The wicked flee when no one is pursuing," she said.

"Sometimes the innocent do a heap of fleeing, too; right, Mont?"

The boy bobbed his head vigorously.

"Was you really in a Chinese opium den?" asked Jed. "I seen pictures of them in the Police Gazette."

"Saw them," Emily corrected, "and I'll not have you reading that trashy magazine. The very idea!"

"No'm," Jed said, hastily redirecting the conversation. "What about this Hand feller, Mont? Is he really seven feet tall?"

"Han," corrected Mont, "an' he look ten feet tall to me!"

"What happened to him, Tom?" Emily asked.

"With his share of the reward money for helping to recover the silver shipment, he could afford to go home to China and live like a king," Tom explained. "But he bought eighteen others out of slavery and hired 'em on to run a laundry! What I still wonder," Tom continued, "is what panicked the gang into sailing so abruptly?"

"Seems I get to answer one," said Colonel Mason, laughing. "They thought that their hired captain turned traitor, but Law never sold them out after all. He was discovered two days later in his hotel room, stinking drunk."

Emily asked, "And what about the army traitor?"

"He will probably hang, ma'am," said Mason.

"I see," said Emily. "And the man Mont saw way back in Richmond; that one glimpse that started this whole chase? He seems very young and more misguided than evil. What will happen to him?"

Tom and Colonel Mason exchanged grins, and then Tom answered, "Seems that the *Chapman* was piloted correctly after all, and that brief voyage took Hastings exactly where he belonged. He will be staying for quite some time as a guest of the Union army . . . at the military prison on Alcatraz."

"And will you be 'staying for quite some time' with us, Tom?" asked Emily with a sudden change of tone that stopped Dawson's revelry in its tracks. The silence that followed had Tom searching for an answer.

"It's good to be . . . home, Emily," Tom said. His tone matched hers, and their eyes met. Neither looked away.

"It wasn't quite home without you," Emily spoke through shining eyes.

Only Colonel Mason had noticed what was *really* being said, but Tom knew that Jed would figure it out if they kept this conversation going. "Sounds like we've got a lot to talk about, Em—*later!*"

THE YEAR OF THE GRIZZLY

This book is
for Luke . . .

1

THE CLANGING OF the church bells in the twin towers at Mission Santa Barbara rolled lazily over the canyons and hillsides. As the deep-pitched cast-iron voices announced the hour of noon, Will Reed looked up from the flank of the calf he had roped and wiped a buckskin-gloved hand across his sweaty forehead.

He pushed the stringy curls of his dark auburn hair up out of his eyes and gestured for his fourteen-year-old son to hurry up with the branding iron. "Vamos, Peter! Just this one more and we can break for mealtime."

"Coming, Father," the thin, serious youth replied. Peter removed the glowing brand depicting the leaning *R* of the Reed family from the blazing coals of oak. The application of the hot iron sizzled on the hide and brought a sharp bleat of complaint from the calf.

After its ears were notched in a pattern to indicate the year 1846, the red calf was allowed to scamper out of the corral and rejoin the rest of the herd. "Bueno!" shouted the short, round-bellied man who opened and shut the corral gate. "That makes a dozen so far. Young Pedro has the makings of a real vaquero."

"Paco," Peter laughed at the heavyset Mission Indian, "you've said the same thing every roundup since I was five and using my reata to catch Mother's geese. When will I *be* a real vaquero?"

Clearing his throat at the question, Peter's father scowled. "Be careful what you wish for," he said. "The other branding teams will do twenty calves to our twelve, and the roundup lasts for weeks."

"And I would be with them if you and Mother did not make me study geometry and practice writing letters!" complained the boy.

Will swatted the dust from his leather chaparejos with a swipe of the stiff-brimmed hat. "What can we do with such a maverick?" he asked Paco, grinning. "His grandfather is a university educated engineer, but all this whelp can think about is horses and cows!"

Paco shook his head in mock despair. "It must be the other side of his nature coming out," he suggested. "His father, it is said, came across the wilderness from America, and put the Spanish caballeros to shame with his riding and roping. And his ojos verdes, his green eyes! They say he was muy enamorado, a great lover, to win the hand of the flower of California, Francesca Rivera y Cruz."

"Enough!" Will shot back. "It is already too hot for such windy tales. Besides, they will have heard the bells at home and dinner will be waiting. Come on!"

He led the way to where his steel-gray horse stamped and fretted in the shade of the tamarack trees next to Peter's buckskin and Paco's mule. "What is disturbing the horses?" Peter began; then another peal of church bells interrupted him. "What can that be? Is it a fire?"

His father shushed him to silence, and the three men listened to the discordant jangling—not the clear tones of the single bell, but a confused and uncertain sound, as if a pile of scrap metal were being dropped onto stone pavement. Underneath it all, a muted rumbling grew, like the passage of a distant stampede.

"It's an earthquake!" shouted Will. "Get away from the horses!" A sharp, convulsive twist in the ground beneath him knocked him off his feet. It tossed his son and Paco into the plunging and rearing mounts, and the horses scattered.

A sickening corkscrew motion, like a square-rigged ship facing a quartering sea, followed the initial shock. Across the plain, Will could see the waves of tremors rolling like ocean swells.

Paco tried to stand just as another crest passed, and he was flung outstretched on the ground. "How long till it quits rolling?" called Peter from where he hugged a tamarack's trunk. "Quién sabe? Who knows?" the Indian replied. "The hinges of the earth are turning, and El Diablo, the devil, is riding out of the underworld."

Don Pedro Rivera y Cruz reached across the heavy oak plank table toward the clay jar of olives. The jar, as if possessed with a mind of its own, edged away from his fingers. "What mischief is this?" Don Pedro muttered to his daughter, who was tasting a kettle of simmering bean and barley stew. Then the shockwave hit, and the earthenware pot rolled off the table and broke on the floor. "Earthquake!" he shouted.

Above the hornillo, the brick oven, a crack appeared in the plaster of the whitewashed adobe. As Francesca stared in amazement, a spider web of lines branched and forked, like a chain of lightning spreading up the wall.

When the rippling net of cracks reached the top of the wall, it exploded in a cloud of plaster dust that showered down on the dark-haired woman. Another tremor hit, flinging her sharply against the edge of the oak table, knocking out her breath and throwing her to the ground. The hornillo shattered, filling the air with smoke and swirling soot and littering the dirt floor with hot coals. Francesca slapped at the smoldering embers that rolled onto her long skirt.

The crack in the wall widened, and globs of mortar fell from the seams of the adobe blocks. The beams of the roof creaked and groaned, and the heavy brick wall leaned inward, threatening to collapse at any moment.

Don Pedro, somehow still on his feet, crossed the small room with a leap and yanked his daughter out of the wreckage of the stove and flung her toward the doorway. She landed half in and half out of the opening, just as the wall split apart with a crack like the noise of a rifle shot, and the adobe blocks began to fall.

The ranchero had no chance to escape. He lunged for the floor and rolled under the stout wooden table. Fragments of heavy clay slabs rained down, and a roaring sound seemed to come from the earth underneath the cookhouse as the roof collapsed into the interior of the building.

Francesca's roll through the doorway was accelerated by another spasm of the earth. She tumbled over and over in the yard between the tall wood frame house and the adobe kitchen.

When at last the ground stopped spinning, Francesca was facing away from the cookhouse. "Father," she called as she stood slowly, fighting the dizziness, "are you all right?" Turning toward the block building, she gave a scream and tottered forward: the structure had completely shattered and fallen into a shapeless mass of rubble. The roof beams protruded from the wreckage like the ribs of a whale carcass.

"Father!" she screamed again, and fell to trying to shift the great blocks of clay from where the entry had been only moments before. Francesca strained to lift a single brick free of the pile and found that she could not; the ruins seemed to have locked together again into a solid mass.

Even when she found a single wooden post that would reluctantly move when she pulled with all her strength, she was forced to stop when another heap of blocks tumbled into the newly made opening. With an anguished cry, Francesca clawed at the fragments of bricks, tossing them aside. Her nails tore and bled in her frenzied struggle to uncover her father. She called his name again and again, but received no answer.

Simona, the cook, and her husband Luis came running out of the house. "Help me!" Francesca pleaded. "Father is buried underneath and I cannot free him!"

Luis looked at the mound of adobe before glancing at Simona. He shook his head sadly.

"No!" Francesca yelled, denying the dreadful suggestion in the unspoken thought. She pounded her fists on the unrelenting bricks. "No! Father! Father!"

The turn of the earth's hinges brought rockslides and avalanches to the hills around Santa Barbara. The peaks rimming the coastal plain sprouted spirals of dust, as if the mountains had broken into a hundred fires.

Will suddenly thought of Francesca and their house. How well had it withstood the quake? His concern multiplied when he recalled his insistence that their new casa be built in the wood-frame manner of his upbringing, rather than the adobe construction of California.

The horses and the mule and the herd of cattle had run from the terror of the tremors. Will could not locate his mount. The only animal of any kind still in sight was one lone steer.

The rangy, rust-colored Chihuahua longhorn shook his head angrily. The four-foot spread of curved and deadly spikes tossed from side to side.

When the quake struck, the herd of cows had stampeded in all directions, except for the single beast that pawed the ground like a fighting bull. Angered at the unexpected movement of the earth, the two-legged man creatures became the target of blame.

The powerful animal lunged at Paco, who fled to the safety of the tamarack tree beside Peter. Together they climbed its spindly branches. There was barely room above the height of the steer's head for both to cling to the narrowing trunk. The steer's horns clashed against the tree, and he gave a bellow of challenge for them to come down and fight.

The crash of the heavy-headed beast against the slender tree was like the force of another earthquake to the man and the boy. A few more such blows, and they would fall beneath his hooves.

Will slapped his hand against his chaps to attract the animal's attention. He did not have time for this disturbance right now. At another moment the predicament might have seemed humorous, but not when he so desperately wanted to check on things at home.

The flapping leather caught the steer's interest and insulted his pride, and he charged. Will coolly inspected the distance to the nearest tree and the space between him and the safety of the corral fence. Both were too far to risk turning his back on the raging animal, so Will stood his ground, expecting to throw himself aside at the last possible instant.

When the separation between Will and the wickedly pointed horns was no more than three body lengths of the onrushing steer, the earth shook once again—an after shock, a concluding exclamation point to punctuate the power of the original quake. No wavelike rolling motion this time, but a single sharp jerk of the land. Will felt as if a rug were being yanked out from under his feet.

His knees flew upward, and he landed abruptly, sprawled on his back in the path of the steer. Paco and Peter were both jolted out of the tamarack.

Fortunately, the tremor played no favorites: the charging animal was also knocked from his feet. His front legs collapsed under him as if he had run off an unexpected cliff. The force of his rush drove the steer's muzzle solidly into the ground.

When Will got to his feet again, the steer was still struggling to get up from its knees. The ranchero watched the beast warily, but its blind rage was all gone. In place of the infuriated pitching of its horn, the animal shook its great head uncertainly as if trying to clear it.

Still staggering, the steer tottered off toward the creek bottom in search of others of its kind. It moved slowly, testing each footstep carefully before committing to it.

Will called out to ask if his son and the Indian were all right, then whistled a sharp signal. He was answered at once by a familiar neigh. Flotada, the gray horse, trotted obediently back into sight. The gelding's flanks were lathered with a nervous sweat. He rolled his eyes and trembled at Will's touch, as if the quivers in the soil had flowed upward into the body of the horse.

Will replaced the bridle and tightened the cinch, then shouted for his son and Paco to retrieve their mounts and follow as soon as possible. A slight touch of his large-rowelled spurs put Flotada into a gallop.

As he rode, Will saw the signs of the devastation caused by the quake. A stone fence bordering the road was knocked to pieces, and the earthen dam of a stock pond had collapsed and drained out all its water. Will urged the gray to greater speed, until only one hill stood between him and the ranch house. He ran a hand through his red hair and shuddered involuntarily as they passed the crest. He was afraid to see what lay before him.

To his surprise and momentary relief, the two-story wooden home seemed completely untouched. Then the curve of his route brought the rear of the estate into view. He drew in his breath sharply; where the adobe cookhouse had stood, there was only a mound of debris, at this distance not even recognizable as having been a building. Beside the ruins two figures stood unmoving, and lying across the heap of blocks was a splash of color that resolved itself into a familiar form. Will's senses spun and, even though the earth was still, he reeled in the saddle.

Francesca! Will jabbed his spurs into Flotada's flanks, and the gelding cleared twenty feet in a leap straight down the hill, lifting his rider over four rows of grapevines and plunging directly across the flower garden.

Will abandoned the horse's back in mid-gallop and threw himself toward Francesca's body. He gathered her in his arms, and she began to sob.

His wife's disheveled dress, tear-stained face, and bloodied fingers told him all he needed to know. Taking her firmly by the shoulders, Will tenderly set her aside, giving her to Simona and Luis to hold. He lifted a great block, then seized the projecting end of one of the roof timbers and used it to lever up a mass of the rubble.

A shaft of light penetrated into the heap of adobe and landed on a corner of the oak table. One edge was raised slightly; a clear space of no more than ten inches in height was left above the dirt floor. In the small crevice, the top of Don Pedro's bald head could be seen, covered with ashes, dirt, and plaster grit.

Deeper into the pile Will dug until he had uncovered the tabletop. Bending his muscled back and lifting with all the strength of his six-foot-three-inch frame, he raised the broad oak table and tossed it behind him.

He stooped to grasp his father-in-law and pull him free, then stopped with a fierce intake of breath. Francesca cried out again, "Father!" and started forward, but Will gestured sharply for Luis to hold her back.

When the tabletop was removed, the truth was plain: the lower half of Don Pedro's body was not merely imprisoned by the fallen bricks; it was crushed beneath them.

The old ranchero's eyelids fluttered; he was still alive! Will could not imagine how it was possible. A ragged breath escaped Don Pedro's lips, no stronger than the faint breeze that stirs the cottonwood leaves.

Will held his stiff-brimmed hat so as to block the sun from his father-in-law's face. The change in light brought Don Pedro's eyes fully open. He struggled to focus them for a moment; then a look of recognition came over his face. "Will," he said softly, "Francesca . . . is she all right?"

"Yes," Will reassured him, "she's fine. Save your strength, Don Pedro. We'll soon have you out." Even as he spoke, Will knew it was hopeless.

The old ranchero knew the truth, and he shook his head in denial. "Before my body . . . is . . . released from these clay bricks," he whispered, "my spirit . . . free from its clay." His voice faded and his body stiffened with a spasm of pain, but he fought it down fiercely. "Your fine new home . . . does it still stand?"

Will assured him that it did. "The wooden frame took the shock," he said. "It was not damaged."

Don Pedro gave a nod of satisfaction. "You were right . . . not use adobe," he wheezed, his breathing more forced and shallow now. "Old ways . . . passing. No quedan ni rastros . . . no vestige will remain."

"Papa," Francesca pleaded, "don't leave us!"

Don Pedro rallied once again at the sound of Francesca's weeping. "Kiss them all for me," he said. Then loudly, "I love you, children—" and his words dissolved in a fit of coughing that left a pink froth on his lips.

Gesturing with a twist of his head for Will to lean close to him, Don Pedro instructed, "Move the stones now, and let me pass." When Will complied, a smile washed over the old ranchero's features. His eyes opened wide, and he stared upward into the bright blue California sky.

2

THE DIRT WAS soft and deep along the country lane that wound through the northern stretches of the great central valley of California. The four mules kicked up the earth underfoot in little explosions of red dust, even though the four travelers were moving slowly.

The lead rider was an Indian named Two Strike, a Delaware who scouted for the United States Army. He was dressed in a blue woolen shirt and army-issue trousers, but he was clearly Indian; two shiny black braids rested on his shoulders. Just as clear was the fact that he was a scout; he paid constant attention to the marks in the dust made by previous travelers, and his searching eyes roved continuously.

Following Two Strike were two men dressed in buckskin shirts and trousers and caps made of animal skins. The first was the younger of the two, Anson McBride by name, nicknamed Cap.

The other man wearing the garb of a trapper from the high lonesome was Tor Fowler. Fowler was tall and angular; hawk-nosed and sharp-chinned. As the Indian scout's eyes swept the path ahead, Fowler's senses registered the brush and trees on either side and silently monitored the road behind. It irritated him that the last man in the column kept up a running monologue of comments and criticism about the dust, the slowness of the travel, and the unnecessary caution.

The talker's name was Davis, a settler who had arrived in California by wagon train. He seemed to think that he could tame the West like he handled store clerks back home in the States—just complain loud and long enough, and things would be run more to his liking.

"Hey, Fowler, what's that Injun up to now?" Davis demanded.

Tor Fowler reined in the mule and stopped in the shade of a cedar. Two Strike, the Delaware scout, had abruptly turned off the road and ridden up a hillside above the track to scan the countryside. He stared especially long and hard at their back trail.

"Reckon he's doin' what Captain Fremont pays him for," responded Fowler.

"Huh!" Davis grunted, gesturing with his rifle up toward the hill, where the Indian peered into the distance. "He looks right impressive, don't he? 'Cept, what's he lookin' for? Ain't no Mex within miles of here. Ain't that right, McBride?"

McBride, the youngest member of the Bear Flag brigade, looked worried. "I ain't sh-shore," he stuttered. "We st-stayed on this road a long t-time, an' maybe we oughta get off it."

"Well, excuse me!" blurted a disgusted Davis, slapping his shapeless felt hat against a thigh covered in greasy, patched homespun. "We ain't gonna get back in two days ner two weeks if that Injun stops ever' mile for a look-see . . . an' now this half-wit thinks we should go skulkin' through the bushes all the way to Pope's ranch an' back." His railing stopped suddenly when Tor Fowler fiercely yanked the mule around and rode toward him.

Fowler's eye bored into Davis's round, pudgy face. He hissed in a low, ominous tone, "How'd you 'scape gettin' your hair lifted before this, Davis? Don't never call Cap McBride half-wit again, hear? He's got more sense than you, stutter or no."

Fowler watched as Davis tightened his grip on the Colt revolving rifle. But any reply Davis thought of making never made it past the knife edge of threat on Fowler's sharp features. "All right, all right," Davis muttered. "No call to get riled. You mountain men is so touchy. I just want to get on with it. Thunderation! Them Mexicans will be busted and the war clean over 'fore we get back into it."

"I don't think so," Fowler replied.

"What's that mean?"

The buckskin-clad trapper lifted his chin toward the knoll above the road and the Indian scout still posed there. "That scout . . . he just give the sign for riders comin'."

"T-tor," Cap McBride asked. "Do we r-run or f-fight?"

Looking to the Indian scout again before replying, Fowler said, "Fight, I reckon, unless we can parley. Two Strike says there's riders ahead of us, too."

Fowler had already selected the brow of the hillside that overhung the road as the place to fort up. A lightning-struck cedar had slabbed off, and part of its trunk rested against some rocks near the edge of the cliff. The steep banks and the thick brush back of the spot made the location defensible, at least for a time.

At Fowler's urging, Cap McBride led the mules farther up the hill into an elderberry thicket. Fowler ordered him to remain there to keep the animals quiet while the other three men prepared for battle.

Fowler, Davis, and the Delaware crouched down behind the cedar log rampart. Davis groused about "skulkin' and hidin' from the cowardly Mexicans," and made a great show of his eagerness for a fight. Fowler thought briefly of correcting the settler, reminding him that these were native Californians fighting on their home ground and that the Americans were the invaders, but he decided it was a waste of time.

Also ignoring Davis's rumblings, Two Strike coolly set about inspecting his weapons. The Indian carried a short-barreled gun, sixty-six caliber. Fowler saw the scout carefully lay the rifle in the fork of a tree branch, and set his powder horn and a row of cast-lead balls in a seam of bark beside it. Two Strike also examined a razor-sharp hand axe, checking its edge before thrusting it back into his belt.

Fowler's rifle, bought at the Hawken family gunshop in St. Louis, rested comfortably across his forearm as it had for thousands of miles. He had carried it across the Rockies more times than he could count. This expedition to California was his third trip in the employ of Captain John Charles Fremont. The Hawken had stopped marauding Pawnees, killed grizzlies, and saved Fowler's life more than once.

Fowler watched with amusement as Davis dithered around, looking up the road in one direction and then peering down in the other. The settler alternated between declaring that nobody was coming, spoiling for a fight, and maintaining to the air that the approaching horsemen would be other Americans anyway, since the Mexicans were too scared to face the Bear Flaggers.

"You got that thing loaded?" Fowler asked dryly, indicating Davis's Colt revolving rifle.

"Huh? Sure enough—fire six times to your one. I bought this new just before I come west with Grigsby's train."

"Ever shot it? You know them newfangled things is dangerous."

Davis looked to Fowler as if swelling pride might overpower good sense, but the echo of cantering hoofbeats shut him up. All three men lowered themselves behind the log as the mounting noise of a large number of horsemen approached.

A dozen riders cantered into view and stopped just below the embankment where the Americans had paused not ten minutes before. Peering through a heap of brush above the level of the cedar log, Fowler examined the enemy troops.

They were a mixed lot, Fowler judged. The two leaders seemed to be a fair sample of the rest of the group. One man was dressed in knee britches of fine cloth and sported a stylish flat-crowned hat. The tack on his well-groomed bay showed silver conchas at every joint and fitting. The man himself was broad of face and pleasant in appearance.

The other man at the front of the column of twos was the complete opposite. His clothing was shabby, and he wore a red bandanna tied over his head and knotted at the back of his neck around his shoulder-length hair. A wisp of scruffy beard clung to his chin. The red horse ridden by this second man was a fine tall animal, but the mochila cloth covering the saddle frame was an old, stained blanket. As the sorrel danced about in the roadway, the mark of Sutter's brand could be seen on its flank. *Stolen, I'll be bound,* Fowler thought.

The rest of the riders were divided between these two extremes—some were well-dressed young caballeros, and others were lean and hungry-looking men with knife-scarred faces. In only one respect did the groups match: none had modern-looking weapons. Some carried old-style muskets and obsolete flintlocks. The rest were armed with lances or pistols only.

The lean man with the scraggly beard spoke, loudly enough that the watchers on the hill could hear. "Don Carrillo," he addressed the well-dressed middle-aged man in Spanish, "the trail of the Americano dogs stops here. They have either turned aside into the woods or doubled back. I told you we should have moved faster. We must find them and exterminate them."

There was a general murmur of assent from the group, but the man addressed as Don Carrillo disagreed. "Juan Padilla," he said, "we wish to capture the Americans, but it is more important to interrogate them, find out their intentions, than to execute them; and General Castro has so ordered. Please remember this."

"Bah!" spat Padilla. "If you have no stomach for this business, then go back to the women. All *true* Californios wish to teach these rattlesnakes a lesson they will never forget."

"You dare to speak thus to me?" countered Carrillo. "You saloonkeeper!"

This is getting interesting, Tor thought. A little dissension among the Californians would make a worthwhile report to Captain Fremont.

"Don't puff up with me, señor rich ranchero. Remember, I was elected co-captain of this troop of lancers."

So intently was Tor Fowler listening to the plans of the troop's next move that he did not see Davis rise up from his kneeling position and slide the Colt over the top of the log. Davis spoke no Spanish, but the settler had correctly concluded that the richly outfitted Carrillo was an important man.

The sound of the single-action hammer being cocked drew Fowler's attention. He threw himself toward Davis, but too late. The roar of the sixty caliber rifle discharging deafened both men as they crashed against the trunk of the tree.

Don Carrillo reeled in his saddle and dropped like a stone to the dusty roadway. "Emboscada!" the horsemen shouted, and the battle was joined. Two Strike's gun fired and a lancer threw up his hands and screamed. A flurry of shots replied from California muskets.

Tor rolled back to his position, picked out a man aiming a pistol and fired. A third horseman clutched his leg, and Padilla shouted, "Retreat, amigos, retreat!"

The fleeing horsemen fired a few shots back over their shoulders, but none took effect. They soon disappeared out of sight around a bend of the road.

Exultant at this victory, Davis jumped up on the cedar log and yelled catcalls after the Californios. "Look at 'em run! What'd I tell you? They won't even stay to fight. Did you see me drop that fat one? Right through the brisket and—hey, why'd you jump me?"

Tor Fowler seethed with rage. It was all he could do not to club the ignorant settler where he stood. "You cussed fool!" he said through gritted teeth. "You may have killed us all. Now get that popgun reloaded and get ready."

"Ready for what? We won, didn't you see? They run off with their tails betwixt their legs."

"They'll be back. By now they figured out that they heard only three different guns, and they know right where we are."

Tor stopped suddenly as he heard a distant rumbling sound and saw a swelling dust cloud floating up above the trees. Both the pounding noise and the swirling haze swept nearer.

When the rank of riders reappeared, they were six across the front, all bearing lances ready. The shafts may have been old and dull from disuse, but the triangular steel points glittered in the sunlight. The churning mass of men and horses surged forward like a single spike-toothed beast bent on the destruction of the Americans.

In contrast to the now-cowering Davis, Tor stood upright and took careful aim. At extreme range he fired and saw a palomino horse stumble but come on. He remained standing still, reloading mechanically as he picked out his next target.

When Two Strike fired, a Californian slumped forward. His lance struck the ground, pitch-poling the man out of his saddle and under the hooves of the on-rushing horses.

Davis fired all six chambers, hitting nothing. His fingers fumbled as he tried to reload and he scattered percussion caps across the tree trunk. Two chambers received no power, two got double charges, and two got powder but no shot. Tor ignored him.

The wave of riders swept closer, urging their mounts up the steep bank without hesitation. The second rank spurred past the bend of the road, then wheeled to attack from the other direction.

A lancer's plunging bay reached the top of the embankment. Instead of jumping over the cedar log, the caballero turned sharply and rode along it, lance point at the ready. Tor fired, and then, with no time to reload, used the Hawken as a club and knocked the lance head aside as the Californio charged past.

Out of the corner of his eye, Tor saw Davis futilely squeeze the trigger on two misloaded chambers. After the two empty clicks, Davis threw the Colt and fled up the hill toward the mules.

At the opposite end of the fallen tree, Two Strike faced a musket with his hatchet. As the rider cantered up the brow of the embankment, the Delaware leaped at the horse's head. It reared up, eyes rolling in terror, and struck out wildly.

One of the flailing hooves knocked Two Strike to the ground. As the Indian struggled to his feet, another Californio rider appeared above the barricades, his pistol aimed at the scout's head.

Two Strike gave a defiant yell and spun the hand axe at the attacker. He missed, and the shot pierced his heart and sent him hurtling down the embankment.

Just that suddenly, it was over. Fowler lay on the ground, a lance thrust against his throat.

Flanked by lancers and followed by a third man with a musket aimed at his head, Fowler stumbled down the embankment and was forced to kneel in the churned dust of the road. Beside him lay the bodies of the leader of the Californios, Don Carrillo, and another man.

Raising his head wearily at a new noise from the hillside, Tor saw Cap McBride prodded down the hill.

"Q-quit stickin' me," Cap protested. "I'm a-g-goin'."

Glad to see that Cap at least appeared unharmed, Tor asked, "What happened? Did they get Davis?"

"N-no!" Cap said with disgust as he was likewise forced to his knees. "He weren't even hurt. He r-run up and kicked me out of the way and r-rode off with all the mules!"

"Silencio!" the man known as Juan Padilla shouted. He spurred his prancing sorrel in a tight circle around the kneeling men.

"Four Fingers," Padilla said to the rider who had killed Two Strike, "how many did we lose?"

"Two killed and four wounded, Capitan," was the report.

"All right," said Padilla abruptly, "shoot that one first." He indicated Cap McBride.

"Hold on!" erupted Fowler in Spanish. "He wasn't even in the fight; and anyway, you don't shoot prisoners!"

"Not all at once," sneered Padilla, shaking Davis's Colt rifle in Fowler's face. "You we may tie to horses and pull apart. What do you say to that, miserio?"

Tor Fowler pleaded for the life of his friend, who was being dragged over toward the earth bank at the roadside. "Prepare to fire," Padilla ordered.

"See you in g-glory," Cap called to Tor. Musket fire rang out, and McBride toppled face first into the road.

With an anguished groan, Fowler dropped his head to his chest. Anticipating his own death, he did not see and barely heard the riders approaching at a gallop.

"What is the meaning of this?" boomed a commanding voice at the head of the newly arrived troop.

"Ah, General Castro," whined Padilla. "We were ambushed by Americanos, but we have defeated them."

"Padilla," Castro warned, "do not trifle with me. By whose order are you executing prisoners? Answer me!" he thundered.

"Don Carrillo's," Padilla lied. "He who was murdered by the first treacherous shot."

"Well, no more," Castro demanded. "The remaining prisoner is coming with me."

3

NORTHWARD, THE DARK green heights of the rounded peaks shimmered in the haze. To the south, a curious trick of the atmosphere caused the low hills of the island of Santa Cruz to loom over the settlement of Santa Barbara as if lying only a short swim away instead of twenty-five miles off shore.

The grass-covered knoll that overlooked Don Pedro Rivera's rancho was itself a tiny island, set between the mountains and the sea. Francesca thought for perhaps the hundredth time that it was in just such a place that she fully understood her father's love of California and his desire to remain and never return to Spain.

As a young girl she had often climbed to this very location to dream of her own future. Through the changing seasons—from wild flower spring to peaceful summer and on into blustery fall and gentle winter—she had grown into a reflection of the beauty and charm of her California home.

The breeze off the ocean was rising, and it ruffled the black lace veil covering Francesca's face as she stood beside her father's newly dug grave. An obelisk of pink granite already marked the spot. Don Pedro had lovingly dedicated this hilltop years earlier when Francesca's mother had passed away.

Her father and mother had come together to the knoll to take the children on outings, to plan the building of their house, and to speculate on their future and that of their chosen homeland. Now they would lie together, side by side, in that place of beauty and peace.

Francesca was flanked by her tall, broad-shouldered husband on one side and her slender son on the other. Their three other children, all younger than Peter, were away at the missionary school in Hawaii. Beside Peter stood his two best friends, the sixteen-year-old twins, Ramon and Carlos Carrillo. Across the grave from her was her brother, Ricardo, his wife Margarita, and their stairstep brace of six children.

At the foot of the grave, a small man in the garb of a Catholic priest led the group of bereaved in the Lord's Prayer. The cleric's diminutive stature and dark brown skin and eyes displayed his Indian heritage.

The small circle of family was surrounded by a much larger group of mourners that included Don Andres Pico, the governor's brother, and Don Abel Stearns. Stearns, a Yankee-born trader, had been living in southern California for almost twenty years and was reputed to be the richest man on the West Coast. He was so widely admired and respected that he had been named subprefect of the pueblo of Los Angeles.

When the service concluded, Don Andres and Stearns drew Will aside. "Don Will," Don Andres said, "we hate to intrude upon your grief, but serious matters have arisen which require that we speak with you."

"Don't fence with him," said Stearns gruffly. "Straight out, Reed, do you know anything about this ragtag bunch of Americans calling themselves the Bear Flag Republic?"

"Only the same rumors that everyone has heard—some American adventures have proclaimed independence from Mexico. I also understand that some U.S. army officer has been encouraging them, but again, it's only hearsay."

"Exactly!" Don Andres burst out, his elaborate side-whiskers bobbing. "It's all hearsay and rumor, promoted by General Castro in Monterey. Listen to this official proclamation." He extracted a folded paper from a deep side pocket of his frock coat and read: "*Countrymen, arise, Divine Providence will guide us to glory.*"

"You see," Stearns explained, "we in the south believe that this fuss may be a pretext for General Castro to increase the size of the militia, ask Mexico City for more troops, and subdue all of California with himself as dictator." Stearns wiped perspiration from his broad forehead with a silk handkerchief, and loosened the knot of the black cravat tied below the stiff-winged shirt collar.

"This is all very interesting," said Will, looking to where Francesca stood hugging Margarita, "but why tell me? You are, as you say, intruding on a time of sorrow and I have never been interested in politics."

"Quite right," apologized Don Andres, bowing.

"Hold on," Stearns said in a no-nonsense tone. "Let's get it all said at once; then he can give us a straight answer. Will you go see the American captain and find out the truth? Fremont's his name, and he's been across the Rockies with surveyors and mountain men like yourself. You two should speak the same language."

"No," said Will with finality. "It does not concern me or mine."

The guard almost shot Davis before recognizing the shambling, gasping form that lurched out of the darkness. The round-faced settler's clothing was torn and full of burrs and foxtails. He was weaponless and walked with a limp, clutching under his arm a crutch improvised from a tree branch. His face was streaked with blood and his hair matted with dried gore from a gash that cut across his forehead and angled up into his scalp.

The guard alerted the camp of the Bear Flaggers. He caught the swaying Davis and led him to the watch fire. Whistling a low exclamation over the settler's injuries, the sentry pressed a cup of coffee into Davis's hands, then brought a bucket of fresh water to wash the wound.

By this time a crowd had gathered around the scene. "What happened, Davis? Where are the others?" asked Andrew Jackson Sinnickson. At five foot ten, and solid as a brick wall, Sinnickson was the leader of this group of the Bear Flag Party.

"Dead," said Davis, shuddering with the horror of the memory. "The Mexicans jumped us. I fought my way clear, but they killed all the others. It was terrible. There must of been fifty of 'em. *Kill all Americanos*,' they was yellin'!"

Sinnickson looked around at the blackness of the Sierran foothill night. "Double the sentries," he ordered, "and put two more men on guard around the horses."

"Got shot in the head," Davis said, indicating the scalp wound. "Shot me clean outta the saddle. I crawled into some bushes and hid out all last night and hiked back here today." There was instant acceptance of this story, although the truth was less dramatic. When Davis had ridden away from the fight, he had looked over his shoulder for pursuers once too often and turned back just as the racing mule had run under a low tree limb.

"Tor Fowler and Cap McBride and the Injun all dead?" said Sinnickson, shaking his head in sorrow and disbelief. "Well, it can't be bloodless now. Grigsby, you and Merritt best ride on over to Captain Fremont and tell him what's happened. Tell him the country's up, and we are requesting the army's aid. Davis," he continued gently, "can you remember any more that might be helpful—anything at all?"

Davis tried his best to look noble and heroic, but only partly succeeded, since he winced at the touch of a washrag on his forehead. "We stood 'em off to start with—yessir, turned 'em back. Ouch! Watch it, will you? An' I heard Fowler say that I had killed a feller name of Car-ill-o or Ka-reyo or somethin'."

"Jose Carrillo? Why, he's a rancher in these parts and supposed to be a moderate man. Was he with them?"

"Right enough," David concluded. "He was their leader."

Captain John C. Fremont ran his slender fingers nervously through his wavy brown hair, then plucked at the top brass button of his dark blue uniform. "So you say hostilities have begun?" he asked Sinnickson, the black-haired leader of the Bear Flaggers.

"Yessir, and it wasn't us who started it, neither. Oh, we had rounded up some horses and made some plans, defensive like, but now it's a real shooting war. We've even had reports that General Castro is advancing against us with a force of six hundred. We need your men and your leadership, Captain."

Fremont looked at Marine Lieutenant Falls. "This puts me in an awkward position, doesn't it, Lieutenant? You see," he explained to Sinnickson, "war is imminent between the United States and Mexico over the annexation of Texas, but it has not yet begun. If I, as an officer of the United States Army, allowed my troops to be used against the Mexicans, I would be committing a breach of international diplomacy."

Sinnickson looked uncomfortably nervous. His prominent Adam's apple bobbed several times before he spoke. "But you can't leave us without protection. We're American citizens, after all. Why, the blood-thirsty Mexicans shot and killed three men in cold blood without any provocation. They may attack our women and children next! You've got to help us!"

Clearing his throat politely, Lieutenant Falls waited for Fremont to acknowledge him. "What is it, Lieutenant? You have a solution?"

"Yessir, I think so," the short, round-shouldered officer said in his whiny voice. "If Mister Sinnickson would step out of the room for just a moment?"

After Sinnickson had obliged, Falls continued. "Sir, the exact wording of the verbal instructions for you from Secretary of State Buchanan was that you were to render aid to American citizens in the event of actual hostilities. Do you hear the wording, sir? Not in the event war is declared, but hostilities. Isn't that what has just happened, sir?"

Fremont brightened visibly. "You're exactly right," he agreed. "My duty is plain. Lieutenant, ask Mister Sinnickson to come back in, and the others as well."

When the group of Americans calling themselves the founders of the Bear Flag Republic had assembled, Fremont explained his conditions for assisting them. Fremont was to be the absolute commander, with all others subject to his orders.

"The first order of business is to capture General Castro. We must strike quickly and not give them time to gather their forces. Those Californio leaders who have already surrendered will remain in custody at Sutter's Fort. From here on we need to move too rapidly to be encumbered by prisoners."

Trading ships of many nations—French, Russian, English and American—had all plied the California waters for decades. Some were legally approved by the Customs House in Monterey. Many more were smugglers' crafts, anxious to take advantage of eager buyers and hundreds of miles of unpatrolled coastline.

As commerce increased, countries encouraged the fair treatment of their citizens by shows of naval might. The British and the Americans in particular kept Pacific squadrons cruising the length of California. It was even rumored that Britain might accept Upper California in payment of old war debts owed by the Mexican government. Of course, officially, Britain had no interest in any stretch of the Pacific coast south of the Oregon territory, and her ships were supposedly present as observers only.

The appearance of Her Britannic Majesty's Ship-of-the-Line, *Juno*, caused no little stir when it anchored off Santa Barbara. Although not as impressive as the eighty-four-gun British frigate, *Collingwood*, which was also sailing in California seas, the *Juno*'s three decks, bristling with cannons, were an imposing sight.

"What do you make of it all, Father?" Will Reed asked the small-statured priest who had spoken at Don Pedro's funeral. "First, Governor Pico arrives from Los Angeles with eighty armed men, and now this warship." The two watched from the white sand beach in front of the sleepy coastal town as *Juno* sailed into the lee of the point before turning sharply upwind and letting go the anchor with a show of British precision.

"My friend," said the dark brown little man, "as to the governor, there is no reason why I should know any better than you; and yet, as regard to the English ship, I believe I have the answer."

The ranchero waited for the explanation as the priest debated about saying more. "You always think more than you speak, Father," Will urged him good-naturedly.

Resuming his reply with a grin and a shrug, the priest offered, "I have been informed by my superiors that a certain priest, a Father McNamara, is to be expected here. As his last location was reported to be Mazatlan, where the British fleet has been anchored, I have followed the rabbit tracks to the rabbit hole and come up with a rabbit."

"Father Francis," laughed Will, "there are times when you still sound more like Blackbird of the Woilu Yokuts than you do a Catholic priest!"

"I am proof," said Father Francis modestly, "that one may be both."

"And you said your visitor's name is Mik-Na-Mee-Ra . . . is he Yokut also?"

"No." Father Francis shook his head, smiling. "Another tribe . . . Irish."

Three gently waving lines of white breakers separated the landing of Santa Barbara from its anchorage. Will and the priest watched as the small boat, called the captain's gig, was fitted out and two men, one in the robes of a cleric and the other in a naval uniform, were rowed ashore.

"And will you be entertaining the visitor?" Will asked.

"No," said Father Francis. "Since attacks by the shaking sickness and by the Mojave tribes have moved my people up into desolate hills, they have many needs. I go now to serve them."

4

THE GOLD BRAID on General Castro's uniform was frayed and faded, and one of his tunic buttons was missing. Even his mutton chop whiskers and gray hair looked thin and threadbare.

His voice was not worn out, though, as he shouted in English at Tor Fowler with a bellow like an angry bull. "Where is Fremont going? What are his plans?"

Fowler was seated in a stiff wooden armchair, his hands bound behind his back with rawhide strings. The chair's legs were uneven, so Fowler rocked forward and back with each blast of the interrogation.

"Don't know, General," he answered truthfully. "I signed on to hunt meat for the camp and to keep track of Injun sign. Never was any call for anybody to tell me nothing important."

Castro seemed impressed with the frankness of Fowler's reply and changed topics. "How many men are armed? What about more troops?" he shouted.

With a look of complete sincerity, Fowler lied, "Man, General, you just can't believe it! Must be close on a thousand in camp already and I heard the lieutenant sayin' that General Kearny was comin' with a thousand more."

Castro rocked back on his heels as if he were the one seated in the wobbly chair. A look of worried consternation ran across his face, and his bushy eyebrows pulled together. The effect was so comical that it took all Fowler's poker playing ability to keep from laughing out loud.

Switching to Spanish, the general addressed the scrawny killer, Juan Padilla, who stood at his elbow. "What do you think, Padilla?" the general demanded. "Is he speaking the truth?"

"We have seen nothing like a thousand men, General," Padilla replied. "But let me tickle his ribs with this," he drew a knife halfway out of the dirty sash knotted around his waist, "and I'll have the truth soon enough."

Castro made an abrupt gesture to Padilla to put away the blade. "He may prove useful as a hostage later. In any case, you do not know this breed," he said. "His kind live with the Indians and think like them—they will die without speaking and spit blood in your face at the end."

The first rifle shot came just as General Castro's camp was stirring for breakfast. Tor Fowler had spent an unpleasant night, unable to swat the cloud of mosquitoes that feasted on him. He was standing, tied with his back to an oak tree, his wrists fastened by a rawhide strap that encircled the trunk. At the whine of the bullet and the report of the gun, he sat down abruptly and slithered around to put the oak between him and the firing.

The Californios bolted out of their tents and made a rush for their stacked weapons. The first man to reach the muskets was dropped with a rifle ball through his leg, and the rest suddenly elected to flop on their stomachs and crawl. Three men ran toward the corral of horses, but two were picked off trying to climb the rail fence, and the third crouched behind a post.

General Castro stormed out of his quarters shouting commands. As Fowler watched, Castro attempted to buckle his sword belt around his middle before hitching up his suspenders and got tangled up. A bullet clanged into the hanging lantern in front of the general's tent, and he dropped, sword and all, behind the oak chest that contained his belongings.

In quick succession, two bullet holes were added to the trunk's fittings. One split a leather strap and flipped the loose end up in the air. Another neatly punched out the lock.

The Californios were returning fire with their muskets, but it was plain that the Americans were out of range of the older weapons. Buckskin and homespunclad figures could be seen walking upright between the trees at two hundred yards distant. A blue-garbed man with a white bandanna tied over his head was waving men into positions.

"Whooee!" Fowler yelled. "Go to it, boys! Hammer and tongs!"

Another bullet clipped a branch above Fowler's head and knocked some leaves and bark down around him. "Hey, General," he called, "how about untying me?"

Castro scowled at him and shouted for his men to circle behind the corral and saddle up.

Working the rawhide binding, Fowler sawed the tie back and forth in an attempt to set himself free. The Californios were feverishly occupied, so escape never looked more likely than now.

Sixteen lancers made a crawling circuit of the corral and managed to saddle their mounts among the jostling and milling horses. Fowler figured that they would make easy targets riding through the gate, since it was too narrow to allow more than one at a time. But he had not counted on the Californios' resourcefulness—or their horsemanship.

With a shout of defiance, four jinetes, expert riders, jumped their horses over the corral fence without bothering about the gate. These were followed by four more and twice again four until all sixteen riders swept across the camp and the open pasture toward the Americans. The tiny pennants on the lance heads waved like flags when the horses jumped, and then fluttered in front of the riders when the weapons were leveled for the charge. Fowler looked on with fascination as the lancers galloped into the hail of rifle bullets now being fired with renewed intensity.

Back and forth Fowler continued sawing at the leather tie until his wrists were bloody. "May have to cut this tree down before I get loose," he muttered to himself.

Another fusillade of shots made the scout look up again and sneak another view around the tree trunk. Two riders were shot out of the saddle, and when one horse was hit, he made an end-over-end roll at full speed. The power of the charge was broken short of the American positions, and the riders were forced to seek shelter in the trees bordering the pasture to try to regroup.

The action by the lancers had succeeded in drawing the Bear Flaggers' attention away from Castro's camp, giving the general time to organize a second wave of horsemen to go in with muskets while he and the rest of the Californio troops withdrew south toward San Francisco Bay.

Still sawing feverishly at the leather strap, Fowler heard another flurry of shots, and two more thudded into the tree behind which he hid. He yanked with all his strength on the rawhide and suddenly jerked up as another bullet unexpectedly hit the binding, freeing him instantly.

The mountain man wasted no time trying to untie his ankles. With his feet still bound together, he began crawling quickly toward a clump of yellow mustard brush just beyond the edge of the camp.

Fowler just reached it when he heard the unmistakable sound of a hammer click. A cold barrel poked him in the ear. It was Padilla with the Colt rifle captured from Davis. "I would like very much to kill you," the wiry little man said with a twisted grin, "but General Castro says you are to come once again with him."

The solid wooden wheels of the ox cart bumped violently over the tiny rocks and dropped with a thud into every pothole. Tor Fowler wished that his captors had tied him into the carreta standing up. As it was, each bounce sent a jolt up his tailbone like being thrown from a mustang onto a granite boulder. Fowler was being transported with the cavalry troops' supplies: sacks of beans, spare saddles, General Castro's trunk, and one prisoner, all clumping along together.

Fowler listened with amusement to the groaning complaints of the ungreased axle. Without their Indian servants, these Californios seemed incapable of the least effort that required manual labor. He had heard it said that if a task could not be done on horseback, then they would not do it at all. At any rate, not one of these horsemen had attempted to grease the axle, even though a bucket of tallow for that purpose hung underneath the carreta.

The cart bumped down a track that ended at a broad expanse of dark water. Fowler guessed it was San Francisco Bay, although he had never seen it before.

General Castro rode up the column on his white horse. "Padilla," he yelled, "take the prisoner and your men and go across the bay. I want Fremont to think that I have gone that way also, but my men and I will ride south from here, driving before us such horses as we can find and recruiting some more lancers."

"Couldn't we sweep around the road and attack Fremont's flank?" Padilla asked. "Do we have to run, General?"

Castro looked thoughtful. "It is the best strategy at present," he said, "until we have raised the whole country and that cursed snail Pico sends us more men. We are not ready to face Fremont's thousand."

Tor Fowler had to duck his head quickly to hide his smile.

Lieutenant Falls stood on the shore of San Francisco Bay not far below the town of San Rafael. He was noisily sucking his buck teeth as he shook his head with displeasure. "It's a bad job," he remarked to Davis. "Castro and his men have escaped across the bay. Now they'll have a chance to regroup —perhaps fortify San Francisco. What I wouldn't give to know his plans."

The breeze blowing across the water was tossing choppy little waves up on shore. Gusts danced on the wide expanse in playful patterns. The wind rippled a stretch of surface half a mile wide, leaving smooth and undisturbed swaths on either side. The passing clouds floating overhead contributed to the show of shifting light and shadow, dividing the waters of the bay into green and blue areas that changed with each moment.

Shading his eyes with a dirty palm, Davis peered across the bay. "What's that?" he asked at last.

"Where?"

"Yonder, straight acrost from us. See that white patch? First I thought it was a wave and then I figured it for a cloud, but now I reckon . . ."

Falls confirmed his guess. "It's a sail, and it's headed right this way, too. Let's get out of sight and see where she lands."

The two men hid themselves behind some rocks above the makeshift pier that served as a landing for San Rafael. It was not long before it was apparent that the triangular sail on the little sloop was tacking so that it would arrive right in front of them.

As the single-masted ship spanked against the tops of the waves, drawing closer to the shore, Falls could see that two men paced the forepart of the deck and a third handled the tiller.

"Slide out toward the road," Falls ordered Davis. "Bring back as many of our boys as you can round up quickly, but do it quietly. Stay out of sight till I holler, in case they've got a bunch below deck. But when I yell, come on up and take 'em."

The fore-and-aft sail fluttered in the breeze and the small ship lost headway, but not much. The last two tacking movements swung the boat away from the pier and then back parallel to the shore. Falls thought that the pilot was going to run alongside the end of the dock, leaving his escape route ready for a quick departure. The sloop's motion toward the pier looked to Falls like a fleeing bird swooping toward a tree branch. The two men on the forward deck had taken places along the rail on the landward side.

The sail dropped and the sloop coasted up beside the wharf. The first man jumped over the rail and landed cleanly. He pivoted suddenly to catch a carpetbag that the other tossed to him. Then it was the second man's turn to leap. His foot snagged some rigging and he tumbled onto the planks of the dock, but he was up quickly as the boat continued to glide past the pier.

The ship's departure was as abrupt as its arrival. Falls watched as the lone remaining figure hoisted the sail taut again and put the tiller over. The two men left standing on the dock each raised a hand in farewell, but the steersman did not acknowledge them. The sloop stood out into the bay sharply, as if dropping off the passengers had been an interruption to the important business of sailing.

Falls drew his pistol and cocked the hammer, glancing down to check the percussion cap. The two Californios moving up the pier were young and carried no weapons openly, but Falls was not taking any chances of running foul of something hidden in the carpetbag.

A moment passed, and in the brief interval the sloop was out of range to be hailed into returning, but the men had not yet reached the landward end of the pier. Stepping out from his place of concealment, Falls leveled his pistol at the chest of one and commanded, "Halto! Or whatever means stop in your lingo."

Startled by the lieutenant's sudden appearance, the pair who had been talking and laughing paused midstride and were silent. They made no attempt to flee. Both lifted their arms in token of surrender, one holding the carpetbag awkwardly at shoulder height before he set it down. Lieutenant Falls looked from one face to the other and thought he was seeing double. They were twins, about sixteen or eighteen years of age. Dressed alike in black knee breeches and short black jackets with silver trim, the brothers matched down to the silver buckles that decorated their boots.

"Señor," said one, tentatively lowering his hands and stepping forward.

"Get back there!" snarled Falls, "and keep your hands up!" The round bald patch on the lieutenant's head turned bright red when he was angry, or scared; it was crimson now.

"Señor," the young Californio meekly tried again, "we speak English. Please to tell us what is wanted—what have we done?"

"I'll ask the questions around here, and you'll answer right sharp if you know what's good for you. What are your names?"

The one who had already spoken continued to reply. "I am Ramon Carrillo and this is my brother Carlos."

"What are you doin', slippin' in secret like this?"

The twins glanced at each other, and then Ramon said, "The manner of our arrival was not of our choosing, señor. The captain, he was afraid to come at all—we had to pay double—and even then we had to jump because he would not stop."

"Yeah? What's he afraid of?"

"He said some crazy Amer . . . some foreigners had caused some trouble on this side of the bay and he did not wish to get mixed up in it."

"Davis!" Falls bellowed, "bring 'em on down. We caught us some spies!"

"Oh no, señor," protested Carlos. "We are coming to visit our uncle, who lives near Commandante Mariano Vallejo in Sonoma."

"Vallejo, eh?" sneered Falls, scratching his thin gray mustache. Davis and half a dozen men with rifles ran up and surrounded the Carrillo brothers. "Well, Vallejo is already our prisoner, and his rancho and his horses belong to us. What do you say to that?"

The twins said nothing at all. Falls, certain that their silence proved their guilt, and puffed up with pride at the capture, ordered the carpetbag dumped and the brothers searched.

"Lookee here, Lieutenant!" Davis exclaimed as he drew a folded sheet of paper from Ramon's jacket pocket. "Some kinda handbill or somethin'."

"Lemme see that," demanded Falls, snatching the paper away from Davis. Falls scanned the printing; then, since he could not read Spanish, he announced the only thing he could make out for certain. "It's signed by General Castro hisself!"

"Well, go on, Lieutenant," requested one of the other soldiers of the Bear Flag brigade, "read it to us."

"It says . . . ." Falls paused; then he plunged ahead. "It says for all Californios to take up arms to kill Americans! Yep, that's what it says. Men, women and children, it says, kill 'em all. Burn their homes, take their belongings, run 'em clear out of California. That's what it says!"

Ramon and Carlos both reacted with horror. "Oh no, señor!" they exclaimed in unison. Then Ramon continued. "It calls on Californios to forget their past differences and band together to fight the invaders, but it says nothing about—"

"There, you see?" said Falls triumphantly. "They admit it! Out of their own mouths, you heard 'em. They were sneakin' across the bay to organize a counterattack—probably to slaughter us all in our sleep!"

"String 'em up!" growled Davis.

"Drown 'em like mongrel pups," suggested another.

"Run!" yelled Ramon, pushing Falls to the ground. He lowered his shoulder and ran into the midsection of a second of his captors before a rifle butt clubbed him to the ground.

Carlos threw himself off the pier and into the chilly waters of the bay. Striking out strongly, he was swimming along the shoreline when the first rifle ball struck him in the back. When the second and the third crashed into his head, he sank without a splash.

"Davis," Falls asked as they stood over Ramon's unconscious form. "Name Carrillo mean anything to you?"

"You bet," said the settler, rubbing the half-healed wound on his forehead. "Carrillo was the name of the leader of the bunch that jumped Tor Fowler and me. . . . I killed him," he concluded proudly.

"Well, what do you know? This scum here is some kin to that feller," nodded Falls, nudging Ramon with the toe of his boot.

"What do you want we should do with him?"

Falls considered a moment. "Captain said we got no time for prisoners," he said. "Drag him over in that gully and shoot him. And remember, they was spies and assassins!"

Tor Fowler had a theory about pain. He believed that one could withstand anything by concentrating all thought somewhere else. It seemed to him that pain could not rob a man of his reasoning without his agreement. If he would just ignore it, then he could go on functioning and surviving.

He had tested his belief before, once when a barbed Pawnee arrow had to be cut out of his back. Another time he had hobbled ten miles across a range of eight-thousand-foot peaks on a newly broken leg. *Keep on thinking and live, or give in to the pain and die.* In Fowler's mind, it was that simple a choice.

But he had to admit that the present torture put a whole new slant on pain. He was hanging face downward, spread-eagle by rawhide straps around his wrists and ankles. The straps were tied over the rafter beams of an adobe hut so that his body sagged under its own weight and tore at his shoulder joints. His breathing was labored and slow.

Concentrate! Ignore the pain! Fowler forced himself to review how he had gotten to this place; but he had almost lost track of how many times his captors had moved him, by forced march on foot and in the carreta, and most recently in the smelly hold of a little trading sloop.

They had thrown him headfirst into the bilge of the small ship and carried him across the bay to the tiny, dirty settlement of Yerba Buena. Upon arrival, Padilla had ordered that Fowler be trussed up like a ham hanging in a smokehouse.

Now that Tor thought about it, there was one thing to be grateful for. The Apaches practiced a similar torture to what he was undergoing now, but with an additional refinement: they hung their victim's head downward over a slow fire.

5

WILL AND FRANCESCA were invited to a reception honoring Father McNamara and the *Juno*'s captain, Blake. The evening's festivities were held at the property of the little Irish doctor, Nicholas Den.

Den stood at the front of the receiving line, enjoying his role as host and introducing the rancheros and merchants to Father McNamara and the warship's captain.

At the opposite end of the row of dignitaries was Governor Pio Pico. With his politician's smile firmly in place on his coarse features, and his ample girth stuffed dangerously into a formal black suit, Pico managed to look jovial and imposing at the same time.

Nicholas Den fairly bounced with the importance of the occasion and, as often happened when the small curly-haired Irishman got excited, his Spanish took on an improbably Irish brogue.

"Don Will and Doña Francesca Reed," he intoned with a ferocious rolling of *r*'s.

McNamara spoke a cultured Spanish as befitted a well-educated man. "Charmed, Doña Reed," he said, bowing. "Don Reed . . . American, yes?"

"Mexican citizen these last sixteen years," replied Will. "And you . . . Irish, like the good doctor here?"

"Aye, but a long way from home, and a long time away as well." McNamara was a large man, as stout as Governor Pico, but a head taller. He had pale skin, much freckled from the California sun. His short brown hair was balding in the crown, and Will thought he looked like a woodcut of Friar Tuck in a book about Robin Hood.

"Father McNamara is here to speak with the governor about Irish colonists coming to live in California," interjected Den with excited self-importance.

Father McNamara shrugged off the comment. "Ireland, my homeland, has many starving folk and not enough farmland to feed them, while I hear that California has plenty of good soil for willing hands to cultivate. But I am really here on a mission for the church."

Will and Francesca passed down the row and reached the governor. The Reeds had met Governor Pico many times before; and while Will did not entirely trust the politician, he had at least a grudging respect for the man who governed as a Californio first and not as a high-handed representative of the government in Mexico City.

"Eighty soldiers escorted you here, Governor?" Will inquired. Pico, beaming through his thick lips at a row of señoritas coyly peeking at him from behind their fans, pretended at first not to hear. But he could not ignore the topic when Will continued. "Two years ago we took up arms against a governor who brought his army with him from Sonora, and we kicked him and his men back south again."

Pico's stubby fingers plucked at the gold and black onyx watch chain draped across his expansive stomach. He was not pleased with the questions, but he attempted to cover up his displeasure by answering lightly, "You will remember that I also participated in the ouster of Governor Micheltorena. Now another man's ego may have gotten too big for him, but I assure you, it isn't mine."

"So you believe that the stories of the American invasion are exaggerated by General Castro for his own purposes?"

"It remains to be seen how much of the present crisis is General Castro's invention. But rest assured, Don Will— whether to put down rebellion or to corral General Castro, I and my men are ready to march." His words were uttered in a light, almost careless tone; and he made a sweeping gesture with both arms, like a bear hug, as he said the word *corral*.

"And the timely arrival of the good captain and the British warship?" added Will, indicating Blake, who was listening without comment. "Does that event also have something to do with the crisis?"

"Purest coincidence only," Pico laughed, holding his ample sides as if to keep the humor confined. "The *Juno*, on which Father McNamara was coming to visit me, put in at San Pedro, only to hear that I was on my way here. Captain Blake was kind enough to sail on to Santa Barbara instead of making Father McNamara await my return to Los Angeles. Ah," he interrupted himself, "I see dinner is ready."

"Hogwash," muttered Will to himself in English.

"Cómo?" asked Francesca, looking cool and beautiful in her white dress. "What did you say?" Her eyes were twinkling, and Will knew she had not only heard his comment but understood it as well.

"Nada—nothing, really. I am just wondering what is so important about a scheme to bring in Irish settlers that Pico would lie about it."

"How do you know he is lying?"

"Because," Will said, pausing in the doorway and leaning close to Francesca's ear as he pretended to straighten the red sash knotted around his waist. "Because Blackbird—Father Francis—told me that Father McNamara was expected here. That means Governor Pico and the Irish priest planned to meet here in Santa Barbara all along."

Enormous quantities of food greeted the guests as they entered the dining hall. Quarters of beef, roasted over oak-coal fires, were sliced into huge steaks and heaped on round wooden serving trays the size of wagon wheels. The Indian servants who carried the trays around the dining hall staggered under the weight of them.

Fragrant mounds of arroz con frijoles—rice and beans, seasoned with chili peppers—were accompanied by steaming heaps of freshly baked corn tortillas. The diners sampled the Zinfandel wines from two different mission vineyards; some from vines already over fifty years old.

At length the still-heaping platters and serving bowls had been carried around a final time and the last filled-to-capacity guest had refused even one more helping. The pewter dishes were cleared away, and the tables and chairs were pushed back to make room for the musicians to come in and tune up.

Will and Francesca went for a walk in the plaza, as did several other couples. "You won't get sleepy before the dance, will you, Señor Reed?" teased Francesca.

"Not a chance, Señora Reed," Will asserted earnestly. "What with you being the most beautiful woman present, I'll have to be on my guard that some young caballero doesn't sweep you away."

"Impossible!" she said, stretching up to kiss him quickly. "I am holding on to the most dashing and handsome man here, and I won't let him go. I saw the eyes that shameless Julieta was making at you."

"Huh!" Will scoffed. "Making eyes at old Pico, I shouldn't wonder, or that British captain."

"I do so wish Peter could have come this evening," Francesca reflected. "He will be sorry he missed the dancing."

"He is being sensible," Will argued. "Since he is leaving tomorrow to join the twins in Sonoma, he needed to stay home this evening to prepare. You know, he is writing out a list of instructions for the care of his herd of cattle during his absence. I like to see him taking his responsibilities seriously."

"So like his father," Francesca murmured.

"And his grandfather," Will added. "Don Pedro would be proud."

The first notes of the jota sounded from the band, calling the strolling couples back to the dance. Will noticed the glint of a tear in Francesca's eye. He guessed that the swirling mixture of violin and guitar conjured up for Francesca visions of the Aragon of her ancestors. No doubt the mysterious strains that drew from the Moors and the gypsies called to her mind the Spain she had never seen, only heard about in the stories of her father's youth. Now she would hear them no more.

The inner circle of ladies faced the outer circle of men. Handclapping and energetic footwork punctuated the jota, the dance that translated as "little details." Pio Pico capered around the dance floor, sweating profusely.

At the next break in the music, Will made his way to the punch bowl. The laughing governor was there ahead of him, with a young señorita hanging on each arm and every word. "Quite a nice fandango, eh, Governor?" said Will in an cheery, offhand way.

"Most excellent," Pico agreed. "Nicholas certainly knows how to entertain. For being a little chino, a curly-headed Irishman, he has become more Californio than many who were born here. Not like some foreigners who think to bring their own culture and force it upon us."

"Perhaps the new crop of Irish will fit in as well," Will observed.

"No doubt, no doubt," agreed the governor, looking anxious to return to the dance floor where the strains of a waltz could be heard.

"Isn't it curious that Father McNamara says his plan is of little importance, and yet it could not wait for your return to Los Angeles?"

Pico was starting to get annoyed. "I don't know what you are trying to suggest, Don Will Reed, but this is a strange line of questions for a man who told my brother and Don Abel Stearns that he had no interest in politics."

"Let us say that I have no political *ambition*," said Will, stressing the last word while staring into Pico's flushed face. "But that does not mean I lack concern for my country."

"Which country?" shot back Pico. "Mexico or the United States?"

"California," Will retorted, bristling.

A cry from the musicians' corner rang out over the laughing crowd. "The bamba! The bamba!" Applause and still greater laughter greeted this announcement.

Three wicker hoops the size of small wine casks were placed in a cleared area of the dance floor. Three young señoritas stepped forward, and each stood inside a hoop. Each was handed a glass of water to balance on her head.

A single guitar began to slowly strum a rhythmic progression of measured notes and minor chords. The girls dipped gracefully and carefully brought the hoops up to knee level. The tempo of the music picked up as each dancer moved first one ankle and then the other in a succession rapid enough to keep the hoop from slipping down. The glasses jostled, but not a single drop of water was spilled.

Faster and faster went the chords as the crowd picked up the beat by clapping their hands. Each girl bent quickly and gave the hoop a spin; the flashing ankles and pointed slippers were joined by the whirling of the bands. One girl, trying to keep up the pace of footwork and manage the spinning hoop, overbalanced and the water glass tumbled off her head. A groan came up from the audience, but it changed to a cheer as the dancer recovered quickly enough to catch the glass before it struck the floor.

The two remaining girls were well matched, and the spectators placed wagers on which would last the longest. The noise of the crowd and the music and the clapping drowned out the staccato sound of horses' hooves ringing on the paving stones of the plaza. None of the partygoers saw the two lathered horses clatter up to the mission in the darkness, nor observed the two men fling themselves to the ground as their mounts slid and skidded to a stop.

Through the rear of the milling throng pushed Peter, calling, "Father!" The crowd, grumbling, parted reluctantly, jostled by the interruption.

Paco shoved two onlookers roughly aside and received angry glares in return. Someone muttered curses about Indios who did not know their place. Another uttered a threat of punishment.

The music was reaching a climactic moment when Peter pushed into the inner circle of the audience and spotted his father and mother on the other side.

"Father!" Peter yelled. "Ramon and Carlos are dead—killed by the Americanos!"

The music jerked to a halt. The crowd noise died away gradually, and then as the message sank in, one of the dancers screamed. In the abrupt silence that followed, the shattering of the water glasses on the stone floor seemed to ring on and on.

The slash of the leather strap across Tor Fowler's back made him jump and yank against the rawhide that tied him to the roof beams. He gave a grunt of pain when the blow landed, but otherwise he made no sound. The sweat of his torture gathered in the tightly knotted furrows of his brow and dripped from the end of his pointed nose onto the black earth of the floor.

Padilla had beaten Fowler before, but this whipping was particularly savage. The former saloonkeeper, Padilla, was matched blow for blow by his accomplice Four Fingers. In between lashes the two men reviled Tor, telling him he deserved death for what the Yankee pigs had done.

The mountain man was grateful that the cutthroats did not beat him in silence. Even though he did not understand what they were talking about, it helped him to ignore the pain as he tried to cipher out their accusations.

He gathered that some of the Bear Flaggers must have killed two young Californios . . . in cold blood, from the sound of things. This news gave Padilla an excuse to be even more cruel than usual.

Finally the pace of blows began to slacken, as Fowler knew it would. The Californios tired of their activity and stopped the beating. Fowler knew what was coming next and braced himself for it.

The knots securing the rawhide ties were let go and he was dropped, face first, onto the floor. Padilla kicked him twice in the ribs and told him to crawl back to his corner, but Fowler could not move. The Californios grasped him roughly and pitched him back to the wall like a discarded cowhide.

Sometime later, an old crone of an Indian woman came into the adobe hut. She brought Fowler a pan of brackish water and a shallow bowl of thin barley gruel. The woman, who never spoke, much less answered questions, fed the broth to Tor like a baby and held the tin of water to his thirsty lips. It would be several hours before he could use his arms again.

"It does not require the gift of prophecy," Father McNamara declared to Governor Pico, "to foresee that California will not remain part of Mexico forever . . . unless some defensive measures are undertaken."

"Yes, yes," nodded Pico impatiently. "Everyone agrees that the American invasion is real and not merely an invention of General Castro's. But what do we do now?"

McNamara looked pointedly at the stoic face of the British Captain Blake and finally received a nod of agreement. "Give us one square league, 4000 acres, for each family and we'll plant a hedge of Irish Catholics strong enough to keep the Methodist wolves at bay."

Pico's bulging eyes turned inward toward his bulbous nose as the strain of mental calculation took place. "You want me to deed . . . 4 *million* acres of land? That's preposterous! In all the area around all the existing pueblos and missions, there is not that much unclaimed property!"

McNamara shook his head and in an ingratiating tone replied, "It is not necessary to disrupt your fine coastal cities. My people are people of the land, willing to settle in the harsh interior. What is it called . . . the valley of the San Joaquin?"

"But it is completely uncivilized . . . a country of wild Indios and wild beasts!"

"Exactly," agreed McNamara. "Ideal for both our purposes, don't you agree?"

Pico pondered. "For such a large transaction, I must confer with the territorial assembly—"

"By all means," the priest concurred. "Only remember, the wolf is at the door, howling to be let in among the sheep. May I suggest at least your tentative approval while the details are being worked out?"

Pico nodded eagerly and stuffed his too-small European style top hat down onto his large head. He bustled from the room, shouting for his carriage driver to bring the caretela.

Father McNamara turned to regard Captain Blake. Broad smiles painted both of their faces. "He doesn't yet understand how completely he has just thrown his lot in with us, does he?" Blake said. McNamara shook his head, still smiling. "But the assembly?" Blake questioned. "Will he be able to get them to agree?"

"Without question. Exchange worthless, unoccupied land for a buffer of one thousand settlers between the ravenous Americans and these pitiful remnants of bygone Spanish glory? My dear captain, we could have asked for 40,000 acres for each family, and they would still agree."

Captain Blake nodded his understanding. "Of course, it doesn't really matter that it would take a year or more to arrange such a colony. The first twenty British subjects will want protection from the American invaders, and the British navy will be honor bound to oblige."

"And what better way to aid and protect than to seize the ports?" McNamara said. "Will it be difficult to locate twenty volunteers for such a project . . . facing wild Indians, wild beasts, wild Americans, and wild Californians, I mean?"

"You have only to ask," Blake replied. "I have *already* dispatched twenty sailors whose ill health made them eager to exchange their shipboard labors for a little time spent living off the land."

"Captain," Father McNamara asked with delight, "where did the governor put that bottle of excellent California brandy? I think a toast is in order."

"Don Abel Stearns wishes to speak with you, Father," reported Peter from the head of the stairs. Will, who was digging through an old sea chest in the attic of his home, turned at the interruption.

"Did he say what he wanted? I am in a terrible hurry, Peter."

"I know, Father, and I told him so, but he insists that it is important."

At that moment, Will's hands grasped the leather-wrapped parcel he had been seeking. He stood up with the rolled bundle. "All right," he said, "now I have what I was looking for. Tell him I'll be right down."

Don Abel was admiring the striking clock on the mantel of the Reeds' fireplace. Will gestured for him to be seated in a chair made entirely of cattle horns lashed together with rawhide.

"Don Will, I know you are anxious to go north and locate the killers of Ramon and Carlos Carrillo, so I will be brief."

Will acknowledged the accuracy of Don Abel's statement with a nod, but said nothing and waited for the merchant to proceed.

"I want to . . . how can I put this? I want to encourage you to go to Captain Fremont with an open mind."

"An open mind about murdering children?" Will burst out. "What are you saying?"

"No, no!" cautioned Don Abel hurriedly. "I mean, I am certain that Fremont is an honorable man and that he will also want to punish the offenders. I hope you will give him a chance to investigate."

"And I hope it will already be done and the murderers under arrest!" snapped Will. "If Fremont has any control at all over that rabble, he should have captured the killers already."

"Correct, correct," said Stearns, "but please remember that the future of this land is properly with the United States and not with Mexico. We don't want Captain Fremont to think that our sentiments run any other way."

"Is that what this visit is about?" Will snorted, standing up abruptly. The leather-covered bundle fell off his lap and spilled its contents: a fringed buckskin jacket and leggings from Will's days as a mountain man. "You think I might make Fremont rethink his support for the revolt? You know what, Stearns? You're absolutely right! If I find out that he or any of his men had anything to do with the murder of the Carrillos, I am going to tell him that all Californios, Yankee or Spanish, will resist him and the so-called Bear Flag rebellion to the last drop of our blood!"

"You cannot be serious," Stearns responded. "We want to belong to America—peacefully, if possible, but by armed conflict if necessary. How can you, an American yourself, feel any differently?"

"Stearns." Will towered over the hawk-nosed man. "You have had your beak in the account books for too long. You cannot see anything but stacks of silver reals. Get out of my house."

Stearns went without protest. Will stood glaring at his back as he left, and his son, who stood in the entryway, closed the door behind Don Abel with somewhat more force than was necessary.

"Peter, I am leaving you in charge of the herds," Will said.

"But I want to go with you," his son replied. "They were my friends."

"I know," Will agreed, "and it is hard for you to remain behind, but it is important. Paco is a crafty mayordomo, and he will help you do what is required."

6

SIX DAYS AFTER the terrible news about the twins had reached Santa Barbara, Will Reed stood on a hill overlooking the little settlement called Yerba Buena. Located on the tip of the peninsula that formed the western enclosure of San Francisco Bay, it was not much more than a miserable collection of shacks and huts. Initially it had sprung up around a Hudson's Bay Company trading post, but had never grown into a thriving city.

The small harbor that provided the anchorage for Yerba Buena was a cove on the eastern shore of the peninsula, just below the ramshackle town. The only ocean-going ship anchored there was a Russian vessel down from Alaska. Its rigging looked dull and in disrepair, and an air of greasy neglect hung over it.

Will arrived seeking answers, but found no one to provide them. All the Mexican authorities had fled southward, including General Castro and his men. The alcalde of Yerba Buena had abandoned his post and taken to his heels. He had heard that the Americanos not only killed children but that they took captured officials and skinned them alive.

No one seemed to know anything about what had actually happened to the Carrillo twins. Leidesdorff, the American vice-consul, was conveniently absent. Robert Ridley, the captain of the port and a Britisher who had adopted California as home, was likewise ignorant of what was happening north of the bay. The Americans were victorious, it seemed, and all of northern California now belonged to them.

Will made up his mind to cross the bay and seek out the American commander. He would demand an explanation of the deaths of the brothers and insist on knowing what was being done to catch the murderers.

But no one would take him across the water. Trading sloops and fishing smacks were available for hire, but no Californio captain was willing to risk coming in range of the American rifles. Will had even offered to pay the captain of the Russian vessel for passage, but the oily-looking officer had only stopped stuffing his face with rice and beans long enough to say that the matter would have to be referred to Sitka and that a response would take six weeks.

In frustration at his wasted day, Will climbed the windy heights above Yerba Buena just as the sun began to set. He stared hard across the straights. Shielding his eyes against the glare on the water, Will traced the line from the cove below him to the far shore, lit in gold and orange by the reflection of the sinking sun.

There was a sail on the horizon. As Will watched, the small craft, no bigger than a whaleboat or the shore launch off a trading vessel, tacked on its course toward the peninsula. The ranchero decided that here at last was someone who had braved the trip to the farther shore at least once and could perhaps be persuaded to go again. Will started down from the heights, leading Flotada by the silver-worked bridle. He paused again on a slightly lower ridge, expecting to see the boat veer around toward the harbor.

Instead of coming to land at Yerba Buena, the vessel grounded directly below the old presidio of San Francisco. Twelve men armed with rifles jumped from the boat. They held their weapons aloft to keep them dry as they waded through knee-deep water, picking their way over rocks to the shore. The last to step from the boat was a young man, clean-shaven, with a thin face and wavy brown hair that showed around the edge of the blue cap he wore. He was dressed in a blue shirt and a fringed buckskin vest.

The men formed into two columns and hiked up the hill toward the presidio. The young man, who was apparently the commander, walked between the two files, carrying a rolled up banner. As Will watched with disbelief, the leader stepped to the center of the compound of tumbledown, crumbling adobe walls and unfurled an American flag. As the twelve men stood respectfully still, the commander evidently spoke some official words that Will could not hear. *Taking possession*, Will thought, and he shook his head at the audacity.

Will's approach to the gate of the old fort was stopped by a man in the uniform of a United States Army lieutenant. There were two guards with the officer, one wearing a long, loose coat of deerskin, knotted around the waist with a rawhide tie. The other had on a shirt of homespun above the dark knee breeches of a sailor, and no shoes.

"Hold it right there," ordered the lieutenant. "Who are you, and what do you want?"

Looking past the odd assortment of men, Will could see small groups of men clustered around the antique brass cannons with which the presidio was armed. The sounds of clanging hammers filled the evening air as the squads of invaders set to work spiking the ancient guns.

"Maybe you didn't hear me? Or is it that you only habla español?" said the lieutenant roughly.

"I speak English or Spanish as needed," Will replied, "but I only speak *with* the commander—take me to him."

The army officer stepped up a pace and peered at Will from his flat-crowned hat to his tooled cowhide boots and silver spurs. "What do you know," the bucktoothed little man observed to no one in particular, "he dresses Mex and talks American. What are you, anyway?"

"Why don't you stop wasting my time?" said Will angrily. "My name is Will Reed. I am related to the two young men, Ramon and Carlos, who were reported killed by the Americans. I am here to find out who was responsible."

Lieutenant Falls looked over his shoulder. Captain Fremont, the man in the fringed vest, was returning to the small boat waiting at the shore. The captain was already out of earshot. "Will Reed, eh?" Falls repeated with a sideways glance from his beady eyes. To the two men with him he remarked, "Stubbs, Bender . . . I think he's a spy . . . take him, boys!"

The soldiers stepped toward Will, expecting to close in from both sides, but he surprised them by jumping straight for the lieutenant. Bearing Falls to the ground, Will jammed a knee hard into the officer's belly. Falls doubled up with an explosion of breath and feebly waved for help.

Stubbs, the man in the sailor pants, grabbed Will from behind, pinning Will's arms to his sides. Will let himself be yanked upright, then he stomped down with all his force on the attacker's bare foot, raking his spur down the man's shin at the same time. With a howl of pain, Stubbs let go his hold and clutched his wounded leg while he hopped around on the other.

Grabbing up his Lancaster rifle, Bender swung it around toward Will. Too close to bring the gun to bear, Bender tried to club the ranchero with it.

Will seized the barrel of the rifle with one hand and clamped his other fist firmly over the hammer to prevent the gun from being fired. A tug-of-war began in earnest, but Will's extra height and superior strength was winning the battle for possession almost at once. Unable to let go for fear that Will would shoot him with his own gun, Bender did the only thing he could think of: he screamed for help.

It took a moment for the terrified shouting to penetrate the ears of the squads still pounding away at the two-hundred-year-old cannons. Peering through the gathering gloom, the raiding party was astonished at the spectacle at the gate. The lieutenant was still on the ground, fumbling with the flap of his holster and gripping his stomach. Stubbs was also sitting on the ground, holding his lacerated knee and moaning. Meanwhile, a big man in Californio dress wrestled for Bender's rifle. "Help!" yelled Bender again. "We caught us a spy!"

Will saw the others drop their hammers and reach for their weapons. He drew Bender up on tiptoe with a sudden jerk upward on the rifle. Planting his boot in the middle of Bender's chest, Will kicked the shorter man backward twenty feet.

Will made no attempt to shoot the rifle. Spinning sharply around, he sprinted for the gate where his ground-tied horse patiently waited.

Just as Will swung into the saddle, Falls freed his pistol from its holster and fired. The fifty-four caliber ball hit Will just below his right elbow. The impact almost flung him completely over the offside of his horse. He reeled in the saddle, snagging the rowell of his spur in the cinch as if riding a bronco. The gray bounded off toward the village of Yerba Buena.

The door of Fowler's adobe hut prison creaked open. Someone stood in the doorway, but Tor Fowler did not raise his head from where he hung face downward in the rawhide straps. The pattern of his imprisonment was set, and he no longer feared torture or expected rescue.

The mountain man knew that Padilla was carrying on with the torture only because he had the power and enjoyed inflicting the pain. There was no real expectation that Fowler would furnish any important information. Fowler also knew that Padilla would stop short of killing him. As long as General Castro wanted Fowler kept as a hostage or for a future prisoner exchange, his life was safe.

A blow on the side of his head swung Fowler against the adobe bricks and his skull bounced off the wall. Muscles that he had thought already numbed to pain awakened at the renewed violence.

A second clout on the head set Fowler's body rocking in the rawhide thongs like a tenderfoot riding a green-broke colt. His moccasined feet thumped against the back wall of the hut and his angular frame began a corkscrew motion.

The third blow whizzed past his ear but did not strike him. Fowler's mind could not grasp why this was so until he heard Padilla's voice, so slurred and thick with drink that the words were almost incomprehensible.

The missed swing had spun Padilla completely around; he tripped over his own feet and sprawled on the floor. Tor's sharp features dangled only a few feet overhead and Padilla mumbled, "Gonna slit your throat, gringo." The Californio pulled his long knife from the sash around his waist and waved it clumsily in front of Tor's nose.

Fowler forced himself to speak calmly and reasonably. "General Castro will not like this—not one bit. You know he told you to keep me safe."

Padilla's unfocused eyes followed the arc of the glittering blade as he waved it in a gesture of denial. "No, no, gringo," he said in a surprisingly soft voice. "*No importante.* The general would not want me to let you escape. If you are killed escaping, what can he say?"

When sober, Padilla was capable of any evil. He was totally without conscience; he stopped at nothing, except for fear of punishment. Now it seemed that the drink had taken that last restraint away.

The rawhide cords suspending Fowler left him hanging at just the right height to have his throat cut. As soon as Padilla could stagger to his feet, it would all be over, unless . . .

Fowler recalled the blows of a moment before. His feet had brushed against the adobe wall. He was that close, and the leather straps had more slack in them. For his plan to work, Padilla needed to be standing close by. Fowler thought he knew just the appeal that would work.

"Do not kill me," Fowler pleaded. "If you took me back to Captain Fremont, he would pay you gold. Two hundred dollars."

Padilla shook his head. He jabbed the point of the blade into the earth and tried to lean on it, but fell back. "Bah! No scout is worth that to his commandante. I am tired of wet-nursing you, gringo. Make your peace."

"Wait!" Fowler said in an urgent tone. "Listen to this—I know where there is gold hidden—more gold than you ever dreamed of—taken off a rich ranchero that we killed."

Padilla's spinning eyes steadied and he blinked slowly and deliberately as if trying to wake up. "Another Yankee lie to save yourself," he sneered.

"No, I swear it. Only one other man besides me knew of it, and he's dead. If I die it'll be lost forever. Don't you know the

Valdez rancho? The old man's gold is buried, and I know where. Let me down and I'll give you half."

Drunken reasoning told Padilla that a man who was lying to save himself would promise all of a treasure, not merely offer half. And Don Valdez was known to be a wealthy ranchero. It was just possible. . . . He stood clumsily and took a step toward Fowler's head. "Do you know what will happen if you are lying, gringo?"

"Yes," said Fowler urgently. He kicked his feet upward hard and bent his body in the middle, ignoring the sudden tearing in his muscles.

Fowler's feet contacted the rear wall and he pushed off with every ounce of force left in his abused carcass. As the forward motion began, he ducked his head.

Directly on target, Fowler's thick skull connected with Padilla's face, which had been only inches from his own. The single blow propelled the Californio backward through the air, until the flight was cut short by the other adobe wall.

Padilla hit heavily, and Fowler heard a crack as the Californio's head struck the bricks.

Between the impact of Fowler's head used as a battering ram on Padilla's chin, and the short arc of the Californio's body that ended against solid adobe, the man was unconscious before his frame pitched forward into the dirt.

Now, how to get free before someone else came, or before Padilla was awake again? Otherwise, Fowler had only postponed the inevitable.

The outcry of pursuit rang in Will's ears, and several more shots were fired after him into the gathering twilight. One splintered against the bricks of an old well just as he rode past, but no other came close.

The shooting fell silent; the Bear Flaggers were too busy running after their quarry to reload. But their speed on foot was no match for Flotada. The great gray horse bounded over a gully and turned up a barranca. The narrow canyon between the two hills dropped mount and rider below the sight of the pursuers as if they had disappeared into the earth.

Will trusted the horse's instincts to keep him away from the chase. His own senses were dulled with the shock of the wound.

The houses of the eighty inhabitants of Yerba Buena were scattered and haphazardly placed. Few streets existed at all, straight or not. The gray horse sensed the need to hide their trail, and he darted from crude hut to adobe home, turning corners without Will's commands. Flotada changed directions three times, always when some structure was between his master and the panting pursuers.

Yerba Buena was deserted. At the sounds of gunfire coming from the direction of the already rumored invasion, those who lived in the little community by the bay elected to stay indoors. Flotada turned two more corners, then entered a narrow passage between a larger building and a small adobe shed.

The last abrupt change of direction proved to be too much for Will's precarious hold. His spur's rowell snapped free of the cinch and he tumbled out of the saddle. Making a last grab for the apple of the horn was futile: he swung his injured arm in a desperate attempt to hang on, but his nerveless fingers brushed uselessly against the leather. He fell heavily onto packed earth.

The gray horse stopped immediately, pawing the ground in an anxious declaration of their need to get farther away. Will tried to rise, pushing himself up on his good arm, then falling back when it collapsed under him. Flotada stamped again and whinnied softly.

Squinting against the pain, Will caught sight of a wooden door hanging from leather-strap hinges. The opening led into the hut that seemed to be a shed or storeroom. "Have to do," Will muttered softly to himself.

He dragged himself upright with the last of his strength, knowing he would not be able to mount the horse again. It was all he could do to yank his Hawken rifle free of the leather scabbard and slip the pouch containing powder and shot from around the horn. The world swayed in a dizzy, looping spiral. "Go! Go!" he roughly urged the horse, "get on with you!"

He flicked the cord of the shot pouch at Flotada, smacking it sharply across the horse's rear. The unexpected rebuke turned Flotada's own nervousness into flight, and Will could hear the gray cantering off down the hill.

Will did not wait to watch the animal's departure. He tucked the rifle awkwardly under his good arm and held its stock pressed tightly against his side as he faced the sagging wooden door.

Will kicked it inward, and thrust the barrel of the rifle forward into the room. When no protest erupted, he stepped inside and leaned wearily against the planks of the door as he shut it behind him.

It took his eyes a while to adjust to the darkness of the shed; then he swung the rifle around and fumbled with the hammer to be certain it was cocked.

The unconscious figure of a man was crumpled against the wall of the hut, almost under Will's feet. He looked and smelled drunk. But it was not this man that riveted Will's attention. He focused instead on a buckskin-covered form that hung suspended in the center of the room like a recently slaughtered deer hung up to be bled.

Will could feel the creeping numbness of the shock and pain of his wound sweeping over him. Even reminding himself about the grim chamber in which he had taken shelter did not enable him to shake off the deepening weariness. He was just about to surrender to unconsciousness when a groan escaped from the hanging figure . . . the carcass that Will had thought was a corpse!

The noise pulled him awake with a start. "Who are you and who did this to you?" Will asked in horror.

Fowler's head jerked upward, his eyes snapping open in the gloom at the question Will had asked in English. "For the love of God," Fowler sputtered, "get me down, Mister!" Will searched the folds of his sash for his knife, but it had been lost during his wild ride. "There . . . on the floor by his hand," Fowler urged, "Hurry!"

Will found Padilla's blade, and with the backhanded slash of his uninjured left hand, he severed the rawhide that held Fowler's feet. The mountain man cried out as the sudden extra weight hit his shoulders and his legs refused to hold him up. "Sorry," Will muttered.

"Just get me loose," gritted Fowler.

Another awkward backhand sweep of the knife, and Fowler dropped to the earth with a thud and a groan. He lay so still for a time that Will wondered if the man had died. Will's own body had now expended its last reserve, and he sank to the floor himself, cradling his wounded right arm.

At last Fowler rolled over onto his back. "I hope you got somethin' to cover that snake there in case he wakes up," he urged. "Else I'll have to crawl on over and slit his throat like he was fixin' to slit mine." When Will did not acknowledge this gruesome warning, Fowler called to him again, "Hey, friend, you all right?"

Through pain-leadened lips, Will said, "Arm's broke . . . shot . . . I'm all played out."

Fowler whistled his dismay.

7

THE SUN WAS finally sinking after a dusty, day-long cattle drive. Peter Reed stood upright in his stirrups and scanned the hills ahead of the trail. He paid particular attention to the gap up ahead toward which he and the Reed vaqueros were moving the herd. The upper reaches of Canyon Perdido touched the wilderness heights of San Marcos Pass.

Grizzlies were not as plentiful as they had been in years past, or so Will Reed had told his son. Of course, according to Will's campfire tales of the early days, every canyon had held an *oso pardo gigantesco*, a great ferocious bear. In legend, each weighed over a thousand pounds and the track of every clawed foot measured eighteen inches in length! Peter chuckled as he recalled the shuddery excitement of his father's stories.

Still, Peter kept a watchful eye on the places where the live oaks, called *encinos*, grew the thickest. Beyond San Marcos Pass, which loomed ahead, the land was wild and rough and little known to the Californios, whose ranchos hugged the coastline. The other side of the mountains was a place of coyotes, rattlesnakes, and condors, and a home from which the grizzly stirred to raid the cattle ranches. Somewhere up ahead lay the seldom-used trail that Peter's father had followed in first coming to Santa Barbara.

Peter could see no immediate danger threatening the herd of two-year-old steers, so he reined aside and waited for Paco to catch up. Already taller at fourteen than the short-statured Indian, the difference in their heights was exaggerated by the mounts they rode. Peter's grulla, crane-colored, gelding towered over Paco's mule.

"I saw you looking over the ground before we brought up the herd," commented the Indian. "It is well to be watchful in this country. It is a place of bad medicine."

The boy looked curiously at the mayordomo. "You speak like one of the Wild Ones instead of like a good Christian, Paco. Are you superstitious?"

"No, only cautious," Paco replied, crossing himself. "I think that evil is real and does linger in some places . . . places it would be best to avoid if it is possible, but which should on no account be entered blindly."

"Why here?" Peter questioned, gesturing toward the slopes covered with coyote brush and chaparral. "This canyon looks no different from many others hereabouts."

"My mind remembers this place," Paco said, reining up and pointing toward a tree-topped mound near the rocky wall of the canyon's mouth. "It was just there that Don Ricardo, your uncle, was almost killed by an oso pardo before your father saved him."

Nodding his acquaintance with this piece of family history, Peter said, "I have seen the scars on Tío Ricardo's forehead, sí. But the story did have a happy ending. Besides, it brought my mother and father together. Surely you do not believe that the spirit of the bear lingers on here."

"No, no," Paco shook his head, "but it is not just the bear. You see, I was also present on that day. I heard your uncle scream . . . saw your father face the oso grande alone, and . . . I fled."

The boy hardly knew what to say or how to respond to this. "I never heard that," he said at last.

The Indian said solemnly, "Don Will is a good man, a great man. He told no one, and have I not been his mayordomo these ten years past?"

In a bend of the canyon, the trickling stream had collected in a pool deep enough to water the herd. "We'll camp here tonight and push over the pass tomorrow," Peter announced; then he looked at Paco with embarrassment. "That is, if you agree, mayordomo."

"No," Paco chided, all the uneasiness of the earlier conversation left behind, "you do not appeal to me for approval. Your father put you in charge of this drive. You have made your decision, Don Peter. If I have comment, I will offer it, but as it happens, you have chosen well."

The other vaqueros brought up the herd and set the leaders to circling. The forward motion soon ceased, and the rangy cattle fell to browsing the grass on the banks of the creek.

Paco pointed out a particularly handsome reddish-brown colt in the caponera, the string of horses. "What do you think of the retinto-colored one? The one there with the curly coat?"

Peter knew that the question was not a casual one. His education in horsemanship had begun as a two-year-old, when his chubby legs had stuck straight out from the horse's back and Paco had walked alongside to hold him upright. Questions about an animal's conformation or habits or training were a kind of test, and a game that Peter enjoyed playing.

The retinto with the curly coat had a long, sleek body and long legs to match. The arch of his neck and the set of his shoulders indicated good bloodlines for a horse that would rein well. The colt's large eyes were interested in his surroundings, and he pricked up his ears when a steer splashed into the creek to graze on the other side.

Peter considered all the factors and gave his judgment. "When he comes into his own, he will be one to ride all day without stopping, and he seems attentive."

"Good," Paco confirmed. "You saw that he has amor al ganado—cow sense. It cannot easily be taught, but a horse that comes by it naturally will leap on the trail of one steer and never lose it."

"And now, mayordomo, why did you call my attention to him in particular?"

"Because, hijito, little son, he is broken to the jáquima, the leather noseband, but has not yet worked in the bit. Your father and I wish you to school him."

Mentioning Peter's father made the request into a command. It meant that Will and the head vaquero had planned this lesson before the drive had even begun. Peter knew that the schooling would not be the horse's alone.

By the time the camp was set, the herd settled, and the simple supper of beef jerky and hard biscuits finished, the glow of the Milky Way filled the California skies.

The night herds were posted, and Peter was just drifting off into sleep when the first sliver of the full moon crept above the ridgeline. As if at a signal, a mountain lion screamed in the barranca, upstream where the canyon narrowed into a rocky gorge.

Peter's eyes snapped open and he slapped his hand down on his blanket, over the saddle carbine that rested beside him. "Gently," cautioned Paco from his bedroll nearby. "You will frighten the cattle more than señor Puma."

Apart from a lone bawling steer, the herd remained quiet. There was none of the confused snorting and bellowing that foreshadowed a stampede. "How far away was that?" Peter asked.

A drowsy reply confirmed that Paco felt no danger. "Far enough. The horses will give the warning if he gets near enough to scent. You may depend on it. Of course . . ." Paco's voice trailed away.

"Of course what?" Peter demanded.

The sleepy afterthought was slow in coming. "Of course, if the lion calls near our camp again tomorrow night, we will have to hunt him."

"Why?"

"Because," came the slurred answer, "on the third night, he will be hunting us."

On that cheerful thought, Paco drifted off to sleep. Peter was counting another set of a thousand stars when it was time for him and the mayordomo to go on watch.

It was the strangest kind of three-way race, and only one of the contestants even knew about the contest. Tor Fowler studied the unconscious Padilla and the silent figure of Will Reed.

Fowler's arms and legs were shot through with fiery pains as circulation returned to his numbed limbs.

Inch by agonizing inch, Fowler stretched out his arms. He dragged his uncooperative body toward Will Reed's weapons. Two feet more to go, one foot, a half. Fowler's fingers closed around the stock of the Hawken rifle. But the weight of Will's body held the rifle prisoner, and Fowler could not jerk it free.

The knife must be his objective then. The room was pitch dark, and Fowler scrabbled in the filth of the hut's floor. He found Padilla's knife near the end of Will's outstretched hand.

Using the weapon to assist him, Fowler plunged its blade into the earth and pulled himself up to it. The dark mass that was Padilla stirred and groaned, and Fowler redoubled his efforts. Like a sailor climbing the tallest mast in the midst of a raging gale, Fowler drew himself hand over hand toward his enemy.

When Fowler was an arm's length away, Padilla's eyes flickered, then opened. For a moment they focused on nothing at all; then Padilla screamed in terror. Fowler knew what Padilla saw: the dark shape of a wild beast with blazing eyes and raking claws that had crawled out of his worst nightmares and was coming to rip out his throat!

The Californio's hands fumbled for a weapon, but found none. Padilla gave a bleat of panic and threw himself backward against the adobe wall just as Fowler stabbed the knife downward.

Fowler struggled to stand. A guttural animal noise came from his throat as he slashed the air again and again. Padilla hurriedly groped his way along the wall to the door. Twice he pushed futilely against it without recollecting that it opened inward.

Fowler's blade sliced both the Californio's legs with a sweeping slash. The wound, not deep, was the goad Padilla needed to escape. Throwing his weight against the ramshackle door, he burst it from its strap hinges and fell out into the night.

The mountain man lit an oil lamp and held it aloft to study the man whose arrival had probably saved his life.

"Come on, man," Tor Fowler urged Will. "We've got to get us both some doctorin'."

Will shook his head. "Not together we can't. You can go back to the army for help, but they want to capture me . . . maybe kill me."

"That's some kinda mistake, you bein' American and all. Why would we be mad at you?"

Will reached up with his good arm and let Fowler help him stand. A swirl of dizziness swept over him, but it passed quickly. "Do you know about the Carrillo twins?" he asked.

"Do I? I should say so!" Fowler agreed emphatically. "I was beat plumb near to death while bein' told what child-killin' murderers us Yankees is! But personally, I never met 'em. Reckon it happened after I got took."

Will nodded. He pulled the sash from around his waist and with Fowler's help used it to fashion a sling to support his wounded arm. "Those boys were my godchildren," he continued. "I came here from Santa Barbara to get to the bottom of what happened."

"Well, what *did* happen? How'd you run foul of our folks?"

Will explained the circumstances at the presidio and how the lieutenant had been at first hostile and then belligerent.

"That Falls," Fowler grunted. "He's as useless as a saddle made for a grizzly, and just about as likely to get somebody kilt. Fancies himself a real military heero headed for politics . . . hopes to hitch onto Fremont's star."

"Then you understand why I can't go back with you."

"No sucha thing," Fowler insisted. "Falls, see, he ain't Cap'n Fremont. The captain is an ambitious man, but he knows what he's about. " 'Sides, him and me been in some rough scrapes before and I saved his bacon. He'll be bound to hear your say if I tell him to."

Will still looked doubtful, but he agreed that his arm needed attention. What was more, it was to see Fremont that he had ridden all the way from Santa Barbara, and here was a man who could make the connection.

"All right," he said at last. "On one condition. Don't tell anybody except Captain Fremont who I am. Ask him to come and see me at the cantina down the street."

The two men had no more than stepped into the dirt lane when they found themselves surrounded by a squad of marines. Lieutenant Falls presented a carbine at point-blank range at Will's stomach, remarking with obvious satisfaction, "Fowler. Good work. Escaped *and* captured the spy!"

"Not so, neither," protested Fowler. "This fella saved *my* life, and—"

"Poor man is deranged," Falls observed to the marines. "Take the prisoner away."

Will knew that protest was futile and that any further attempt to fight his way clear would get him shot down on the spot. He let himself be led away quietly.

"Lieutenant," said Fowler, thinking quickly, "I'm warnin' you. This is an important fella with a secret message for Captain Fremont. Ain't nothin' better happen to him!"

Falls regarded Fowler and Will with a look compounded of suspicion and cautious self-interest. "Captain Fremont has already departed, leaving me in charge," he said. "All right, lock him up." Then he added in a grudging tone, "*Just* lock him up."

8

PETER YAWNED INTO his morning cup of coffee and stared at the tin platter of cornmeal mush without taking a bite. "Eat! Eat!" Paco scolded. "One cannot conduct the jornada, the cattle drive, without nourishment."

The curly-haired retinto horse was caught and brought to Peter for saddling. "It is a perfect time to try him with the bit," Paco said. "He was first bitted up exactly one month ago, and now it is time to advance his schooling. Every true vaquero knows that the best reining caballos are given the bit in the full of the moon."

Paco watched as Peter examined the mouth of the reddish-brown gelding before turning to the canvas on which were displayed the various bits. The boy chose a silver-mounted bridle. Attached to it was a mild-curved mouthpiece called "the mustache of the Moor" from its drooping shape. In the center of the cross bar were two barrel-shaped rollers made of copper.

"Bueno," nodded Paco with approval. "Exactly the bit with which the retinto has been standing each day in the corral."

The curly-coated horse took the metal bar in his mouth without objection, and soon little whirring noises could be heard. The colt was spinning the copper barrels with his tongue, indicating his contentment.

Peter saddled the horse with care, tightening the center-fire cinch and leading the animal around in the small circle known as the pasos de la muerte, the steps of death. Many a rider had come to grief when a cinch-binding horse came over backward as the rider's weight was added to the saddle.

Removing the silk mascada scarf from around his neck, Peter tucked it into the bridle over the horse's eyes as a makeshift blinder. He did not know if this precaution was necessary, but it was a point of honor to discover the colt's personality and secrets without asking too many questions.

Stepping lightly into the stirrups, Peter mounted and settled quickly into the high-backed, apple-horned saddle. The retinto stood perfectly still in the clean morning air and flicked his ears back toward his rider. Peter adjusted his grip on the reins and nodded for Paco to remove the scarf.

The spur chain jingled once as Peter tapped his heel against the colt and urged it into a walk. The horse wheeled left and right in response to Peter's directions, and he found no trace of obstinacy or rebellion as the horse worked in the bit.

"Shall we start the herd moving?" Paco inquired.

"Por favor. I'll take the colt across the canyon and back to work on his rein. We won't want to try him with the cattle until tomorrow."

"Bueno," Paco agreed, "and perhaps you may be able to bring back meat for the camp." He handed Peter a rifle, and watched with affection and approval as the boy rode out of sight.

The colt took eagerly to the trail, trotting across the creek and looking around him with an intelligent interest. Peter followed the twisting path away from camp and started the horse up the climb that led out of the canyon and onto a mesa beyond.

A pair of finches chattered in the buckthorn brush. The boy instantly recognized their noisy calls and was reminded of the childhood tales told him by his mother. The finch's red breast, Francesca had said, was caused by blood dripping from the brow of the crucified Christ. A pair of the small birds, so the story went, had flown to the head of Jesus on the cross and plucked out the crown of thorns one by one. God allowed the blood to permanently stain their chest feathers as a remembrance of the time when men had no pity on the Lord of

Glory, but two of the least members of creation showed compassion for their Maker.

Both Peter and the rust-colored horse turned their faces toward the twittering sounds in the scrub. The colt nodded his head toward their perch, seeming to acknowledge the finches' greeting. "Ah," said Peter aloud, "so you know the story also? We will be compadres, you and I. Also, I like your curly coat. I think your name should be Chino—Curly. What do you think?"

The trail reached the mesa rim and leveled out as it angled across the plateau. The brushy undergrowth thickened, with gooseberry patches replacing the coyote brush. As Peter scanned the dense growth, his attention was drawn to a clump of heavy thorned cover at the base of a huge boulder that jutted out of the landscape like a stone sailing ship set on end.

Peter's eyes traveled past the location, then flickered back again and he studied the berry thicket intently. Was it a rabbit in the brush, or perhaps only the flitting of another small bird that had caught his notice? Both horse and rider stopped and stared, peering at the unseen animal. Slowly the camouflaged outline of a deer bedded down behind the gooseberry thicket took shape. Peter stepped off Chino's back and carefully lifted the Hall saddle carbine out of its scabbard.

Dropping the reins to the ground, Peter stood away from the colt and took aim. He cocked the hammer while judging which set of branches were actually antlers, and where the point of the buck's shoulder was located. The boy took a deep breath and let it out slowly, then took another and held it, just as his father had taught him.

The boom of the sixty caliber rifle shattered the morning stillness. At the sudden explosion, the buck leaped up from the bushes as if by the release of a spring, but Peter had no chance to judge his success. Behind him, Chino reared and plunged, reared again and came down on the reins. The colt jerked away from the abrupt tearing in his mouth, breaking the bridle and scattering silver conchas across the hillside.

The horse snorted with fear as Peter lunged at him in a grab for the reins. Chino reared again and struck out with a forefoot, and Peter threw himself backward out of the way. The retinto colt whirled then and ran off, back the way they had come.

Peter sat up and watched the horse's flight. He kicked himself mentally as he retrieved the fallen rifle. The hammer had broken off and the stock had two deep scratches in it. From the dirt near a broken piece of rein he picked up a silver ornament and tossed it morosely up and caught it. What would Paco say? Worse, what would his father say? Peter knew better than to fire a gun next to an untried colt. He should have tied the horse to a stump and then moved away before firing, but the horse's good nature and cooperative spirit had made Peter careless. Carelessness got people killed, his father had taught him. Well, Peter might wish he were dead, but he was not, so he had better pick up what he could and hike on back to the herd and face the consequences. Peter hoped that the colt would find his way back, or else the boy would be in even bigger trouble.

With the broken rifle over his shoulder and two dusty silver conchas in his pocket, Peter turned to follow the vanished horse when a thought struck him. He had fired at the buck, but he did not know whether his bullet had struck the animal or not. The boy fervently hoped that his shot had been successful so that he at least would not have to go back empty-handed.

Peter returned to the location from which he had fired the shot. At first he could see no trace of the buck. He placed his feet in the same tracks again and sighted along the rifle barrel toward the gooseberry patch. Nothing was stirring there now. He swung the barrel slowly to the left, tracing the buck's leap and trying to remember where his last glimpse of the deer had been.

He hoped he had either killed the animal cleanly or missed it completely. Now that he was afoot, he doubted if he could trail the buck if it were only wounded; and anyway, he had no weapon with which to shoot again.

Walking toward the brush pile, Peter circled it on the uphill side, in the direction of the buck's leap. He looked in each clump of thorns and weeds as he passed, but saw no sign that the deer had ever been there, much less had been shot. Peter glanced back at the point from which he had fired, judging the correctness of his course and the amount of distance he had covered.

He was far beyond where he believed the animal could possibly have been when he saw it: a single drop of bright red blood glistening on a shiny gray-green gooseberry leaf. An instant's excitement that his aim had been true gave way to remorse. He had let the deer get away wounded, after all, to suffer and fall victim to some predator.

In a last attempt to locate the buck, Peter set up a stick beside the telltale drop of blood, then backtracked the deer to where it had been lying. Turning around once more, the boy sighted up the hill in a straight line from where he stood, past the marker stick . . . and saw the deer.

It had made perhaps two more jumps during the time when Peter's attention was distracted by the plunging horse, and then it had come to rest in the crevice formed by a slivered chunk of the granite boulder.

Peter walked slowly up to the carcass, thinking about what he must do next. He could not carry the entire deer back to camp, but he could manage to take a hindquarter back with him. Perhaps there was even some way he could use the broken reins to hoist the remaining meat up out of the reach of scavengers until it could be retrieved later.

Standing over the buck, Peter was mentally preparing himself for the gutting and cleaning that must come next in order that the meat would not spoil. He knelt over his boot top to withdraw the hunting knife he carried there.

When he stooped to draw the blade, he heard the tiniest whisper of a sound, directly over his head. Peter's head snapped up and he found himself looking into the pale, amber eyes of a mountain lion. His direct gaze caught the big cat just before springing. The cougar regarded him from near the top of the boulder, where it lay in the shadow of a rocky ledge, and snarled . . . not a scream or ear-splitting roar, but a low, menacing rumble that ended with a coughing sound.

The cougar snarled again, louder this time, and flashed a threatening glimpse of spiked fangs. Peter understood the lion's anger. It had not been on the rock above the brush-choked ravine by chance; no, it too had been stalking the buck until Peter had stolen the kill. But the lion did not intend to part with his meal without a fight.

Very slowly and deliberately, Peter stood erect and began backing away from the base of the boulder. He recalled what he had been taught about never turning his back on a lion. Cougars hunt by stealth and surprise and will attack even humans from behind, given the opportunity. The boy placed each step carefully. He did not want to glance away from the mountain lion, not even for an instant, but he could not risk tangling his foot in the brush and taking a tumble, either. Peter remembered the *Leatherstocking Tales* read to him by his mother; it seemed that Cooper's characters were always falling down when pursued, and Peter did not want this to happen to him.

The lion shifted on its perch and stretched out a great paw toward the deer carcass in an unspoken statement of claim. Then as if reaching a decision, the great cat jumped lightly down from the boulder. It looked once over its shoulder at the dead deer, then fixed its yellow gaze on Peter and began moving slowly toward him.

The boy had backed up about halfway across the brushy slope when he found himself against a tangled gooseberry thicket so dense that he could not push through it. The lion was still padding toward him, but Peter could not risk turning to look for a path across. Instead, he began to move sideways, crablike, hoping to come to a clearer place where he could resume his getaway.

A crashing of branches from the upslope direction drew the attention of both the lion and the boy. A light breeze was blowing up the little draw, or the cougar might have scented the second intruder sooner, but there was no mistake now. Ambling across the brush piles and smashing them down with total disregard for the thorns was a large sow grizzly with a very small cub alongside.

The bear was evidently following the blood smell from the buck, for she was moving with purpose directly toward the carcass, pausing only to sniff the air and correct her course. The lion lashed out an angry snarl that ripped through the morning stillness like a saw blade through lumber.

Giving a wuff of alarm and swatting the cub to get it back behind her, the grizzly stood upright on her hind legs. She shook her massive head and peered around through squinted eyes, the very picture of a myopic matron refusing to take any nonsense.

Peter looked around with alarm. There were no trees to climb near enough that the bear would not be able to reach him first. In fact, the only place of safety close by was the granite monolith, and the lion stood between him and the rock. Peter crouched down right where he was and hoped that he would escape the humpbacked bear's attention.

So far the plan seemed to be working. The mother and cub were still zeroed in on the scent of the deer, and the lion demanded the grizzly's notice by letting loose another full-throated scream. The mother bear snarled and growled in reply, and dropped to all fours again to charge.

The lion jumped back toward the rock ahead of the grizzly's rush and grabbed up the deer by the hind leg. The cat tried to drag the carcass away, but the antlers wedged in the crevice of the rock and would not budge.

The bear charged up with a bellowing roar and swung a paw at the lion in a blow that would have crushed the cougar if it had connected. At the last possible instant, the cat gave up its hold on the deer leg and leaped over the fractured chunk of rock. The two opponents glared and snarled at each other, no farther apart than the width of a tabletop. The lion's ears were flattened against its skull, and it roared and hissed its defiance of the bear.

Peter began to back away again from the scene. He would have no better opportunity than right now to make himself scarce. The grizzly had grasped the deer, her superior weight drawing it free of the crack in the rock where the lion had failed. The cat snarled and slashed and threatened, but the bear, unperturbed, was bent on drawing in the prize.

The boy might have been able to withdraw from the confrontation had it not been for the curiosity of the bear cub. Since Mama had forced the cub to stay back out of harm's way, he had cast around and come across Peter's scent. The grizzly cub shuffled and sniffed his way over the bushes, directly toward the retreating boy. Peter stumbled into a heap of dried gooseberry brambles that crackled underfoot. As if suddenly noticing the absence of her baby, the mother bear whirled around with the mangled body of the deer hanging limply from her jaws.

The rush of the grizzly toward Peter made her earlier charge toward the lion look like a peaceful stroll. With the momentum of an avalanche she galloped across the mesa, her mouth full of venison, bellowing all the while for the cub to get out of the way.

Peter was certain that this was his finish; then, out of the corner of his eye, he saw a streak of tawny lightning. The lion had given up the idea of trying to retrieve the buck, but it was not going to leave empty-handed either. The bear cub squalled as the mountain lion's fangs closed around his neck, and the cougar went bounding away up the slope.

The charging grizzly stopped abruptly and skidded into a sudden turn, reversing direction. In her distress at this new development, she dropped the deer carcass from her grasp and tore off across the mesa in pursuit of the cougar and the stolen cub.

9

"**W**HEW," MUTTERED PETER, wiping his face with his mascada. "A deer, a lion, *and* a grizzly. It is true, what Paco says, 'Cuando Dios da . . .' when God gives, He gives with a full hand!"

The deer carcass looked to be too mangled and chewed to be worth bothering with. The order of business now was to rejoin the herd and relocate the missing colt—with the saddle still intact, he hoped.

Peter started back across the mesa, pushing aside the coyote brush and retracing the spidery line of the trail. In a hundred yards, a thought struck him and he stopped to consider.

By now the herd was probably already on the move, going farther up the canyon toward the high pastures. If he followed his own trail back, he would come in way behind the location of the next night's camp. This plan would have been reasonable on horseback, since a mounted man can travel farther and faster than a drifting herd of cattle. But on foot, that was another matter altogether.

Peter decided that an angle toward the northeast would cut into the canyon of the jornada. Trail drives are noisy, dusty affairs with slapping leather and plumes of airborne dirt. Once striking the correct arroyo, Peter believed that he would have no difficulty locating the camp.

Taking his bearings, Peter turned so that the sun stood just ahead of his right shoulder; then he started up the slope. He picked out a peak on the horizon that was directly in line with his nose and began hiking.

It was still before noon, but the air was already shimmery with the heat. Cicadas singing in the brush stopped when Peter's shadow passed over them and then resumed their buzzing when he trudged on.

The broken and useless rifle slung over his shoulder was a weight he would gladly have traded for a canteen of water, but he knew better than to leave it behind. A couple hours' walk that was all. With a little luck, the story of his encounter with la osa and señor puma just might protect him from punishment. He hoped so; to a young caballero, the reception he would get arriving in camp on foot was going to be punishment enough.

The canyon that appeared over the next ridge when Peter crossed it was narrow and deep. It had no stream of water flowing in its rocky depths and so could not be the one the herd was following.

By now the sun was directly overhead and it was impossible for Peter to set his course by it. He concluded that it did not really matter, since he had to cross the barranca anyway, and certainly would find the right canyon just over the next ridge.

But the next ridgeline revealed only another narrow, dry arroyo, clearly still not the right one. Worse, while Peter could descend into the canyon, climbing out again up the near vertical wall on the opposite side was not possible. He would have to follow the canyon farther up to locate a way out of the steep embankment.

Walking through the age-old sand of the dry wash, Peter found himself following a looping path. Flash floods had carved the deep canyon, but in slicing through the sandstone layers they had gone around other, harder material, turning the stream bed into a tortuous serpentine. Far above him, through gaps too high to reach, Peter could see towering sandstone columns sculpted by the wind into strange, wavy sentinels.

Peter wondered how far off course he must be. This forbidding landscape did not have the appearance of pasture land. The wall on his right by which he had descended into the canyon dropped lower and lower as he paced along. The bank receded to a low berm, and the hills on that side retreated as the width of the canyon expanded into a small valley. Peter continued hiking, almost oblivious to the newly flat terrain on that side, for his attention was focused on the north.

In fact, his decision to climb out of the flood water's path was not made because he thought of reversing his course but because he hoped to get a wider perspective of the barrier he faced.

Over the bank of the dry stream bed at last, Peter found himself on a level plain covered with small gray-green brush. The flat stretched away to the south and east until it merged with the hazy brown and yellow streaks that were the vague outline of distant hills.

The low bushes crushed when he walked over them, giving off a sharp pungent aroma, not unpleasant, but penetrating. *Sage*, he thought, *like Mother uses in the kitchen*.

The boy now knew that he had completely missed his rendezvous with the herd. He had somehow overshot the mark and would have no choice but to backtrack his own trail. But a greater concern came first. Peter recognized that he needed water—and soon. The way back was a long distance to a stream.

Up ahead, a line of alamos, cottonwoods, presented the possibility of moisture. If not a pool, perhaps at least a spring. Peter changed his direction to line up directly with the little clump of trees.

For a long time, Peter trudged across the sage-covered field without looking up. He amused himself by watching his shadow flow over the brush and mount the ground-squirrel mounds as it marched along ahead of him.

The boy was not alarmed at his predicament. The nights were not cold enough for the lack of a fire to be a problem, and tomorrow he could retrace his steps. He regretted having refused Paco's advice; he wished now he had eaten breakfast. Still, water was the pressing issue. Tomorrow he would meet up with someone looking for him and then there would be food.

Glancing up from his shadow and his thoughts, Peter corrected his course slightly and checked his progress toward the cottonwoods.

The dark dots on the horizon grew into tree shapes. The images wavered with the heat waves reflected off the red soil. The upper half of each tree appeared to be floating, while the lower half had disappeared.

Floating alongside the trees were two brown dome-like bodies that hovered above the ground. Peter stared and squinted, trying to determine exactly what he was seeing. In appearance, the forms were like two extremely large brown bears, sleeping near the line of trees.

The recent experience with the bear and the lion made the boy cautious. If there was water near the cottonwoods, then it could very well be a place where grizzlies came to drink.

Peter stood inspecting the shapes, then advanced a little and studied them again. A change in the light and shadow revealed a third domed shape and then a fourth and a fifth. Understanding flooded Peter's mind, but he did not know whether to be relieved or more anxious. The group of rounded images shimmering in the afternoon sun were huts— the dwellings of a tribe of what Peter called the Wild Ones . . . Indians.

There was no turning back. Peter needed water and he needed it now. That an Indian rancheria existed by the line of cottonwoods meant a certainty of finding water, and Peter meant to have it.

The dome-shaped huts grew in his vision and increased in number as he got closer. They were oddly placed in irregular groups. Peter was curious as to why he saw no people out and about. The afternoon was wearing on, but it was not late enough or cool enough for the people to stay indoors. *Perhaps this is a deserted village*, Peter thought. *I hope they didn't leave because the water ran out.*

No dogs barked at his approach, no horses stamped, no children played, no adults watched him, and yet . . . Peter had the eerie feeling that the village, though clearly deserted, had only recently been abandoned.

At the edge of the cleared ground that marked the collection of huts, the village was tucked into a fold of hillside where a rockfall released a spring. There was not enough water to run down the creek bed, but there was a trickle of the precious liquid that dripped steadily down from the ledges and filled a good-sized pool. The overflow of the pond made its way downstream only a few yards before it was swallowed by the thirsty sand. It was barely enough to supply a village of this size and keep the cottonwoods alive as well. Perhaps the people *had* moved on.

Peter went directly to the spring. He eyed the stagnant basin with its covering of yellow-green scum, and then turned to the rocky ledge. Cupping his hands beneath the seep, Peter waited patiently for a handful of water to drip into his grasp. He drank it greedily, waited for his palms to refill, and drank again.

His eyes glanced downward as he waited for his hands to fill the third time. At first nothing seemed out of the ordinary, but then his mind focused on what his eyes saw: There was a footprint directly under the drip of the spring. In the sandy verge of the pool was the imprint of five large naked toes.

Staring at his own feet, encased in soft leather boots, Peter came to the inescapable conclusion. Not only was there at least one other person around the camp, but the dripping water would have obliterated the track in no more than ten or fifteen minutes. Whoever it was could not be far away.

Peter tried to backtrack the trail, but other footprints could not be seen. Beyond the line of the alamo trees, a dust devil danced and hopped its way over the sage. The dry, thin dirt would not hold a track long against the sweeping breeze, except in a sheltered place such as near the rocks.

The way the wind swished through the camp, there was no true lee side to be sheltered, and no more distinct prints met Peter's eye. He circled one hut, then another and a third without finding any evidence of another human.

"Hola," he called. "Is anybody here?" There was no answer but the rustle of the cottonwood leaves. Discarded baskets and tools lay scattered about. An odor of decay assaulted Peter's nose, and he did not enter any of the buildings.

Next to the third deserted hovel was a circular heap of rubble where a hut had burned to the ground. Most of the ashes had been blown away by the wind, but fragments of charred timber remained. Peter studied the location for a moment, then went past another abandoned structure, which also had a burned-out hulk beside it.

He passed another hut, buzzing with a cloud of flies, and then two more burned spaces. The boy thought how strange it was for the village to suffer so many fires, and yet not lose *all* the buildings. He stood beside a fifth burned place and examined the debris. A broken clay pot was overturned in the center of the rubble. Peter idly kicked at the shard with his toe.

The pot fragment rolled over to reveal a human skull. Its empty eye sockets stared up at Peter, and even without the lower jaw there seemed to be a malicious grin to its expression.

Peter ran toward the edge of the camp, passing standing huts and burned-out ruins without looking. He did not stop running until he was beyond the last of the domed houses and was outside the village next to a long, low mound of earth.

He forced himself to stop; his breath was coming in ragged gasps and his heart was pounding in his ears. What was he afraid of? Old dead bones could not hurt anyone, nor was Peter a child to be frightened anymore by Paco's ghost stories about headless vaqueros and haunted caves.

He dropped down on the mound next to a discarded deer hide to rest and think, to regain the composure that he thought an almost-adult should have. He laid down the broken gun and reviewed the situation: some disaster had hit this village, with multiple fires that had claimed at least one victim. Also, as lately as a few minutes before his arrival, there had been some person—not a ghost but a living, barefoot human—walking in the camp. *Now what?* he thought.

As if in answer to his unspoken question, the earth beneath him moaned. Not a quick groaning sound like Peter had heard when tree limbs rub together in a wind storm, but a long, drawn-out sigh of misery.

Peter jumped up from the mound. From the highest part of the long barrow of earth, near its center, a puff of smoke drifted up. At the same time, the deer hide lying on the ground stirred and shook as if something were coming out. *The demon caballero riding forth!*

Adult composure or not, Peter was *not* remaining to see what actually came out of the ground. He was already up and running back toward the spring when he remembered the rifle.

It was a credit to Peter's discipline, if not his courage, that he turned around and raced back to reclaim the gun. He had just reached it when the deer hide shook itself free of some clods of earth that had rolled down on it and it flipped open to reveal a tunnel into the mound. Peter stood transfixed as a small bony hand was followed by a sleeve of coarse gray cloth and then the familiar small form of . . .

"Father Francis!" Peter cried with relief. "What are you doing here? And what is this place? Where is everybody?"

The priest was just as dumbfounded as the boy. "Don Peter," he said, brushing off his robe and standing up to look around. "Is your father here?" His face was lined and drawn and his expression anxious.

In a few clipped phrases, Peter explained how he came to be lost and wander into the village. The priest then shook his head with a sorrowful expression. "You cannot remain here, Peter. It may cost you your life."

"Why? What is it?"

"Smallpox," came the weary, toneless answer. "The village is dying."

Father Francis had only a few moments in which to explain about the village and its desperate condition. "I alone am able to care for the people calling for water in their dreadful fevers."

Only a month earlier the village had been thriving. Bustling with the summer activities of preparing hides and gathering chia seeds for meal, the Yokuts had welcomed a group of twenty British sailors who said they had come to settle.

Always hospitable, the Yokuts noted that the sailors were sickly and weak and many exhibited small sores and pock marks. The Indian elders had done what they could to supply the needs of the newcomers and treated them with such medicine as was known.

Two weeks later, the first of the Yokuts fell ill. The next day two more and the following day six. The traditional Yokut ceremony of burning the bodies of the dead inside their huts with all their belongings had been carried out at a pace that accelerated daily. What prevented the rancheria from being totally reduced to ashes was only that no people remained who were strong enough to carry out the cremations. Only Father Francis was untouched by the disease, and he was too busy caring for the sick and dying to bother with the dead, now piled in two of the remaining huts.

"Only two of the Britishers died," Father Francis said, "but the rest fled—back to their ships, I suppose."

"But why have all the sick people gone into the hole in the ground?"

"It is our way," Father Francis replied. "The sweat lodge has always been our cure for sickness, and now all who are left alive have gone there."

Peter looked around at the dusty valley and the slight frame of the careworn priest. "You need help," the boy said. "I will stay to aid you."

"God bless you, my son," Father Francis said sincerely. His body swayed as he made the sign of the cross. "But it cannot be. I will not risk your life—" He stopped suddenly and said, "Perhaps God has sent you here for a greater purpose than you can know." The priest retreated abruptly into the bowels of the earth.

When he emerged again a moment later, he had a tiny bundle, wrapped in doeskin. Father Francis stood before Peter, who watched curiously as the priest tucked back a fold of soft white hide to reveal the face of a baby.

"His name is Limik—*Falcon*, the same as my grandfather," Father Francis said. "He is only two days old. My cousin's baby."

"But his mother?" asked Peter.

The priest shook his head sadly. "She will not live another night. I despaired of keeping this little one alive, but now I see that heaven has sent you for that reason."

Peter drew back sharply. "Me?" he asked incredulously. "You want *me* to care for this baby?"

A strand of fluff from a cottonwood tree drifted down out of the sky and landed across the baby's nose. Impulsively, Peter reached over to pluck the strand away. Limik, who had been gnawing on his fist, opened his hand and grasped Peter's little finger in a grip surprisingly strong.

The young ranchero gulped. "All right," he said. "What do I do?"

The lines of white surf had already disappeared and the red tile roofs and whitewashed adobe walls were fading into the backdrop of dusty green California hills as the *Juno* stood away from Santa Barbara.

Father McNamara and Captain Blake stood and regarded the receding shoreline. Blake said gloomily, "I do not relish having to report to Admiral Seymour on the complete failure of our mission here."

Father McNamara was more sanguine. "Tut, Captain," he said, "it is not your fault that events proceeded so rapidly. Who would have foreseen that the Americans would be prepared enough to achieve their seizure of San Francisco, San Diego, and Monterey, all within one month? They will be lounging about the Pueblo of Los Angeles and wandering through Santa Barbara in another week."

"But the scheme to colonize!" Blake exclaimed, dashing his fist against the taffrail. "It should have worked!"

"Yes. It is a pity that your sailors were not able to perform as expected. But let me cheer you up with another plan which I expect to lay before Admiral Seymour."

"What might that be?"

"Ah, a capital scheme to be sure . . . controlling the crossroads of the Pacific, I call it. Tell me, Captain, have you ever been to the Sandwich Islands, discovered by the inestimable Captain Cook? I believe in the native tongue the land is called Ohwyhee. . . ."

10

THE BOOM OF the twelve-inch cannon echoed around the Santa Barbara roadstead. The arrival signal rolled past the mission, up San Marcos Pass, and back again. The report reverberated in the ears of Nicholas Den as he sat in his counting house. The curly-haired Irish ranchero was reviewing columns of figures for "California bank notes." Each entry represented cowhides worth two dollars, American. "What ship can that be?" he muttered to himself. "Julio," he called to his Indian servant, "fetch my telescope."

Den's eyes crinkled at the corners in the pleasant anticipation of some trading to be done. He climbed the stairs to the flat roof of his office two steps at a time. "Could it be the *Juno* back from Monterey in only a week?" he thought aloud. "If it is, they'll be wanting twenty head or so for meat."

"Don Nicholas," said Julio, handing him the spyglass, "I do not recognize this ship. She is a frigate, sí?"

"Not so fast," corrected Nicholas Den, snapping open the brass telescope and fitting it to his eyes. "We'll know in a moment. She must be one of Admiral Seymour's—" He let out a gasp. "That's not a British ship—they're flying the Stars and Stripes . . . she's American!"

The word spread quickly through the settlement and into the countryside beyond, bringing a crowd of curious onlookers to the beach.

"Can you make out the name of the vessel?" someone asked Don Nicholas.

"She's swinging around now . . . yes," he said, "the *Congress*."

The small boat being rowed ashore from the frigate looked to be in danger of swamping. Besides the six sailors manning the oars, there were ten men carrying muskets with the muzzles held rigidly upright.

As the boat swept onto the sand, two of the sailors jumped overboard to guide the boat farther on the shore. When the little vessel was beached, it was dragged up past the high watermark, and only then did its distinguished-looking passenger get out.

The man who stepped out of the boat onto the Santa Barbara landing was no taller than Don Nicholas and thinner of face and body. He was wearing the full dress uniform of a commodore of the United States Navy. Despite the warm summer temperature, every brass button of his double-breasted coat was secured, right up to the high, stiff collar worked with gold. His gold epaulets glinted and gleamed in the sunlight as he proceeded directly to where Don Nicholas stood.

"Sir," he said formally in English, "I am seeking the alcalde of this place, Don Nicholas Den. Can you help me locate him?"

"It depends," Don Nicholas replied, shifting uncomfortably. "What do you want him for?"

"Why, to announce my arrival and give him my compliments," the youthful-looking man with the aristocratic nose said with a touch of sarcasm. "No matter . . . I have other pressing business. Mr. Mitchell, if you please."

"Fall in!" commanded a midshipman in a high, nervous treble.

Leaving the sailors beside the boat, a double file of marines escorted the naval commander and midshipmen up away from the beach. The crowd of curious Barbareños followed, but at a respectful distance. After all, the soldiers' muskets were fixed with bayonets, and their field packs and grim expressions suggested that they meant business.

The main thoroughfare of Santa Barbara was little more than a muddy track more suited to carreta oxcarts than to precise military formations. The Americanos knew exactly where they were going, however, and stepped out smartly, even when they had to wade across Mission Creek.

The formation followed the rutted highway directly to the old adobe presidio. There were no Mexican soldiers present, since the remaining few guards had been withdrawn when Governor Pico had retreated to Los Angeles only a few days before.

The courtyard was empty except for a forgotten goat and a flock of chickens pecking in the dirt. The whole fort had an air of dilapidation and abandonment. The slumping adobe walls could have been deserted for a century instead of just a week.

The commodore looked around uncertainly, as if wondering how to demand the surrender of a town when there was no opposition. "Mr. Mitchell," he said at last, "I'll have our flag run up the flagpole, if you please."

"Begging your pardon, sir," apologized the middie. "But there is no flagpole, sir."

The young American officer tugged on his bushy sideburns and frowned. "All right, then," he concluded, "we'll just march until we find one!"

After slogging down narrow lanes even more rutted than the main highway, the detachment of troops came to a halt in front of a two-story adobe casa. It looked like many other nondescript tan brick buildings in Santa Barbara, with one notable exception: it had a flagpole. The slender mast was actually a semaphore staff that its owner, Don Nicholas Den, kept to exchange signal flag greetings with ships in the harbor, but it would do.

"Mr. Mitchell, you will post the colors," ordered the commodore.

The middie saluted sharply and called the detail to attention. The red, white, and blue of Old Glory was soon hoisted to the peak.

Much whispered commentary erupted from the crowd and Don Nicholas stepped forward in protest. "Sir," he said stiffly, "what do you think you are doing?"

"Well, señor alcalde, mayor. You *are* Nicholas Den, aren't you?" inquired the commodore.

Don Nicholas stumbled back a pace. "How did you—"

The naval officer brushed the question aside in favor of answering the earlier challenge. "I am Commodore Stockton of the United States Navy. Inasmuch as the United States and the country of Mexico are now at war, I am hereby taking possession of the Santa Barbara presidial district."

As soon as the word of Commodore Stockton's invasion reached the Reed Rancho, Francesca ordered her gray Barileno mare saddled, and she set off for town. No word had come from Will, nor news about him. But he had gone seeking Americans, and it was to the Americans that she would go for information.

Stockton had set up his headquarters in Nicholas Den's office and was proceeding to treat Santa Barbara as conquered territory. Francesca was stopped by a sentry outside Don Nicholas's doorway, but that did not prevent her from overhearing the conversation within. "And I expect you, Don Nicholas," a high-pitched, nasal voice was saying, "to be responsible for keeping the peace. I will be departing shortly to continue the campaign, but I will leave Midshipman Mitchell and Lieutenant Falls, along with a platoon of marines."

"Commodore," an unhappy-sounding Don Nicholas sputtered, "I must protest! How can you force me, a Mexican citizen, to administer the laws of a foreign invader? It is against all the rules of the civilized world!"

"Civilized world be hanged!" the nasal voice retorted. "I intend to see that order is maintained in Santa Barbara, by force if necessary. If you wish such an unfortunate consequence to be avoided, you will do your utmost to make certain that the citizenry remain cooperative and peaceable." The finality of both words and tone left no doubt in Francesca's mind that she had just heard the last pronouncement on the subject. "Now," the voice continued in a quiet volume, "as to quarters for my men. Your own rancho, Dos Pueblos, is just outside of town. Is that correct?" A short man in a crisp blue uniform paced in front of the doorway.

Don Nicholas sputtered again and choked. His bulging eyes and beet-red face gave a good imitation of a man suffering apoplexy. But he was saved from responding by a marine guard announcing that a lady wished to speak with Commodore Stockton.

The officer spun on his heel to face Francesca. The words that he did not wish to be disturbed were on his lips, but Francesca watched him check himself and saw his gaze inspect her face and figure. Striking a military pose with one hand behind his back and the other grasping his jacket lapel, the banty rooster of a man addressed her. "What may I do for you, señora?"

Seizing on the interruption, Don Nicholas said smoothly, "May I present Doña Francesca? Her husband is an American, and their rancho is even closer to Santa Barbara and more spacious than my own humble casa."

"Wonderful," said Stockton, eyeing Francesca. "Your husband is American? Where is he? Is he in favor of our, uh, activities?"

Francesca fixed the commodore with a steady gaze of her dark eyes. "It is about my husband that I have come to see you, sir," she said. "My husband, Don Will Reed, went north some time ago to inquire into the reported deaths of our godchildren, Ramon and Carlos Carrillo. I have not heard from him since. Do you know his whereabouts, or if he made contact with the American commander named Fremont?"

Stockton's face grew grim. "I know something of the death of the Carrillos," he said. "I must tell you, madam, that they were executed as spies, and if your husband had any connection—"

"They were *not* spies!" Francesca snapped, her eyes flashing. "They were barely older than my own son! And what of my husband? Do you know of him?"

"Know *of* him? Yes, I know of him . . . he attacked Captain Fremont's landing party in Yerba Buena. He is a pris-

oner, madam, and after trial will face further imprisonment—
or worse."

Francesca's already pale skin turned ashen, and she groped
for the office chair into which Don Nicholas guided her. "You
cannot mean it," she murmured, shaking her head. "It cannot
be so."

Stockton looked stern. "Don Nicholas," he said with finality, "under the circumstances, I think it entirely appropriate
to adopt your suggestion. Lieutenant Falls and half the troops
will be billeted at the Reed rancho."

Staring at the wood-planked floor, Francesca bit her lip and
held a lace handkerchief to her eyes. She said nothing at the
outrage and barely heard Don Nicholas inquire, "And the
rest?"

"I think that some should remain closer to the center of the
town. Yes, I'd say the remaining troops can bivouac right here
in your office building."

"They are thieves and cutthroats, these Americanos," declared Simona, the cook in the Reed household. With one
infant on her hip and a toddler trailing after, Simona helped
Francesca stash the most precious household belongings into
a large trunk. Luis, her diminutive vaquero husband, was already hard at work digging a hole in the floor of the stall
reserved for the master's horse, Flotada.

Silver table service, tea sets, goblets, and candelabra were
wrapped in delicate lace and linens. All the weapons, including table knives, were placed into the trunk lest the Americanos carry out their threat to arrest every citizen caught with a
weapon of any kind.

Her face grim, Francesca warned Simona, "Tell Luis that
these Americanos are greatly afraid of vaqueros. They know
how accomplished our men are with their reatas, and now
have made the rule that anyone with a reata will be publicly
whipped or arrested. We will bury the reatas in the trunk as
well."

"They are loco!" fumed Simona as she hurried out the door. "If Don Will were here, they would not treat us like prisoners."

Francesca was secretly relieved that Will was not here, even if it meant he was in jail. Certainly he would not stand for the endless list of regulations that the American Lieutenant Falls had imposed upon the "conquered" people:

BY ORDER OF THE AMERICAN COMMANDER LT. FALLS

1. Shops will be closed at sundown
2. No alcohol will be sold
3. A strict 10 P.M. curfew will be enforced
4. No meetings to be held
5. No two people may be on the street together
6. No assembly of more than two people
7. No carrying of firearms
8. No carrying of reatas or tailing of steers

American Commander Lt. Falls will act as civil judge in the absence of Commodore Stockton. All violations of the above regulations are punishable by whippings, imprisonment, or death. Houses may be searched if a suspicion of wrongdoing exists.

The scrawny, arrogant Lieutenant Falls had dictated his rules as he paced back and forth on the porch of city hall. Written in English and posted on the wall of every shop and home in Santa Barbara, the regulations were then read aloud in Spanish from the rooftops. Clusters of astonished citizens had listened, then looked at one another in the realization that anyone standing among a group of three or more could instantly be arrested and punished.

The crowd had simply evaporated. No doubt every Santa Barbara resident had hurried home to do the same thing Francesca was doing now. Every valuable would have to be hidden. The new laws were not laws meant to protect from harm. They were simply designed to grant absolute power to the strutting little tyrant who would soon be moving into Francesca's own home.

Simona returned with the reatas, which she wrapped in a sheet and placed at the top of the chest. "Luis says he understands why the Americanos fear our skill with the reata," she said to Francesca. "But why have they made a law against the tailing of steers?" She shook her head at the madness of such a proclamation.

Francesca laughed a short, bitter laugh. "Perhaps these Americano cows have tails beneath their uniforms. Perhaps they have seen the way our vaqueros can flip a steer by simply cranking its tail. No doubt this Lieutenant Falls is afraid Luis will crank the man's tail and he will live up to his American name."

That explanation was as reasonable as any, since the whole list seemed to border on insanity.

"Don Reed would tail this strutting calf if he were home! Did you see him parade around as though he were some handsome mayordomo on a prancing stallion? His teeth poking out from those thick lips! And he has only half his hair. Skinny neck and a pot belly, too! A very poor specimen of Americano, if you ask me. It is a good thing we know Don Reed, or we could think them all piggish and pitiful and . . . *loco*!" She finished where the conversation had begun.

"If he is loco, then perhaps he is also very dangerous, Simona." Francesca closed the trunk and snapped the lock closed. "I have heard my father speak of men such as this Lieutenant Falls before. He sees danger in every look and believes that each whispered word is about himself. He feels that he is much despised—"

"And so he is!"

"Ah, but he does not believe that such hatred is justified. His whole existence depends on fighting some personal enemy. For this reason, men like Falls work very hard at making enemies of all men. It is a twisted mind. A twisted and dangerous life." Francesca glanced worriedly out the window. "We must be careful, Simona. He has made himself the law. If we offend him, we are subject to his revenge."

"The fact that we were here first offends him."

"Think of your children. Smile and keep silent until someone sane returns to put an end to this madness." She was glad that Peter was in the hills, relieved that Will was far beyond the reach of this little madman. She would pray for Will's release and safe return, but not if homecoming meant greater danger!

The company of eight marines rode toward the Reed rancho as Francesca and Simona stood on the porch. Luis hurriedly spread straw to cover the turned earth in Flotada's stall.

On the shoulder and rump of every horse, Francesca recognized the brands of the finest ranchos in the country. She was justified in burying her belongings. These vile men took what they wanted.

Simona noticed the brands at the same moment. Through gritted teeth the plump cook declared, "Thieves and cutthroats, señora Reed. They should be riding wild burros! American pigs!"

"Whatever you say," Francesca reminded her, "say it with a sweet smile. They do not speak our language, Simona, but this Lieutenant Falls fancies himself to be both judge and lawgiver. No doubt he studies the expression on our faces even now." She raised her chin slightly and smiled like a gentlewoman welcoming guests to the hacienda—no trace of the bitter resentment of this violation . . . not a hint of the disdain she felt for the pitiful little Americano lieutenant. He flapped awkwardly against the saddle and tugged at the reins of the magnificent horse he rode.

"It is pathetic to see when the horse is finer than the one on his back," said Simona in Spanish. Her face was also a reflection of genuine hospitality as the riders approached.

"The horse should be riding señor Falls, I think," agreed Francesca. "The animal knows more than the man in this case."

The eight marines pulled their mounts to a halt before the porch. Francesca and Simona both curtsied in unison.

"Good afternoon, madam," said a breathless Falls as his nervous horse pranced about the yard and fought the harsh tugging on the bit. "You have prepared for us?"

"Welcome to the Reed Rancho, Lieutenant," Francesca said graciously. "I have moved my belongings to the servant quarters. You and your men are welcome here. My husband, who is an American also, will be pleased that you have chosen our home to reside in during your stay."

"Your English is quite good," said Falls, jerking the horse around in a tight circle. "I will thank you to speak only English in the presence of me and my men at all times."

"But my servants do not speak your language, señor Falls. What if I must speak to them in front of you?"

"Well then . . . you will provide us with a proper English translation in such a case. We cannot have you Mexicans conniving behind our backs, can we?"

With a gracious nod, Francesca agreed. "As you wish, señor."

"And I am not a *señor*. I am no Mexican, madam, but an American officer."

Again the nod. Then Simona asked in Spanish, "What does this *cabro* say, Doña Reed?" She continued to smile demurely at the officer, who was unaware that cabro meant *goat*.

"May I explain to my servant what you have just told me?" Francesca asked.

"Tell her," Falls ordered.

Francesca did so in Spanish. "The cabro says that I am to speak only English to him and give him the translation of every Spanish word uttered in his presence."

"Sí," agreed Simona with a nod at the American. There was no change in her expression. "Caporal de cabestros." Simona uttered the salute, *Captain of Oxen,* with respect.

"What did she say?" Falls demanded.

"She calls you Captain of Horsemen, an honored title," Francesca answered. Indeed, the word for *oxen* was quite close to the word *caballero,* horseman. "Does the title please you, Lieutenant? If so, it is a simple title for my servants to use. Their tongues cannot master the difficulties of your language, I fear."

Yes. He liked it. *Caporal de cabestros.* It had a ring to it.

With a self-satisfied smile, the Captain of Oxen set his muddy boots in the home of Will and Francesca Reed.

11

TOR FOWLER WAS leading a gray horse as he approached the guard outside the adobe block hut—the same hut in which he had lately been held. Will was now confined there; an iron gate had replaced the wooden door. "Davis," Fowler said, peering at the guard as if in disbelief, "is that you?"

Davis hastily put down a tin plate of beans and wiped grease from his whisker-stubbled chin. "Hello, Fowler," he said nervously. "I heerd you was back."

"Yup," Fowler agreed. "You know that feller in there," he said, pointing to the hut. "He saved my life."

"I heerd something like that," Davis nodded. "But he's a turncoat what's to be sent to Sutter's with the other prisoners."

Fowler nodded and studied Davis's face intently so long that the settler fidgeted, shuffling his feet. "What're you lookin' at, anyhow?" he demanded at last.

"They tell me you was nearly killed, shot in the head, escaping. Same time I got took prisoner. That so?"

The smallest mark remained on Davis's forehead from where the tree limb had batted him to the ground. A twitching hand rubbed over the spot and traced around it as if pretending the wound were larger. "Yup," Davis said at last.

"Got you promoted too?"

Davis bobbed his head. "Corporal of Californie Volunteers," he said, "ever since we took care of them Carrillo assassin fellers." Then as if drawing renewed confidence from remembering his rank, he demanded, "What do you want here, Fowler?"

"Hear that?" Fowler asked, jerking his chin toward the sound of a cannon fire salute. "Captain Montgomery is comin' ashore to read a proclamation. Probably be a regular fiesta after."

"So?" said Davis unhappily. "I got to guard this here prisoner." He hefted an army-issue musket. "And I don't need no help from you."

"Thought you might like to go on down to the party and leave me on guard a spell." Fowler's voice sounded surprised at Davis's hostility. The barest droop of an eyelid over a gray eye was directed at the doorway.

"What kinda danged fool do you take me for? Everybody knows you favor lettin' this fella loose!" A move closer by Fowler made Davis draw the musket up to chest height and cock the hammer back. "That's far enough," he warned.

Fowler held up both empty hands, palms outward. "Whatever are you scared of, Davis?" he said innocently, taking one more pace nearer.

Unconsciously, Davis backed up a step and his shoulders touched the iron gate across the door. "I'm warnin' you," he said, and he raised the musket to his shoulder.

From behind him, Will's hand shot out through the grating and grasped the barrel of the musket. The gun erupted with a roar, striking nothing, its blast blending with the rolling cannon fire. Will yanked back hard on the weapon, pinning the settler by the neck to the metal frame.

Eyes bulging and hands waving frantically, Davis saw Fowler take one more step. He even saw the haymaker that started down by Fowler's side and flashed in an overhand arc toward his nose. Briefly he saw shooting stars, then the settler saw nothing as Will let him slip to the ground.

"That was for Cap McBride and Two Strike," Fowler muttered, rummaging through Davis's pockets and coming out with the key to free Will.

"Thanks," Will offered, emerging into the sunlight. "Now tell me where that fellow Falls has gone, and we're all square."

Fowler shook his head. "I'm still comin' with you," he said. "Nothin' left for me around here. Castro's moved south; Fremont, too. I figure there'll be a fight round Santa Barbara somewheres."

Will started. "My home!" he said. "What about Falls?"

Gray eyes locked on green. "Left by ship," Fowler said. "Fremont sent him ahead to Santa Barbara to cut off Castro's retreat."

A crowd of spectators gathered on the dirt field that passed as Yerba Buena's public square. Russian sailors, whaling men, Frenchmen off a merchant vessel, and American traders all jostled for a better view, but there were few Californios. The Spanish-speaking residents mostly stayed indoors.

Those who stood before the Customs House could see boats being lowered from the United States ship *Potsmouth*. Seventy black-hatted sailors rowed ashore at Clark's Point at one end of the arc of Yerba Buena cove.

To the brittle noise of one drum and the shrill prattle of one fife, the files of men marched to the square. Down came the Mexican Flag, and the Stars and Stripes was hoisted in its place.

But the banner at which a small knot of Californios were staring was neither of these. At the rear of the crowd stood Juan Padilla, flanked by a dozen men. Their wide poblano hat brims were pulled low over their eyes, and under their serapes they held pistols. The flag at which Padilla directed his attention was a white sheet with a red stripe along its bottom edge. The crudely lettered words *California Republic* paralleled the stripe. In the center of the flag was a hulking shape meant to be a grizzly bear.

One of Padilla's friends made an obscene comment and the men laughed, the sound covered by the cheering of the rest of the crowd. "Looks like a cochino prieto, a black *pig*, to me," Padilla added.

"What do we do now, Capitan?" whispered Four Fingers hoarsely. "Do we ride south to aid General Castro?"

Padilla repeated the obscene remark that had been applied to the Bear Flag. "We ride south," he agreed, "but we go only to aid ourselves! Vámanos!"

Peter stopped pounding the chia-grass seed long enough to pick up the tiny wailing Limik and rock him for a moment. "Just wait a bit," Peter soothed. "I'll have food for you soon."

He stirred the pounded seeds into a gourd bowl half full of water. Using a pair of wooden tongs, Peter picked up a clean round stone that had been heating by a fire of mesquite wood. He dropped the stone into the bowl of porridge and stirred it until it began to steam.

"You are hungry all the time, Limik," he said, "but that's all right because you will grow up strong." Peter dipped his finger in the porridge, then let the baby suck the thick gruel. Limik wrinkled his face as if to say that the meal was not altogether to his liking, but he continued eating. "I know we need milk, but there is nothing I can do about that now."

Father Francis stumbled out of the sweat lodge. His robes were drenched in perspiration and his brown complexion had turned almost as gray as his robes. He was exhausted.

Stooping beside the trickle of water from the spring, Father Francis splashed a few drops over his own face, then thrust a gourd under the flow to let it fill. When the bowl was nearly full, he turned to go back to his charges, but stopped beside Peter and the baby as if he had just seen them. A weary smile played across his face, and his eyes lightened just a touch. He stretched out his hand as if to place it on the baby's head, then drew it back quickly without contact. "They say this sickness is spread by the touch," he croaked.

Across the plain, up from the canyon, four swirls of dust appeared. At first they seemed to be nothing more than dust devils in some curious parallel flight, but soon they resolved into riders, coming at a hard gallop. Peter pointed them out to Father Francis. The priest shaded his eyes and squinted, then asked, "Can you make them out, my son?"

Covering Limik carefully in his doeskin wrapper, Peter laid the baby down on a hide, then hopped up on a ledge of rock.

"The lead rider is on a tall mule," the young ranchero said. "It looks like . . . Paco!"

In a few minutes the Reed mayordomo and two vaqueros rode into the Yokut camp. They had brought Peter's horse, Chino, with them.

"Peter! Hijito, little son! Where have you been?" Paco managed to sound angry and relieved in the same breath. "Your horse wandered in without his rider, and we found not only oso tracks but also puma tracks over yours. Now here you are, miles away from . . . what is that?"

The flow of questions and rebukes ceased abruptly as the thin wail of baby Limik came up from the bundle on the ground. Paco's mule snorted and cross stepped sideways as a small brown arm broke free of its doeskin wrap and waved angrily in the air. "Father Francis," Paco addressed the priest, "where are all the Indios? And how long has Don Peter been here?"

Father Francis waited patiently for the stream of words to subside again before explaining. When he had finished, the two vaqueros had purposely backed their mounts several paces toward the edge of camp and Paco was looking nervous. "So you see," concluded the priest, "Don Peter was sent by God to serve the needs of this little one. And now that you have arrived, Paco, you must take them both back to Santa Barbara at once."

"But what about you?" Peter blurted out. "You alone cannot care for everyone."

The gray robe, once a perfect fit around the sinewy arms and legs of Father Francis, appeared to have grown. The folds of coarse cloth swallowed up the little man. "No," the priest said, "there are very few left now . . . I will manage."

At that moment the cowl slipped backward, exposing the drawn features of Father Francis. And in the hollow of his neck, at the base of his throat, a single yellow dot. The priest saw Peter's stare. "Peter, my son, do you remember what follows the rodeo, the roundup?"

Peter looked surprised at a question that seemed so out of place, but he answered respectfully, "Sí, what follows is de escoger y desechar, the choosing and the discarding."

"Just so," Father Francis agreed. "You and I have both been chosen, Don Peter, but we must go to different fields for a time."

The boy bit his lip. "Will I see you again?" he managed to say.

"Of course," replied Father Francis, smiling once more. "In the Rodeo Grande. Isn't there always a parada de escojidos, a parade of the selected ones? We will be there together, you and I."

A deep saddlebag was emptied of its provisions: jerked beef and small sacks of rice and cornmeal. The pack was lined with rabbit fur, and then baby Limik was carefully tucked inside. The bag was secured to Paco's saddle, and Peter mounted Chino. "I will miss you," the young ranchero said to the priest.

"Vayan con Dios," Father Francis said softly. "Go with God."

It was inevitable that the American officer Falls would become the object of quiet ridicule on the Reed Rancho as well as in the town of Santa Barbara. Greeted by young and old alike as *el cabro*, the goat, the salute was always uttered in such a respectful tone that the little tyrant did not catch on. He was told, and believed, that cabro meant *leader*.

"*Buenos días, el cabro*," said priest and mission Indian and schoolchild alike. *Good day, you goat.*

He always nodded his too-large head in acknowledgment, although he did not speak. Later, he ordered Francesca to let it be known that he liked this title better than the one which meant Captain of Horsemen because it was shorter and easier for him to keep track of. Too many Spanish words made him uncomfortable, even when those words were meant to convey his authority of the community of Barbareños.

This small conspiracy among the citizens somehow helped to ease the tension of the almost intolerable oppression.

When a runaway steer tore through the main street of Santa Barbara and was halted when a vaquero tailed it to the ground, *el cabro* Falls carried out his threat and had the vaquero publicly whipped. From windows and doorways, citizens watched the whipping with hostile eyes. Forbidden to gather together for solace or action against such injustice, they comforted themselves by smiling and greeting *el cabro* at every opportunity.

Each new outrage was met with this quiet inner resistance. Not every Americano could be so loco! After all, señor Reed was a kind and good man. Certainly this Lieutenant Falls was some sort of aberration, a *diablero*, a demonic lunatic who would sink back to hell before the summer was past.

He added the proclamation that there would be no church services. Visits to the mission were restricted to one worshiper at a time. The citizens complied, entering the sanctuary one person at a time, lighting candles one at a time, until all the prayers and all the candles added up to one great hope— that soon the oppression of *el cabro* would be lifted from the tiny village.

12

IT WAS LATE when Peter and Paco rode into the syca-more-bordered lane that led up to Casa Reed. The two va-queros had accompanied the young ranchero and his mayordomo only as far as the mouth of the canyon before turning back to rejoin the herd.

Baby Limik was sleeping in his makeshift cradle. Fed not an hour before on a mixture of chia gruel and cow's milk, he was happily sucking his thumb and being rocked by the gentle motion of the mule.

"Wait a moment," requested Paco, gesturing for Peter to stop. "I must walk a bit or my leg will stiffen completely."

"I thought you said vaqueros were too tough to notice a little thing like a kick in the shins," Peter teased.

Paco was not amused. "Next time, *I* will mind the reatas and *you* may milk the wild cow! Caramba! That hurts!"

"It was all for a good cause; and anyway, there won't be a next time. Mother will know of someone to nurse the child, probably tonight. *If,*" he added with emphasis, "we don't daw-dle too long in getting home."

Remounting the mule, Paco said, "You know, young Pedrito, you have a cruel streak about you." Then the mayordomo leaned over to check the slumbering infant. Peter could not see the tenderness that crept across the Indian va-quero's weathered face, but he could hear the man's gruff voice soften when he said, "We must take good care of him, Don Pedro. He is our godchild, you know. Perhaps the last of all his people."

Peter shuddered at the remembrance of the terrible loneli-ness and the stench of death that clung to the Yokut village. "Come along then," he said with fervor, "let's get home."

The lights of Peter's house had just come into view around a bend in the lane when a voice from the darkness ordered in English, "Halt! Who goes there?"

"Quién va? Quién es?" called Paco, echoing the same challenge in Spanish.

"Halt or I'll shoot," came the order again.

"Wait, Paco!" cried Peter. "Think of Limik!"

It was a timely reminder. Paco was on the verge of spurring the mule and riding down the voice from the shadows.

"Get down and lead your animals," came the command. "Walk on up to the house there, nice and easy-like."

The metal triangle hanging on the porch for calling the vaqueros to meals began an insistent ringing. The sounds of the shouted confrontation on the road had reached the soldiers in the Reed home. There was a muffled stir of cursing and swearing, the thump of boots running out onto the hardwood porch mixing with the flap of bare feet.

"That's far enough," called the sentry from behind Peter and Paco.

On the porch, Peter could see a disheveled array of soldiers in various stages of undress. Some stood with uniform blouses hanging out, and others wore suspenders over bare chests.

In the center of the group posed a little man with round shoulders. A rumpled ring of hair stood straight out all around his crown as if he had slept standing on his head. He held a pistol in front of his bulging pot belly.

"What is this, Hollis? What have we got here?" demanded the little man.

"Well, sir, Lieutenant Falls, sir, I caught these two sneakin' up on the house."

"We were not sneaking!" Peter corrected. "This is my home. What are *you* doing here? And where is my mother?"

"Ah, the coyote pup!" said Falls, snorting. "I'll ask the questions here, sonny boy, unless you want the same treatment your father got!"

The Americanos of Commodore Stockton had stolen every ham from the smokehouse of Will Reed before they sailed away. The commodore himself had tasted a fresh-cooked slice of the stuff and declared that Señor Reed's mind might be addled from living among the Mexicans, but that only a truehearted American knew how to smoke a ham so well.

Lieutenant Falls, however, had a different impression of the Reed family. He envisioned a different purpose for the empty smokehouse; adobe walls and slit windows made it a perfect jail.

Francesca faced off with the pompous little man who held his pistol tight at the back of Peter's neck.

"This is madness!" she declared. "You cannot take my son prisoner in his own home!"

"He has broken the regulations, madam, and he is my prisoner!"

Conscious of the cold steel against his flesh, Peter did not speak or move. He kept his gaze riveted on his mother, whose eyes burned with fury and indignation at the injustice.

"But he did not know your rules! How *could* he know them? He has only just returned home!"

Oblivious to her protest, Falls licked his buck teeth in thought and then began to recite his orders. "It is plain as anything. He broke the rules. Out after ten o'clock. Carrying a weapon. Traveling with a companion. Strictly against the rules."

Baby Limik, being nursed by the cook, gave a contented cry from the parlor. Francesca gestured toward the sound.

"Traveling with this child, señor! Bringing this baby home so that it might be cared for! He has told you how he and Paco came to be on the road so late! Are you a man without reason?"

Again, Falls ticked off the broken rules. "On the road after ten o'clock. Traveling with a companion. Carrying a weapon . . . I can name another dozen regulations broken if you like, madam. Enough to get this boy of yours strung up. Neither Commodore Stockton nor any other American will doubt my reason in this. Your son is plainly a menace. A danger to me and my men here!" His eyes flared as he said these words, and Francesca could see that he actually believed what he was telling her. She stood face-to-face with a madman who hid his insanity behind rules and regulations and imagined threats.

Peter also understood. He looked at her with an expression like Will's, telling her that she must tread gently. Here was a coiled snake, prepared to strike. Like a rattler, Lieutenant Falls perceived any step too near as a danger and a challenge to his petty tyranny. And there could be no doubt that he would kill without provocation if he believed he was being threatened.

"I insist that my son's case be heard by Commodore Stockton! You are the commandante, but the commodore is the governor." She played to his self-importance now, submitting to his imagined authority while appealing to a higher authority to decide the issue.

The ploy seemed to placate Falls. He stepped back a pace from Peter, removing the muzzle of the weapon from his neck. "Now you see, madam. I am only doing my job. Rules are rules. I obey authority, and so must you. If the rules are broken, it is my job to enforce them. It is for Commodore Stockton to interpret the fate of your son, whether he is hanged or imprisoned. Rules are rules, you see. My duty . . ."

Francesca had seen enough to know that Falls, when pushed, was quite capable of executing his own interpretation and judgment of the rules. A chill of fear coursed through her.

"If Peter gives his word of honor that he will not run away, may he not remain your prisoner in this house?"

To this, Falls shook his head. "I already explained to you, madam, that prisoners would be confined to the smokehouse. He's lucky I do not simply hang him and this Indian from that oak tree and be done with the bother. Commodore Stockton would not question me if I did. They broke the rules. No matter whose son he might be. No matter. Men have been known to use the cover of carrying a child as hostage to protect themselves when they intend to do harm to the authorities." This was a new possibility. An interpretation which he enjoyed contemplating. Perhaps that was the real reason Peter had been traveling with the baby.

Francesca saw the madness flash through his eyes again. How might she stop it from taking root? She stepped closer to Peter, taking him by the arm as though he were a child caught in a prank.

"Well then, Peter, you shall have to stay in the smokehouse. The Commandante Falls must obey authority no matter what the circumstances, even though the rules were violated in innocence. But he is not an inhumane man—simply an officer forced to do some distasteful things. He will allow me to feed you and Paco, and bring you bedding. You must go along to the smokehouse. You and Paco. It is the law, and we must obey as Commandante Falls obeys."

Placated by her soft voice and seeming compliance, Falls flashed his buck teeth in a proud smile. He squared his sloping shoulders and nodded his head to her in what he imagined was a chivalrous manner. "Well now, madam, I see that you have some sense. You understand I am just doing my job."

"I would like to walk beside my son to the jail." Francesca took Peter's arm. "I have not seen him in a while and would like his company if only for these few moments. A mother's wish, Commandante Falls." She said this so sweetly that he did not deny her. Even so, he still held the pistol aimed squarely at the back of Peter's head as they marched out to the smokehouse.

The little bay horse Will had purchased near Yerba Buena for Fowler to ride could not keep up with Flotada. The ranchero, now dressed in his buckskins, chafed at the delay. The farther south they rode, the more it sounded as though the war would soon be on the front doorstep of his home, if it was not already.

With Yerba Buena and Monterey both controlled by the Bear Flaggers, return to Santa Barbara by ship was out of the question. Will's splinted arm was bound tightly to his chest, but it was his own impatience that caused him the greatest irritation.

Once again it was necessary to rein in Flotada, whose easy canter ate up the miles, to allow the winded bay to catch his breath. "Fowler," Will said, "either I need to go on alone or we need to get you better mounted."

Tor Fowler slowed the laboring brown horse to a walk and felt the animal's sides heaving. "We can't afford to get parted," he said firmly. "You'd be in trouble with an American outfit or with them Mexes that held me prisoner, either one. Besides, I can't go back till we meet up with Fremont and explain . . . I'm a deserter, see?"

"All right then, it's a change of mounts that's needed. We'll see what we can find."

They rode along the Salinas River, south of Monterey. The course of the stream bed would eventually lead them into the heart of what the old Spaniards had named the *Temblor*, the earthquake range. But the part through which they rode was a wide, dusty valley, dotted with oak trees, small ranches, and occasional grizzly bears.

A wisp of smoke from one of the branch arroyos drew Will's attention. "Let's see if we can do some quick trading," he called to Tor, and turned aside into the canyon.

A hot breeze swirled the smell of smoke down to the riders. There was something else on the wind besides smoke, something that made Flotada snort and stiffen his knees in his trot as though protesting their course.

The ranchero sensed the tension in the spirited horse and caught the need for caution in approaching the ranch. Fowler carried Will's Hawken rifle, while Will clenched a pistol in his left hand along with the reins.

The dwelling was on a bench of land above the canyon. Motioning for Will to halt his horse at the near approach, Tor rode past on the trail till he flanked the home at another gully.

Will heard the perfectly imitated plaintive song of a dove: low note, middle note, three sustained low notes. So realistic was the call that Will waited for the sound to be repeated just to be certain it was really the signal.

Then, putting the spurs to Flotada, Will urged the gray into instant movement. Up the trail they sprinted, then turned aside to climb a bank at the last second so as to appear from an unexpected direction.

The ranch house was a smoldering ruin. The roof had been burned, and its collapse had pulled down two of the adobe walls. In the dirt of the cleared space before the door lay a dead man. Flies buzzed around his face and swarmed thickly on the dark blood that pooled under his chest. In his hands he clutched no weapons, only beef jerky and a stack of tortillas. The shattered remains of a clay water jug were scattered around.

"He was bringing them something to eat when they shot him down," Fowler said angrily. The mountain man stepped down off the bay, which he tied to a corral post. The gate had been yanked free of the fence and the tracks of five or six stampeded horses showed in the dust. "Run off all the stock, too," Tor concluded.

Examining the dead man while Fowler went into what remained of the house, Will called, "This man's been dead only since yesterday. They may be only hours ahead of us."

Fowler stepped back out of the ruined adobe and circled around the narrow bench of land, checking behind the corral fence.

Will saw him stop beside a row of trees, then turn away suddenly and lean on the rail as if sick. "There's a woman here," Fowler called. "They . . . she . . . she's dead too."

Two mounds of earth stretched side by side beneath the shade of a nearby live oak. "Best we can do for now," Will said, putting the shovel in the ground at the head of one grave. "We still need to find you a better horse. We'll get somebody to fetch the priest to tell their kin."

"I bet the devils who did this are running off all the stock," Fowler observed. "From their tracks I'd say a dozen men were here. They could be raiding all the ranchos hereabouts and driving a herd along with them."

Will saw Flotada's ears prick forward, and the horse gazed pointedly toward a willow grove below the hillside. Indicating for Fowler to be silent, Will stepped next to the trunk of the oak. Laying the pistol across his splinted arm, he drew a bead on the center of the grove.

When he glanced back toward Fowler, Will saw that the mountain man was already ghosting from tree to tree down the slope. In the patches of light and shadow thrown down by the willows and the oaks, Fowler's tawny buckskin form was zig-zagging, lionlike, from cover to cover.

Fowler was no more than halfway down the slope when Will heard a rustling in the willows, followed by the nicker of a horse. Both men froze, guns at the ready, then a riderless buckskin horse limped out of the brush.

It was a tall lineback buckskin with a dark mane and four black legs. Fowler and Will still watched the willows intently until certain this was no trick. At last the flinty-faced scout approached the gelding and slipped a rawhide string around his neck. The horse stood patiently waiting, favoring a foreleg and holding his weight up off it.

"This'd be one the cutthroats rode in here," Fowler remarked, pointing to the outline left by a sweat-soaked saddle blanket. "Left him 'cause he's lamed."

Will inspected the horse's brand as Fowler ran his hands gingerly down the injured leg. "I know this brand," Will remarked. "This is one of Mariano Vallejo's prize animals, from his ranch near Sonoma."

"Well, lookee here," Fowler said, picking up the hoof and digging into the sole with his sheath knife. A jagged shard of clay pot fell out into his hand. "Probably came from the busted water jug when they killed that feller. Reckon he'll be sound again now."

The horse planted his forefoot firmly on the ground to indicate that Fowler's conclusion was correct. "Get your stuff and get mounted," Will said. "You won't have any trouble keeping up now."

13

THE HERD OF horses being driven along left a trail as plain to the two experienced trackers as a well-marked roadway. The tracks headed south, keeping to the washes and gullies, out of sight of the main road and following the line of hills.

At one point the trail forked, with the milling mass of horses being diverted into low-lying pasture near a spring. The tracks of three horses with riders, noticeable because they stayed three abreast and did not cross one another's paths, continued on. "I 'spect they left the others hereabouts with the stolen stock while them three reconnoitered up yonder," commented Fowler, waving his arms toward a hill that loomed just ahead.

"It could be worse than that," Will observed. "Seems somebody in that group knows this country like I do. There's another rancho just over that rise."

The American scout and the California rancher exchanged looks. Each saw mirrored in the other's strong features his own grim thoughts: *What would they find across the hill?*

The two men checked their weapons and separated at the base of the hill to again make their approaches from opposite directions. Will's route led to a low-lying saddle. There was very little cover once Flotada had climbed out of the cottonwoods and mesquite along the creek bottom—almost a bare hillside with a few clumps of brush and granite boulders. Will dismounted, tied the gray horse to a tree branch and crept up the hillside. If his memory served, the ranch was just on the other side.

Tor Fowler saw all this from his vantage point high on the hillside to the west. He and the buckskin had climbed almost straight up the slope before moving toward the ridgeline that lay between him and the ranch. Fowler watched Will's cautious progress up the bare hill of dry grass and foxtails. Automatically his eyes traced Will's probable path from boulder to boulder until it topped the rise.

There, just at the summit of the hill, in a small cluster of rocks, a flash of light caught his eye. It could have been sun glinting off a patch of quartz or an outcropping of mica, but as the scout watched, the flash was repeated. This time he could detect movement as well. Fowler was certain he was looking at the reflection off a gun barrel.

The watcher was obviously posted to guard the hillside up which Will was sneaking. Even if he had not seen Will Reed yet, there was no way the ranchero could cross the largest bare space near the ridgeline without being spotted and shot.

Fowler could fire a warning shot of his own that would alert his friend, but if the other murderers were nearby it would bring them all into the action. "Ain't no kinda choice," he muttered to the buckskin. "Come on then, hoss," he said. "Let's go down there to help him."

As fast and as noiselessly as possible, Fowler and the buckskin plunged down the slope. As they went, Tor was grateful that the sun was westering. Its descent toward the hills behind him would make him harder to spot if the guard should glance his way.

The next time Fowler had a clear view of the ridgeline, he had dropped too low to see Will. But the scout could guess his friend's whereabouts: The watcher in the circle of rocks was standing now, swinging his rifle from point to point as he covered Will's approach, holding his fire till he was certain of killing range.

A woodpecker hammered on a hollow tree nearby, marking the passing like the ticking of a fast-running clock. Fowler knew that the explosion of a rifle would soon be the chime that ended the hour, perhaps marking the death of Will Reed as well.

Flicking the reins against the buckskin's rear with a loud pop, horse and rider exploded downhill toward the waiting assassin. Fowler began screaming at the top of his lungs to distract the watcher, who stood to draw a bead on the unsuspecting Will.

The figure in the rocks whirled around, startled by the spectacle—a tall apparition whose leather clothing blended with the animal he rode until both appeared as one. The charging beast thundered down the hill, as unstoppable as an avalanche and just as deadly.

Firing one futile shot that came nowhere near Fowler, the guard made no attempt to reload. He threw down his rifle and fled. Tor was behind him at once, the buckskin's pounding hooves right at his heels.

The man was brought up against a rock, his sombrero gone and one sandal missing. "Don't even twitch," Fowler ordered, leveling the rifle across the saddle horn, "unless you figure having a big hole in your chest would make for interestin' conversation."

"No hablo inglés, señor," the man said, holding his empty hands aloft.

Fowler noted the ragged cutoff homespun trousers and the single remaining hemp sandal. "Hey, Reed," Fowler yelled, "come up here pronto!"

Will soon appeared atop the ridge. "Somehow I don't figure this feller for one of them horse-thievin' murderers," Fowler said.

A few moments of conversation explained the true situation. The paisano, whose name was Feliz, was guarding against the *return* of the horse thieves. They had raided the rancho only the day before. "My brother, he is shot at the door of our casa, but he manages to wound one of the ladrones, the robbers. They do not see me and they ride away when we start shooting. We think perhaps they will circle back and try again, and so, I watch."

Will asked if they could have food and water. He explained about what they had found at the neighboring rancho.

Feliz gasped; then his face hardened. "My brother is only a little wounded," he said. "He can stay to guard our rancho, and I will ride with you. We will hang those malditos, or shoot them down like wild dogs. Give me but an hour, and six will ride with you."

News of Padilla's bandits reached the Reed Rancho when a half-starved young vaquero stumbled out of the mountains in search of refuge. Instead, he was captured by Falls, refused food or water, and forced to march at gunpoint to the rancho.

He collapsed on the steps of the servants' quarters as Falls glared down at him. "He pretends not to understand English." Falls did not step down from his horse as Francesca and Simona rushed to aid the half-conscious vaquero.

"Agua," begged the prisoner, who was no older than Peter.

"Hey there!" Falls commanded as Simona brought the drinking gourd. "He can have water after he explains who he is and where he comes from."

Francesca glared at Falls and took the gourd from Simona. Never taking her eyes from the little tyrant, she held the water to the lips of the vaquero, who drank eagerly.

"It is not wise to defy me, madam," warned Falls.

"He will not be able to tell you anything unless he drinks."

Falls stepped from his horse, took two steps, and kicked the gourd from the man's hands. "If he wants any more he will tell me what I want to know."

Holding the young man's head, Francesca spoke to him softly, carefully explaining the presence of Falls. The vaquero licked his parched lips and lay his head in Francesca's arms.

"The Americanos here," he croaked. "And the bandits of Padilla just to the north. Both . . . they take what they wish. Rape our mothers and sisters and kill . . . everyone . . . except I alone escaped." He closed his eyes. His chin trembled with emotion as the vision of horror replayed in his mind. *"Por el bien del país* . . . Padilla claims he kills for the good of the country. Just as this one." He opened his eyes to glare at Falls. "This *diablo huero*, the white devil who denies me water."

"Is Padilla coming this way?" Francesca asked as Falls leaned closer, trying to comprehend if their conversation contained some treachery.

"He goes where he wishes." The vaquero closed his eyes again as though he had no strength to hold them open.

Francesca instructed Simona to prepare food and draw water to soak the vaquero's bloody feet.

Falls stomped onto the porch. "You must tell me in English what you are saying! What is this Mexican spy telling you, madam? I demand to know the truth!"

"He is the only survivor of an attack by a bandit troop headed by a villain named Padilla." She answered honestly, but Falls had already made up his mind. He had written his own tale of how the half-dead young man came to the Reed Rancho.

"Lies, I am certain. It is obvious . . . he is a survivor, all right, but no doubt he has survived a battle against our American forces! Look at him! Mexican! You cannot expect me to be such a fool as to believe that there is some rogue Mexican bandit on the rampage in the north, killing his own people?" He snorted his derision at such a thought.

"Think whatever you wish, el cabro!" Francesca snapped, smoothing back the vaquero's matted hair. "Look at him! He is in no condition to lie!"

"Unless he has been on the run from our American forces and now finds himself my prisoner. Reason enough for a Mexican to invent such a tale!" He called to the guards at the smokehouse. "We have another prisoner! On the double!"

Francesca leaned over the vaquero protectively. "He is injured! He needs food and care or he may die! I cannot allow you to do this! We will care for him here!"

Falls placed his boot on the arm of the limp vaquero. "You cannot allow me, madam?" He sneered at her defiance. "You question my authority?"

"I question your humanity!" Francesca spat. "And your sanity in such a case!"

Simona emerged with a plate of corn bread and a bowl of cold soup. Falls struck the tray from the hands of the startled cook.

"I did not give permission for him to be fed. Unless he tells the truth, he shall not be fed, madam! That is the final word."

"And if he has told you all there is to tell?"

"Bandits? Absurd! He has met this fate at the hands of my countrymen. He is fleeing justice and thinks I am stupid enough to believe that he should be allowed to stay in a house and be fed and nursed to strength so he can kill us when our backs are turned! I am no fool, madam."

"He must be fed."

"In our little jail, perhaps. When he confesses, perhaps. When I give my permission. Then . . . perhaps, madam, he will be fed. Now stand back from him or you shall find I can be a harsh man . . . even with stiff-necked women." He clenched his fists as though he would strike her.

Simona pulled at her shoulder. "Por favor, señora Reed!" she cried.

Francesca lowered her eyes and moved away from the unconscious vaquero. He was half dragged, half carried to the smokehouse and thrown in like a sack of potatoes. Then the door was slammed shut and locked again.

14

THE ROUNDED SLOPES, covered with dense chaparral, trailed streamers of wet, gray fog. "I smell the ocean in this mist," Fowler said. "Is it that near?"

Gesturing toward the west, Will Reed indicated the line of hills that rose above the saddle they were crossing. "No more than fifteen, maybe twenty miles that direction. Reminds me of home."

What he did not say was that home was always uppermost in his thoughts, and had been for the endless miles of riding. Will wished he could see across the intervening space, see Francesca and know that she was safe and their home untouched by either the lunatic Falls or the evil-hearted Padilla. Will comforted himself more than once on the foresight of having sent Peter out of harm's way.

Behind the two Americans rode a score of vaqueros and rancheros gathered from the valley as the men rode south. All agreed that the safety of their families was more important than the politics of nations or the nationality of the perpetrators. They were bound together by their honor to rid the countryside of malditos and ladrones, evil men and thieves. *Por el bien del país* . . . for the good of the country.

Will shook himself out of his reverie. "Down below this pass is the little mission town of San Luis Obispo. We'll get food and rest the horses there, then press on south. With hard riding and God's help we can make Santa Barbara by tomorrow."

Down the slope they rode until the mission itself came into view. The church sat on a knob that stood out in the surrounding bowl of green hillsides and jagged rocky outcroppings. One wing of the building, two stories high, stood at right angles to a low colonnaded portico. The mission and the church looked peaceful; a decided contrast to the uneasiness in Will's heart.

With only a mile of green pastures edged in yellow bee plant and mustard weed yet to cross, a line of riders emerged from the cottonwoods bordering the small creek below the mission. The mounted men obviously intended to challenge the progress of Will's group; the newcomers spread out in a line directly across the ranchero's path. Will called a halt and both sides studied the other intently.

After a long moment Fowler announced, "It ain't Padilla. Them's buckskins on that tall fella, and the others ain't dressed Mexican neither. Yup, they's Americans."

There was a hasty conference with Will's band. "What will you do, Don Reed?" he was asked. "They are your country-men."

Will shook his head. "California is my country. We did not come to fight the war to decide which nation will rule," he said. "We will not fight these men if they will let us pass. But if they will not—" He shrugged. "Then see to my family after."

Holding aloft a saddle blanket in token of parley, Tor Fowler and Will rode across the field toward the waiting line of men. As they drew closer Fowler glanced at Will's sling-bound arm and commented, "Get ready to make a run for it. I recognize that tall, skinny fella. That's Andrew Jackson Sinnickson, one of the Bear Flag leaders."

"That's close enough, Fowler," ordered the swarthy-com-plected Sinnickson when the men were still twenty yards apart. "I never figured you for a traitor."

"Sinnickson," Fowler replied, "me and Will Reed here got a story to tell you. You have the reputation of being a fair man. What say you listen first and make up your mind after?"

Fifteen minutes later Sinnickson asked, "God's truth then, Fowler? Davis lied about who started the fighting, and Falls murdered two youngsters in cold blood, but right now you're trailing a gang of cutthroat Mexicans?"

Will answered for them both. "That's it," he said simply. "There's wickedness on both sides, and it looks like Santa Barbara and my family are about to be caught in the middle. Will you let us pass?"

Pondering for a minute, Sinnickson dropped his head in thought, like a great carrion bird perched on a limb. At last he said, "Pass, nothing. It's time the grizzly banner stood for what's right. We'll ride with you."

After an hour of rest and some food, the group of riders who had followed Will Reed and Tor Fowler from the north were ready to move on southward. But when they rode out of the grassy bottom land dedicated to Saint Louis the Bishop, their numbers had swollen by twenty more.

Behind the leading rank of mountain men in tawny buckskin rode the oddest collection of fighters California had ever seen. Elegantly dressed rancheros astride impatient stallions were flanked by frontiersmen in loose coats of leather tied with rawhide strings. The untrimmed hair of the rough trappers escaped their drooping hats, and their wiry beards were a sharp contrast to the rancheros' smooth faces. Raggedly clothed *paisanos*, the simple farmers and ranchers of California, rode their short, stocky horses next to stony-faced Indian scouts.

If the California Republic was to have any meaning, Sinnickson had explained to the group, all men who desired to live peaceably had to be able to receive justice and oppose evil, wherever it was found. Will was grateful for the strength of men at his back, but as they rode out, his thoughts all lay on what he would find ahead.

Simona nursed baby Limik as Francesca prepared the evening meal for prisoners and guards as well.

"Every day you fix supper for these Americano pigs," Simona said indignantly. "Let me prepare it, señora Reed, and I shall add a drop or two of something special to their beans. Then we shall see how well they are able to guard the smokehouse!"

"You think I have not been tempted to do as much?" Francesca sighed as she dished up the corn bread. "Then I imagined what that devil Falls would do if he suspected we poisoned their food. No, Simona. We must try to outsmart *señor Diablo Huero*, Lord White Devil, until Will returns. He would want us to stay calm and outthink this fellow until my good husband can put things right. Then I believe this Lieutenant Falls will find himself in grave trouble with the Americano leaders. If we can last . . ." Her brow furrowed. "I must hold my tongue with this beast."

"He is *muy peligroso*, very dangerous, señora Reed. I am frightened to think what he might do."

Francesca nodded and tucked Will's Bible into the pocket of her apron. The condition of the young vaquero had worsened since yesterday, and Peter said he begged for a priest. Falls had forbidden a priest to be summoned, but surely Peter could comfort the young man by reading from the Holy Scriptures. She had bribed the guard by making a fine berry cobbler. Falls had ridden into Santa Barbara. Could they object to her giving the Bible to Peter?

"Who goes there?" The youngest of the two marine guards challenged her as she approached.

"I have brought your supper," Francesca answered sweetly.

"I smelled that corn bread coming before you got halfway here," called the second guard cheerfully. They were pleasant enough with Francesca, but she knew they were much like dogs, wagging happily until the moment their master ordered them to attack.

"Simona and I made a cobbler for you today." She offered them the heaping plates, then waited silently as they unlocked the door of the smokehouse.

"You'll have to show us your pockets, ma'am. Them's the rules, and Lieutenant Falls will have our heads if we don't follow them."

She pulled the pockets of her apron out for them to examine and produced the well-worn Bible. "My son has asked for his father's Bible to read in these long days of his confinement. Surely you cannot object."

They thumbed through it, exchanged glances and shrugged. "It ain't like it's a weapon, now, is it?" Stepping aside, they let her pass into the gloomy interior of the cell.

The sweet scent of woodsmoke and ham greeted her. Peter and Paco were against the far wall. The young vaquero, who was called José, lay on a blanket in the center of the enclosure. In spite of the thick adobe walls, the air was close and too warm. The light from the guards' lantern shone on the haggard faces of the prisoners. Francesca was forbidden to speak in Spanish. Violation of this order would be reported in spite of berry cobbler bribes, and Falls would punish the prisoners by withholding their food.

"Two minutes, Missus Reed," called the guard.

Two minutes. Just long enough to kneel and check José's weak pulse.

"Has he eaten since yesterday?" Francesca asked Peter.

"Only a bite. I think . . . he wants to die, Mother. This Padilla is very bad. José tells us that his sisters and mother were . . . murdered. And I think he has given up all hope."

Francesca gave Peter the Bible. "You must find hope here. Read to him. This is our only comfort, Peter. Your father would say the same if he were here. This is our best weapon."

Peter held the Bible to the light. He nodded and then embraced the book. "All men seem evil to me now, Mother. All . . . the Americanos of my father's homeland. Men like Padilla, who are from this, my own country. Who is for us, Mother? And who is for the innocent one . . . like baby Limik? These days the darkness seems to consume everything."

"It has always been the same, Peter." She touched his forehead as though she were tucking him in. "There have always been men like Lieutenant Falls who make themselves grand by bullying others. And there have always been those like Padilla . . . and the British who brought plagues upon a gentle people without a thought or care that their whole world has vanished now." She passed the plate to Paco. "God's Word is filled with such stories. Injustice. Evil. But I tell you this, Peter, the Lord is still God and these men will stand before Him as judge. Sometimes that is the only hope we have left to cling to in this world."

"Thirty seconds, Missus Reed," came the warning.

"Es la hora de rezar," she whispered. "It is time for prayer, Peter!"

"What was that you're saying Missus Reed? You speaking Mexican, are you?" The lantern behind her was raised higher.

"Just reminding my son to say his prayers," she replied with a strained cheerfulness. She kissed Peter on his forehead. "Pray, Peter. Pray that the Lord will deliver us from evil just like you carried the baby home to our care."

The boy nodded. "Yes, Mother, I will."

"Time! Out you go, Missus Reed. Visiting is over!"

15

TWO OF MITCHELL'S sailors and a pair of Falls' marines were deeply involved in their game of horseshoes. The score was three games to two in favor of the marines when the clatter of hooves and swirling dust alerted them to the approach of horses.

All reached for their rifles in alarm at the racket, but it was difficult to feel very apprehensive. After all, Santa Barbara had been peaceful under Falls' restrictive rules. If the Barbareños were not happy, at least they had not shown open hostility. Still, it was best to be on guard, so no one relaxed until the new arrivals appeared as a herd of horses only, rather than a troop of mounted men.

The American sailor on guard duty on the outskirts of the parade ground next to the old presidio gave the order to halt, but in the mass of milling animals it was unclear where there were humans to hear the command. "Halt!" he ordered again when a rider at last came into view.

Four Fingers looked disgusted with the blue jacket's tone. "Qué dice la vaca? What does the cow say?" he muttered. His right hand crept downward to the reata, and he shook out a loop on the side of the horse where the guard could not see.

The sentry, who spoke no Spanish, knew only that the rider gave no sign of complying and was openly carrying a knife. Its handle could be seen protruding above the sash around the waist of Four Fingers. The sailor raised the still uncocked weapon to his shoulder and repeated the order to halt.

The hand that gave Four Fingers his name flashed across the neck of his sorrel horse. The loop hit the guard in the face with such force that he wondered if one of his friends had thrown a horseshoe at him.

In the next second the loop flipped around his shoulders, pinning his arms to his sides. Before his rifle even hit the ground, the sailor was jerked off his feet and dragged across the parade ground.

"Ha!" shouted Padilla with delight, waving his sombrero over his shoulder. "Bring them on, amigos," he yelled to the other riders. "Stampede!"

The herd of thirty stomping, kicking horses veered sharply onto the parade ground, scattering the sailors and marines. Two shots were fired, but neither hit anything.

Padilla drove his strawberry roan directly at a fleeing marine. "Golpe de caballo!" Padilla exulted as the horse's shoulder struck the American in the back and knocked him down on his face. "Golpe de caballo!" he called to his comrades. "Strike with the horse!"

Four Fingers spurred his mount toward the abandoned fort. The Americans were fleeing in that direction, and Four Fingers wanted to deny them the shelter of the crumbling adobe walls. The pace of the red horse was slowed by his kicking and crow-hopping at the weight of the still-struggling man being dragged behind. Four Fingers never slackened his gallop, but with a nonchalant air, he loosened the dally around the horn and let the reata slip to the ground. Two of the stampeding horses jumped the torn and bruised figure without touching him, and he hugged the earth and remained flat on his belly.

The slight delay had given two of the Americans the chance to reach the cover of the presidio. The pair still had their rifles and, once out of the immediate terror of the stampede, they began a deliberate and methodical process of firing and reloading.

The battle of the parade ground was over just that suddenly. Padilla wheeled the roan toward the edge of the field as soon as the firing started. He waved the Colt revolving rifle, and the others joined him there, out of the effective range of the Americans' weapons.

Gesturing for Four Fingers to ride to his side, Padilla said to the other banditos, "Keep the herd here, amigos, and watch that the Americanos do not break out. We will find out the strength of the Yankee dogs in the pueblo and return here for you."

As he and Four Fingers set off on the short ride into town, Padilla complimented his second-in-command. "That was a marvelous cast you made, amigo. Truly you are a lazadore bravo!"

Four Fingers made a deprecating gesture. "Not so good, Capitan. I did not hit what I was aiming for."

"You caught the gringo completely around his body," argued Padilla. "What more would you have?"

"Ah," sighed Four Fingers, "I was trying for his neck!"

The afternoon heat was stifling as Francesca carried the midday meal to the smokehouse jail.

The chains on Peter's ankles had been forged by the Santa Barbara blacksmith only yesterday. Francesca blinked back tears of fury as the door of the smokehouse slammed shut, leaving her son and Paco in utter darkness.

"I will come back with supper for you," she said in Spanish, breaking the English-only rule of Falls.

"And a lamp, Mother." Peter's voice sounded small, yet unafraid.

Falls nudged her hard away from the slit window. "You are to speak only in English, madam!" Falls growled. "I have spoken to you about that before. This prisoner is already under suspicion. How do I know if he is passing you some information? Perhaps some word from the enemy."

Francesca whirled around to face him, her patience finally at an end. "And who is the enemy, el cabro! Qué grosero! How insolent you are to speak of enemies when you sleep in the bed of my son and he is chained to the walls of his father's smokehouse! You steal our food and then lock my son into this place as though he were nothing more than meat! I ask you again, el cabro, Who is the enemy in this country? It is not Peter. Nor Paco. Nor myself. It is not we who have stolen and persecuted and even forbidden the gathering to worship God!"

Her outburst startled the little man. He had not expected such a reaction. "What I do I do for the sake of my duty. For the good of the country." He drew himself up. "You are ungrateful, madam. I could have this upstart hanged for a spy. No one would question my decision. I have executed others no older than he for the good of the country and no one questioned—"

"Por el bien del país!" she scoffed.

"English, madam!"

"For the good of the country, you say? I have heard this lie before. You know nothing of this country or of our ways. You have seen our land and desired to take it."

"And we shall have it, madam. No matter if you wish it not to happen. You and that traitorous husband of yours, who is also rotting in jail in the north!" He enjoyed watching the blow of this information.

Silenced, Francesca suddenly felt sick. "What do you know of my husband?"

He chuckled—a low, mocking laugh. Her pain was his amusement for the day. "He went to investigate the execution of two young spies, did he not? Two spies no older than your son, madam. Executed for the good of the country."

"Ramon and Carlos . . ." She faltered, looking at a man whose soul was the blackest she had ever known in a human. "It was you . . . you killed them."

He shrugged, unconcerned. "The country is full of spies . . . and former Americans. Traitors. Like your husband, madam. Perhaps like your own son?"

The threat was clear. What he had done to others he would do again. Perhaps he had also murdered Will. "Why are you here?"

"I thought my purpose was obvious, madam." He gestured toward the door of the smokehouse. "To hang the dead meat over a slow fire before it spoils and stinks up the land. I, madam, am a patriot. Here for my country. We will have no opposition left when the task is complete."

"*Usted es un diablero lunático!* You are a demon lunatic!"

"Perhaps, madam. But I am efficient, am I not?" Her accusation amused him. He was not surprised at her outburst any longer. She was a wife and a mother, after all. No doubt she knew the twins he had shot down in the north. And she was not an American. She could not understand that this land must be joined to the United States at all costs.

"I do not believe all Americanos are so cruel as you. You do not do this for the sake of the land. You kill and bully because it gives you great pleasure to do so. The rest is only an excuse. Fear God, you demon. His judgment is true."

To this he laughed. "So. It is as I suspected, madam. You are a little hypocrite yourself. You have opposed me all along." He stepped near, and she could smell his foul breath. "Well, now, that puts a different light on the relationship. Does it not? No more pretending, madam." He grabbed her arm. "Now we can maybe get to know each other a little better. On honest terms. Come along with me."

She cried out as he pulled her toward the bushes. In the smokehouse Peter shouted for him to stop, to leave Francesca alone!

Francesca lashed out at Falls, kicking him hard in the leg. She dug her nails into his arm and struck his face as he tried to kiss her.

"You think I care?" He enjoyed her struggle, slapping her hard across the cheek and jerking her hair until she screamed from the pain.

Helpless in his prison, Peter slammed his fists against the adobe walls. The ring of his chains echoed like the thrashing of an animal caught in a steel trap.

"*Let her go! In the name of God! Let my mother go!*"

Again she struck at Falls, this time drawing blood. He twisted her wrist, bringing her to her knees. Touching his cheek, he looked at his own blood and then wiped it on her face as she wept.

"Do not do this to me!" she begged. "Do not dishonor me!"

"Hear how she whines." He showed his teeth. "I have not enjoyed such sport in a long time, madam. Yes! Fight me! Fight me, then! You will not be laughing behind your hand when I am finished with you!" He gave another hard twist of her wrist and hooked his fingers in the lace collar of her dress. "I enjoy an honest fight, mada—"

Falls did not see the determined figure behind him. The large iron skillet in Simona's hand came down on his head and rang like the sound of a gong when it connected.

The eyes of *el cabro* rolled back in his head. He swayed above Francesca for an instant and then collapsed in a heap on the ground.

Simona gave his head another solid blow with the skillet for good measure. She towered over him as Francesca scrambled away, standing far back from his motionless form.

"Un mulo muy malo!" Simona declared. "A very evil mule, this animal!" She flourished the skillet and turned to her mistress. "He will learn not to turn his back on a woman with a skillet!" At the sight of Francesca's swollen cheek, her confident demeanor vanished. "Oh, Doña Reed!" she cried. "If only we had not buried the guns, I would shoot this devil myself!"

Francesca embraced Simona. "You have done well. This fool did not imagine to banish frying pans from Santa Barbara! You have tailed the steer, Simona! Now we must get the keys and release Peter and Paco, then decide what we must do before the other Americanos come back!"

The bells of the mission clanged wildly as Francesca and Simona struggled to free the prisoners from the smokehouse. "I will keep trying, Simona," Francesca said. "You go see what this alarm is about."

Up the lane ran a ragged band of marines. There were only a handful of them, and half had no weapons. "Lieutenant! Lieutenant! The Mexicans have busted loose in a rampage down to the—where's Lieutenant Falls?" Hollis demanded of Simona.

"Cómo?" she said, all innocence. "No hablo, señor."

"Blast it all, woman! Uh, donda esta Lieutenant Falls? Falls . . . you know, el cabro?"

"Ah, sí, el cabro," Simona nodded. With her frying pan she gestured back down the hill toward town.

"You mean he ain't here?"

From around the side of the hacienda nearest the smokehouse came the sound of a hammer pounding against links of chain. "What's goin' on in there?" Hollis wondered aloud. "Come on," he said to the six other panting soldiers, "let's check around here real quick. Somethin' ain't right."

They rushed toward the smokehouse, with Simona loudly protesting in Spanish that el cabro had left. The smokehouse cell was open, and Francesca was hammering at the chains that bound Peter's legs.

"Hold it right there," demanded Hollis, leveling his carbine at the group. "What have you done with the lieutenant?"

From the oleander bushes came a slurred reply. "I'm right here."

Out of the brush staggered Falls, holding one hand against the back of his head and swearing loudly when he stepped into the bright sunlight. Two lines of blood had trickled from his scalp around to the corners of his mouth, painting him with a grotesque smile like a monstrous clown. "These lousy Mexicans tried to kill me," he said. "We're gonna shoot 'em all, right now. Line 'em up against the wall." He gestured with his gore-covered right hand toward the smokehouse.

"Lieutenant," said the young marine nervously. "Sir, we was just run out of Santa Barbara by a gang of armed Mexicans. Mitchell's holed up down at the mission, but the rest of us couldn't make that, so we high-tailed it up here. We think they'll be comin' after us too."

Falls glanced around at the rancho. "Too few of us to defend this place," he said. "We'll retreat up into the hills. Make 'em pay to get at us."

"What about these prisoners, sir?"

"Lock 'em up again," Falls said, "all except this one." He grasped Francesca roughly by the arm with his bloody hand. "She's coming with us."

Padilla and his men arrived at the Reed Rancho with a pack of horses and mules piled high with plunder. From the top of one hastily wrapped canvas protruded a golden candlestick.

"Ah," said Four Fingers in an admiring tone as he looked up at the Reed home. "I will enjoy getting acquainted with this house."

"Later," Padilla snapped. "First we take care of the Americano soldiers. We know they came this way."

The prisoners locked in the smokehouse were calling for help. Peter was yelling the loudest of all. "Get us out of here!" he shouted. "The crazy Americano lieutenant has taken my mother and gone up to the canyons with her."

"So?" said Padilla with interest, though he made no move to unlock the cell. "How many men did he have with him?"

"No more than six or seven," Peter replied. "Let me out—I must go help my mother."

"Is she pretty, your mother?" said Padilla with a leer. "Don't worry, boy, I will help her myself."

16

PADILLA LED THE charge through the arroyo that led up toward the Santa Ynez mountains. The hill rose abruptly, much steeper, and the bandit leader knew they must be gaining on the Americanos. Just past a line of live oaks, the gang broke into the open of a hillside covered in dry brownish grass and brush that reached to the horses' bellies.

Above them the long slope was mostly bare of trees, except for a grove of oaks about halfway up. The last two in a line of blue-clad forms could just be seen disappearing into the shadows under the trees. "We have them!" Padilla exulted. He waved the Colt rifle in an overhead arc. "At them, amigos!" he shouted.

But even mounted as they were, the incline of the hillside and the thick brush made the uphill attack slow work. Before the bandits had closed even half the distance to the trees, shots began to ring out from the Americanos' position.

Four Fingers heard a slug whistle past his ear, and another maldito took a bullet in his thigh. Padilla was still urging his men onward when the rifle fire seemed to converge on him. In quick succession one slug cut his reins, striking the roan in the neck, a second went through his hat, and a third struck the horn of the saddle. He wheeled and sawed the useless reins as the horse gave a terrified scream and toppled over down the slope.

Kicking his feet free of the stirrups as the roan fell thrashing to the ground, Padilla leaped clear, keeping the rifle uppermost as he landed. Lying in a prone position, he returned the gunfire, getting off three quick shots before sliding off down the hill to rejoin his men.

"Now what, Capitan?" Four Fingers wanted to know. "The gringos have the advantage of us. Why don't we leave them, the cowardly pigs, and return to more important business?"

"No!" Padilla insisted. "Do you want it said that we could not take care of a pack of Americano curs?"

"I do not care what someone says to me if he is willing to take my place and be shot at. Ayee! That one bullet burned my ear, it came so close!"

"That's it!" Padilla exclaimed. He felt the breeze that blew up the hill from the sea. "Perfect," he said.

"What are you saying?"

"Give me your piedras de lumbre, the flint-and-steel," Padilla demanded. "We'll burn them out!"

The wave of riders that swept around the Reed hacienda completely encircled the house. Paco cautioned Peter to make no noise that would give away their presence until it was known who these men were. Still shackled, Peter wrenched around and pressed his face against the narrow crack in the boards of the smokehouse door and tried to make out the identity of the newcomers.

It was confusing. Some were dressed like the boy's neighbors and relatives in Santa Barbara, but just as Peter prepared to call out to them, a wild and fierce-looking American came into view. Paco and Luis jostled the boy as all tried to peer through the cracks. Peter angrily ordered them to stand aside!

One ruffian with his arm bound in a dirty bandanna and with the hems of his clothing trailing buckskin fringe jumped off his horse amid the crowd. The man vaulted the steps to the back porch of the house three at a time. Peter was about to yell a protest, then checked himself and gasped: This backwoodsman was riding Flotada!

Then Peter heard a familiar voice yelling, "Francesca! Francesca, where are you?"

"Father!" he called, pounding on the wall of the smokehouse. "Father, over here!" But his cries went unheard. Amid the din and chaos of the milling horses, no one could hear the boy's shout.

Frustrated, Peter watched through the crack as his father conferred with another man dressed in frontier leather. Will gestured angrily at the ground torn up by the pawing horses, then pointed up and down the coast. It took no words for Peter to understand the anguish that the muddled trail caused the man who was desperate to locate Francesca!

"Father!" Peter shouted again. Exhausted, he sank back against the wall. No one was coming; they were all about to ride away without ever knowing that he was there. "Father," Peter said once more, his voice barely above a whisper, "help me."

Suddenly the noise outside the smokehouse subsided. At first Peter thought his father and the other men had left; then he heard the sound of footsteps coming across the hard-packed earth directly toward Peter's prison.

Peter held his breath. With a roar and a deafening clang, a single shot took the lock off the smokehouse door.

When the dust cleared, Peter saw his father standing in the doorway, silhouetted against the bright light outside.

Leaving Sinnickson to bring the rest of the troop of riders, Will mounted Flotada with Peter on behind. Over his shoulder Will called out, "I can get ahead of them, head them off." Even with the double burden, the mighty gray horse sprang away from the trail and up a steep ridgeline, leaving behind all the others except one. At his side, stride for stride, galloped Tor Fowler on the buckskin.

The wind of their passage whipped away words like the spray over the prow of a ship under full sail. Peter dug his fingers into his father's shoulder and pointed toward a thick, black column of smoke rising from the arroyo that snaked upward toward the heights. Will nodded sharply, and Flotada instantly caught the clashing fears of both his riders. *What if they were too late*? The Barileno steed, in whom the blood of his Andalusian forebears still ran true, redoubled his efforts and thundered up the mountainside.

The first wispy tendrils of drifting smoke reached Francesca's nose before Falls had recognized the threat. He was still posturing in front of his men and bragging. "The Mexicans have no stomach for fighting. Pretty soon Mitchell and the rest of our boys will venture out from town and we'll catch these bandits between us."

It had taken only a moment for the thick dry underbrush to catch fire. Then a heap of chaparral blazed up with an explosion like a bucket of coal oil thrown onto a blacksmith's forge, and the flames raced up the hill.

"We've got to get out of here!" said the marine named Hollis. "Quick!"

Still Falls hesitated.

"Come on, Lieutenant! We can't stay here!"

"Wait," said Falls. "I've got to think. If we go out of the cover of the trees, they'll ride us down."

"No time for thinking, sir. If we stay here, we'll be cooked alive like roosting pigeons."

"Wait," demanded Falls again. "Don't they know they're endangering the woman's life? Don't they care?"

"They are *bandits*, like the boy José tried to tell you," Francesca hissed. "Now let me go while there is still time." She gestured up the hill. "There is a place of bare rock. We can find safety if we hurry."

A thick cloud of brownish-gray smoke began to roll through the grove of trees. "We got to go, Lieutenant," said Hollis again, and took Francesca's arm. "C'mon, ma'am," he urged. "You show us the way, and I'll help you up."

"No!" Falls snarled. "She's my prisoner. It's a trick to get us killed; don't you see, a trick!"

Hollis ignored him and started up the slope with Francesca. A heavier wall of dense smoke poured across the hillside like a wave of dirty seawater.

Falls snapped back the hammer on his carbine and fired at Hollis. Beside her, Francesca felt Hollis's grip tighten suddenly and then fall away. "Go on," he choked. "He's crazy." The marine slumped to the ground.

Francesca ran through the trees, reaching the clear hillside at the top of the grove. The sound of gunfire, mingled with the roar of the inferno on the hillside below, swept toward her. She blundered into a gully, gagging and coughing from the smoke and struggling to fight her way clear of the brush.

A swirl of wind parted the column of fumes overhead. In that instant Francesca could see the barren pinnacle of rock that was her goal, and she corrected her course toward it. Another bramble-choked gully appeared across her path and Francesca hesitated, not sure whether to force a way across or look for a way around.

In that moment's hesitation came a noise from behind her. Out of the wall of smoke stumbled Falls, his face a mask of soot and dried blood, his clothing torn. He had lost his rifle. His eyes had a frantic light, like a rabid wolf, a demonic figure come to life from the painted panels in the mission church.

Spirals of flame lit up the pall of smoke behind him. Incoherent ravings rumbled from his mouth, and he prepared to spring toward Francesca.

Francesca raised her arms to ward off the leap of the American lieutenant. In the next instant she felt her arms surrounded and pinned to her sides.

But it was not Falls's loathsome embrace that grasped her around the middle—it was the expertly cast reata of her son, who stood on the pinnacle of safety above her head. "Hold tight, Mother," Peter called.

Beside her son was her husband, pulling her to safety with mighty yanks of his strong left arm. "Hang on, Francesca," he urged. "We've got you."

Francesca felt herself being lifted and swung over the gully, away from Falls and away from the flames. Looking up in amazement, she saw Will, her son, and a third man she did not know, reeling her upward with mighty pulls that raised her a yard at a time.

Falls made a futile jump after Francesca that sent him sprawling into the midst of the brambles. He floundered for a moment before pulling himself, torn and bleeding, to the other side.

Emerging from the chaparral without an instant to spare as the flames raced up the gully, Falls began to climb the rock face. Behind him the heat of a thousand furnaces charred the back of his uniform and singed the hair on his head.

The lieutenant was halfway up the stone strata when another figure appeared behind the wall of flame. Padilla, fleeing from the forty horsemen who had caught him in his own trap, had hurriedly reloaded his rifle and was ascending the ridgeline right on the heels of the flames, in hopes of escaping the riders. He did not know Falls, but saw in the lieutenant's form someone who was standing in the way of his escape.

Padilla raised the Colt revolving rifle to his shoulder and fired. At first it seemed to have no effect on the climber, and Padilla wondered if he had somehow missed. He aimed and prepared to fire again, but stopped as Falls began to peel away from the rock face.

Little by little the American's hands and feet let go, and his body crumped backward. He turned a somersault, and then his carcass crashed into the blazing brush of the arroyo.

Glancing around quickly, Padilla searched for a spot where the fast-moving flames were already dying down and he could cross to the other side. A bullet struck the ground near his feet. The shot had come from above! Throwing his head back in disbelief, Padilla saw Tor Fowler reloading a rifle on the knoll above him.

The cursed Americano! Padilla would finish him now, before the fool even had a chance to reload. He threw the Colt up to his shoulder, drew a bead on the front of Fowler's buckskin shirt, and pulled the trigger.

The hammer landed squarely, exploding the percussion cap. The powder of the cylinder under the hammer ignited with a roar . . . and so did the next cylinder, and the next and the next in uncontrolled chain firing. The frame and the barrel of the Colt disintegrated, taking Padilla's face and arms with them. With an unearthly scream, Padilla toppled forward and rolled into the inferno in the gully, stopping only when his corpse bumped against another body in the flames.

The shot intended for Tor Fowler hammered into the stock of the rifle, down near the ground. The weapon flew out of the mountain man's hands, but did not distract him from seeing Padilla's end. "I told Davis them rifles ain't safe," he muttered as he watched the two bodies disappear into the roaring flames. He shook his head. "Not even havin' company for the trip will help where them two is goin'."

EPILOGUE

WILL REGARDED TOR Fowler on the prancing buck-skin horse. "You're a good man, Fowler," he said. "Why not give a pass to the rest of this war and stay here in Santa Barbara?"

Fowler shook his head. "I figger to clear my name with Captain, no, *Governor* Fremont," he corrected himself. "'Sides, mebbe I can speak up for doin' right by you Californios."

"Why don't you ride with *us*?" Sinnickson asked Will. "The three of us together might convince both sides to leave off fighting."

"Sorry," Will said, his good arm around Francesca. Peter stood close beside him. "But do what you can. Enough innocent folks have been hurt already." He gestured toward the infant Limik, sleeping in Simona's arms. "When the shaking out is all over, come on back and we'll build something good. Vayan con Dios," he said. "Go with God."

SHOOTING STAR

"For the great-grandson of
Andrew Jackson Sinnickson—
H.T. (Tommy) Turner

—with love and thanks—"

PROLOGUE*

Shiloh, Arkansas
September 24, 1910

THE GOLD CASE of the old Rockford pocket watch lay open beside the huge stack of manuscript pages heaped on the old man's desk. Soft ticking provided a gentle rhythm behind the urgent scratching of pen against notepaper. The thin golden watch hands swept across the ivory face, as if to remind the writer that time was passing too quickly for him. Time was running out. Only a thousand pages of his life had been written, and surely it would take ten thousand more to tell the whole story!

He paused and glared at the watch. No. It was not the timepiece that was the enemy but *Time*. . . . The old man cocked a bushy eyebrow and tugged his drooping mustache as he recalled how he had come to carry the watch and the heavy gold watch chain and the California-minted ten-dollar gold-piece watch fob. It was a tale the children never tired of hearing. One of their favorites, and yet the old man had not yet put the story down on paper. He held off writing it as though he could bribe the watch and slow down the steady forward movement of its hands. *"And when I've written about you, old friend,"* he often whispered to the timepiece, *"then I'll shut your golden case and send you to Jim to carry. I shall lay down my pen at last, and you may mark the hour of my passing as just another tick of your cycle."*

---

* As taken from the Prologue to *A Thousand Shall Fall*.

But the watch made no promise in return, as though it did not care if the story of pocket watch and chain and fob were ever written.

But there were other tales to tell. The dark eyes of the old man flitted to the black fist-sized stone paperweight that prevented the wind from scattering the legacy in the heap of papers before him.

It was the story of this stone that the old man now struggled to recount. The most important story of his eighty-six years was in that hunk of iron and nickel! It had saved his life when he was twenty-six years old. It had given him the gift of sixty more years to live. It had made possible the sons and a daughter and grandsons to gather at his knee and beg, *"Tell us the story of the star, Grandpa Sinnickson! Tell it again!"*

For sixty years he had hefted up the stone and cried, *"Well now, boys! Listen up! This may look like just a black rock to you, but it's more than that! It ain't gold, but it's more than gold! This ain't an ordinary stone, no sir! This is a star! Yessir, boys! You heard me right! A star! Straight from heaven it came, blazing across the sky on the darkest night of my life! With a tail of fire a mile long, it screamed down to earth and saved my life in a most miraculous way! Listen up now, boys, and I'll tell you about it. For it is the truth, and I stand alive here as witness to it!"* And then they would pass the star from hand to hand. The eyes of young and old grew wide at the story of danger and death and the miracle of the falling star.

Perhaps of all the stories, this was the most often repeated. This was the most important tale to be written down because *it made all the rest of his life possible.* . . .

The high shrill cry of the Hartford train echoed across the valley of Shiloh, interrupting his reverie. The old man peered at the watch a moment.

"Late again," he grumbled, snatching up the timepiece and striding to part the curtains of his bedroom window.

Just above the golden tops of the autumn trees, a dark gray plume marked the progress of the locomotive. Far across the valley the tall straight row of birch trees trembled and swayed as if to bow toward the train.

"The boys are playing in the trees again," the old man muttered. Glancing at his watch again, he whispered a warning, "You're late, boys. Get on down. Get home before your father gets wind you're having a good time. Hurry home now, boys!"

As if they heard his distant heart, the two small boys in the birch trees began their descent. Bending the slender trunks low, they rode the treetops to the ground and tumbled onto the field.

The old man mopped his brow in relief as he watched the two red-shirted figures dash up the hill toward home. Perhaps their father, who had no timepiece, would not know they were late.

For a long time the old man stood at the window and stared across the dusky fields at the birch trees. He had planted those trees with his own hands. A tall straight row of birch trees for his grandsons to climb and ride. Too bad their father did not believe that small boys were created to climb and whoop and laugh. . . .

Sam Tucker would leave a legacy of harshness, of distance and cruelty, for his sons. It was for this reason that their grandpa, the old man, worked day and night on the tales of his own life.

Clicking the watch face closed, he turned from the window and returned to his task. Filling his pen with ink, he tapped the nib on the blotter. It was easier to tell the story aloud than it was to put it down on silent paper, and so he whispered the words as he wrote at the top of the page. . . .

To Grandson Birch
from
Grandfather Andrew Jackson Sinnickson:

Already I have written one thousand pages, and yet
I find I have come only to my twenty-sixth year.
This may yet be the most important tale of all my
legacy, however, as in it I learned by the miracle of
a falling star how God delivers those who trust Him.
Read on, Birch, for it is a story you seem not to tire
of. Perhaps one day you will have sons of your own
you may read these words to. Then you will tell them
early what I have learned late: 'A thousand shall
fall at thy side and ten thousand at thy right hand,
but it shall not come nigh thee . . . '"

September 24, 1910

1

JACK POWERS. NOW there is a name to frighten children into behaving. "Straighten up!" the Californio mothers would say, "or Jack Powers will get you!"

Long before Joaquin Murrieta rode into legend on a flashy stallion named Revenge, and much earlier than Black Bart ever penned his first poem, Powers was well known and feared. From the southern California cantinas of the City of the Angels, to the miners' hovels of Angel's Camp in the Sierras, Powers had a name as the genuine article: the first and worst of the California bad men.

I first crossed trails with Powers in the sleepy sunlit presidio town of Santa Barbara. Powers was a sergeant in Stevenson's regiment—New York boys they were—sent to garrison Santa Barbara against rebellion in the spring of '47. They were a crude, cutthroat band right from the beginning. Recruited straight out of Hell's Kitchen and the Bowery, the regiment drank their enlistment bonus and did not sober up till they were a day and a night out of New York Harbor.

By the time the stinking tub of a transport dropped her hook off the point, the toughs of Company F had had three and a half months of hard tack and green salt beef to regret their decision to enlist. They came ashore sober, angry, and spoiling for drink and fight. Powers was the worst, because he intended to give them plenty of both and make a profit in the doing.

Sergeant Jack Powers was supposed to be in charge of discipline for Company F. That's like setting a diamond-back rattler to ride herd on a nest of sidewinders. Within a week of Company F's arrival, there were two dozen new cantinas selling rotgut liquor to the soldiers. Within two weeks, every one of them was paying extortion money to Powers. This added cost of doing business, the cantina owners reasoned, was better than having their places burned, as happened to two who resisted, or being found floating face down in the ocean off Goleta, as with a third.

For all that, I might still have avoided tangling with Powers if I had not volunteered to accompany Will Reed's cook, Simona, into town that fine April morning.

My paint mare, Shawnee, was stepping out right smart, enjoying the feel of the salt breeze off the big water. I had to hold her in check to keep from outpacing the squawking and groaning oxcart. "Simona," I said, "haven't you got any way to make that beast go faster?"

"No, Señor Andrew," she said, "but the cabestro will move no slower either, and he always gets where he is going."

She added a comment about how this ox could find his way to and from town without any guidance, but her words were almost lost in the most frightful wail yet from the solid wood wheels.

"Don't you folks ever grease those wheels?" I asked.

"Sí," she said, "but you can hear Señor Carreta asking for more."

"What do you mean?"

"Listen, señor," Simona said with a straight face. "He says, 'Quiero sebo, quiero sebo.'" Her words were a perfect mimic of the high-pitched squawk of the cart. "I want tallow, I want tallow," and she laughed right in my face.

Well, I got to laughing too—the sort of laugh that comes from purely feeling good. When I get tickled like that, my laugh isn't exactly quiet either.

We were passing one of those canvas cantinas that had sprung up since Company F's arrival, and just then a knot of unshaven, red-eyed, slack-jawed drunks fell through the door flap and out into the street. They reminded me of a squirming pile of maggots tumbling all over each other, except these maggots were halfway dressed as United States soldiers.

The one who landed uppermost in the heap squinted up at me and said, "What are you laughin' at, you dirty Injun?"

Now I never was one to get riled easy, especially not on account of some drunk's slurred comment. As my Cherokee father used to say, "You can win a dispute with a skunk, but in the end you will smell like him."

So I just leaned over out of my saddle and real gentle like said, "'Pears to me you fellas already got all the trouble you need. I'm just passing by."

I was fixing to let it go at that when a big, red-haired lunk with a sunburned face got up from the pile. He looked at Simona heading on down the road and then he said to me, "What's that perty woman doin' with somebody as ugly as you? Hey, señoreeter," he called, "come on back and get to know a real man."

Sometimes even a skunk puts his nose where it doesn't belong. Then it doesn't do any good ignoring him and hoping he'll go away; best to run him off at once. I wheeled Shawnee around and put her into a parade canter, a slow gallop, with her legs churning hard.

I headed right into that heap of blue-jacket maggots. Shawnee knocked one over with her shoulder while stomping on another. I kicked the third one out of the way and sent him sprawling over a guy rope. "Now lay there and listen," I advised them. "Señora Simona, that's missus to you, is a nice lady. Drunk or sober, you'd best not be insulting her where I can hear it." As I spoke, I dropped my hand to the coil of rawhide whip looped around my saddle horn.

That was when I first laid eyes on Jack Powers. The tent flap was flung back and a spruce-looking uniformed man with a big nose and a fleshy face stepped out. In one hand he held some cards. In the other fist was a Paterson Colt, and its .36-caliber barrel was pointed right at my breastbone. "Hold it right there," he ordered.

"Ease up a mite, Sergeant," I said. "I didn't really hurt your boys any. I was just teaching them some California manners."

"Get down off that horse," Powers ordered with a sneer. "You're under arrest for assaulting soldiers of the United

States Army." To his men he added, "Pat, Ed, get up from there." Then he repeated his order to me to get down.

I turned Shawnee so as to step down with my back to those men. I will tell you plain, my spine half-expected a lead slug any second, but I needed to hide my whip hand as I shook out the lash.

"C'mon, hurry it up," I heard one of the drunks growl. He grabbed hold of one of my buckskin leggings. That's how I knew when to turn, because with that red-haired soldier right between me and Powers, the sergeant wouldn't dare shoot.

A sudden flick of the whip got Powers around the wrist of the hand gripping the gun. The Paterson discharged up into the air and then flew over into a patch of weeds.

I reversed my grip and drove the twelve-inch hickory wood handle into the forehead of the red-haired fellow, and he dropped like a stone.

Shawnee was dancing and kicking up the dust, and when the other two soldiers tried to close with me, she cut one of them off. It was too tight a space for lash work now, so I stabbed the drunk named Ed in the gut with the hickory handle. His breath went out, and as he doubled over I hooked my left fist into the point of his chin. The shoulder that had caught the lance tip in the last battle of the war with Mexico didn't like that and let me know it, but the blow served its purpose.

The third soldier circled out of range of Shawnee's hooves and tried to come at me with a knife. I needed to hurry. I could see Powers cussing and scrabbling in the dust, trying to recover the revolver from where it had landed in a mess of prickly pear cactus.

It's amazing how much force you can put into a twelve-inch piece of hickory if you've a mind to. I smashed one blow over the soldier's knife grip, then backhanded the man across the nose.

Powers was coming up with the pistol, so it was needful to turn my attention back to him. This time I let the popper on the bullwhip do my talking for me. The thin strip of knotted buckskin crossed Powers' cheek, splitting the flesh in a welt that stopped just short of his right eye.

The sergeant threw up his hand to his cheek, and the gun dropped again in the dirt. "Leave it there," I said, "or next time I won't spare your sight."

"Señor Andrew!" called Simona as she rattled back up to the scene. Only this time she had Colonel Stevenson with her.

"Sergeant!" ordered the colonel. "Bring your men to attention at once!"

"Colonel, this man . . ." Powers started in, but it was obvious his words didn't carry any weight with his commander.

"Forget it, Sergeant. The señora has already told me about the drunken insults. Besides, do you know who this man is? Andrew Jackson Sinnickson has scouted for Colonel Fremont alongside of Kit Carson. Sergeant, those three men are on report, and put your own name down as well. Now, make your apologies."

There was some grumbling, but no open argument from the three soldiers or their sergeant. A few muttered words passed for apologies, and that seemed to satisfy the colonel.

But when I was coiling up the whip and got over next to Powers, this is what he said, "You may be holding all the cards right now, but there'll be other hands dealt."

2

FIFTEEN MONTHS LATER I had all but forgot about
Jack Powers and his threat. I had my own cattle spread all
right, but things had not exactly worked out according to my
calculations.

I was running a herd of about two hundred head, mostly
rangy old rust-colored steers. They looked like the hide was
stretched over their bones without any meat in between. I had
picked up the land on the west side of California's Great
Valley by settling an old ranchero's debt to a Yankee money
lender.

I called my place Rancho Libre, or Freedom Ranch, figur-
ing to honor both my American side and the Spanish speakers. Freedom grew well enough in the sage and creosote bush-
covered hills, but precious little else did. Fact is, I should have
named the spread Rancho Liebre, which sounds almost the
same but means Rabbit Ranch. The only critters that thrived
and grew to remarkable size were the jackrabbits.

To make matters worse, the hide business slumped. There
was still no market for the meat, and after twenty years as
dependable as the sunrise, hides were selling for less than two
dollars apiece.

The solitude of the place gave me lots of time to think on
what my future might hold. For companionship I had only the
rabbits and a half-breed boy named Joaquin, whom I won in a
card game. I didn't really own him, you understand, but he
was only twelve and had nowhere else to go, and anyway,
that's a tale for another time.

I also had a dog. At least I think he was *part* dog. Mostly he
looked coyote by the set of his muzzle and the prick of his

ears. He had a brush wolf's coat and tail, but with some added spots of tan mixed amongst the gray. He was thicker of body and short of limb too. Anyway, however careless of his parentage he might have been, he had adopted me. He trotted up to my campfire one night without so much as a by-your-leave, waited politely for supper, and stayed ever since.

Joaquin and I had built a brush hut with a canvas roof. It was to keep thieving critters away from our meager supplies. It did give us a place to sleep out of the rain, but April to October we slept out-of-doors.

The winter of my spell at Rancho Libre had been one of too little rain. The feed for the cows was thin, and all summer we had to keep moving them from one little canyon to the next.

We had a big fire blazing at the head of the draw, and after a supper of roasted rabbit, Joaquin had already drifted off to sleep. We took turn-about keeping watch. The few calves we had we could scarce afford to lose to the coyotes or the occasional bear or cougar down from the high country.

I was nodding myself, so I got up to throw another stick of mesquite on the fire. All at once Dog sat up and looked out over the dark valley. Then I heard it too—the clinking sound of stones struck by shod hooves. It came from the direction of the Tejon, or what they call the Badger Pass.

I shook Joaquin awake, gesturing for him to remain quiet. Boy and Dog faded back into the shadows away from the fire's glare.

My whip was coiled and hanging from my belt. I took my Allen over-and-under and moved silently on moccasined feet down the draw toward the herd.

As yet the cattle had made no stir. I passed quickly to the mouth of the draw and hunkered down to wait. The night was a dark one, with no moon, yet the sky was blazing with the light of millions of stars.

Now we had nothing worth stealing, and so little to fear from any robber. Still, only men in trouble or in a big hurry travel on moonless nights. This traveler, whoever he was, seemed headed straight for our camp.

A man's night vision is not as good as many of the Lord's creatures have, but his hearing can be a powerful tool if he's trained to use it. My Cherokee father had taught me to tell the shuffling run of the raccoon from the quick patter of the fox. I knew all the sounds the animals make going about their nightly routines.

Shawnee, my paint mare, who was grazing nearby, confirmed my thoughts about the intruder by lifting her head and snorting softly. The solitary rider was coming in cautiously from the east. He had dismounted and was leading his horse, and Shawnee stared at a dark clump of brush that had grown broader in the past minute.

Speaking might draw a bullet if mischief was meant, so I waited to see what was up. Presently there came a chuckle out of the darkness, and a gravelly voice said, "I swear, Andrew, you are as keen as ever, but you still got that dang piebald pony. Her white patches stand out like lanterns."

"Tor Fowler," I said. "What cause have you got for sneaking up thisaway?"

"I wasn't for certain it was you," he grumbled. "There's folks in this country now that'll take a friendly howdy and answer back with buckshot."

"Come to the fire," I said, and he needed no further urging.

He seized on some leftover rabbit like he'd been without food for a week and devoted himself entirely to the business of eating. Joaquin came back into the light and stared in wide-eyed wonder at this apparition.

Tor Fowler was a mountain man and a wanderer. He still sported the fringed buckskins of one who was more at home with the solitude of the great peaks than the company of men. He had come west as a scout for Fremont. Fowler and I had been together in the days of the War with Mexico. At its conclusion, when I saw the chance to settle down and build something, he saw creeping civilization and felt the urge to drift back into the mountains.

When he had filled himself moderately full, he sat back and wiped his pointed chin on the sleeve of his jacket. His eyes above the sharp beak of his nose twinkled back into mine and gave the lie to the otherwise hardness of his features.

"Guess you wonder what brung me?" he said at last.

"I figured you'd tell me when you were ready," I acknowledged. " 'Seek to know another's business and you'll always learn more than you care to,' Pastor Metcalfe used to say."

Fowler nodded sagely. "True enough, but what I've got to say is like to be everybody's business afore long. Have you heard tell of the gold strike up Coloma way?"

"Gold strike?" I could feel my eyebrows raise clear up to the top of my forehead. "Fowler, you are about the last man on earth I'd expect to believe in fairy tales."

"Knew you'd say that," Fowler replied, unruffled. "Try this on for size: Do you remember that Sutter fella that kept all them Injuns like slaves to work his wheat fields?"

"Sure. Styled himself captain. Even dressed up a hundred scrawny Nishinam in moth-eaten Russian army uniforms. Called them his soldiers."

"The very same," Fowler agreed, with a sidelong glance at me. "Well, all them Injuns have dropped their hoes and their fancy green coats and skedaddled."

"All of them?"

"Ever' one. Sutter's screamin' and nobody pays him any mind. Why, even some Germans he hired to build his mills just up and tossed away their hammers and saws to grab up picks and shovels."

I considered the words Fowler spoke. This wasn't the first time people had expected to find mineral wealth in the Sierras. Way back in Old Spanish days, three hundred years before, California was reputed to be a land so rich that even the tools and weapons were made of gold. 'Course, the same stories told of how Queen Calafia ruled over a kingdom inhabited only by women! "Fowler," I said, talking politely, "Don Will Reed told me how, in '41 or '42, some vaquero pulled up a handful of wild onions and found gold dust in amongst the roots. Don Will said it was true, but the little pocket played out and never amounted to much."

A crafty grin stole across Fowler's face. With his pointed features it gave him a strong resemblance to a fox. He'd probably have approved of the comparison, but I held it back just the same.

As the boy and I watched, Fowler reached inside his buckskin jacket. Lifting a small doe-hide pouch that hung around his neck, he pulled it over his head and hefted its weight. "Come on over here, son," he said to Joaquin. He passed the leather sack to the boy and gestured for Joaquin to shake it into his hand. We all scooted up next to the firelight to see. Even Dog crowded in, his ears all pricked up and his head cocked to one side.

Joaquin pried the knotted strings apart and up-ended the pouch. Into his palm dropped not one, but a dozen dull gleaming lumps. The smallest was the size of a pea, while the biggest approached the dimensions of the last joint of Fowler's brown, scarred thumb.

"Dug 'em out of a place no bigger than this," Fowler said, using his wiry arms to show a space the size of a washtub.

"Is it really oro, señor? Really gold?" asked Joaquin. The boy's voice trembled a little.

"Tested and proved," Fowler vowed. "That big rascal is worth close to thirty dollars all by hisself. Altogether you're holdin' maybe a hundred fifty, two hundred dollars' worth."

"All right, Joaquin, enough gawking," I said sternly. "You and Dog make a circle of the herd and then come back for some shut-eye."

"But Señor Andrew," Joaquin started to protest.

"No arguments. Get going." The boy handed the shiny pebbles back with some reluctance, I thought.

When Joaquin was out of earshot, I asked Fowler why he had come so far to bring me this news. "You must have ridden three hundred miles to tell me about your good fortune," I said. "Why?"

Fowler looked over his shoulder at the gloomy dark of the hillside before replying. "I'll tell you straight out," he said at last. "These here nuggets does strange things to folks." He searched my face as if reading trail signs. "It won't pay a man to work alone in them wild canyons—but it surely would be worse for him to be amongst partners he couldn't rely on."

I nodded my agreement with this assessment and encouraged him to go on. "Well, sir, there's nought but four men in this old world I'd trust to partner up with where gold is concerned. Two of them is off somewheres in the high lonesome, and the other two is you and Will Reed."

Having the approval of a man like Tor Fowler is akin to the honor of having the President hang a medal around your neck. Or rather, it's like being complimented on the keenness of your eyesight by an eagle.

"Thanks," I said, "but are things truly so lawless?"

"Not so far," he admitted. "The finding is still easy but the elbow room only so-so. And greed can't be made to hold still. Before I came south there was already folks from Monterrey and Frisco comin' up to stake claims. And I seen two bunches square off over a promising hunk of creek bed."

"Anybody killed?"

"Not for want of tryin'. When the score was five to two of folks still standin', the losers moved downstream a ways."

"I've got my ranching to think of," I protested. "I can't just turn my herd loose."

Fowler looked amused, but he had the good grace to hide it. I'm certain that the same image of the rangy cows flashed through his mind as was etched in my own. "I'd not expect you to leave your herd," he said, tugging at a shaggy forelock. "I come here first to sound you out afore ridin' on to Santa Barbara to see Will Reed. You are interested, ain'tcha?"

I started to argue, but my heart wasn't in it. Ranching was not exactly turning out like I expected. "Let me have another look at your poke," I requested.

A grin crept over Tor Fowler's lean features. "I'll do better than that," he said. "I'll leave half of it here with you . . . partner."

Fowler rolled up next to the fire and slept. Joaquin and I took turn-about on guard, and when I came back at gray dawn from my last watch, Fowler was already up and gone.

It didn't surprise me any that he had not said goodbye. Mountain men were always wisps of smoke in their ways of coming and going. Not sleeping past dawn nor announcing a departure were two hard-learned lessons of survival that I'll not begrudge a man.

Joaquin seemed to think he might have dreamed the whole thing. I saw him wake and rub his eyes; then as the recollection struck him, he looked around for Fowler. Stretching his hands out toward the smoldering fire, he turned one palm upward as he remembered the nuggets. "Señor," he asked me, "was your amigo, Señor Fowler, was he really here last night?"

I unbuttoned a flap pocket of my flannel shirt and passed over one of the golden lumps left me by my new partner.

3

IT TOOK TOR Fowler only three days to ride to Santa
Barbara and back. When he returned, he was accompanied by
a pair of Don Will Reed's vaqueros and a loaded pack mule.

"Hello the camp," Fowler hollered, riding up in broad daylight. "Where's that Sinnickson feller who's about to be a rich
man?"

Fowler explained that Will Reed, while fascinated with the
gold and plainly itching to go for the adventure of it, could
not leave home. "Seems that the Señora Francesca is in a
delicate condition," Fowler said, "and Will don't think it right
to leave her."

"And you," I said to the vaqueros. "Did he send you to go
in his place?"

"No, Señor Andrew," responded the one named Rodrigo.
"Don Will sent us to drive your cattle to his San Marcos
range. He says to tell you we will keep them safe against your
return."

"Right neighborly of Don Will too," commented Fowler.
"Said for us to take right off. Even sent us some supplies." He
indicated the mule.

"Seems everything's settled then, with one exception," I
said. "Joaquin, I want you to go with the herd and stay with
the Reed family until I return."

"Oh no, señor!" protested Joaquin with alarm. "You and I
are compadres, partners, you said, just like you and Señor
Fowler are partners. You must not leave me behind!"

"Now, Joaquin," I began, trying to reason with the boy.
"This won't be a pleasure trip. Things may get rough. Best
you remain—"

"No, Señor Andrew," he said firmly. "If you make me go to the Reed rancho, I will run away to come and look for you."

I looked to Fowler for help, but he just shrugged. "Puts me in mind of me and you, Andrew," he said. "Guess he don't leave us no choice but to take him along."

We traveled north for three days, skirting the western edge of the swampy lands and following the course of the San Joaquin River. The morning of the fourth day found us across the stream bed from a tent settlement by the name of Tuleburg. Apt name too for a place that only rose above the cattails to the height of a canvas-covered ridgepole. It was near the junction of the San Joaquin and the Calaveras and looked more like a haphazardly laid-out army post than a town.

But humans being what they are, everybody tries to invest his efforts, no matter how modest, with a little grandeur. (Like me and my big plans for Rancho Libre, I reckon.) Anyway, this miserable collection of motley gray awnings and shacks was already styling itself a city. There was even a move afoot to rename the place for Commodore Stockton of Bear Flag War fame.

Fowler braced a merchant to inquire if anyone had asked Stockton for his permission, but the shopkeeper did not see the humor in it.

We were of a mind to push on to the location of Fowler's find on the south fork of the American, but talk around Tuleburg stopped us.

"Whereabouts you gents figure to make your pile?" inquired a fat man selling two-bit shovels for ten dollars apiece.

"Up Coloma way," said Fowler vaguely.

"A pity," commented the chubby hardware salesman with a shake of his head that made his jowls quiver.

"Why? What's wrong with it?" I demanded.

"Nothing. Nothing at all, 'cept it's altogether overrun with folks. Shiploads of whalers, army deserters, scads of foreigners from outlandish places like Peru . . . even kanakas from

the cannibal islands. You won't find room enough to swing a
cat. No sir, none atall."

"So? Why tell us? You got a better idea?"

"Just thought you might want to turn up the Calaveras.
Some mighty fine big strikes up yonder. Yessir, brand new."

"So's you can sit downstream here and sell ever'body their
supplies? No thank you," Fowler said. "We don't need your
advice."

"Ease up, Fowler," I suggested. Then to the merchant I
inquired, "This new strike got a name?"

"Angel's Camp," was the reply.

After we had passed on out of earshot I turned to Fowler.
"What do you think really?" I asked him. "Do we go on or
turn up the creek here?"

"I just don't like ever'body knowin' my business," he said.
"Sutter's land was gettin' awful overrun. Let's go see what
Angel's Camp has to offer for a couple old sinners like us."

The trail we followed up into the Calaveras country had
plainly been hacked out of the wilderness not long before.
The path was not yet passable to wagons or wheeled carts of
any kind. In fact, it was scarcely wide enough for two loaded
mules to pass each other. Portions of the way wound through
hewn-down clumps of elderberry bushes. The debris of the
discarded branches, heavy with fruit, still littered the ground.

Fowler pointed out the wasted and rotting piles of dark red
berries. "Shameful," he said. "Injuns hereabouts make their
winter stores up outta poundin' acorn meal and bear fat together with elderberry juice. Keeps right well too."

Ahead of us as we rode, another traveler bound for the
mines came into view. He was a smallish man, dressed re-
spectably in a black suit. He was leading a loaded mule, while
he himself rode "shank's mare."

The path just before us crested a knob of bare rock, then
made a sharp turn away from the edge of a sheer dropoff. The
stream bed lay about eighty feet below, and another eighty
feet or so of hillside hung above us.

The lone prospector was struggling with his dark-coated Mexican mule. It had chosen the exact worst place, as mules and humans often do, to turn balky.

"Come on now," the man demanded in a clipped and nasally voice. He dug in his heels and pulled on the lead rope as he backed up the hill. The mule responded in kind, squatting on its haunches and bracing its forelegs against the stone face of the cliff.

Fowler, who was riding in the lead of our threesome, called a halt. As I have said, the trail was too narrow for us to get around the obstruction, so all we could do was keep out of the way of the battle.

We had dismounted and were watching the struggle with some amusement when from behind us I heard the low "hoo, hoo, hoo" of a horned owl. It must have registered with Fowler at the same instant as me, because he whipped his Hawken out of its beaded scabbard just as I pivoted the Allen up and cocked both hammers.

You see, as my Cherokee daddy taught me, when a nightbird calls in daylight, it's time to wake up! A low rumble and a pattering sound, like a light rain, sounded from above us on the cliff. It gained rapidly in volume and intensity as the rumble became a roar. "Rock slide," I yelled, slapping Shawnee on the rump to get her moving and hollering for Joaquin to get down. With an enemy behind us, there was nothing to do but hug the ground and pray.

All three of our horses and our pack mule went clattering back down the trail. A boulder the size of my head came bounding down the hillside. It was aiming straight for Joaquin when I grabbed him by the arm and rolled over and over with him to get out of the block's path.

Not six feet from us the rock struck something and gave an immense leap into the air, like someone who just sat on a bee. The stone careened overhead in a high arc and flew off into the canyon. After that first flying headache, the hillside seemed alive with bouncing rocks.

A yell erupted from the throat of the stranger. His panicked mule swung around violently and swept the man about like a game of crack-the-whip.

It was an act of providence that saved the man's life. His grip broke free of the lead rope that he'd been tugging on, and the sudden motion flung him aside some distance away from the mule.

Not five seconds later, the main force of the avalanche swept right over where he had been standing. The mule gave a high-pitched scream of terror and was carried over the precipice in the blink of an eye.

All this happened in less time than it takes to tell. The roar of the slide had changed back to the pattering of odd stones and loose gravel before the body of the unfortunate mule had scarce hit bottom. Fowler and I were already sighting over our rifles in expectation of the attack that would follow this ambush.

There was a movement near the top of the hill, and Fowler and I fired almost in the same heartbeat. It was too far to make out plain, but a swarthy-complected figure in a buckskin shirt cried out, then turned and ran up over the hill and out of sight.

"Stay with Fowler!" I yelled to Joaquin, and I took off after our horses and all our belongings. You may wonder how I could charge off that way, since there was no way of knowing how many enemies were waiting for me and without having had a chance to reload. The answer is simple: I was so hopping mad, I didn't stop to think about it! Anyway, I still had the shotgun barrel of the Allen primed and ready. I was not about to let any cowardly murderous thieves succeed in getting away with our possessions if I could prevent it.

I ran along, zigging and zagging down the slope, hoping to take the thieves unawares by appearing from an unexpected direction. I knew Shawnee would not have run far, and I hoped that the other animals would take their cues from her and stop when she did.

The next level spot I came to was a clearing ringed by oaks and elderberry bushes. In the center of the circle of brush were our three horses. They were milling around, stamping and snorting like steam engines. But there was no trace of the pack mule and all our supplies.

I debated with myself over mounting up and riding after the robbers, but the hot anger was off me by then, replaced by more temperate reasoning. I wouldn't gain much by spurring after them alone, not when Fowler and I could follow them plain enough after he was mounted again.

About this time, Dog came trotting up with a scrap of buckskin clenched between his teeth. He dropped his trophy at my feet and wagged. "You did good," I praised him. "Here I was wondering where you'd got off to, and you were on the job all the time."

I picked up the fragment of leather and the lead ropes of the three horses and started back up the trail. Halfway to the rockslide I met Fowler headed down. "You all right?" he asked.

"Only half," I admitted. "They got away with the mule, but Dog here gave them something to remember us by. Where's Joaquin?"

"Left him with Ames. That's the feller that almost took a swan dive with *his* mule. Yankee from the sound of him. Piece of rock grazed him across the head, an' he's lucky he ain't kilt. Joaquin's patchin' him up. We can send them along to camp while we get on the trail of those bushwhackers."

The rest of the way back, Fowler and I discussed the attack. "Injuns, you figger?" Fowler asked, squinting at the shredded fabric.

"Hard to say. By his coloring, dark like mine, the one who caused the slide might have been Indian, but he could have been Mexican or Spaniard. He lit a shuck too quick for me to get a good look. I never saw any others. Dog left his regards on one, but this piece of buckskin could have come from you just as easy as an Indian."

"Anybody mad enough at you to want to kill you?"

I laughed. "Not so far as I know. How about you?"

Fowler gave the matter serious reflection. "Some folks I know ain't gonna go outta their way to shake my hand or buy me a seegar, but I don't recollect anyone after my scalp personal like."

When we came up to the slide, Joaquin was tying off the knot on a strip of shirttail that he had wound around the bleeding man's head. The slightly built figure in black was seated on the ground gritting his teeth. One side of his head was swelled up in one place the size of an apple, and the man's complexion was gray as the rock dust.

The man stuck out his hand. "I'm obliged to you and this boy," he said in a Yankeefied voice. With evident difficulty he struggled to his feet. "Ee-yup. Best get on with rounding up my—" Ames swayed and would have pitched over on his face if Tor and I had not caught him.

"Guess that settles what we do next," Fowler said with a shrug as he tossed the unconscious Mr. Ames across his shoulder. "We'd best take this one and Joaquin on to Angel's Camp, an' then we'll get to trackin'."

4

I THINK IT safe to record that our entry into any town or village back in the States would have occasioned quite a stir. Consider our appearance: A mixed-breed boy and a brown and weathered buckskin-clad trapper, leading a horse with an unconscious man tied onto the saddle. These were followed by a down-at-the-heels rancher riding on an Indian pony, with a half-grown wolf pup ranging alongside.

And yet, for California in 1848, not only did our assemblage not cause any commotion, we did not even provoke any comments! Anyone who had ridden into Angel's Camp that autumn afternoon would have recognized the reason at once. Nothing in our dress, manner, or composition would have been the least out of the ordinary. Fact is, while no one paid us any heed, we all found ourselves staring around quite a bit.

A pretty little valley, ringed by low hills, lay before us. The nearer slopes were studded with gnarled oaks and gooseberry patches, while the farther wore manzanita thickets and tall, shapely pines. The center of our view was a bare plain where two creeks converged, or rather, what would have been a bare plain if it had not been covered with tents and canvas awnings, rude huts, and brush lean-tos. And the architects of those human habitations—now there was a sight!

A split plank footbridge crossed the larger channel of the two creeks, and over this rustic roadway passed a parade to equal the sideshow of any circus. Three men, lately of some infantry regiment as demonstrated by the remains of their tattered uniforms, were likewise marked as deserters by the lack of any company insignia.

Waiting for the ex-soldiers to pass was a short man whose knees were escaping through the rents in his trousers even as his curly black hair escaped from under the odd bonnet-shaped hat he wore. A plain tan vest was an ill match for his overly large gray-striped frock coat.

Behind this fashionable Californian were two tall men in long serapes that reached to their knees. Flat-crowned, broad-brimmed hats and a haughty and aristocratic manner made me guess that their homeland was the Argentine.

And what did these assorted specimens of God's infinite wit have in common? They were all miners; true examples of the strange breed known as prospectors. Between the six there were five shovels, three picks, four tin pans, and a determined air of invincible good fortune. What's more, these six were just the sample on display, so to speak. In the creek bed and on the hillsides all around, there were a hundred more, swinging their picks and swirling the pans.

But we had no time to reflect on these impressions. There was the injured Mr. Ames to be seen to and the not inconsequential matter of our stolen property.

We directed our course toward the most imposing structure visible. This was, I regret to say, nothing more than a long, low tent covered in stained gray sailcloth. Three sides were sheltered by the canvas awning, but the fourth was open to the elements.

When we got closer, we could see that our target was in fact some sort of public building, since a stream of miners were coming and going from the premises. "Hello the tent," Fowler called out.

"Store, if you please, or trading post," retorted the man who responded to Fowler's salutation. "Either sounds more dignified than 'tent.'"

"That's as may be," Fowler returned, "but I'm seeking a doctor or what passes for one around here, and if I can't find him in this tent, then it don't matter what you call it!"

"Easy, friend," said the portly proprietor through teeth clamped around a short-stemmed pipe. "I didn't see you had wounded. Bring him in; this is as civilized as it gets." Then to the interior of the tent he shouted, "Patrick, clean off that counter—we got an injured man here!"

Now I like to think that I don't surprise easy, and I try my dead level best not to show consternation even when I feel it, but the identity of that storekeeper's assistant surely did give me pause. You see, it was Patrick Dunn, one of those New York soldier fellows with whom I'd clashed back in Santa Barbara.

If he recognized me, he gave no sign of it. At the time, I thought that either he'd been too drunk during the brawl to remember me, or perhaps he'd just decided to let the past lay. Anyway, I figured if he was content to leave it alone, so should I.

Dunn busied himself moving a stack of flannel shirts and a crate of plug tobacco off the rough-hewn plank table. We stretched Ames out, and the store's owner examined the Yankee's head. Ames was still unconscious, but his color was better. He flinched and moaned some when the wound was unbandaged and cleaned, and it started to bleed again.

During the procedure, the man doing the doctoring introduced himself. "Name's Angel," he said. "Henry Angel. This is my store. Doc Den is over at Murphy's Diggings today seeing to a man that came near to cutting his thumb off, but I reckon I can stitch this fellow up. How'd this happen?"

As I filled him in on our experience with the rockslide and the robbery, I watched his face grow grim. "Thievin' Digger Indians," he said. "They just get bolder and bolder. Well, it's got to stop."

I tried to explain that the identity of the attackers was by no means certain and that Fowler and I could track them with the aid of Dog, but he seemed not to be listening. "Patrick," he ordered Dunn, "round up a half dozen of the boys and we'll go teach those savages a lesson."

Henry Angel and the other Angel's Campers had it set in their minds that the local Miwok Indian tribe was behind the attack on our party. It was the miners' intention to see that retribution was carried out. In the words of a man named Cannon, a burly prospector who wore his long black beard tucked into the front of his red flannel shirt, "It was them thievin' Digger Injuns, I tell you! We oughta ride straight to their village and burn 'em out!"

Angel had Patrick Dunn remain behind to watch over his store. Privately, I thought this was setting the fox to guard the henhouse, but I kept my peace. As long as Dunn was acting the part of an upright citizen, there seemed to be no cause to butt in.

We rode out then, Angel and Fowler and me in the lead, followed by Cannon and the others. Ames, with his freshly stitched and bandaged scalp, was tucked into a cot. I left Joaquin and Dog with orders to watch over him.

We were within half a mile of the site of the ambush when Fowler called for a halt. He directed the miners to follow a trail that veered off down toward the creek. "What's up?" Angel wanted to know. "I thought you said they jumped you up on the main road."

"Did say that," replied Fowler tersely. "Reckoned you could go by where the mule belongin' to that Ames feller musta landed. See if you can salvage some of his things, whilst Andrew and me pick up the track up top."

I knew without being told that Fowler was trying to keep the miners from attacking the Indian camp. Led by Cannon, the prospectors were of a mind to shoot first and raise questions after. Such an attitude isn't healthy for those on the receiving end. It would be the shank of the afternoon in one more hour. If Fowler's device worked, the Angel's Campers might spend long enough gathering up the scattered supplies that it would then be time to head back.

There were few noteworthy clues on the high ledge above the trail. We found where the swarthy-faced attacker had tied his mount while he prepared the ambush and where he had used a redwood limb to tip over the rock to start the slide. Beyond that we found nothing to identify the race of the man. "I don't know, Andrew," Tor Fowler said. "Does this strike you as Miwok doings? I've fought plenty of Injuns in my time, but I never saw anything as bald-faced as this."

I agreed with him. "They must have known that an ambush of white men this close to a mining camp would bring destruction down on their heads, doublequick. Even if they weren't expecting any of us to survive, who else is there around to blame?"

"That's the point, ain't it?" he mused. "No matter who done it, the Injuns'll catch the blame."

"All the more reason for us to track down the real culprits," I said.

We started to follow the trail that we were certain would lead back to the site of Dog's encounter with the robbers. We were no more than a hundred yards along the ridge when the peaceful afternoon was shattered by a sound like a herd of buffalo crashing through the brush of the creek bed. Wild whoops and the explosions of gunfire followed close behind.

"Come on!" Fowler shouted, spurring his bay. "Someone's catching it!"

Across the slide rock we flew, sparks bursting from Shawnee's shoes as we clattered slantwise down the slope. I was practically lying along Shawnee's backbone to keep my weight back on her skidding haunches. I had the reins out at arms' length, like steering by the tiller of a sailing ship, but the fact is, I was relying totally on her instincts to get us through.

We swung sharply to the left, narrowly avoiding a drop of a hundred feet or more. Shawnee's hooves somehow found a ledge that was no more than a crack in the rock face. In between jolting gasps for breath, I found myself wondering who it was we were risking our necks for, and if they would even appreciate it should we come to grief on their account before reaching the bottom.

A flurry of gunfire up the canyon a ways told us of the ongoing battle. A flock of doves burst out of their roost in the cottonwoods at what was then eye level for Fowler and me. "Hold on, Andrew!" he called over his shoulder as he and the bay plunged ahead. I could not see past the body of his horse to know what he was warning me about, and perhaps it was just as well. We had run out of hillside, and the last of our headlong charge carried us through a dozen feet of air.

Shawnee took the jump in fine shape, landing in deep sand with scarcely a break in her gallop. Wheeling around like a cavalry squad on parade, Fowler and I set off toward the screen of trees and brush that obscured our view of the fight. I shucked the scabbard of the Allen. Out of the corner of my eye I noted Fowler draw his rifle as well. As we got closer, we heard cries of fear and shouts of rage mingled with the explosions.

Our swoop toward the conflict was cut short by a small dark-haired figure in buckskin and faded flannel that burst from the willows right under my nose. I saw an ax waving in the air, but as I brought the Allen to bear, Shawnee reared and spoiled my aim. The menacing figure jogged aside, making me hurry my sights. I had just drawn a bead again when Fowler's cry stopped me. "Don't shoot, Andrew," he yelled. "It's a woman!"

And so it proved. The slight form that scampered off into the brush and out of sight had a reedwork basket strapped to her back. Over the rim of the hamper, an infant-sized fist could be seen waving defiantly.

I grinned weakly and waved my thanks at Fowler. I wanted to think that even without his warning, my own senses would have prevented a mishap, but then I remembered that Shawnee's unexpected motion had also been needed to keep me from firing. I breathed a prayer of thanks, but the nearness of the tragedy made my stomach churn.

We charged on into the battle, fearful of what we would find, and found that the reality was worse than we feared. An unearthly keening had joined the other noises. It was a high-pitched wail that began at the level of a wolf's howl and went straight up to the screech of a red-tailed hawk.

The portion of the creek bottom toward which we rode was an island at a wetter season of year. At the time of which I write, it was a low knoll of cottonwoods and willows surrounded by a rocky plain through which ran a thin trickle of water. The hillock was ringed by Angel's Campers with their rifles cocked and steady on a small knot of Indians that had retreated to the clump of trees.

I've lived with Indians and I've fought Indians, but I never before saw anything so one-sided dignified with the word battle. A wounded Miwok man sat on the ground, hugging a bullet-shattered forearm and rocking softly with the pain. Another dead man was draped over a boulder. There were three bullet holes in his back. In his back!

The shrieking sound was coming from the throat of a Miwok woman who was huddled over the limp body of a small boy. A young Miwok woman and two children stood looking on, their eyes wide with fright.

At the moment we rode up, Cannon was saying, "What are we waiting for? I say we shoot 'em down and put a stop to their thievin' *and* that caterwaulin', the filthy savages." Without waiting for any agreement on the part of the others, he raised his Hall carbine to his shoulder.

Fowler never paused in the headlong rush of the bay. Without drawing rein the least bit, his gelding barrelled into Cannon's mount. It was a classic *golpe de caballo*, the strike with the horse, that would have done credit to one of Will Reed's vaqueros.

Cannon's arms went straight up and the rifle flew from his hands, the shot exploding into the air as it went. The black-bearded miner followed the carbine in flight, landing heavily on the river-rounded stones with a cry of pain.

A friend of Cannon's made to swing his revolver around to bear on Fowler, but I was ready for him. My lash flicked out and around his wrist, and soon after he joined his partner on the canyon's rocky floor.

"You'd both best lie there awhile," Fowler ordered, swinging his rifle around the group.

"And if the rest of you don't want to join them," I added, "you'd better keep real still."

"What is this?" Henry Angel said. "I don't get it. We come out here to catch the snakes that attacked you boys. We nab them red-handed lootin' Ames's supplies, and now you stick up for them. It don't make sense!"

"How do you know that this particular bunch of Indians ambushed us?" I asked.

"Just look!" spouted Cannon from his place on the ground. He abandoned caution in favor of rage. "They got their hands full of mining gear!"

The squaw who was standing dropped a tin pan as if it had turned blazing hot in her grasp. It clattered and banged on the rocks, but brought the wailing to a sudden stop. The woman with the dead child continued moaning, but softly.

I said, "You understand English? You speak it?"

"I speak," replied the woman who dropped the pan. "We find dead mule and no man around. We no kill."

"Pack of lyin' rats," Cannon announced.

"Friend," Fowler said, "I ain't gonna warn you again not to interrupt," and Cannon subsided.

"We no kill," the squaw repeated. "We find only."

"Where were you coming from before you found this?"

The woman gestured downstream. "We pick berries. Fill baskets. Go home."

I pointed toward a reed-carrying basket and motioned for her to upend it. As she obliged, several gallons of dark red berries spilled across the creek bed, blending into the dark red blood of the dead man.

"All right," Angel observed, "but that doesn't prove anything. They could still have caused the rockslide when they saw a way to get something more valuable than berries." Several of the miners nodded their agreement, especially Cannon.

I ignored this and continued to question the woman. "Did you see anything on your way here?" I asked. "Meet anyone?"

She thought for a minute, then said, "Two men. A mule, going toward valley."

"Indian?"

She shook her head no. "One Spanish, one white."

"So what?" Ames said. "You don't know that those two, if they really existed, had your animal. Loaded pack mules are all over these hills."

"Think hard," I urged the woman. "Did anything seem wrong with those two men?"

She looked puzzled at the question; then a light of comprehension widened her eyes. "White man's britches," she said. "Seat torn out."

I reached inside my shirt then. Retrieving the scrap of buckskin brought me by Dog, I held it aloft for all to see. One by one, the miners looked from the leather fragment to the woman holding her dead son. Cannon's friend hastily mounted up, and the five turned their mounts around and started up the trail toward home, leaving Angel and Cannon with Fowler and me and the Miwoks. Fowler gestured with his rifle for Cannon to pick himself up and get on his horse.

Fowler looked as stern as only a mountain man that was part grizzly bear could look. He stared pointedly at Cannon and Angel, then turned to study the Miwok man who was struggling to stand and the mother gathering up the body of her child. Angel did not miss the suggestion in Fowler's look. "We can help you to your camp," he said.

"No!" said the younger woman fiercely, gesturing with her fist at Cannon. "You not touch them!"

We four white men turned our horses then, riding away from that place of grief and cruel injustice. Fowler urged his bay up between Cannon and Angel. "Seems those 'savages,' as you call them, got a sight more dignity than you," Fowler observed. "She spit in your eye, didn't she?"

Cannon hawked and spat noisily. "Lousy vermin. Still shoulda kilt 'em. Teach the rest a lesson."

Fowler never looked over or gave any sign. He just unloaded a backhanded blow against Cannon's temple with a fist like a smith's hammer. The bearded man was again swept from his saddle, this time landing on his head. He looked around stupidly as his horse ran off toward camp. "Thought you'd say that," Fowler observed as we rode on.

Tor and I left Henry Angel behind to fetch Cannon's mount. Far up the trail we did not speak, yet I knew we were of like minds. Calaveras Canyon, which the old Spaniards had called *Skulls*, had certainly lived up to its grim name. The site of an ancient Indian battle, this place had been littered with human bones left to bleach in the sun. Like Calvary of old,

Calaveras had become the scene of a new crucifixion. A man and a child had been murdered, and the white man's law offered no punishment for the crime. To butcher a Miwok Indian for sport or target practice was no worse than shooting a bear. To kill an Indian suspected of thieving was considered a white man's duty!

"'Twas almost Eden when I first come here," Tor muttered at last. "If we live a while, Andrew, there won't be no more Injuns left for swine like Cannon to kill."

I nodded and followed Tor as he spurred his mount up the embankment and off the trail into the cover of the woods. Although we did not speak of it aloud, we felt the nearness of evil at our backs.

5

THERE WERE MORE remarks made in Angel's Camp of white men sticking up for the despised Digger Injuns than of the fact that two innocent people had been killed and another seriously hurt. If Fowler and I were not exactly shunned, nobody was overanxious for our company, either.

That suited us just fine. Ames was awake and feeling as well as could be expected for a man who had come within an inch of having his head split open like a ripe melon.

But they don't call Yankees "hardheaded" for nothing. Ames was up and around after only one day. He said that the inside of his skull was buzzing louder than his family's cloth mill back home. "Reckon you saved my life," he managed to remark to Fowler and me. "Ee-yup. I'm mighty grateful."

When Ames heard that our supplies had been stolen in the same attack made on him, he insisted that we share equally in his recovered provisions. We found ourselves outfitted once again, as good as before.

Ames was a trader in dry goods. He had been in the Kingdom of Hawaii for several years, operating an outpost of his family's business, when he heard about the California gold.

With typical Yankee shrewdness, Ames had recognized at once that the miners would only bring a limited amount of supplies with them. They would need to replace boots, clothing, and equipment, and they would want it from the nearest source they could find.

"You won't find me breaking my back, no sir," he said. "You boys will be bringing gold straight to me without me digging a lick."

Ames had come alone to the diggings with only a single mule load of supplies in order to get the lay of the land. He had a ship full of goods waiting in San Francisco for his word to freight them up into the hills.

"I'll snoop around here for a few days and look into the competition," Ames said, meaning Henry Angel's store. "Then we'll see. I might move on up a ways."

The creek banks around Angel's Camp were humming with the activity of mining. Fowler and I had to travel a day's journey farther upstream to locate a likely stretch of as yet unoccupied creek. We decided to commence prospecting there.

The first order of business was to stake our claim. At this time, the commonly agreed on rules for the Calaveras region allowed each miner to claim a space ten-feet square. We marked the corners of three adjoining squares, one each for Fowler and me and a third for Joaquin, by writing our names on scraps of paper nailed to posts along the stream bank. In appearance our claim was then a thirty-foot rectangle that extended ten feet in width up from the water's southern edge.

My claim, which was the farthest upstream, commenced just at the middle of a sharp bend in the stream. We had agreed for each man to examine the prospects of his own claim first; then we would concentrate on whichever square showed the most promise.

I filled my first pan with dirt from the bank and carried it to the icy water. Squatting down beside the creek, I swirled the water around and around, washing the mud and the lighter gravel over the side. When this had been done until only the heaviest material remained, I tilted the pan toward the sunlight and poked around in it with my forefinger.

"No chispa," muttered a disappointed Joaquin, looking over my shoulder. "No spark."

"Don't be too sure," I said. From the iron particles that remained I separated a heavy flake of material. I scratched it with my knife and it did not shatter; between my teeth it felt soft and not gritty. "It's gold, right enough," I announced. "I heard tell that this Calaveras gold was real dark, almost black."

That panful of dirt contained twelve flecks or bits of gold—scarcely enough to cover my fingertip with a button-sized circle of the precious metal, but this was still a good prospect, since the real pocket was not to be expected on the surface.

It took two days to dig down to bedrock, saving all the dirt that came out of that hole for later washing. When we hit a layer of quartz, we knew we had reached our limit.

Unlike Fowler's experience, there were no nuggets lying in the bottom of the ancient stream bed. We found a few pieces the size of kernels of wheat tucked into a crack in the quartz face, but nothing to get real excited about.

Resolving to see how the excavated dirt would pan out, we began to work through that chore next. We would then decide whether to continue working these claims or abandon them in favor of moving the search somewhere else.

Our first week of panning the heap of dirt brought us two ounces of the coarse, black flakes, or about thirty dollars' worth at the going rate. Not a fortune by any account, but not a bust either.

I reminded myself that I owned a herd of steers that I couldn't clear two dollars apiece for, if that, and five dollars for a day's work didn't seem half bad.

We didn't actually divide it up right then, of course. That gold went into the leather pouch that Tor Fowler still wore around his neck.

Panning is backbreaking, muscle-tearing, finger-numbing work. Hunkering down on your haunches for eight or ten hours with your feet slipping into a snow-melt stream is no Sunday social. Right off we saw that we needed to build a rocker.

Fowler felled a cedar tree and cut a round from it that we slabbed into passable planks. It wasn't that this was so altogether easy as it sounds—rather it was the anticipation that it would improve our gold-finding ability that made the work pass pleasantly.

A rocker looks for all the world like a baby's cradle, which is its other common name. The earth to be washed is loaded into a kind of hopper at the top. When water is poured over it, the gold-bearing dirt sifts through a crack down to a slanted board set with cross-bars called riffles to catch the gold. The curved runners on which the thing sets and an upright handle allow the whole device—water, mud, gold, and all—to be rocked from side to side. It is the back and forth motion of the water that separates the gold from the soil.

Fowler fitted the last of the whittled cedar pegs into the holes cut to secure the handle, then stood back to admire our creation. "Whew, Andrew," he observed. "It's a good thing this ain't really for no baby. No child would want to be rocked in this contraption! Why, he'd up and die of shame afore he'd let hisself be humiliated thisaway!"

I will admit that it was a touch lopsided. "Let's see how she works," I said. "Even an ugly old buggy perks up when it has gold fittings."

Three men is just the right number to work a rocker. One hauls the pay dirt, one lifts the uncountable buckets of water required to run through it, and the third keeps the cradle in motion. Fowler and me took turnabout working the rocker and hauling the water. Joaquin loaded in a shovelful of dirt every so often and cleaned the gold dust off the riffles and into our poke, so his part wasn't too tough.

It isn't that the cradle makes the work so much easier, it's just that you can sift your way through so much more dirt in a day's time. We ended our first month in the diggings with three hundred dollars of gold dust, a working system for proceeding, and an all-fired hankering for something to eat besides bean and jerky stew.

"Warm tortillas," Joaquin daydreamed aloud. "Pollo con arroz, chicken and rice like Señora Simona fixes at the Reed rancho. Strawberry jam . . ."

Fowler nodded his head at the recollection. "Mighty tasty," he agreed, "but I'd like to have that chicken fried and served up with a mess of biscuits. What say, Andrew? Do you favor the cooking of lower California or the lower Arkansas?"

"I approve of both your choices," I said, my stomach voicing its agreement. "But as for me, give me a piece of beefsteak."

Our imaginary feast was interrupted by an unpleasant, unexpected arrival. A horseman riding at top speed descended the bank of the stream across from us and splashed headlong into the creek. Dog jumped up, barking fiercely, his ruff raised stiffly above his shoulders.

The rider that clattered noisily into our camp was Patrick Dunn. He rode in with his revolver drawn and leveled in our faces. "Call off that wolf, Sinnickson," he demanded, "or I'll shoot him down."

We were nowhere close to our stacked rifles. I let my fingers creep down to the coiled whip hanging from my belt. Out of the corner of my eye, I saw Tor Fowler drop his hand from his knee to the top of the boot where two inches of knife hilt protruded.

At that tense moment, two more riders appeared at the back of our camp. "Not this time, Sinnickson. I told you there'd be other hands dealt. Move your hands up slowly and keep them in plain sight." It was Jack Powers. To the other man with him, Powers ordered, "Ed, get their weapons."

"Hold on there!" Fowler demanded. "Who are you, and what's this all about?"

"We're looking for a pack mule that belongs to Patrick here," Powers said. "It was stolen from him."

"Well, just open yore eyes, you no-good highbinder. Do you see a mule critter in this here camp?"

Powers grudgingly admitted that he did not. "But I know Sinnickson's type. Jew name, Sinnickson?" His ruddy cheeks glowed with a delighted sneer. "You'd figure a Heb for a sneak thief, right, boys?"

Fowler's fists clenched, and the line of his jaw tightened. From the look in his eye, I could tell he was fixing to remove the saddle from Powers' horse without having Powers get off first.

"Leave it," I said. "It's not worth getting shot over."

"Smart Jew-boy, huh?" Patrick Dunn laughed.

Patrick's brother Ed took my whip and Fowler's boot knife, then moved crabwise around our camp to the stacked rifles. He had a .50-caliber hogleg in his hand for protection against dangerous folks like us, but it seemed to me that he kept its muzzle and his attention focused on Dog. Dog was still bristled and growling low in his throat.

"Well, I guess we can't hang you for mule thieves today," Powers said, leaning heavily on the last word. "But we can't leave without correcting this unlawful claim."

"What's that supposed to mean?" I said.

Powers rubbed his gun hand through his swept-back silvery-gray hair. "I see you've illegally claimed more of this stream than you're entitled. How'd you ever think you'd get away with claiming three claims for only two men?"

"We've got three partners. One claim for each partner, just like the mining regs say."

Powers pretended to look around and scan the hillsides while Patrick Dunn laughed loudly. Ed joined in the laughter, but his had a nervous quality.

"Three partners? I only see two broken-down miners and one no-account half-breed boy. Don't you know that Injuns can't hold claims?"

"Joaquin worked his claim, same as us," I said.

Powers shook his head in mock sympathy. "Pity you don't get to town more often," he said. "There have been some changes made. I'll wager your claim isn't even registered properly."

"Registered!" Fowler exploded. "Our stakes are up, plain as day!"

"So they are," Powers noted. "Ed, Pat, take care of that." Patrick Dunn whooped and rode around the claim, ripping out our stakes and hurling them on our campfire. He threw a loop of rope around the rocker, then dragged it over on its side. Galloping a ways downstream, the bouncing and bumping cradle held its own till he ran it up against a boulder and it splintered to pieces.

So much rage and frustration boiled up in me then that the bitter taste of hot bile rose into my mouth. It felt like an

animal caught in a steel-jawed trap, to be taken unawares and
forced to stand by while our camp was destroyed. My face
must have shown the anger, for it was Tor's turn to caution
me. "Steady, Andrew," he muttered, "for the sake of the
boy."

Patrick Dunn proceeded to retrieve his loop, then dropped
it over our tent pole. Another whooping gallop and the canvas was ripped to pieces. Our belongings were scattered and
most ended up sunk in the stream.

Powers nodded his approval, while Ed Dunn looked on and
agitatedly fingered his revolver. When Patrick returned, he
made as if to toss his noose over Joaquin's head. Caution all
gone, I had my shout for Dog and leap for Ed's gun all
planned when Powers called it off.

"Leave him be, Pat," he said. Then to me he remarked, "I
guess this about evens the score, eh, Sinnickson?"

Ed threw whip, knife, and rifles in the creek, then mounted
his horse, and the three rode off up the stream. We watched
them out of sight, then set to gathering the demolished camp
into some kind of order again. All the time I was thinking how
Powers was right about this hand, but after this the game was
still far from over.

6

WE HAD INTENDED to work the claims until our supplies ran out in a few weeks. The encounter with Jack Powers and the Dunn brothers changed our plans. Beans and hardtack destroyed; precious cornmeal trampled in the mud. After putting our camp back into some kind of order, we surveyed the wreckage and decided that if we wanted to eat, we had to head for Angel's Camp pronto. Fortunately, we had not been robbed. We kept our gold dust in a two-quart canning jar tucked away in the hollow stump of an old oak tree on the bank of the creek. Every evening after dark we had made deposits at our "bank." Now we figured it was time for a withdrawal.

We divided three hundred dollars in gold dust equally between the three of us.

Tor hefted his share with satisfaction. "Beats herdin' cows, now don't it, boys? Let's see . . . at two dollars a hide it peers to me I'm carryin' fifty cattle in this here poke. Yessir, it shore do beat anythin' I ever seen b'fore!"

I had to agree with him on that. We had pulled more out of the Calaveras in one month than I could have made from my little herd in two years. Joaquin, who had worked as hard at the claim as a grown man, never imagined that he would possess so much wealth! One hundred dollars in gold would buy him passage on a schooner to Hawaii and a real education in the mission school. Schooling was the only way to answer ignorant bullies like Jack Powers and the Dunn brothers. One day, I explained to Joaquin, he might return to California as a man of learning. A judge, perhaps. Or maybe governor of the whole state. He could spit in the eye of any bigot and say his success began along a ten-foot stretch of Calaveras Creek!

The thought of overcoming skunks like Jack Powers fired the boy's imagination. Remembering the tales of Mr. Ames about Hawaii, he gazed far to the west, as though he could already see himself at home among the brown-skinned Sandwichers on their island. I resolved to speak with Ames on the matter of Joaquin's schooling at the first opportunity. Eagerly, the boy placed his poke in my care, asking only that he might have one pinch of the stuff to purchase a jar of jam when we returned to Angel's Camp.

Having been absent from Angel's Camp for a month, however, I had no idea just how much gold dust it would take to buy even a small jar of jam.

The place had sprawled out four times bigger than when we left. Canvas tents, fashioned from the sails of abandoned ships, sprouted like mushrooms on both sides of the creek. The streets were mud bogs criss-crossed here and there by logs with the bark still on them. Crudely lettered signs hung above the tent flaps, bearing the names of stores and saloons and cafes and even a barbershop. The tinkle of banjo music drifted up to the rise as we looked down in wonder at the transfiguration. I rubbed a hand over the coarse black beard that sprouted below my hawk's beak nose and eyed the huge oak barrel painted to resemble a fat barber pole.

"A shave," I said, remembering hot towels and clean lather of a distant life.

"Fried chicken." Tor tugged his long whiskers and cocked an eye at the ragged sign outside a ragged tent advertising HOME COOKING.

"Strawberry jam," cried the newly wealthy Joaquin, licking his lips and pointing straight to the big sign above the AMES DRY GOODS AND SUNDRIES. "Just like the kind Señora Reed makes!"

The waters of the Calaveras were brown and murky from the work and traffic of hundreds of men. The shantytown was hardly more than a pest hole, but to each of us it was a vision of civilization, comfort, and luxury. All of these things were to be bought for a price. As we were soon to discover, even small luxuries were worth their weight in gold!

The dry goods store of Mr. Ames was crammed into a tent created from the weathered canvas of a square-rigged ship. The ship was owned by the Ames Trading Company in Honolulu and had sailed to San Francisco stuffed full of merchandise and Hawaiian workmen. It was Ames's plan to dismantle the vessel and build a proper store from its timbers in San Francisco that winter. Meanwhile, a second schooner from the islands would keep the San Francisco company well supplied with Yankee broadcloth and all the goods the tribe of miners would desire. The tent in Angel's Camp was the forward outpost for what the little Yankee saw as a thriving empire of commerce. Three wagonloads of supplies had arrived the day before, and the tent was crammed with crates of merchandise stacked from floor to ridgepole. Miners crammed the space between the boxes, shouting at Ames for the price of blankets or boots or shovels.

Tor scowled in at the mob through the tent flap. "Looks to me like Ames is near to having a riot on his hands. Ain't so shore I'm up to a fresh brawl without a bite to eat first."

Joaquin grimaced as he saw two miners inside wrestling over a shovel. One had drawn a blade halfway from his belt when the two men were forcibly separated by an enormous dark-skinned Kanaka, whose bushy black hair brushed the canvas ceiling of the tent. I estimated that the Hawaiian was over six and a half feet tall and thick as an old oak tree. He made even my six-foot one-hundred-eighty-pound frame feel small. His features were coarse, and he scowled like a bouncer in a bawdy house. Such a savage face and enormous stature drove all thought of their quarrel from the minds of the two arguing customers. Both released the shovel and stepped back as if they had just met a grizzly bear face-to-face. At this moment Ames parted the crowd and appeared like King Solomon to resolve the matter. We remained outside the store and watched the event through the flap.

"Well done, Boki," Ames congratulated the Hawaiian, then raised his hands to the crowd, which now lapsed into respectful silence. "Now listen up," Ames instructed the men. "No arguments in my store or Boki here will crack your skulls and throw you out in the street. I run a respectable, law-abiding dry goods store. No guns, knives, clubs, or fists will be allowed. You want my merchandise, you'll act civilized."

"But that there is the last shovel!" cried a mud-caked miner from the back of the tent. "I been diggin' with my cook pot. When you gonna get more shovels in?"

"I grabbed that there shovel first," cried one of the grizzly combatants. "Then he come along and—" His hand returned to the hilt of his knife, and Boki snatched him up by the scruff of his neck. Before we could say howdy, Boki tossed that man out the tent flap. He flew by us and landed spraddle in the mud. It appeared that Boki was the law for the time being. Men shuffled and sniffed and looked down at the toes of their boots. I had seen such looks on the faces of guilty schoolboys caught smoking behind the barn.

"Well, gentlemen?" cried little Ames from beneath the shadow of his giant. "What's it to be? You get in line or Boki gives you the boot. There ain't a place between here and Boston has what we got to sell. The line forms there." He pointed at the tent flap and at us. His eyes lingered on us for a moment, and then his pinched face broke into a grin as the mob broke up and formed a line back out the tent and into the mud of the street. "Well, now!" he cried. "Well! Well! My friends! My friends!" He gathered us in even as his scowling customers shuffled into line. "You're back early by my reckoning. You struck it rich then? Come in to spend a little jack at my humble establishment?"

"We come to spend a little all right," I said in wonder at the scene before me. "Although it 'peers to me that you're the one who's struck it rich."

"A gold mine," he agreed, mussing the hair of Joaquin and thumping Dog on the head. "Anything a man could need right here. Everything a man could want . . . or nearly . . . if he's willing to pay for it." He nudged the toe of my ragged boot. "Three dollars for your road stompers go for forty dollars up here. Ee-yup. You in the market, Andrew?" His eyes glinted with amusement as I blinked back at him in astonishment.

"That's near half my poke!" cried Tor, clutching the little bag of gold dust in his coat pocket.

Someone mumbled behind me. "Ten dollars he charges for a fifty-cent shovel."

Then another surly grumble, "One dollar fer one onion. Figure that."

Ames cheerfully replied, "Onions all the way from the Sandwich Islands, lads."

"Mighty expensive sandwiches they make, too," Tor muttered.

Ames rubbed his hands together. "Well, lads," he said to us. "What'll it be? Seeing how you saved my life, I'll take you to the head of the line."

I figured that I had just enough to buy a sack of onions if that was what I had in mind. I shook my head, knowing that we would have to recalculate what provisions we could afford to buy.

Joaquin looked hopefully into the face of the storekeeper. "Please, señor. I have been dreaming of Señora Reed's strawberry jam. You have jam, Señor Ames? I have a dollar to spend."

Overhearing the child, someone called back, "An ounce of jam is an ounce of gold dust, kid. Ain't you heard the rules for half-breeds around here?"

Ames whirled around. "Who said that?" he demanded. "Boki! What lowdown skunk thinks he's going to set the prices in my store?"

Boki pointed down at a red-shirted fellow holding a sack of beans. "This one," Boki replied in a surprisingly soft, melodious voice.

"Beans you're buying?" Ames menaced. "Ain't you heard the price of beans for dirty-bearded fellows wearing red shirts has gone up? That'll cost you one pound of dust for every pound of beans. Put up or get out!"

With Boki to back him up, Ames could set his own prices. And if he wished, he could even choose to sell a quart of precious jam to a boy for a pinch of gold dust. This is exactly what Ames decided to do.

As the offended miner tossed down the sack of beans and stalked out, Ames growled, "He's one of Jack Powers' gang. Skunks, all of them. Even if he paid me a pound of gold for a pound of vittles, I'd rather not sell to the likes of him."

And so it was that we discovered that Ames and Angel's Camp had become unhappily acquainted with Jack Powers while we had been gone.

"Jack Powers is the very reason we've come into town early," I explained.

"Him and the Dunn brothers wrecked our camp." Tor eyed the retreating gang member. "We ain't et in a while."

At that, Ames left the store in the capable hands of Boki and two other Hawaiians and led the way through the mire to HOMECOOKING CAFE. Joaquin followed after, bearing his jar of strawberry jam.

The proprietor of the Homecooking Cafe was a rotund, heavy-jowled man, whose bald knob of a head was enclosed by a fringing thicket of bristling gray hair. He had a canvas apron tied high up across his chest, and while we approached the front of his establishment, he was transferring another layer of grease from his hands to the cloth.

Tor whispered to me over my shoulder, "Pay it no mind, Andrew. It don't appear that his cookin' has hurt him none!"

The owner beamed as he greeted us. "Welcome, gents. Mister Ames. Sit down, sit down."

We seated ourselves on a variety of what passed for chairs —two empty crates, the top half of a cracker barrel and an old trunk. Two rough plank tables ran the complete length of the tent and completed the dining arrangements.

"What'll you have?"

"Now yore talkin'," Tor said eagerly. "Fried chicken for me."

The man shook his head. "Sorry, I can't oblige. We ain't got no chicken."

"Biscuits?" asked Joaquin hopefully, waving the jar of jam.

The host of the Homecooking Cafe thrust out his lower lip
and folded his arms across the grease-stained apron. "Nope."

Fowler sounded a touch testy when he said, "Wal now, why
don't you just tell us what you do have 'stead of us guessin'."

"Beef or beans," was the response.

We three partners looked at one another while Ames
watched us with amusement. "No beans," I replied for the
group. "How's the beef?"

"Excellent choice! Four steaks, coming up." He gave Ames
a broad wink and departed toward the back flap of the tent.
As he passed through we could see a black cook tending a
steaming pot next to an open fire. A dressed beef carcass was
hanging just beyond the fire. "Mose!" the owner shouted at
his cook, "throw four more slabs on the grill!"

"Just like Mama used to make," Fowler observed wryly.

Despite the disappointing news about the menu, we were
pleased with the prospect of heartier fare than we had eaten
in weeks. I took some ribbing on account of my preference
being the only choice available, but it was all in fun.

The wait while our dinner was being cooked gave Ames a
chance to catch us up on the news of the camp. "Some Mexican fellas from down Sonora way found a seven-pound chunk
of gold and quartz. Figures to be worth five hundred dollars,
maybe more. How you three doing?"

I was a little chagrined when I answered. "We thought we
were doing all right, but after looking at the prices of
things—" I stopped so as not to offend Ames, but he only
grinned and said that he knew, and weren't the prices ridicu-
lous. I went on then, "Anyway, I guess we're making expenses."

"I told you that it was easier finding gold in miners' pockets
than in the streams hereabouts," Ames said forthrightly.
Then his face darkened. "But I sell honest goods. There's
many who deal in second-rate, cheap-john—weevily flour and
salt pork that would have gagged General Washington's men
at Valley Forge."

"Jack Powers, for instance?" I asked.

"Ah, Powers!" Ames almost spat out the name. "He sits in his tent gambling and scheming like a spider in a web. Make no mistake—his influence runs deep hereabouts. He's made a pile from the crooked card games he's staked and from watered-down Who Hit John in saloons that look to him for protection."

"Is he so hard to read that folks haven't got him figgered?" Tor asked. "Seems to me he'd be run outta most places."

Ames shook his head. "There's a class of men in the diggings who work one day and then go to hunting easier ways to fill their wallets. Powers caters to them . . . stakes them to drinks and meals in exchange for their support. He rallies them around causes he favors, like running foreigners off their claims over trumped-up charges so he can take them over and sell them to some greenhorn."

The tent flap gapped open again, and a heaping platter of sizzling beefsteak was propelled into the room by the smiling owner. The trencher on which the seared meat rested was a salvaged barrelhead, but little we minded that. The aroma that accompanied the sight of our meal set our mouths to watering and stomachs to rumbling.

The proprietor set the platter down with a flourish, and the plank table actually groaned under the weight. "That'll be an ounce," he said as we grinned at each other in anticipation, "*each*." Our grins turned to grimaces of consternation.

Fowler's eyes were fixed on the topmost steak, and when he spoke it appeared that he was addressing his words to the chunk of meat. "Fifteen dollars? That's highway robbery."

The owner of the Homecooking Cafe looked ready to snatch the serving dish back out of jeopardy when Ames spoke up. "It's all right, John. This meal is on me."

Smiles erupted on all our faces, including the host. "Mighty nice of you, Mister Ames, considering that you already supplied the beef."

"What'd he mean?" Tor asked after the owner had gone to greet some newly arrived customers. "Are you in the cattle business, too?"

I was eagerly slicing into my steak. I did not care who had raised the beef or sold it or cooked it. All I wanted to do was eat it. I noticed how dull my hunting knife was behaving and made a mental reservation to see to sharpening it.

"You might say I'm in the cattle business," Ames said. "I sold John a spare team of oxen after my load of provisions got here."

"You don't say," I mumbled around an especially chewy hunk of steak. I saw Tor's jaw muscles working away, and Joaquin seemed to be in particular concentration over his portion.

"Yessir," Ames went on, "at these jewelry prices for meat, I wished I could get my hands on a whole herd."

Fowler, Joaquin, and I all stopped mid-chew and stared at each other. "Do you," I mumbled, having to shift the load to the other side of my cheek. "You mean to say an old cow critter like this that was leather clear through his middle sells for fifteen dollars a steak?"

Ames nodded.

Fowler worked his quid of gristle around till it was safe to swallow, and then inquired, "What does that figger out to on the hoof?"

"Well, John paid me a hundred apiece for the team, but real beefstock would fetch more. Why? Do you boys know where you can get your hands on a herd?"

"Right here!" said Joaquin, bouncing up. "Señor Ames, Señor Andrew is a ranchero. He owns a herd *himself*."

"Could it be?" I wondered aloud to Tor. "Could we have had the makings of our fortune right under our noses all along?"

"And Don Will Reed," Fowler added. "Don't forget him. He'll be wantin' to throw in with us when he hears about this."

"But is it possible?" I wondered aloud. "Nobody's ever driven a herd up from southern California before. Not that I ever heard tell of anyway. Could we do it?"

Fowler looked me square in the eye and here is what he said, "How much you figure your herd is worth for hides?"

and then, "What's two hundred head times a hundred dollars each figger out to?"

Joaquin whooped and started dancing around the table chanting, "A hundred a head! A hundred a head!" Fowler joined him in an impromptu Virginia reel. The ruckus was so tremendous that John and the cook both hurried inside to see if we were tearing up the place.

7

I WAS PACING back and forth in front of the tent flap. My mind was a whirl of calculations: distances from one river crossing to the next, where we could find the best feed along the way, how many vaqueros we would need. A sudden flurry of noise from the street outside the Homecooking Cafe drew my attention.

Almost involuntarily I stepped through the canvas opening to see what was up. My thoughts were really three hundred miles away, so it took a few moments for what I was seeing to register with me.

Patrick Dunn was riding into town, and he had a prisoner in tow. The description is exact because the man, a tall fellow in South American garb, stumbled on foot at the end of a rope attached to Dunn's saddle. The prisoner's hands were tied together in front of him, and he fought to keep his balance in the slimy mud of the roadway. Patrick's brother Ed followed along behind, leading a pack mule.

Apparently the capture had not gone altogether smoothly. Patrick Dunn's left eye was swollen shut, and Ed had what looked like a knife slash across his right forearm.

A circle of babbling and angry-sounding miners accompanied the trio, and when Patrick pulled up in front of a gambling tent, the crowd flowed around the scene like a tide of muddy flannel. As the hubbub grew, more prospectors dropped their tools or their liquor bottles or their cards and joined the audience.

Patrick Dunn got off his horse and called into the gambling establishment for Jack Powers. "Mister Powers, sir. We caught him."

Dunn spoke as respectfully as if he were addressing a judge in a New York courtroom. Here in the Sierras, the judge was self-appointed and his bench was an overturned crate marked *Johnson's Baking Soda*. His honor's muddy boots rested in the churned Calaveras clay, and the heavily bearded spectators in their worn dungarees hardly made for a respectable legal setting.

In contrast, the prisoner at the bar was a tall, haughty-looking man. He was wearing a dark brown woolen poncho, banded across the ends with stripes of blue and yellow. The serape was secured around his middle with a six-inch-wide leather belt.

Below the flat-crowned, stiff-brimmed hat were the features of a man more accustomed to giving orders than of being ordered about. He looked more capable of sitting in judgment on all the rest of the assembly than the other way around.

The man's appearance was bruised and puffy, and a once straight nose was canted to the side. His cheeks were stained with gore, and his wrists were raw and dripped blood from the hemp cords.

The contrast between the florid-faced Bowery toughs and this man of proud bearing was ludicrous in the extreme. But the circumstances themselves were no laughing matter.

In the diggings, even petty thievery was not tolerated. A first offense, no matter how slight, was punished severely. The theft of money or mining equipment merited fifty lashes or branding or disfigurement of the ears or nose. Second-time offenders were summarily hanged.

The rules were even tougher for the theft of a horse or pack animal. All a man's possessions and, in fact, his wherewithal to survive in the wilds were transported on the back of some four-footed beast. It meant that death was the standard punishment for being caught once.

I moved closer so as to hear the proceedings.

"Good work, Pat," Powers praised his lieutenant. "Caught him with the evidence, eh?"

"Yessir, Mister Powers. This greaser was actually leading the mule when we caught up with him. Put up a fight too and tried to stab Ed there with a knife."

The tall prisoner addressed Powers in refined Spanish. "If you are the alcalde, señor, you will instruct these ruffians to release me at once! I am Guillermo Navarro, lately of Buenos Aires. My family fled to Chile to escape the tyrant Rosas. I am in California to recoup—"

"Patrick," Powers sneered, "shut that gibberish up, will you?"

"Gladly," Dunn said, and he cuffed the still-bound Navarro with a backhand across the mouth. The unexpected blow staggered the prisoner and silenced him, but his eyes blazed with a fierce hatred.

"Just a minute," I said, shouldering my way between two stocky miners. "Does he get a say in this or no?"

Powers looked mighty displeased at the interruption. I believed then and still do that he actually understood some of Navarro's words. But with the Spanish-speakers cowed into silence, Powers anticipated no opposition to watching the scene play out according to his own script.

Looking me over thoughtfully, Powers remarked, "Choosing to side against your own kind again, are you, Sinnickson? A man could get a bad reputation doing that too often around here." A rumble in the crowd told me that the story of the attack on the Miwoks had changed some in the retelling.

Powers went on. "Or maybe thieves of all colors *are* more *your* kind, eh, Sinnickson?" He laid a lot of stress on my name when he pronounced it.

"Just hear him out," I said. "This man comes from a wealthy, high-class family in his homeland." To Navarro I said, "Go ahead, señor. I will translate for you."

Navarro inclined his head in a nod of appreciation and resumed his speech. "I came to California to recover my family's lost fortune. When I located a claim and established my camp, I discovered that I needed cash for supplies more than I needed a mule. So I sold the mule to—" Here he stopped and pointed at Patrick Dunn. I explained to the crowd what had been said so far.

"He sold it to me all right," growled Dunn, "but how did he get the mule back again? Ask him that."

I put this question to Navarro, who shrugged and replied, "When I awoke yesterday, the mule was grazing again near my camp. He must have broken free and returned to the last place that he regarded as home."

When I translated this, there was a general stir in the crowd. Nothing definite, just a clearing of throats, shuffling feet—that sort of thing.

I judged that a number of the onlookers were inclined to believe Navarro's story. What is more, his calm manner while telling his side spoke well for him. For a man facing death, he looked neither shifty nor cringing. He spoke uprightly, like one with truth on his side.

Powers scowled. It was not in his interests to have his bully-boys lose face in front of the miners. To Patrick Dunn, Powers said, "How was the mule secured when you had him last?"

"Tied up tight to a picket line and hobbled."

"And what did you find in the morning?"

"The hobbles were slashed off and the lead rope was cut!"

"Hold on!" I said. "Does anyone else vouch for this?"

"Are you calling me a liar?" Patrick roared. "Taking a stinking greaser's word over mine!"

Here Powers chose to appear judicious, even fair. "It's a good question, Patrick," he said. "Can anyone support your story?"

"Sure," Dunn bellowed. "My brother saw it, same as me. Ain't that right, Ed?"

Ed Dunn looked at his boots and mumbled something that no one could hear.

"What was that?" Powers demanded. "Speak up."

Talking quickly, as if in a hurry to get it over with, Ed said, "It's the truth." He shot Navarro a momentary look that had emotions I could not read, then went back to staring at his feet. He rubbed his left hand over and over his wounded right arm.

"Hand the greaser!" shouted a voice to my left.

"Stinkin' foreigners makin' off with all our gold and stealin' too!"

"What are we waitin' for? Hang him now!"

"String him up!"

"Wait!" I yelled. "How do you know—" Then I stopped, since I could not make my voice heard over the crowd.

I laid hold of my whip handle. I figured I could clear a space around Navarro long enough to buy him some time.

A calloused grip caught my wrist and yanked my hand away from the lash. The fiercely bearded face of the man named Cannon thrust into my own. "Not this time, Sinnickson!" he roared, then something crashed into the back of my head, and I dropped like a stone.

How long I lay unconscious in the filth of the Angel's Camp street, I don't know. Not long perhaps, for they told me later that what followed took only a minute or two at most.

When I woke up, my head was ringing like two dozen blacksmiths were hammering inside it. When I started to stand, the best I could manage was to get up on one elbow.

In front of me, not twenty yards away, dangled the lifeless body of Guillermo Navarro. He was hoisted into eternity at the end of a rope slung over an oak limb. All around the street was deserted. Even Powers and his vermin had disappeared.

Joaquin came running to me, followed by Fowler and, more slowly, Ames and Boki. "Señor Andrew," Joaquin gasped, "are you all right?"

"Just help me up," I slurred. My next look went to Fowler. I wanted to ask him where he had been, why he had not come to help. He saw and answered my unspoken questions.

"I'm awful sorry, Andrew," he said, biting his words off short. "This big feller held me back." He stabbed his thumb at Boki's massive girth. "He grabbed me from behind and sat on me."

I gave Boki a look of anger and reproach, but it was Ames who answered for him. "Don't be blaming Boki, Andrew," he said. "I told him to keep Tor back, and I held on to the boy myself. Yessir, and a mighty good thing too. If you three had interfered, they'd have hanged all of you, sure."

8

THE GROUND WAS pocked with places where prospectors had dug in search of gold, then abandoned. Heaps of brown earth and broken rocks made the clearing look as if it were a colony of giant ants instead of a graveyard. Soil barren of gold was the only ground fit for burying the dead miners of the Calaveras gold fields.

Wood planks were too precious to use for building a coffin, and so we cut down the body of Guillermo Navarro and wrapped him in a red woolen blanket for burial. He was carried to his makeshift grave on the shoulders of half a dozen of his countrymen. Only another dozen Spanish speakers joined the solemn procession up the hill. Tor and I followed behind with Joaquin. Ames, who provided the shroud, came after with Boki. There were no other mourners. Those who might have come under different circumstances were too frightened by what they had witnessed to associate themselves with the proud and noble Navarro even at his graveside.

"I assume he was a Catholic gent," said Ames as they laid Navarro's body in the damp hole.

There was no priest for a hundred miles. The sad fact that the dead man would be launched into eternity without a decent burial distressed each of his comrades. They looked sadly from man to man and asked who would say the proper words for their friend. There was no one to speak. None who knew how to pray. There was not a copy of the Good Book among them. Hats in hand they simply gazed over the rim of the grave at the body.

I understood their language well and explained to Ames and Boki the problem. "Easy enough to cut him down and put him in the ground, but there isn't a one of them who knows what to say. No Scriptures to read from, I reckon."

Tor furrowed his brow. "It ain't fittin' a feller to git hisself hung without reason and then can't git hisself buried proper on the same day. You go on, Andrew. Say somethin', why don't you? You know the words in the Good Book. Go on and say what you know about it."

I had indeed gotten my own schooling fresh out of reading the Good Book. I had not had any primer except Matthew, Mark, Luke, and John. As a child I had hated memorizing scriptures every day, and I had resented the message those words had taught. But I was grown now. Sadder and wiser from living in a world such as this. Long since I had learned that nothing was certain in life from one moment to the next, and that the only thing I could truly count on were those words I had been forced to learn as a child. Yet I hesitated to speak. After all, Navarro was not my companion. I had never met him before the hour of his death. What could I say?

The question was answered for me. Tor stepped up and nodded to the small assembly. He spoke in the Spanish language. Truth to tell, his Spanish was much more refined than when he spoke in his own tongue.

"My friends. We are new to your small circle, but in our hearts we are one with you in this tragic hour. Great injustice has happened here, and how are we to answer to it?"

"We have no priest, señor," cried a short man dressed in a poncho similar to that which Navarro had worn. "For us there is no justice. They killed Guillermo only because they wanted his claim and he would not sell it."

"This is true," enjoined another. .

There were nods of agreement all around.

The man in the poncho continued. "We are simple men. Guillermo Navarro was a great man among us in our homeland. What can we say to put his soul at peace? If it was one of us in that grave, he would know the words even without a priest. He once studied for the priesthood but married instead. He is . . . was . . . the father of three young sons. What can we say? Bad men have done this thing to a good man. Where is there justice? Where is God that He would allow such a thing?"

"Well, Andrew?" Tor questioned me. "You know the Book backward and forward. Can you speak to this?"

"It isn't my place," I replied in English.

Tor did not accept my answer. He put a hand on my shoulder, then addressed the others. "Here is one American who tried to stop the lynching of your friend. He is a learned man and perhaps can speak the words of a priest if you permit—"

A chorus of "Sí! Sí! Tell us the words, señor!" erupted from the company while I frantically searched my heart for some answer.

After a time, the group fell silent. Wind scraped the treetops and made a hushed, whispering sound. I looked at the red shroud and then at the rugged hills of the Calaveras, and I prayed that the good Lord would speak not only to the men around me, but also to my own bitter heart as well.

"This place is called Calvary," I began in Spanish. "Named after a place where long ago the one truly innocent man in all the world was murdered." It was cool, but beads of sweat stood out on my brow. I switched into English, for my memories of Scripture flowed better that way, while Tor translated my words for the others. "Seems to me that Jesus who died on Calvary knows just what happened here today. Seems He experienced some of the same as Guillermo Navarro here at the hands of a mob. Folks accused Jesus of things He was not guilty of. Hired guns were paid to bring false testimony against Him. He was tied up and beaten. He was paraded through the streets. His friends were afraid to speak for Him . . . afraid of dying themselves. . . ."

At this a sob erupted from the man in the poncho. He cried out the name of his friend and dropped to his knees on the mound of earth beside the grave. "How can you forgive me, my friend? I should have fought! I should have died with you! Oh, I am a coward! A coward!"

There were others among the group who wept silently and reflected on their own fear and failure. I remembered Peter who had cursed and denied he even knew the Lord, and for just a moment I glimpsed the true meaning of the first Calvary. My own words were not enough.

"It has always happened that men are full of death and darkness. We know the kind of lust that justifies murder and the kind of fear that keeps us from standing up for what is right. We who stand here alive are responsible for the death of an innocent man. No. I do not speak of Navarro. I speak of the One at whose feet Guillermo Navarro now bows. I speak of Jesus, The Innocent, who died at Calvary because your sins and my sins shouted across the ages, 'Crucify Him! Hang Him from a tree!' "

Tears flowed from the eyes of the men as Tor repeated this.

"I have failed!" cried Navarro's friend. "What can I do? What?"

"Remember what Jesus said as He died: 'Father, forgive them, for they know not what they do.' He was thinking of this moment when He spoke those words. He was seeing me and you. He was watching the men who hanged Navarro. . . . His friends took Him down and buried Him. They mourned for three days, but then Jesus rose from the dead. He is still alive. He says that one day every knee shall bow and every tongue confess that He is Lord. . . . Those who have loved Him . . . like Guillermo Navarro . . . will see heaven. Those who have denied Him, who have not asked forgiveness for their sins, will wake up one day in hell. All the gold in Calaveras Canyon will not save them. One day they will be dust like your friend, but their eternal souls will wish that it was they who died this day instead of this innocent man. This I believe. The Lord is merciful to those who love Him. His eyes see all things. Pity the men who have done this. Rejoice for Guillermo Navarro, for his place in eternity is forever established. His battle is fought and won and finished on Calvary."

We sang a hymn then and prayed some. Each man knelt and asked forgiveness for their failures and many sins. Each left that barren, desolate place with something new born in his heart. We were forgiven. We somehow had a glimpse of Christ's death for us on faraway Calvary. There was much in my own heart that was forever altered on that terrible day. I knew I would never forget the grief that an innocent man was lynched before my eyes. Something in me cried, "Never again!" No. As long as I had breath in me, I would not stand and see another Calvary. . . .

9

THE AROMA OF sage and autumn oak leaves mingled with the scent of sea air. As we rode across the vast Santa Barbara rancho of Will Reed, Shawnee seemed to recognize each steer and heifer of my herd. She nodded at the black, slat-sided, long-horned beasts as if to greet them. Perking her ears and nickering softly, she let me know that she was pleased to be home again; pleased to be in familiar pastures with the prospect of doing what she was born to do. As for Dog, he seemed to agree with my sharp little mount. There was a spring to his step as we passed by the herd. His mouth was open in a dog-smile that made Joaquin laugh with pleasure.

"Look, Señor Andrew!" the boy called. "Dog smiles at Señor Toro." He pointed at the rangy steer as the critter raised its head from the dry grass and eyed Dog suspiciously. "And Señor Toro remembers Dog nipping his heels, I think. He seems not too happy that his shaggy master has come back from the gold fields!"

Tor hooted. "Gold on the hoof, Andrew. Reckon that ol' Toro ain't gonna be none too happy when he figgers out Dog is takin' him north to be et up!"

"We just won't tell 'em till it's too late," I enjoined. I did not say so, but it did feel mighty fine seeing those old familiar hides again. Like my horse, I knew I was not born to spend my life grubbing for gold in an icy-cold stream. Herding cattle was something I knew. I had done it when my only prospect was to make two dollars a hide for shoe leather. Now I looked out across the Santa Barbara hills and saw my fortune.

My herd mingled with that of Will Reed's. Since I had purchased them from the Reed rancho, many of my heifers bore Will's leaning R brand. I had added two notches to the right ear of each as well as my own Lazy S brand. Will had given me a good price on those heifers, and I hoped now to return the favor. Had he heard of the hungry miners of the Calaveras? Had he looked out over his thousands of cattle and imagined the worth of his stock? Such a vast herd could feed every one of the prospectors in the north this year and for many years to come.

Tor tugged his beard thoughtfully as he eyed the grazing beasts of the hillsides. "Andrew," he ventured cautiously. "You ain't got but two hunert cattle. Now that's more'n I got, which makes you a rich man."

"We're partners, Tor. Didn't you come looking for me when you heard about the gold strike?"

"It didn't exactly work out the way I figgered."

"Sure it did. We just found a different sort of gold. We're partners, and there's the end of it."

He nodded slowly. "What are we fixin' to do after we sell this bunch? I mean . . . they're fine fer a start. But I don't fancy bein' a rancher for a month and then goin' out of business."

I had spent the miles considering this very problem and had come up with a plan. "I've got it all figured out, partner," I said as we topped the rise and the white frame home of Will Reed came into view below us.

At first glance the place seemed exactly as it had when we left it. The two-story white New England-style home seemed out of place in the midst of the brown, oak-studded valley. I had heard once that Will had seen a picture of just such a house when he was a young man. After his marriage to Francesca he had ordered every plank, nail, and window from Boston and had them shipped around the Horn. Will Reed was a man who put muscle and action to his dreams. I hoped that he would do the same when he heard my plan.

The rubble of an old adobe cookhouse lay where it had fallen during the quake of '46. Smoke rose from the chimney of the new wood-frame cookhouse, and we caught the scent of bacon on the breeze. Tor raised his face to the aroma and patted his belly. "Been dreamin' of Simona's bacon and biscuits. I'd of given a bag of gold dust just for a bite of her cookin'!" He urged his mount to a slow canter down the gently sloping lane.

The sun glinted on the red hair of two young men as they strolled out of the barn and looked toward our dust.

"By the color of their hair, that'll be two of Will's boys, I reckon," Tor remarked as I rode at his side. "He's got hisself a whole litter of red-headed younguns. I ain't met but a few since most is in Hawaii at school. These'uns must be just returned."

At this information, Joaquin's face brightened. He leaned forward in his saddle as though to look more closely at the two Reed brothers. I lifted my hand in greeting. A tentative wave replied. As we came nearer, I saw that the older brother was perhaps fifteen or sixteen years old. The younger was little more than Joaquin's age—twelve or thirteen. They could not have finished their term at the mission school in Hawaii. Why, then, had they come home to California? I felt a vague sense of uneasiness at that thought. Had some family tragedy come upon the peaceful rancho in our absence? Was Will all right? Francesca?

Truth to tell, the rancho seemed too quiet. Normally the barns and corrals were a swarm of activity. Vaqueros came and went with unbroken regularity. The only people in sight this morning were the two brothers, who eyed our approach with evident suspicion.

"Where is everyone?" I wondered aloud.

"It ain't Sunday. Ain't in church," Tor responded, scanning the hills and herds beyond. He pointed toward two vaqueros on the rise bringing in strays. Weeks before, there would have been a dozen hanging around the cookhouse waiting for the dinner bell.

"Somethin's up, Andrew," Tor said. "Mebbe this ain't gonna be as easy as we figgered."

There was an odd, deserted air about the place. Too many cattle. Not enough vaqueros. I remembered the tales we had heard of the sailors deserting their ships and leaving them to rot in San Francisco Bay while entire crews struck out for the gold fields. Could that be happening here as well?

At that instant, the tall, muscular form of Will Reed appeared in the opening of the barn. His eldest son, Peter, joined him a moment later. I knew Peter well from the days of the Bear Flag revolt. Nineteen years old now, Peter was as tall as his father and as strong as a grizzly. He recognized my piebald horse instantly and shouted my name.

"Andrew!"

Will laughed at the sight of us, as though he had known all along that we would be back soon. We were a grubby-looking bunch. The best bath we had managed was a dip in the Rio Bravo three days before.

"Home from the gold fields so soon?" Will greeted us with an edge of amusement in his voice. "Struck it rich already, have you?"

Interest sparked on the faces of the younger brothers. They eyed us with open curiosity.

"What I want to know, Will Reed," Tor grinned and eyed the smoke from the cookhouse chimney, "we ain't missed breakfast, have we?"

One platter was heaped high with fried eggs; a mountain of bacon was piled on the other. Fresh melons, warm tortillas, butter, and strawberry jam were all washed down with cool buttermilk and coffee with thick cream.

We ate the feast as though we had not eaten anything at all since we left. Simona cocked a disapproving eye at Tor as she placed another plate of eggs in front of him. His mouth was too stuffed to say thanks, and he grunted like a hog at the trough.

Simona scowled at Tor and opened her mouth as if to scold him, but Francesca silenced her with a stern look. "Our guests will be needing more bacon, Simona. See to it, por favor."

I always said that Francesca Reed was a first-class lady. She ignored the fact that we seemed to have forgotten our table manners, but all the while she kept her sons eating proper by just raising an eyebrow at the three of them. Napkins in place, silverware held just so; they said their "please and thank you, ma'am" and "will you pass the butter" like proper gentlefolk, while we stuffed our grizzly faces. Peter, James, and John they were called, and they were just as polite as apostles, too. Will and Francesca kept them from asking questions until we three were working on our second plateful of food. Joaquin wiped his mouth on his sleeve and blew his nose on his napkin.

"Mother?" John muttered in disgust, as if he did not care to share breakfast with the half-starved, half-breed boy across the table from him. The thought crossed my mind that I had neglected the boy's upbringing in some ways. I was about to send Joaquin out to eat in the cookhouse when Francesca intervened.

"You have had some great adventures in the gold fields, Joaquin?" she asked kindly. Her sons leaned forward attentively, seeming to forget Joaquin's ill manners.

The boy talked around his mouthful of eggs and babbled on about the first gold dust he had panned from the Calaveras. "Plenty of gold, Señora Reed," he said. "But no eggs. You see? The miners are paying one dollar in gold dust to buy even one small egg. I have eaten three weeks of gold dust this morning," he added happily.

"This is true?" Francesca turned to me.

"Yes, ma'am. One dollar for an egg. And a stringy steak is worth a whole ounce of gold," I explained. Tor mumbled confirmation.

"Are they all as hungry as you, then?" Will was amused. "I'm not surprised. A man can't eat gold dust, can he?" He nodded his head at his sons as though he had been telling them this before we brought our tales of hunger and hardship home. "Like I said this morning, boys, every vaquero who lit out of here will be back soon enough. Won't take them long. You'll see. Give them a few weeks scrounging around in the cold water and nothing to eat but hardtack and grizzly bear meat . . . they'll wish they could get their hands on a Leaning R steer."

"Ah-ha!" Tor and I interrupted at the same instant.

"The very thing we came to speak to you about, Will!" I cried, mindful that the subject had come first from him.

Will nodded, not yet comprehending my meaning. "I'll wager you've met up with more than one of my men up there. Seventy-five of the best vaqueros in the country . . . two thirds of my men . . . just bolted one night and left us short-handed during branding time. I'll not wish them luck, but when they come crawling back, I'll put them back to honest employment. Feed them and—"

"Feed them!" I cried, perhaps too eagerly. "The very thing!"

It was then that I unfolded my great plan for feeding the hungry miners of the gold fields. They were paying real gold for overcooked cart oxen. What would happen if they laid eyes on the Leaning R brand of Will Reed coming up the trail?

Will let me go on through two more cups of coffee and then jerked me back to reality. "A thousand head, Andrew? Three hundred miles through the tules and the rivers of the big valley?" He shook his head. "It sounds difficult, but possible . . . except for one small detail."

Had I left something out? "What is it?"

"There are no vaqueros left to help you drive the herd." He gave a slight shrug. "My sons have come home from school to help me here on the rancho. There are perhaps two dozen other vaqueros who did not desert. Most have families. They have been on the rancho for several generations. I can't go myself, you see." He gestured toward Francesca, whose baby was due any time. "We cannot spare any more men."

It was Peter who drew himself up and challenged his father's reasoning on this point. "But, Father, if we take one thousand head to the north, that will be one thousand less we have to tend here at the rancho. Could you not spare a few of us for such an enterprise?"

"A few of us?" Will glared down his nose at Peter.

The younger brothers jumped in. "Yes, Father! We can do it! The branding is finished! We managed all of that short-handed, didn't we?"

I had not spoken of the lawlessness of the gold camps. No word of the murders or lynchings had been mentioned. Nor had the name and evil dominion of Jack Powers been raised. Somehow, however, Francesca Reed sensed that there was much more yet untold of our story. She raised her chin defiantly to her sons. "Your father needs you here," she insisted. "That is all that I shall say on the matter. You are just children. You cannot go to such a place."

John set up a gruff protest. "Children!" he scoffed. "Look at him!" He pointed at Joaquin, who suddenly became a hero. "He is younger than I! He has been there and back! He has a gold claim on the Calaveras River! He has been a partner to Señor Andrew and Señor Tor! Do not call us children, Mother!"

Silence at the table. Will cleared his throat. "I reckon I was a lot younger than Peter when I set out to come west." He narrowed his eyes in thought. "It was the stuff to make a man of me."

"Will?" Francesca warned, seeing the wheels turning in his mind. "They are not you. Peter is older. Yes. But James and John are . . ."

"Good hands," Will finished. "And I reckon such an adventure might come to a happy conclusion for them were they to ride at the side of Andrew and Tor. And there is great fortune to be made, even if it is only half as much as Andrew tells us." He turned to me. "I get two dollars a hide for my stock. Ten thousand head are grazing on my rancho. I will send one thousand to the north and split the profit with you and Tor. We can spare Peter, James, and John, and I'll find vaqueros to make a dozen hands for the drive. What do you say?"

He put out his hand as the boys whooped and Francesca looked daggers at all of us. In this way the deal was set. In our jubilation, we could not guess that the misgivings of Francesca Reed held real portent of the danger we were to face in the coming weeks.

10

WILL REED CHOSE seven of his remaining vaqueros to accompany his sons and us north. They were not selected because of great skill, he explained, but because they were single men. There were no wives or children to leave behind in their journey.

Were they loyal? Men we could count on? To this Will shrugged his shoulders and replied that these had come to the rancho after nearly every other vaquero had vamoosed at the first rumor of gold. If that was loyalty, then he supposed they were faithful as old dogs.

They were also as mangy looking as old dogs. A scruffier-looking lot I had seldom seen. Alzado, who seemed to tell the others what to do, looked mean enough to top a grizzly bear in a "Who's Uglier" contest. One look at the long knife stuck in his boot top made me rub my throat and think a while about sleeping real light on the journey.

"You need anything done," Will said confidently, "just ask Alzado."

Five other vaqueros—Rodriguez, Garcia, Ramos, Sanchez, and Ortiz—were a close second in appearance and smell to Alzado. The last man on the crew was named Gomez. He was softer than the rest, dressed somewhat cleaner, and bowed and smiled a lot to Will, his sons, and now to Tor and me as well.

"Pure toady," Tor muttered as Gomez disappeared around the corner of the barn. "Makes me want to wipe my boots off, he does. Give me a tobacco-spittin' grasshopper like Alzado over that smooth, puffed-up toad any day." He shook his head. "Truth to tell, I ain't real sure of any of these fellers,

Andrew. I say we take the Reed boys an' you an' me an' Joaquin, and leave these 'uns behind."

I considered the proposal, but a thousand head of cattle meant that we needed more than two grown men and four boys to handle the drive. I reminded Tor of the fact that these seven had remained on the rancho and not jumped ship like their compadres. Tor did not seem comforted by this fact all the same.

It took a week to gather the herd and cut out the young heifers from the steers. Will was not overeager to sell off breeding stock. A wise decision. Keeping his heifers here in the south meant fewer calves in the north. If this was to be a truly profitable enterprise, he said, we had to consider such matters.

All in all, the herd was a much handsomer-looking lot than our vaqueros. Those cows smelled a mite better too, but we put our doubts aside and after a long benediction from the mission priest, we headed out of Santa Barbara.

On the advice of Will, we did not head straight north along the King's Highway that linked the string of missions along the coast. That route was crawling with highwaymen, he told us. Thieves and cutthroats who paid homage to Jack Powers were thick along that way. Even if we managed to drive the herd past them, no doubt word would reach Powers that a thousand head of cattle were moving north on the coast. If the bandit king ever put two and two together, Will rightly said, the herd would be stolen and we would be lucky to escape with *our* hides, let alone the cowhides.

For this reason we chose to drive the herd over the mountains and straight up through the marshy San Joaquin Valley. It was a more difficult journey, to be sure, but the country was inhabited by only a few remaining bands of Yokut Indians. Gentle folk, the Yokuts would pose no threat to us. Tor and I had often remarked how many of them had died off from white man's diseases and the malarial mosquitos brought from the north by French trappers. Taking our herd to the gold fields through the Central Valley might make for a more difficult trip, but at least we would not have to fight men as

well as the elements. It was our hope that our arrival in the
north would be met by great amazement and hungry miners
with pockets filled with gold!

I've never been one to get the wind up easily. I'm not superstitious, nor does the night breeze sighing in the cedars
give me the "williwaws," as Tor Fowler would have said. Still,
the experience of our first night on the cattle drive did provide ample reason to think that things were not going to be
smooth.

One day out of the comforts of Santa Barbara, we were
pushing the herd into the narrow defile of Gaviota Pass. The
"Canyon of the Seagulls" had come to the world's attention
two years earlier, since it was there that the Californios had
laid an ambush for Colonel Fremont. You can bet my
thoughts went back to those days, because Tor, Will Reed,
and I had each had a hand in preventing the success of the
trap.

Anyway, on this occasion, with a thousand head of cattle
and a largely unknown group of men, I had little time to dwell
on past history. Gaviota was still a wild place, with a primitive,
dangerous feel to it. Its rocky canyons and steep, narrow trail
were favored by outlaws, renegades, and grizzly bears for the
waylaying of unwary travelers.

We rolled the herd up for the night into a blind arroyo. We
had not pushed as far as I would have liked, but Tor reminded
me that cow-critters and men alike both need a little time to
settle into a routine. The first passage had to convince both
the herd and the vaqueros that it was easier to keep walking
forward than to get punished for standing and bellowing to go
home.

I posted the first two night herders with instructions to call
their relief in two hours. We could have kept more men on
watch together, but with the drive all bedded down and
placid, there seemed no reason to give up more sleep.

I've heard it said that the toughest watch is the one just
before dawn, but in my experience, this is not so. The anticipation of the first glint of gray light along the eastern rim of

the world always seemed to sharpen my senses—watching for it, you see.

For me, the hardest part of the dark hours is between two A.M. and four. Seems like every sound is magnified and every worry too. You keep thinking about how far off the daybreak is, and what you most want is to get next to the fire and sleep. There must be something to it, because Pastor Metcalfe always got called out in those hours to attend some poor old soul's shuffle off this mortal coil.

Which is why I assigned myself that shift on purpose. The three Reed brothers took the first watch. They were fast asleep beside the fire when Tor shook me awake at two by the set of the Big Dipper. "Everything all right?" I asked.

"Sure, nice an' quiet. Not even a breeze stirrin'," he said, but with an added comment left hanging in his voice.

"But what?"

"Can't put my finger on it exactly. Peter said there was somethin' in the air durin' his watch. Jest a feelin', he said. Ever'thing near the mouth of the canyon seems settled, but up where the arroyo backs up to the rocks I get an urge to look over my shoulder some."

"Indians, you think?"

"Not likely. Not here. 'Sides, they can read Will Reed's brand, same as us. If they wanted a beef, they'd just sashay in and ask for one. No, it's somethin' else."

"Grizzly?"

Fowler shrugged and yawned. "I'll leave you to it," he said, rolling up in his bedroll. His vaquero partner had already turned in, and Fowler was sawing logs even before I shook Joaquin awake.

I told the boy of Fowler's cautioning words. "Do you wish us to ride with you, señor?" he asked. By "us" he meant him and Dog, who had been sleeping across Joaquin's feet.

"No," I said quietly. "You and Dog sit up here by the fire. I'll ride the circle once and come back."

The farthest back piece of the canyon pinched off against a rock wall, topped by a high, brushy hillside. It was plastered with chaparral and sage and would have made tough going for a limber squirrel, let alone a man on horseback. For that reason, it felt as secure as a corral fence at the rear of the herd, and yet the hairs on my neck prickled.

Shawnee had made no sound to indicate that anything was amiss, but her ears pricked back and forth as if searching for an expected but missing sound. "Easy," I cautioned her. "Let's just sit and look around a spell." No breeze meant no scents on the coolish night air, unless we got up close, so quiet watchfulness was the order of things.

After a time, I was ready to write it off to an uncommon case of the jitters when a steer lying off a ways from the herd caught my attention. Sometimes the lack of movement can be just as telling as a twitch or a wiggle. This animal was lying too flat and too still—dead, without doubt.

I nudged Shawnee up closer. She moved reluctantly as the warm smell of fresh blood reached us both at last. Dark, raking marks stood out on the neck and shoulder of the rust-colored hide, and the corkscrewed position of the head told the rest of the story—mountain lion! Big, smart, and fearless, I judged, from the way he had brought down the steer with a single blow and in complete silence. Of even greater interest to me was the cat's present whereabouts.

The Allen over-and-under was already in my hand, and Shawnee backed away from the kill without being told to. You see, lions prefer to strike from behind, and neither my paint mare nor I intended to give this one any opportunity.

Shawnee walked us very deliberately around the herd in the direction of the fire. We did not want to compound the loss of the steer by flying through the drove in the middle of the night and causing a panic that might end in a stampede. In point of fact, even after reaching the fireside, I did not shout an alarm. Rather, I motioned Joaquin to join me, then roused Tor.

He had the mountain man's knack of coming instantly awake, and after a few words of explanation had a grasp of the situation. "Well, Andrew," he said, peering away from the fire into the dark canyon, "could be a young cat. Mayhap you skeered this here cougar away from his kill."

I shook my head. "Shawnee or I would have heard him go, the brush being so thick and all."

"Figger yore right . . . which means the other explanation must fit."

"What, Señor Fowler? What does it mean?" asked Joaquin, his eyes round as saucers.

"He means that what we've got is an outlaw lion. A young one might be run off from his prey that easy. An older one would usually stay and fight for it, or else he'd have already drug it off in the brush. But this one didn't do either. He just killed for the sport," I explained.

"And he . . ." Joaquin kind of stuttered and reached out to hug Dog around the neck.

"Right," I agreed. "He'll be back. If we don't deal with him, he'll kill again . . . maybe tonight, maybe tomorrow night . . . but he'll follow the herd till he gets tired of the game."

I saw a shiver start at the base of Joaquin's spine and work its way up till it came out his shoulders with a final shudder. To his credit all he said was, "What do we do about it, Señor Andrew?"

Tor nodded his approval, and I gave the boy a squeeze on his arm. "What *you* need to do," I said, "is stay here with Dog. I don't know if I could keep him from running that cat, and either he'd get hurt or the herd spooked or both."

We woke the Yaqui vaquero by the name of Alzado, which means "warrior." He was a sullen-seeming cuss who grunted more than he spoke, and that but seldom, but he was fearless. Built lean and tough and with all the pride of a people who had never submitted to the Spanish conquest of their homeland, the Yaqui was feared by the others, but much admired too. Out of a band about whom little was known, he seemed the most steady to take out into the darkness to face a rogue lion.

We each took a brand from the fire and again we rode slow and easy back to the spot where I had found the steer. But when we got to the place, there was no carcass to be found. Dismounting, we left the Yaqui holding the horses, while Tor and I scoured the ground. "Could you have mistook the place,

Andrew?" Tor asked. "On a dark night such as this, one clump of brush looks pretty like another."

"No," I argued, "I'm certain this was it." We raised the firebrands overhead to give us a wider ring of view. "Look here," I said. "There's blood here on the grass."

I pointed downward at the stain that looked pitch black against the shadowy brush, but Fowler was not watching where I directed. "No doubt yore right," he said, "but in that case he's kilt another one." Fowler's outstretched right arm gestured beyond the glare of the torches some few yards to where another steer's body lay prone on the grass.

It was all I could do to keep from swearing. Not only was this the first night of the drive, but I had scarce been gone ten minutes since viewing the previous victim. It was with relief then that I saw the downed creature move. "Look, Tor," I said. "You're wrong."

We had already taken a few paces in the direction of the animal. Its horned head lifted and pivoted in our direction, wobbling awkwardly as if drunk. That's when we saw the baleful yellow eyes staring back at us over the neck of the steer. In the flickering glow of our burning branches, we watched as a huge cougar raised the head of the dead steer by the grip of his powerful jaws clamped around its throat.

The cat sprang upright, dragging the six-hundred-pound cow as if it were nothing. Tor and I both fired, but our shots took effect only on the dead carcass. The lion flung its prey aside and bounded into the chaparral with a defiant roar and a crash. It was gone for now, but we knew it would be back.

11

THERE WAS NO further sleeping done that night. The vaqueros, roused by the sounds of our gunfire, rushed about with some confusion.

The Reed brothers, showing the character typical of their parents, were in favor of setting out on the trail of the big cat at once. Opposing this was the opinion of some others who felt such a plan was *muy malo*, very bad. In fact, Gomez and Rodriguez were ready to call it quits and return to Santa Barbara.

The plan we actually adopted was more cautious than the one but less cowardly than the other. Tor and I formed a picket line of men around the rear of the herd to guard against the lion's return. It was our intention to wait for first light, and then track the animal to where it holed up for the day.

There were no more disturbances, even though we watched until gray dawn reduced the number of visible stars to three. It was a very grumpy group of men who stretched out the kinks and gave up the vigil.

I instructed Peter Reed to ride the point and lead the herd out of the arroyo and up the trail. Tor and I would set out to do the tracking. We were accompanied by the Yaqui, Alzado.

During the night watch, the fawning vaquero Gomez had been one to raise his voice in support of abandoning the drive, but he sang a different tune when the sun came up. "Please, Señor Andrew," he begged, "allow me to accompany you. In my country I am known as a great hunter."

I caught Fowler's raised eyebrow and considered that perhaps the man needed an opportunity to redeem himself, but could not agree. We three would track the cougar till noon, then break off the hunt and rejoin the herd. All the rest were needed for the drive. "No," I said. "You and Joaquin take charge of the remuda."

I planned to return to the point where the puma had bounded away into the darkness, intending to follow the trail of the big cat. Fowler and Alzado set off directly toward a rocky pinnacle that looked to be a likely spot for a den.

"Señor Andrew," Gomez called out, riding after me. "I have something to tell you." He cast a furtive glance toward the pair of riders ahead and noted that Tor and the Yaqui were out of earshot before continuing.

"Not necessary," I said, taking his caution for embarrassment. "I already know what you are going to say."

The vaquero swept off his sombrero with its sugar-loaf crown and rubbed his hand across his forehead. "You do?" he asked.

"Sure," I replied. "Don't give it a thought. I don't like my sleep interrupted by a thieving lion, nor a band of hostiles, nor a snake in my bedroll, for that matter."

Gomez stroked his thin, black mustache with a quick, nervous gesture. "Señor is making the joke?" he said.

Now it was my turn to be confused. "What are you driving at, then, if this isn't about last night?"

Gomez reined his palomino alongside. There was a moment's jostling of horses as Shawnee laid back her ears and with bared teeth warned the gelding off from coming too close.

When the stomping settled, Gomez gestured for me to lean over. In a conspiratorial voice he whispered, "It is about the fierce one, the Yaqui."

"Alzado? What about him?"

"He is not to be trusted, señor."

"What do you mean?"

"I have seen him before, señor, in the company of malditos, bad men and robbers. He is hot-tempered and will kill when the mood is on him."

"So?" I said, trying to sound less concerned than I really felt. "Has he made threats against me or mine . . . or you, perhaps?"

Gomez looked as if I'd kicked him in his pride; as if my words cast suspicion on his motives (which of course they did). "Ah no, señor. I only wished to be of service. But if my words are not welcome, then I will keep my own counsel."

"Just see that you keep a sharp eye out for that lion," I said. I pointed downward to a pug mark the size of a horse's hoofprint. "He's big and mean too, and he's been a lot more trouble up to now than Alzado."

Gomez drew himself up haughtily and spun the palomino around in the direction of the herd of replacement mounts. As I looked on, Peter Reed shouted the orders that roused the men and the cattle and set both upon the trail. Then I turned to the task of picking my way along the increasingly steep dry wash as it wound up into the wild.

The sun had climbed high in the sky when I reined Shawnee to a halt and reflected on the lion. His tracks had led me on a meandering path, looping in and out of the low hills. Twice I had come upon the bloody remains of other steers killed and dragged into the brush. Three times I lost his trail entirely, having to go back to the last clear print and then ride widening spirals around until I picked up the marks again.

He seemed to have been going nowhere in particular. The commotion around the camp and the shots fired had not scared him into hightailing for home, that much was certain.

Shawnee and I circled another low hill, then were led up to its crest. The barest hint of a crushed place in the weeds showed where the lion had stretched out to take his ease. "What was he playing at?" I remarked to Shawnee. I stood up in the stirrups and found myself gazing out over the canyon where we had spent the night. The dust of the drive had already disappeared, and it was time to think about riding after my herd.

All at once it struck me. Not only had we not scared this particular lion back into the high country, we had not even driven him away from his sport. Or at least not far away.

While we had stood guard, he had spent the remainder of the night prowling around our camp, looking for an unprotected way in. While we had been watching for him, he had circled all of us. The thought was enough to give a man the willies.

Tracking him now seemed pointless. We would have to outguess him and get there first, or he would continue to be trouble. I set off into another canyon, toward where I expected to find Tor and the Indian.

Shawnee and I were some little way up a steep hill when we heard the gunshot. I had just turned my head to check my bearings when the ringing echoes bounced down through the canyon, and Shawnee took off as if she had been the bullet fired from the gun.

Up a narrow trail we raced, following the barely visible track of an ancient path that curved across the chaparral-covered slope. Around the base of a windcarved, sandstone spire we charged, and then out of the corner of my eye, I caught the briefest glimpse of a figure lurking on a ledge.

The next instant, a knife flashed in front of my face and a forearm like a bar of iron struck me across the neck. Shawnee plunged, unbalanced, rearing and shaking herself, while I parted company with my saddle and lit with a crash in a patch of sage and greasewood.

Instinctively, both my hands closed around the wrist of the attacker's hand that held the knife. Over and over we rolled, fighting for possession of the blade, for what seemed like an eternity, before I ended on top and pressed the point downward toward my assailant's throat.

"Don't, Andrew!" Tor's voice shouted. "Let him up!"

The savage face panting a few inches beneath my own belonged to Alzado; so did the twelve-inch sharpened steel. "He tried to kill me!" I yelled back.

"Not so, neither! Look up on the trail—on the rock just ahead."

The snarling jaws of the great mountain lion parted in a scream of hatred and pain. He crouched in a crevice right beside where Shawnee's next few strides would have carried us if we had not been swept off the trail by Alzado's leap.

While my head was still spinning and my breath was coming in short jerks, Fowler took careful aim and fired. Even at the moment of his death, the mountain lion jumped straight outward at his pursuers . . . a defiant lunge of barred claws that carried him across twenty feet of space before he hit the ground, dead.

"That cat was crazy—more so than ever, since I wounded him and let him get away," Tor explained. "If Alzado hadn't jumped when he did, I don't know what mighta happened."

"Why didn't you yell or something?" I said.

"No time," Alzado gasped. "Then, no breath." He added, "Señor is hombre fuerte."

A strong man, he had called me, and I knew he was reliving just how close the point of the knife had been to his throat.

"I'm sorry for the mistake," I said, stretching out my hand and pulling him to his feet. "And mighty in your debt, too."

Alzado shrugged. "It was nothing," he said.

"Nothing!" Tor snorted, raising the dead lion's head and pulling back the lips to expose two-inch-long fangs. "That wounded cat was ducking in and out of the brush and the boulders, an' Alzado was right behind him on the blood trail with nothing but that pigsticker in his hand."

"Where's your gun?" I asked him.

"I have none."

"Well, you do now," I said. I handed him the Allen. The barest hint of a smile wrinkled the corners of his mouth, and then it was back to business as usual. "Gracias," he said, and then, "I will skin the leon."

Shawnee's and Tor's mounts rolled their eyes and trotted a nervous distance away from Alzado's big bay. Even minus his insides, the cougar's rolled-up hide made a large bundle behind the Yaqui's saddle. We three rode in a jovial mood, congratulating ourselves on the success of our effort and discussing the cunning of the adversary. I also noted an occasional admiring glance downward by Alzado as he studied his new rifle. Each time I saw that look, it made me check my boot top where the bone hilt of a newly acquired Yaqui knife protruded.

By the swirling dust on the horizon, we knew that our line had been true and that we had almost reached the drive. It crossed my mind that there would be some new stories to tell around the cook fire this night, and perhaps the morale of all would get a boost.

Behind the mass of dark shapes that was the herd proper was a separate, smaller bunch of animals that made up the remuda. Joaquin was driving the string of horses into a grassy hollow enclosed by willows for a noon rest. I nodded approvingly to myself, and directed our course that way.

I was looking again at the rolled-up lion skin and thinking how impressed Joaquin would be. As we rode over the rim of the small bowl, the horse herd appeared right below us. I saw Joaquin's small figure snatch something up off the ground and point it toward us. A puff of smoke clouded his face and something clipped a lock of Tor's hair. A second later the report of the rifle reached us.

I set Shawnee at a gallop and waved my arms while shouting, "Don't shoot! It's us! Joaquin, don't shoot!"

The warning was unnecessary. A cuff from Gomez caught Joaquin upside the head and knocked him sprawling. The vaquero grabbed the boy up again and shook him fiercely. "Stupid, stupid boy!" he yelled in Joaquin's face. "You almost killed Señor Fowler!"

Gomez had drawn back his fist to strike the boy again when I reined Shawnee to a halt of flashing hooves and flung myself off her back. "That's enough!" I ordered. "Joaquin, why did you shoot at us?"

Tears were streaming down the boy's cheeks, and his throat was too constricted to answer. "Señor Andrew, I . . . he—" He stopped, too choked to say more. Then he turned and ran off.

12

THE NEXT SEVERAL days slipped by without incident as we moved the herd through the mountains by way of Tejon Pass. The terrain was rough and progress slow. A cold wind blew in our faces, while above us the light of the sun was darkened by the migration of millions of wild geese and ducks. This served as a reminder that winter was just around the corner. We had to deliver the herd in the north before the first snow arrived or face being stranded for the winter in the valley.

Peter, James, and John Reed worked with the skill and grit I had seen demonstrated by the best Californio vaqueros. They made even the hardest work into sport. Each hour was filled with contests in riding and roping. When matching their skill against the other riders, the brothers worked together like three fingers on the same hand. Dozens of times each day I could hear their laughter echo across the herd. They were polite to others of our little band, but there was the strong bond of kinship that naturally excluded anyone else from entering their tight circle. The other vaqueros treated the Reed brothers with respect due to young princes in line to inherit a great kingdom. Alzado would not think twice about barking commands to Joaquin, yet he pressed his thin lips together and held his peace when Peter, James, or John rode by. Many times I noticed conversations would die away when the Reed brothers, Tor, or I would come within earshot. Often, furtive, uncomfortable looks would follow. At first I believed that this attitude was in deference to our authority, and then I began to wonder exactly what the vaqueros were speaking of that they did not wish for us to hear. Joaquin's behavior became silent and almost fearful in the presence of these men.

Perhaps it was the prospect of weeks of this slow and tedious journey that affected the riders, I reasoned. And then the laughter of the Reed brothers reminded me that some among us were enjoying the adventure. Why then did the vaqueros seem so resentful as we topped the rise and began our descent down into the great San Joaquin Valley of Central California? Why the hard looks boring into the backs of Tor and me? Why the reluctant nod when we gave the order for some common task? As I looked out over the enormous, cloud-filled valley below me, I could not help but wonder again if Will Reed had chosen these vaqueros wisely. Without families to return to on the rancho, what was to tie these men to the herd and the job before us? More than once I imagined I glimpsed the thought of mutiny in their eyes. Resentment seethed just below the surface and was put aside only when the fierce Alzado rode among them shouting orders.

The chill I felt was more than a change in the weather. It seemed that I was not the only one to notice.

Cattle picked their way down the rocky slopes. Ten thousand feet above the herd, the din of a million honking geese covered the sound of bawling cows. I did not hear the approach of Tor's horse until he was beside me. Tor jerked a thumb skyward and shook his head as though he had water in his ears. He shouted to make himself heard above the roar.

"Don't look now, but somethin's up between Alzado and that smilin' sneak Gomez."

I started to look over my shoulder, but Tor stopped me with a shake of his head.

"I said don't look," he instructed. "Best pay 'em no mind. But they had some words. Came to blows in the saddle. Alzado knocked Gomez off his horse. There'll be blood spilt over it if I know anythin'."

"Been building toward it," I remarked, gazing out over the top of the clouds as if we were discussing the valley.

"The vaqueros don't seem overfond of Alzado, that's for certain. They're skeert of him. Maybe that ain't all bad. I'm a little skeert of him, too." He grinned sheepishly. "A right unusual feller. I don't trust him. But then I don't trust none of the rest of 'em neither. Mebbe they'll jest fight among themselves and leave us out of it."

"Don't mind that as long as we get the herd where it's going," I agreed.

Tor looked toward Joaquin, who was riding alone on the far side of the herd. "The boy ain't said two words since the other day. Don't look nobody in the eye. Ducks and runs ever'time anybody comes near. What do you make of it, Andrew?"

"He feels foolish, I reckon."

Tor tugged his beard. "I got me a feelin' . . . mebbe somethin' else."

"You tried talking to him?"

"Don't do no good. You'd best keep yer eye peeled, Andrew. I got me a real feelin'. Trouble's on the wind. We're headed into foggy territory, and somethin' don't sit right here with that Alzado and Gomez and the rest of the mob."

"And Joaquin?"

"Keep 'im close, Andrew. My bones is a tellin' me that boy knows somethin' he wishes he didn't know. Mebbe it's somethin' to do with us and the herd, and mebbe it ain't. But it bears watchin'."

There was no use pretending I had not noticed the way Joaquin ate off by himself and rode alone and spoke no word to anyone. No use pretending I had not noticed his hands trembling when Alzado or Gomez rode by. Tor's warning was only a confirmation of the same uneasiness I had been feeling for days.

13

THE CLACKING OF a thousand pair of long, curved horns resounded from the herd like the clash of sabres in battle. The cattle seemed to sense the broad, swift barrier of the river just ahead of us. They bawled and tossed their heads nervously as we drove them on.

The river was called Rio Bravo by the first Spanish explorers. The north and south fork came together high in the Sierras and then roared down from the mountain through a steep, rocky gorge to tumble out onto the valley floor. Since those early days, the Powerful River has been renamed Kern, as though it were as tame as a small brook. But the roar of its waters has been the last sound in the ears of many men. Even where the river appears peaceful, the placid flow conceals a treacherous undercurrent ripping just beneath the surface. Maybe the Spaniards called the river "Bravo" because it took a strong man to ford it. To the west, it became shallow as it emptied into the marshes of the valley floor. Mud bogs and mires of quicksand made it impossible for us to cross there. Indians told of whole herds of elk being trapped and dying in the swamps after following a buck that strayed only a few yards from the trail.

Instead of risking such danger, we skirted the southern rim of the valley, moving on high ground toward the mouth of the river canyon. The torrent exploded from this boulder-strewn funnel and then seemed to collect itself in quiet pools before it sighed and moved on. There was one possible fording place that Tor and I knew of. I had made the passage several times on Shawnee. With the water low, we had driven my small herd across it easily. But rains had swelled the waters since then.

The river was a quarter mile wide now, and deep enough that it would have to be swum. It was one thing to wade across a shallow flow. This was another matter entirely. Above us to the east, the current was impassable. Below us to the west lay the quicksand. We scratched our heads and looked the situation over. Were we brave enough to face the river?

Alzado spurred his big bay gelding to the edge of the bank. He stared at the far shore for an instant, then, making the sign of the cross, he plunged ahead, whooping as the horse hit the water. Urged on by Alzado's shouts and the sting of a quirt on its butt, the horse cut through the water without looking back. Straight across he swam as Alzado held its mane and yipped like a coyote. Emerging on the opposite side of the flow, the soaking vaquero reined the horse around, stood in his stirrups, and raised his sombrero in victory. He cupped his hand around his mouth and called over to us. "She is nothing, Señor Andrew! Deep, yes. But slow and lazy!"

As if to prove his point, he again rode down the bank and spurred his animal into the river to swim back. Brave Alzado had matched the Bravo with apparent ease. He called the treacherous stream "a woman" and in his mocking smile dared us all to follow after.

I unsheathed my bullwhip as all others of our troop took positions at the sides and rear of the herd. Dog was called to jump onto the saddle with Joaquin. I turned to the boy, who seemed not so eager as the Reed brothers for this adventure.

"Stay right with me, Joaquin," I commanded. "Do you hear me, boy? No matter what happens, you keep your horse tight behind me."

Joaquin nodded curtly and wrapped his fingers in Dog's leather collar. "We will follow you, Señor Andrew," he replied grimly. "Me and Dog are not afraid."

I knew Joaquin was not much of a swimmer. He was not even much for taking a bath in a water trough, and we were in for quite a baptism here. The cattle bellowed their protest as we lassoed the horns of the leaders and whipped and whooped them into the river from all sides. They made a black, bobbing counter current, heads raised and horns tangled. The Reed boys brought up the rear. Alzado, Rodriguez, and Garcia took the high side of the current with me and Joaquin. I spotted Tor on the down side with the soft, frightened-looking Gomez close behind him. Sanchez and Ortiz followed after.

Icy water soaked my buckskins and filled my boots. Popping my whip behind the ears of the reluctant steers kept their course straight. The first of the animals emerged on the northern shore, bawled and shook themselves, then trotted forward.

Alzado turned and plunged back into the water to keep the central core of the group moving. I started to follow him, but it was at that moment I noticed that Tor was in trouble. He had lassoed an enormous animal around the horns. The critter was foundering! Caught up in some undertow, the beast had rolled over and now was tangled in the reata. To my horror, I saw that the reata was also looped around Tor's saddle horn and somehow caught beneath his stirrup leather. He and his strong bay horse were being pulled downstream. Gomez, who was within a few yards of my friend, did not seem to notice, or if he saw Tor's predicament, he offered no assistance. I shouted and rode through the herd as the head of Tor's mount screwed around in a desperate attempt to struggle free. With no more than a nudge, Shawnee leapt from the embankment and swam toward Tor as though she knew the urgency. For an instant I saw Tor's hand raise up. Light glinted on the blade of his knife as he tried to cut his mount loose from the reata. And then suddenly Tor and his horse parted company. The horse righted itself and, after a moment of confusion, swam toward shore. I could plainly see that the cinch on the saddle had broken. Tor bobbed up once and then went under. The wayward steer paddled on, dragging the saddle after.

"Tor!" I shouted. Gomez paid no mind to the struggle of my drowning comrade. He urged his mount in a straight line toward dry land while Tor splashed and gasped and sank a second time from sight. The churning hooves of a thousand beeves swept past him. One blow would be enough to finish him off! Two more steers broke away to tumble downstream just ahead of me. Where was Tor? I cracked my whip, urging Shawnee onward, although she could swim no faster. The waters were murky brown. I could not see Tor. Had he been sucked beneath the cattle? Was he swept away?

"Gomez!" I cried as the vaquero passed me. "Get back! Tor has fallen." The Mexican seemed not to hear me.

Seconds dragged by. Too long for a man to be beneath the water without a breath! I called out to heaven for help! Was the life of Tor Fowler to end in such a way?

I spotted a fragment of red flannel just beneath the surface. "Tor!" I shouted, turning Shawnee toward the spark of color that gave me hope! Twenty feet from me the hand of Tor groped upward. Then his face emerged for one feeble breath before he rolled and sank out of my sight again. Fearful that Shawnee might strike him with a hoof, I leapt from her back without thinking. My bullwhip still coiled in my hand, I struck out to where I had seen the color. Diving beneath the surface, I reached through the water hoping to grasp him. Nothing! Another quick breath and then I went under again. This time, my fingers brushed his limp body. I grasped him by the belt and struggled to hold him up. Only now did my own desperate situation come to mind. Here I was, only a fair swimmer, holding an unconscious man in the middle of a river! My lungs ached for air! I surfaced, gasped, half-shouted with terror and joy at what I saw!

There was little Joaquin on his horse, only ten feet from us! He had obeyed my command to stick tight on my tail. Now he held Shawnee by the reins and cried out to me!

"Your whip! Señor Andrew!"

Catching his intent, I managed to toss out the lash. He caught hold of the tip and looped it around his horn.

I strengthened my hold on Tor and held fast to the whip handle as the boy towed us toward dry land. Only then did he release Shawnee, who cut a path through the water ahead of us.

I did not let go of the bullwhip or Tor until we were dragged twenty yards up the embankment. Cold and shaken, I lay in the sand until a circle of riders came around, and Dog whined and licked my face. Tor coughed and moaned and asked if he were dead.

We had survived, thanks to Joaquin. And no thanks to Gomez.

I stood slowly and looked at the boy. "What were you doing out there, Joaquin," I scowled. "Don't you know you could have been killed?"

"You said I should follow you, Señor Andrew," he replied. There was a renewed confidence in the boy. He had redeemed himself as well as Tor and me that day.

The herd milled aimlessly about on the north shore of the Rio Bravo, but Tor and I were too tired to care. I waved feebly for Joaquin. "Tell Peter to make camp here," I coughed. "This is as far as we go today." The boy scampered off, relief written on his face.

Tor retched and coughed up some river water. He was hugging a boulder with his face pressed against it. It was a gesture I understood. Things were still swirling some for me as well. "What happened, Andrew?" he said.

"Your cinch busted," I said. "It's a good thing Joaquin took me so at my word, or you and I would both have been in trouble, pard."

Dragging himself upright, Tor stood swaying unhappily and frowning. "What's your all-fired hurry?" I wanted to know.

"Got a problem," he said quietly. "That cinch was new."

While all the men were shaking out their belongings to dry, Fowler and I had an inconspicuous meeting with Peter Reed. The eldest brother had caught up with the wayward steer, still dragging Tor's reata and the waterlogged saddle.

Fowler looked with disgust at the battered leather. "Tore it up . . . just flat tore it up. But looky here."

He was right. The horsehair girth was still intact, the metal buckle ring shining. Not a single strand had parted. Tor ran his hand upward to the leather strap that secured the girth to the saddle. "Now look at this."

Peter and I saw where the leather had ripped across when the weight of the steer and the force of tons of water had pulled against the reata. Fowler flipped the strap over in his hand. There, on the back and at a place that would have been out of sight up under the skirt of the saddle was the faint but still perceptible mark of a knife. "This didn't happen of its own self," Tor growled. "Somebody give it a good start and then waited for somethin' to happen."

"But who?" Peter wondered aloud. "Who would have done such a thing?"

"And when was it done?" I added. "There's no way to tell from this."

"What should we do?" was Peter's next question.

"Here's my thinking on it," Tor said. "Some lowdown snake has took great pains to see to it that this looked like a accident. Let's just let him go on a thinkin' thataway."

I studied the roiling waters that had so nearly cost two lives, then looked again at the knife mark. "You're right," I agreed at last. "Let's play this close and see who tries to up the ante next."

"Shall I tell my brothers, or Joaquin?" Peter wanted to know.

"No," I said. "The less who know we're on to it, the smaller the chance of giving the game away. We have to keep this just between us three." It was to prove a fatal mistake.

14

SUNLIGHT BROKE THROUGH the morning haze and warmed our backs as we rode on. Lizards awoke and slithered out onto boulders and fallen logs to soak up the last bit of sun before winter closed in.

The feel of Indian summer might have warmed my spirits as well, but there was a chill in my soul that had nothing to do with temperature. I found myself studying each man among us, mentally calculating what motive there might be for attempting to murder Tor. Why stage an accident when a knife between the ribs in the dark night would accomplish the same purpose? I doubted each man in turn and then all of them together. After a time I talked myself into doubting my doubts. Perhaps the cinch had been cut halfway through long before we ever left on the drive. Maybe our vaqueros had nothing to do with it. Wasn't it possible that the leather cinch had been scored by some disgruntled enemy back in Angel's Camp? The man who had done the deed was certainly patient if that was the case. He had been counting on the fact that one day there would be just enough strain on the leather that it would snap at a crucial moment and take Tor with it.

"You're payin' more mind to the hired help than the cattle," Tor commented, riding up beside me. His gaze followed mine to Alzado as the Indian shouted and cursed a wayward steer.

"I expect you're right," I agreed. I had not been thinking much about business. "Trying to figure who it is. Or if it's all of them. Or maybe none of them. Maybe this is an old score," I said hopefully.

"Ain't all of 'em." Tor kept his eyes on Alzado and then scanned the other vaqueros who rode in pairs and singly all around us. "But it's some of 'em."

"How can you know that?"

"'Cause if it was the bunch of 'em what wanted us dead, there wouldn't be much to stop 'em. They'd of stuck us to the ground while we was sleepin' if they had a mind to. No sir, Andrew, it ain't all of 'em. Mebbe most of 'em is in on this, but there's some of 'em who ain't. Elsewise they wouldn't wait to make a move." He drew a finger across his throat to make his point. "If they aim to rustle the cattle and kill us all at once, I reckon they'll wait till we're closer to the gold fields. After all, we're still some use for drivin'. Takes lots of men to move a herd like this. They won't want us all dead till they see the end of the trail."

"You figure they aim to steal the herd?"

"Can't figger no other reason why they'd want to pick us off one by one."

"You ought to feel real proud, Tor." I tried to make light of our predicament. "They tried to kill you first. I guess that means they're most scared of you."

He did not smile, but looked across the mass of swaying critters. "It's a matter of cuttin' the wolves out of the pack, Andrew. We got to be mighty careful about now. Don't want to bring down the good 'uns with the rotten apples, if you take my meanin'."

"I can't tell the good ones from the spoilt ones," I said. "And that's what's got me bothered."

We both looked at Alzado at the same instant. There was something menacing in the manner of the Yaqui. His face was a scowl set in leather and stone. He was feared by the others; hated by Gomez.

I opened my mouth to speak, thought better of it, and then blurted out my thought, "He could have let that lion kill me. Saved himself the trouble. That would have been one less of us to do in."

Tor nodded thoughtfully. "I been figgerin' on that one too, Andrew. Don't make no sense . . . except . . . we was only a day's ride from the Reed Rancho. If you'd been kilt, we would have turned back for sure. Taken the herd right back to the rancho. Nope. If Alzado is leader of the pack of wolves, he's thinkin' like a wolf, too. Draw the prey away from the main herd. See? Here we are a hunert miles from Will Reed and his help. You, me, Peter, and three boys. It won't take much when they figger we ain't a use to 'em no more."

I frowned and narrowed my eyes as Alzado whooped and whipped his mount to a gallop to head off another stray. Tor's reasoning made sense. And there was that warning from Gomez that Alzado kept company with bandidos. But what about Gomez? I trusted the groveling little snake even less than I trusted Alzado. "You said that Gomez and Alzado got into it the other day?"

"I don't trust neither of them two," Tor muttered. "They wasn't arguing about how to throw a loop, I'll wager. More likely they was fightin' over when to throw it and whose neck they was goin' to throw it around, if you folla me." He rubbed his neck in a nervous gesture, as though he had already imagined his neck in a noose.

"You think there are any others besides those two?"

"Them two for sure. Well, I'm almost sure. As for the rest of 'em . . . I don't know. I just figger I ain't gonna be sleepin' none too sound till we get these critters checked into somebody else's corral." He shook his head. "A new kind of claim jumper. Here in the valley there ain't no law to stop 'em, neither." He patted the stock of his rifle. "Jest this kind of law. And I'm keepin' her loaded and ready, too." Now he smiled reproachfully at me. "'Course you gave your Allen rifle to our friend Alzado, didn't you? Love your enemy, Andrew, but don't give 'im your rifle, I always say."

Tor did not have to remind me of my foolish gesture of gratitude. A dozen times that afternoon I found myself regretting that I had traded my rifle for Alzado's knife. I looked down at the smooth antler handle of the weapon protruding from my boot top, and then I looked at the stock of the Allen in its sheath on Alzado's saddle. I could not help but wonder now if my old Allen might soon be used against me.

15

WE WERE CAMPED along a nameless creek that wandered down from the high Sierras. The Reed brothers stood first watch while the rest of us gathered in close to the fire and tried to get some sleep after a supper of bacon and beans.

There was not much conversation. These men were mostly strays. Lonesome critters without home or family, they worked on one rancho and then another, never staying long in any set place. Sometimes their pasts found common ground. Garcia and Sanchez talked softly about a cantina girl named Rosa from down Sonora way. The two men had never met each other before coming to the Reed rancho, but both had loved Rosa. Both had gotten drunk in that cantina. Both had been beaten and robbed. Could their beloved Rosa have been a part of the plot? This common betrayal somehow made them brothers. They cast around in their memories to compare what other places they might have in common. Nothing. Only Rosa and the Sonora cantina. It was enough for a long conversation. I fell asleep listening to their soft laughter and the crackle of the fire.

When I awoke, all was silent. The blaze had died to embers, and I judged it to be another hour before my watch began. Another hour to sleep, I thought, snuggling deeper into my blanket. I opened one eye and looked at the orange coals. If I stayed put, the fire would die before Tor's watch was up, and we'd all sleep cold and have cold breakfast in the morning. There was a small heap of dry sticks outside our circle. I hoped that someone else would wake up and stoke the fire, but no one seemed to notice the chill but me.

I pulled my blanket around me and sat up slowly. My boots were drying next to the fire. I picked up the right one, shook it out and slipped it over my bare foot. Standing, I started to put on my left boot as well. My fingers grasped the upper leather and my toes were just above the opening when I felt the tanned hide tremble and caught a glimpse of something moving—slithering—inside my boot. I gasped, tossed the thing away from me just as the air was filled with a bright buzzing sound like bacon frying.

"Rather!" I cried, stumbling back as the creature spilled from my boot and coiled on top of it. I had not fallen back far enough. The snake fixed its black, evil eyes on my outstretched leg. It buzzed afresh, and every man in the camp lay stock-still and watching.

From across the fire pit Peter Reed whispered in a hoarse voice. "Don't move, Señor Andrew. No one move."

Don't move? I wanted to holler and run for a mile. Yet less than a yard from my big toe that rattler held me prisoner. I dared not speak and held my breath as I watched Peter's shadowed form reach cautiously for his rifle.

Even as I lay there, I knew for certain that the deadly creature had not gotten into my boot without help from some two-legged snake in the camp. I was not supposed to find it until a set of fangs pierced my foot. Even if I had shaken it out, it would have landed right next to me.

Peter stood slowly and raised his weapon to his shoulder. If he did not split the head of the thing with the first shot, I was still a dead man. Even wounded it would strike me.

The hammer clicked back. Every sound was a threat to the rattler. It moved its flat, hideous head from side to side as if to see which part of my flesh was best to bite. The buzz of its rattles quickened until the air was full of the warning.

All around me I could see the firelight glinting in the eyes of the silent spectators watching me. Which one of them had planned this little performance? Whoever he was, his intent was more vile than that of the snake that faced me now.

"Peter . . ." James Reed muttered his brother's name fearfully.

Beads of perspiration stood out on my forehead and trickled into my eyes. In an instant I expected to feel the fire of
fangs ripping into me. Drawing a slow breath, I silently
prayed that the aim of Peter Reed would be true. The young
man's eyes narrowed as he stared at the back of the swaying
dark head of the viper. His muscles tensed, and then the air
exploded with fire and smoke. The head of the rattler tore
away and flew past my face. Its jaws opened and closed as
though to strike even though separated from the writhing
body. The headless thing flipped and fell across my legs. I
shouted and grasped at it, tossing it into the fire where it still
struggled in death amid the embers.

Alzado leapt to his feet and, grabbing up a stick, rescued
the body of the snake from the heat. He laid it belly up on a
rock, cut off the rattles, and tossed them to me like a prize.

"Twelve buttons," Alzado said. There was a hint of a smile
on his leathery face. He was plainly amused by what had
happened. "Keep it for luck."

I was about to say that I needed all the luck I could get
when Peter stepped forward. He swept his rifle around at
each smiling vaquero until their smirks disappeared. It was
his way of saying that he would blow the head off of any
human snake if the need arose. The men shrugged or looked
away uncomfortably, as though to say they understood.

Alzado skinned the snake and fried the white meat. I did
not eat any, but I tied the twelve-button rattle around my
neck by a leather string as a reminder that the real snake
among us was still alive.

"Wake up, Andrew!" Tor shook me awake, and believe me,
after the experience with the snake, it did not take much.

"What is it?"

"Rodriguez is gone!"

"Gone? What do you mean, gone?"

"Made off with the palomino horse that Gomez rides.
Prob'ly the fastest mount here, savin' yore Shawnee, of
course."

"Are you certain he's not around somewhere?"

"Positive. He was s'posed to be the guard that I relieved for the last watch. When I got out there, he was already gone. Well, I just figgered he slipped into camp a little early or I'd missed him on the other side of the drove, but the others say he didn't come back atall."

I eyed my boots with renewed curiosity and touched the rattles tied around my neck. "Do you think that means he's been the one trying to cross us up?"

Tor considered this notion, then said, "Possible, or maybe that's what we're s'posed to think so as to make us let down our guard. Or mayhap he was a good'un run off by fear of the others. Naw, Andrew, I reckon we don't know much more than we did, 'ceptin' now we're short one hand and one powerful fast horse."

Not for the first time I wondered if we needed some help. "Maybe you should ride on ahead and fetch Ames with some more hands," I suggested. "Maybe Rodriguez works for Powers."

Fowler shushed me with a look and jerked his chin to the side. There, casually coiling a lariat, but well within earshot, was the brooding figure of Alzado.

16

THE LIGHT IN Peter Reed's green eyes danced in the reflected glitter of the stream called Mariposas. The fall air was full of a drifting cloud of orange and black wings.

"Butterflies," he said. A grin marched across his freckled features. "That's the stream's name. My grandfather told me that the old Spanish explorers had never seen so many butterflies as in the meadows on the banks of this place."

"It is an amazing sight," I agreed. "And for those pious men to leave off using the names of saints when they went to make note of this river says that they were very impressed indeed."

We were long past the near calamity and only a few days travel from our destination. The spirit of high adventure with which the Reed brothers had begun the drive had reasserted itself.

"Thank you, Señor Andrew," Peter said, "for bringing me. I have often imagined this spot, but never knew when I might get to see it."

The stream of water curved around a little oak-topped knoll. The herd settled in to feed on a rich, grassy meadow, while we made our camp on top of the rise. Thousands of butterflies floated into the grove of trees until they clustered on the trunks like heavy drapery. Peter and I stood and watched as the sun went down and the men gathered for supper.

The vaqueros sat apart and talked among themselves. Tor kept the Reed boys and Joaquin spellbound with his tall tales of life in the mountains. He told them the story of how he had experienced an especially difficult time saddling an uncooperative mule on one extremely foggy night, only to have daylight reveal that he was riding a grizzly bear. I think Joaquin and John, the youngest Reed, believed him.

Our discussion came round to the boys' future plans. Joaquin was excited to learn that John would be returning to school in the Kingdom of Hawaii. After just one month in the island kingdom, John assured Joaquin, he would swim like a dolphin and glide his canoe over the sea like a flying fish.

James, the middle brother, would be entering Harvard to study law. "Father says that now that California belongs to the United States, we must have at least one in the family who knows Yankee law, and I'm elected."

I turned to Peter, who was watching his brothers with some amusement and yet, I thought, a touch of sadness. "What are your plans, Peter?"

The young man took a deep breath. Before replying, he brushed a hunk of dark red hair back off his forehead. "Father says I am to go to the States with James. He says we need more Yankee business sense." Peter sighed heavily.

"And you ain't happy to be goin'?" Tor asked. "Where'd you druther go?"

"Go?" Peter said. "I don't want to leave at all. I love California. It has everything—the seashore, the high mountains, the herds and the rodeos, the places still waiting to be explored. . . . If I live to be a hundred, I could never see it all. I'll go to please Father, but I'll be back to stay."

He stood up and unfolded the heavy leather chapederos on which he had been sitting. Peter buckled them on, readying himself to take his turn as night herder when Alzado and Sanchez came in.

The Yaqui arrived just as Peter returned from saddling his curly-coated horse. As they entered the circle of firelight, I noticed that the animal was limping.

"Hold on, Peter," I said. "Chino is favoring his near hind hoof."

A quick examination showed no obvious injury, but it was plain that the horse would see no duty that night. Peter started to lead Chino back to the remuda in order to select another mount when Alzado stopped him. "Take my horse, Don Peter," the Yaqui offered. "We have only walked a little, and he is still fresh."

"Gracias, Alzado. Shall we swap the saddles?"

"No importante. You are of a height with me. Just take him, if you wish."

It was a couple hours later that the wind came up out of the east. The fire had died down and everyone was asleep, except Peter and the other night herder, Gomez. As near as I could later figure, Peter had posted himself on Alzado's bay at the north end of the herd. It was a place where the oaks from the knoll trooped down to drink with the willows.

The Santa Ana winds blow up out of the eastern deserts of California. They whistle through the mountain passes and down the western slopes, sometimes blowing dust in mile-high clouds. The east wind always makes people and critters restless. Sailors look to their anchor rodes, and herds stir and mill about. Most times the wind dies down after a while, and the unease passes.

This one came up all of a sudden. From perfect stillness, the night changed to high streaky clouds racing overhead. Clumps of butterflies were ripped off the tree bark. They bumbled in confusion across the pitch-black meadow, colliding with the noses of startled cows.

For all that, there was no great cause for alarm. The herd had done twenty miles that day. They were tired, well fed, and would not be easily roused. A little quiet talking or singing and they would have quieted right down. I know this is true, and have thought it over many times through the years.

It was the gunshot that ended all hope of calling things back. Somewhere around the south end of the drove, a rifle exploded. Besides the shattering noise, the flash was like a lightning strike in its brilliance.

How can I picture the awful dread with which a stampede is regarded? I could compare it to an avalanche, to a runaway steam locomotive, or to an earthquake and a tornado rolled into one, but no description is really adequate.

The vaqueros awoke with a rumble that they felt in their souls even before the bellowing roars had penetrated their sleep-muffled hearing. "El ganado! El ganado!" they cried. "The cattle!" At that moment, the expression no longer called to mind a placid, cud-chewing band of stupid animals. From a drowsy jumble of fitful complaints, the herd was transformed into a single beast with four thousand legs and two thousand tossing horns, but only a single thought—to get far away from that terrible blast as quickly and as directly as possible.

At that moment, any plan to reach a horse and head off the charging mass of beef was discarded in the same second that it entered the mind. The only idea of any interest was to save oneself any way at all.

I struggled free of the ground sheet in which I was wrapped and saw Joaquin nearby still wrestling to get out of his bedroll. I picked him up, canvas covering and all, tossed him toward the branch of an oak and yelled, "Climb!"

By the flickers of the dying embers, I saw Tor do the same with John Reed. My attention changed then to the hundred or so head of cows that seemed to be headed directly for me. Individual hooves could not be heard, not the bawling of separate throats. All sound massed together in a noise so fearful that one felt overrun and trampled even before the first wave of steers reached the little knoll.

Dodging the fastest of the wild-eyed critters drove me away from the trees that had branches close to the ground. I found myself beside an immense water oak of perhaps sixty-foot height and twenty of girth. It gave me protection from the initial rush, but like a wave that rolls both up and back the beach, a stampede carries away all imagined places of safety that it touches.

Over my head, but higher than I could jump, a large snag of a limb jutted out. I always sleep with my coiled blacksnake whip close to hand, and as on other occasions, this habit saved my life. A flick upward looped the whip around the limb, and I shinnied up as I have never climbed before. The spiked tip of an angrily pitching horn gored the calf of my leg, but then I was up and out of harm's way.

From my perch I looked out over a floodtide of steers that trampled bedrolls, belongings, and even the remains of the fire. Smaller trees shuddered and collapsed under the onslaught, and the larger ones resounded from the repeated collisions until it was all one could do to hang on.

Across the meadow, over by the stream, the moonlight reflected off the water. Silhouetted against that patch of silver illumination, I saw Peter Reed on the bay horse. He was urging his mount in twisting and corkscrewing, trying to move with the flow of a new peril as he was carried along the creek, but it seemed that he would win free to the far side of the water. Up the steep bank should be safety.

I saw the bay rear and plunge, once and then again. I saw Peter's shadow rocking with the jolts of the bucking ride. Then the shapes merged with the great beast called stampede, and I could not see either the horse or the rider anymore.

When the rush had passed, we climbed down from our perches and out of whatever other crevices had presented themselves as refuges. In the head count around the remains of our camp, all were accounted for except Peter. By some miracle, there were no serious injuries. The hole poked in my leg was typical. There were cuts and bruises in plenty, but no broken bones. Being camped on the little hill had saved us, I guess. It had slowed down the charge enough for each of us to find a place of safety.

John cried and begged for us to go looking for Peter. I whispered to Tor what I had seen, and then we told the boys to stay and pick up what they could salvage of the supplies while the adults searched.

Dog was missing, too. Every minute or so, Joaquin would whistle and call for him, but he was nowhere around.

Just before we set out on foot, I saw Tor having words with Gomez. The vaquero was the only one of us still mounted, all the other horses having been run off by the stampede. I could not hear what was said, but I saw Gomez waving his arms, then pointing at the sky, the vanished herd of cattle, his horse, and lastly his rifle. When Fowler rejoined me, he made no comment, but shook his head with grim disgust. Tor and I concentrated on the area closest to where I had caught my last glimpse of Peter. There was a chance that he had gotten into the lee of a downed log or crawled in a hole. Perhaps he was injured or unconscious, but alive somewhere.

Even carrying blazing pine knots as torches, we found nothing until almost dawn. We had walked much farther along the stream than I thought was reasonable, but we did not want to turn back while any hope remained. How could we face the boys without knowing?

It was the bay horse that we came to first. Turned broadside to the force of the stampede, the bay had been carried along the creek like a twig on the crest of a flood. The saddle was missing.

A whine reached our ears from just west of the stream. Tor and I broke into a stumbling run. Around the next bend, half hidden by a clump of elderberries up on the bank, we came upon Dog. He acknowledged us with another whine, but did not come to greet us. He sat very still, his head cocked to one side. One forepaw rested on the lifeless body of Peter Reed.

Rolled up and tied over Tor's shoulder was the largest remaining fragment of his bedroll. After standing a moment in painful silence, we spread out the tarp and wrapped the young man's form to carry back to camp. "Come along, Dog," I said. Dog remained by a mound of earth near where he had found Peter. "Come on," I insisted. "What's the matter with you?"

Dog whined and began to dig into the mound. By the time I looked to see what he was seeking, he had uncovered what was left of Alzado's saddle. The thin light of the Sierra morning answered my question right off: The cinch leather had been cut part way through, high up and out of sight.

17

MURDER HAD BEEN done to Peter Reed and murder was in my heart for the man who killed him. I slung the scored leather cinch strap over my shoulder to use as evidence in the trial of Alzado. Yet I had determined already that there would be no court, no judge, no jury in this case. I would kill him myself and with the same cold-bloodedness he had shown toward young Peter Reed.

Dog trotted alongside as we carried Peter's body back toward camp. Neither Tor nor I spoke for a long while. My thoughts flew to Francesca and Will Reed. All the gold in California could not buy them back their firstborn son! Nineteen years of love and hopes now lay trampled—wrapped in a tarp and slung between us like an empty sack. Will had trusted us with his sons. Francesca's fears had proved right. Three brothers had left home, and now only two would be returning. The sense of my own failure filled me like bitter gall. Alzado would pay for this grief with his own life, I determined. Tor had come to the same conclusion.

"Alzado," Tor muttered, "lamed the boy's horse and scored the cinch. Same as he done mine afore the river crossin'. Put that there rattler in your boot. Peter shot the wrong snake."

I nodded, but did not reply. Words failed me as we topped the rise and looked down on the little knoll where James and John Reed waited for news of their brother. They stood side by side, off a ways from the vaqueros and Joaquin. Their backs were toward us. Looking southward, no doubt their thoughts had also turned toward home—to Francesca and Will. I dreaded the moment when they would look back and see the burden we carried with us.

"Gomez!" spat Tor. "Fit for hangin' right along with Alzado. Dropped his gun, he says. Fired off accidental, he says. Spooked the herd. An accident, he says. Well, I say he was in on it with Alzado. Murder. The boy woulda made it if this cinch hadn't been cut. No jury gonna see it otherwise."

Below us, the men were standing, kneeling, or sitting in a tight circle. I counted only five men. Gomez, who had been the only one of us left with a horse, seemed to be missing. Had he ridden off like Rodriguez?

"Whoa up there, Andrew," Tor said, and we stopped for a better look. Lowering the body to the ground, we ducked behind a heap of boulders to reconnoiter what we now felt was an enemy camp. "There's Joaquin." The boy sat alone and forlorn on a fallen log. "The Reed boys . . ." Tor frowned. "I count only five vaqueros."

For a few seconds I studied the forms of the men below us. Hats, the slope of shoulders, shirts, and shapes told us that all were present on the hill but one. . . . "Alzado is gone," I said.

"So's that big chestnut Gomez was riding," Tor added. "Our pigeon has flown the coop."

When his oilcloth coat gaped open, it was easy to spot Gomez's bright yellow shirt from among the others. The center of attention, he was sitting on the ground and cradling a blood-stained arm.

"Alzado," I said as hate boiled up in me. "He's stolen Gomez's horse."

"That'll mean he got away with the only rifle that ain't been trampled. Gone to fetch his gang, unless I miss my guess."

If Gomez was part of the conspiracy, why had he been left behind? The framework of facts left much unexplained. Bullwhip on my belt and knife in my boot, I once again hefted Peter's body, and we started the descent into our shattered camp.

It was Joaquin who first spotted our coming. He raised his arm and shouted. James and John spun around to look, ran a few steps, then froze in the horror of what they saw. Making the sign of the cross, they sank to their knees.

Leaving the wounded Gomez on the knoll, Sanchez, Garcia, Ramos, and Ortiz ran to meet us. All four vaqueros were babbling at once.

"Alzado the Yaqui!"

"He and Gomez—"

"They argue—"

"Alzado pulls a knife!"

"He stabs poor Gomez—"

"He steals Gomez's horse!"

"Alzado is gone, Señor Andrew!"

Ramos and Ortiz offered to carry Peter, but we did not relinquish the body until we reached the knoll. We placed the boy beneath the shade of an oak tree. Joaquin brought a blanket to cover the blood-soaked shroud as James and John held tightly to each other and staggered to Peter's side.

Gomez shouted at me, "I tell you, Señor Andrew." He bellowed and cradled his wounded arm. "I warn you that Alzado is a very bad man! You did not listen to me! I gave you warning!"

Tor whirled on the whimpering toady. "Shut up, Gomez! You ain't in the clear in this affair, neither!"

Gomez puckered his mouth like a petulant child and looked mournfully down at his arm. "You do not see I am wounded? Alzado has stolen my horse—no doubt to ride for bandidos who will kill us all and steal the herd!"

Impatient with these cries, Tor snatched the cinch from my shoulder and strode toward Gomez. Grabbing the vaquero up by his shirt front, he waved the severed leather under his nose. "What do you know about this?"

"Nothing!" cried Gomez in terror. The other vaqueros stepped back, exchanging fearful looks.

"Nothing?" Tor shook him like a rag doll. "The leather cut nearly clean through. Just like mine was at the river. And it was your gun what started the stampede!"

"An accident! I swear, señor! I dropped my gun! It was an accident! No, señor! It is Alzado who is the bandido! Alzado who has done this evil thing! I have nothing to do with Alzado! You see . . ." He waved his bloody arm like a flag of surrender. "He tells me to get off my horse. He says he is leaving! I fight him, and he stabs me and steals my horse! I am left here wounded! Nearly killed! Can you not see, señor?" he begged. "I have done nothing wrong. I only tried to warn you. . . ."

James Reed looked up from the body of his brother. "It happened the way Gomez is telling it," James managed to speak. "No explanation from Alzado. At first I thought he was going to ride after the remuda. But he rode out of here hell-for-leather, and he didn't come back. Like Gomez told it."

Tor scowled down into the terrified face of Gomez, and then gave him one more shake, sending him sprawling back on the ground. I heard Tor mutter in a menacing voice, "Mebbe it's so and mebbe it ain't, you little worm. Fact is, 'twas your gun what started the stampede. I'll get back to that later."

James looked hard at the cinch and then at the covered remains of Peter. "Ah, Peter," he choked. "What will I say to Mother? What will I tell Father?"

With Alzado gone, fled on Gomez's horse, we were completely without mounts. That thought alone was enough to rekindle the flame of hatred I felt for the treacherous Yaqui. How were we to begin recovering from the disaster of the stampede and Peter's tragic death? Regardless of what else we may have sensed, the answer in practical terms was "on foot."

I dispatched the vaqueros to search for our horses. Things would level out some once we were remounted, but there was no telling how far the animals might have run in the terror of the night. Gomez started to whine about how his arm was hurting him, but I gave him no slack on that account. I knew the wound to be minor, no matter his complaints, and sent him out with the rest.

What came next was harder still. James and John were gathered around the canvas containing the body of their brother. Joaquin stood awkwardly by, unable to speak but unwilling to leave his friends. James looked up at my approach.

"The first three horses we recover are yours," I said. "No matter whose they are, they are yours to take Peter back home. I'll send one of the vaqueros along, or Tor." Fowler nodded his agreement.

"Take Peter home," James repeated hollowly. "Yes, we need to do that. He'll be buried next to Grandfather."

"I'm more sorry than I can say, boys. Peter was just telling me yesterday how glad he was to be here, but I wish now we had turned back at the first sign of trouble."

John sniffed. "When I got scared and wanted to go home, Peter told me not to be a baby. He said being a quitter would shame Father. Peter would never have left without finishing the drive."

"Well," I said simply, "we can't always control how things turn out. If it wasn't that I need to see to saving the rest of the herd for your father, I'd throw in the hand now, too."

"No!" James said sharply. "We're not throwing in this hand!"

"Now, James," I began, "nobody expects—"

"No!" he said again, cutting me off. "We are here in Father's place, and I'm the oldest now, so I decide. I say our job is helping with the herd and catching up to Alzado. Father would be disappointed with anything less."

"But, boys, what about Peter? And your parents need to be told."

James shook his head decisively. "What's done can't be changed, so our folks don't have to hear about Peter till they also hear that we did what was needed. Besides, Peter liked this spot. It's a good enough resting place for now."

Tor, James, and I fashioned crude shovels from tree branches. We dug into a sandy space in the south side of the hill that was overhung by an earthen bank. Joaquin and John found two straight sticks, and these they bound together in the form of a cross by using leather strips salvaged from the remnants of busted reins.

We arranged Peter Reed's body in the cutout under the overhang and rolled up some rocks with which to cover the spot. When all was ready, James hesitated when his little brother said, "I don't know, James. We don't have a priest. What if this isn't holy ground?"

James looked around at the sky and the giant, patient oaks, then listened for a moment to the scolding call of a bluejay. "This is right," he said. "God is here, even if a priest isn't."

Slanting beams of sunlight brightened the hillside as we dug into the bank, collapsing it over the grave. We rolled the granite rocks atop the place, and when it was neat, John and Joaquin set up the cross. "Now," James said, "where do we begin tracking Alzado?"

18

JAMES WAS RIGHT. We could not linger around Peter Reed's grave. Already it was time to think of finding the horses and the herd. Attending to business, so to speak.

Folks fresh from the States or other civilized countries often believe that we of the West are short of a normal set of human emotions. We are described as unfeeling by those with more sheltered lives.

Let me record that such a charge is a slanderous lie. Unless a westerner is a hardened criminal or has abused liquor, he has no lack of feelings. Nor have our sensibilities been blunted. It is necessity that drives us to set aside emotions and press on.

I put the boys to work collecting all the remnants of provision and tack. Now every morsel of jerked beef and every scrap of bridle was precious.

Tor and I cobbled together pieces of reins and strips of leather cut from trampled saddles. We were making jaquimas, bridlepieces, which the gringos call hackamores, that would work without bits by pressure on the horses' noses and jaws.

Around noon the vaqueros returned, having located neither mounts nor steers. They were a footsore lot—walking far in high-heeled, pointed-toed boots was never done for pleasure.

I watched Gomez flop down with his back against an oak. So that he could sit without his pistol grip pressing into his gut, he pulled it from his belt and laid it beside him.

Gomez called Joaquin to him. The boy had recovered a stuff sack full of jerky and was distributing the dried meat to the men. The vaquero gestured for the boy to come closer, then spoke something to him. I saw Joaquin's limbs grow stiff and his spine turn rigid, as if he was hearing something that terrified him.

I wanted to go immediately and find out what was up, but decided to speak to the boy privately first. I poked idly about in the dirt, as if I were recovering something of use. To my surprise, there in the dust were two small fragments of Bible pages. My copy of the Good Book, which had traveled with me for more years than I could recall, now was torn to shreds and scattered. I stuffed the fragments of paper into my pocket without looking at them.

After Joaquin completed his rounds to all the vaqueros, I joined him near the fire. "What did he say to you?" I asked.

"Who, Señor Andrew?" He spoke as if he did not take my meaning, but his eyes flickered toward where Gomez lay.

"What are you afraid of, Joaquin? What did he say to you?"

Again his frame stiffened, and he glanced quickly at the vaquero who was toying idly with his pistol. The bandaged knife wound did not seem to be causing Gomez any great distress.

"He said that we must hurry to find the horses. He says that Alzado has most certainly gone for the rest of Jack Powers' gang, and they will be returning to kill us and steal the herd."

I listened to the last sentence as I was already walking away from Joaquin over to Gomez's relaxed form. "Gomez," I called out, "what do you know of Powers? What are you hiding?"

"I? I am not hiding anything, señor," he said innocently. "I have heard it said that Alzado, the cursed savage, belongs to an outlaw band whose leader is the American Powers. If it is true, señor, it will mean much trouble for us."

Settled some by this explanation, I demanded, "But why frighten the boy? Why didn't you tell me directly?"

Gomez shrugged. "It is only hearsay, señor. I was just telling the muchacho of the great need to hurry and locate the horses. Perhaps he is easily frightened because of the stampede."

I reached down and grasped Gomez by the arm. I will admit that I took hold of the wrist on the wounded side on purpose. With one yank I stood the vaquero upright, spilling his pistol from his lap and his jerky into the dirt.

"You're exactly right about the need to hurry," I said. "Bring your food. You and I will go search together, and you can tell me all you know or have heard."

Gomez could not very well refuse a direct order from the boss, no matter how tired he was. He made a great show of wincing when he touched his injured arm, but he tramped along out of the camp by my side. I whistled for Dog to join us, and we three set out. I carried one of our improvised bridles and Gomez carried another.

Once unleashed, Gomez's tongue babbled like the stream beside which we hiked. "There is much I know of Alzado, señor, but much more that is spoken of Jack Powers around the cantinas of the City of the Queen of the Angels, Los Angeles. Powers has used his skill at cards to gain enough money to hire some very bad men. It is said that he will soon rule the gold camps, far from any law that could touch him."

I nodded grimly at the remembrance of how Jack Powers had made himself out to be the law. "Go on," I said.

"This Powers has men who rob and kill along El Camino Real. He has those in the cantinas who report of who has much gold, and soon—" Gomez drew his thumb across his neck and made throat-cutting noises.

"And Alzado?" I asked. "Why an Indian vaquero?"

Gomez looked around as if he expected to see the Yaqui lurking behind a tree. "Powers is very clever. He knows he must have fresh horses with which his malditos may flee their crimes. On each rancho of renown, he keeps those who will steal the best mounts."

I looked down at the knife hilt showing above my boot top. To think of the cutthroat Yaqui around Will and Francesca's home made me shudder . . . almost as bad as the thought of how far he had ridden with me unaware of his nature.

Dog had been ranging along on either side of us as we hiked. At my command he would explore branching side canyons and dive into thickets. He had on this occasion been out of sight long enough, and I whistled for him to return.

Imagine my delight when instead of Dog's recall, my signal was acknowledged by a bugle from Shawnee. Through the manzanita she came, sorrel and white flashing, leading a band of six horses with her.

Her tail was flagged, and she was obviously proud of herself. "So that's what kept you," I said, rubbing her nose. "You stopped to gather your friends."

My paint mare willingly accepted the unfamiliar bridle, while Gomez had somewhat more difficulty with his mount. "Drive these others back to camp," I said as the vaquero finished wrestling with the jaquima. "I'll have another look round for the cattle."

But where had Dog gotten off to? With Shawnee beneath me again, even though we were minus a saddle, things felt a lot better. I pointed Shawnee straight up the highest hill I could see close by in order to survey the countryside.

When we reached shale rock, we wound around the cone-shaped peak, spiraling upward till we emerged above the tree line. There below us was spread the terrain of the Sierras, like a map in a geography book. Looking south I could see the little knoll where we had camped and where Peter Reed now lay buried.

My eyes traced the wandering path of the creek to the point where Tor and I had discovered Peter's body, and still farther to where I had met up with Shawnee. I probed beyond that point, searching for the shapes of the cattle, and for Dog.

The afternoon sun glared on granite and sand, making it difficult to see. I nudged Shawnee forward a few paces, then shaded my eyes. There was a particular side canyon I was interested in because of a familiar coyote shape that crouched in the narrow throat of the arroyo.

"Now, why would he. . . ?" I mused aloud. A single cloud of no great size drifted obligingly across the sun. As the glare

faded, the back wall of the box canyon jumped into high relief. Standing out against the granite walls were the dark
forms of hundreds of cattle, milling about within the confines
of the little valley and guarded by the patient watchfulness of
Dog.

19

I HAVE HEARD it said that one of the cruelest tortures wrought upon a man is to deprive him of sleep for long periods of time. Tor and I had not allowed our eyes to close for almost forty-eight hours. While the others slept and worked in shifts, we dared not rest. The menacing thought of Jack Powers was always before us. How long did we have before Alzado reached Powers with the news of our approach? How long before Powers and his henchmen rode out to greet us? Although we were forced to depend on the remaining vaqueros, we dared not trust them.

By the light of our second campfire, the sleepless days and hours closed in on us.

"You're done up, Andrew," Tor said in a low voice as he sat beside me on a log.

"That I am." I could not argue. "And so are you, pard." Tor's eyes were ringed with dark circles. "You look like you've been hit in the face with a board."

He managed a faint smile. "You ain't gonna win no beauty prizes, neither." We both looked over our sleeping comrades with envy. Gomez and Ortiz stood watch over the herd now. Tor was set to join them, while I was to remain watchful here at the camp for two hours and then exchange places with Tor at midnight.

Tor rubbed his hand wearily over his eyes and gave his head a shake as if to clear away the grogginess. He muttered, "We ain't gonna be no use to nobody if'n we don't get some shut-eye. Why don't you sleep here a couple hours, Andrew? I'll wake you at the end of my watch, and you can take lookout while I sleep. Long as one or t'other of us is out with the herd and keepin' guard, it don't make no sense that t'other one of us can't rest a bit."

It was not so much the herd we were watching but the vaqueros. We both knew that. We trusted no one, even though we needed their help. Could it hurt if one of us slept for a bit as long as the other was alert?

In my muddled brain Tor's offer made sense. I nodded agreement, but I do not remember speaking to him. Sinking down, I let my head rest against the log. Tor dropped a tattered blanket on me, and I called Dog to come lie beside me. I closed my eyes with the knowledge that four-footed critters like Dog have some God-given sense that lets them be on guard even as they sleep. At the first whiff of danger my shaggy companion would alert me. One hand closed around the handle of my knife. The other rested on the ruff of Dog's neck. I was lost in profound sleep before Tor took his first step out of camp.

The sounds of the night mingled with my dreams. Far away I heard the night time bawling of cattle, and I dreamed myself riding among them. *I sat in my saddle. The Allen rifle was ready across my thighs. Shawnee moved effortlessly as I urged her around the perimeter. Then it was daylight, and somehow I was back in Santa Barbara on the Reed Rancho. Will Reed waved at me from where he rode on the far side of the herd. Peter was next to him on the curly-coated Chino. Sunlight glinted on his dark red hair, and he turned his face full toward me and smiled. I was relieved by this kindly sight of him, and I imagined that the stampede and the death of Peter had all been a nightmare! How good and true it seemed to be herding the cattle with the boy again! The nightmare of reality was turned around in my vision to become a vapor that I joyfully dismissed. "Buenos días Peter!" I called, and I felt myself smile. There was no Alzado. No Gomez. No threat of Jack Powers or the lawless violence of the gold fields. . . .*

But suddenly the vision changed. I raised my eyes to see a rider approaching behind Peter. Dust rose like smoke from a vast fire behind the galloping bay. I strained to see who it was coming on so fast at Peter's back! A sense of dread filled me as I recog-

nized the shape of Alzado, and then I saw him bring the Allen rifle up to his shoulder and take aim! I tried to shout a warning to Peter! I tried to call out the attacker's name! I reached for the Allen and realized with horror that I had given my rifle to Alzado! The fierce Yaqui now held Peter and me in the sights of my own gun!

"Look behind you!" I heard the cry.

Was it my voice shouting the alarm to Peter? Was I calling for the boy to face the Indian?

I opened my mouth. No sound escaped. In that instant I realized that it was Alzado who was shouting. Not to Peter Reed, but to me! Peter dissolved into a bloody, broken mass before my eyes!

"Look behind you, Señor Andrew!" screamed Alzado. "Turn! Turn! Open your eyes!"

I turned at his urging and saw the grinning face of Gomez on the hill behind me. Beside Gomez were the other vaqueros in a line. They parted, and Jack Powers rode out to lead them.

The earth rumbled, and I heard the low growl of Dog. I felt the warning of his snarl beneath my hand.

"Look behind you!" The voices of Peter and Alzado joined as one.

The dream erupted into reality as Dog leapt to his feet barking at the perimeter of the camp. My eyes snapped open.

"Look behind you!" shouted James Reed, tangled in his bedroll.

I scrambled for my Allen, then realized once again what was real and what was vision. Faces came into focus. I heard the hammer of a pistol click back and whirled to see the bloody form of Tor Fowler as he was shoved forward to fall at my feet. From the shadows, the grinning smirk of Gomez caught the firelight. He leveled his pistol at my gut, then waved it at the barred fangs of Dog.

"Do not shoot!" cried Joaquin. "You promised if I did not tell you would not kill—"

Gomez laughed at the boy and at the shocked look in my eyes.

"Did I say such a promise?"

Dog barked and made as if to lunge. "Dog!" I commanded, and with a gesture sent the animal back into the gloom of the brush. Gomez fired once, but I heard the chapparal cracking as Dog retreated. He had not been hit.

Tor lay in the dust and raised his head. "Andrew . . ." he moaned. "Sorry . . . pard . . . I dozed and they—" Ortiz kicked him hard in the belly, silencing him.

Gomez sneered more broadly as the other vaqueros joined him, holding each of the boys in their gun sights. Ramos had the look of a man ashamed. Ortiz and Sanchez took pleasure in our helplessness.

Joaquin clasped his hands together and dropped to his knees to beg for our lives. "I did as you told me, Gomez!" he wept. "I did not tell Señor Andrew!"

Ortiz leaned over and slapped the boy hard across the face, sending him sprawling back with a cry of pain.

"Enough!" I shouted. Gomez replied with a pistol shot aimed between my feet.

"You are in no position to say what is enough," Gomez replied with amusement. He smoothed his thin mustache and shoved his sombrero back on his head in a self-assured gesture. "You have never been in a position to say what was enough. That privilege has always been mine. Only you did not know it, Señor Andrew." He bowed in a mocking way.

"Alzado?" I asked.

"The fierce Yaqui?" Gomez laughed. "A spineless coward, that one, mi amigo. He would not join us. I spoke to him early about our little business arrangement. He refused to be a part of it."

"And so it was you who cut his cinch."

Again the mocking bow and the smile that told everything. "A shame Don Peter got in the way. Ah, well. One less to worry about."

"Murderer!" Young John Reed lunged at Gomez as James tried to hold him back. With one blow, Sanchez knocked the boy unconscious to the ground.

"You are the leader of these children," Gomez said. "Silence them, or the next one will die." His fingers were white

around the pistol grip. "I am growing weary of the game." He
was not bluffing.

"Keep still," I issued the order quietly. A sense of my own
foolishness filled me. I had been ready to lynch Alzado, who
was the only man among seven vaqueros who had done no
harm! Now the five who remained held guns to our bellies
while Gomez painted the whole picture.

"This one," Gomez waved the gun at Tor, who remained
unconscious. "Sí. A broken cinch? I have no taste for murder,
you see. But a faulty cinch? What is that but carelessness? An
accident. I can take no blame that he did not check. Acci-
dents. I drop my gun and the herd stampeded. It was not I
who caused Peter Reed to fall." He looked at James as the
boy stared at him with unguarded hatred.

It was plain to me that in spite of his claims to not be a
murderer, Gomez planned all along to murder us and take
the herd. He had used us much in the way we had used him in
order to move the herd close to the northern gold camps.
Now our usefulness was at an end.

"You Americanos," he continued, "you steal all of California from us." He nodded toward his compatriots, and I knew
this speech was meant for them as much as for us prisoners.
"You steal the land. You steal the gold. You steal the cattle.
No? Now we Californios take back the cattle. Just a few,
señor." Gomez's face broke into a vermin's smile. "And then
we will have a little of the gold, too. A small herd. Don Will
Reed is a great man. He will hardly miss one thousand head,
is this not so?"

"He will not care for a thousand head of cattle. . . . But if
his sons are harmed, I know Don Will Reed will hunt you like
a dog and see you hang for this," I replied. Then, glancing at
the others, I added, "He will not rest until you are all dangling from an oak tree to rot at the end of a noose."

Such words had the effect I wished. The vaqueros looked
fearfully at one another and then at Gomez. "I had nothing to
do with the death of Peter Reed!" cried Ramos.

"We care only for the herd. For the gold," declared Ortiz
gruffly. "We have nothing to do with the killing of men."

James cradled the head of his brother. "My father will see you all dead for what happened to Peter!" he cried.

"An accident!" Gomez spread his too-soft hands in protest. "I tell you it was no more than that! Meant to get Alzado out of the way!"

James opened his mouth as if to accuse again. I silenced the boy with a sharp look. Here was our only hope. "Sí," I agreed with Gomez. "Yes. No one can argue that. You meant no harm to poor Peter. An accident. You could not have known. Will Reed is a man of reason. For the lives of his sons and his friends, he would gladly offer you this ransom of one thousand beeves. What is that to him, Gomez? As long as we are set free. Unharmed." I directed my words to the other vaqueros who seized upon the lesser crime of rustling as though it was nothing compared to murder. What were a few cattle of a rich man, after all? Will Reed would not mind so much, would he? Not so long as James and John and Will Reed's friends were safe.

They began babbling at once to Gomez that they wanted no part in murder. Don Will Reed was a powerful man. He would not forgive harm done to his sons. The bandits united against the unspoken threat of our deaths. Gomez had lost the fight by his own argument that he was not a killer . . . merely a Californio patriot taking back what rightly belonged to other Californios!

I did not bring up the fact that the brigand he worked for was one of the American soldiers who had fought against the Californios with violence that defied description. No need to bring up the origins of Jack Powers now. Our captors somehow believed that they might escape justice by leaving us unharmed! The truth was that every last one of them would be hunted and captured and brought to justice. Inwardly I memorized the features of each face and the sound of each voice as I vowed that I would lead the hunt one day! For the time being, though, our lives were spared.

"I am no assassin, mi amigo," Gomez demurred again. He shrugged. "That is not to say I will not shoot out your knees if you resist me now." He motioned with the gun. "Sit down.

Take your boots off." I obeyed, and he gestured broadly. "Yes. That's it. All of you. Take your boots off. Sí. And the boots of Tor Fowler, if you please, señor?"

Our boots were thrust into a sack and tied to a horse. "Even used boots are worth something in the gold camp, I hear," Gomez laughed. "I shall sell them at a good price, to be sure."

After this he and his gang bound us tightly with leather thongs and then separated us, tying each of us to our own tree so that we could not help one another escape. Tor moaned and opened his eyes as Gomez mounted his horse and raised his arm in a rigid gesture of contempt.

"Hasta la vista, Americanos," Gomez laughed. "By the time you get free or are found, we will be rich men and long gone! Gracias, amigos! I shall think of you with amusement in days to come!"

Sunlight topped the jagged peaks of the Sierras as dust from the departing herd blended with the violet haze of dawn.

20

I COUNTED IT A miracle that the five of us were still alive. But we were in need of another miracle—and soon. Trussed up like calves at a branding, barefoot and unarmed, there was no guarantee that we would not die here. I imagined some future traveler stumbling upon these five oak trees and five human skeletons grinning back.

My legs had no feeling below the knees. My fingers had gone numb right off, leaving it impossible for me to attempt to work the knot. No doubt the bandits had tied us with tourniquet-like tightness for this reason. What good would it do for us to have been left alive, only to die of starvation and thirst? Gomez, while claiming he was not a murdered, was killing us slowly by the same methods I had seen among the cruel Mojave Indians of the high desert. Left like this, we were dead men all the same without some help.

Tor came conscious and realized our predicament. I was at the top of the knoll, and he was at the bottom, facing the broad view of the valley. He could not see any of the rest of us. We were all scattered across the slope.

"Anybody there?" he called. A chorus of voices replied.

"Andrew."

"James."

"John."

And then a voice filled with remorse. "Joaquin."

"That's good," Tor's voice rang out. "Nice day, ain't it, Andrew?"

It was good to hear humor in Tor's voice. At least the thieves had not knocked that out of him.

"I've been sitting here thinking how glad I am it's not too hot," I shouted back.

"You're right on that score. I'm sittin' about a yard from a red anthill. On a hot day they'd be comin' out to take some sun and a piece of my hide, I reckon. Ain't but a few of the little beggars out on a day like this. They ain't got a whiff of me yet, neither."

I had also noticed a large anthill just spitting distance from my bare feet. In the cold morning air, the critters were barely moving. As the day warmed, I knew they would emerge a thousand strong. A moment later John called out that there was a colony to the right of where he was sitting, and James reported a nest of yellow jackets just above where he was tied. Joaquin said nothing at all, until I called to him.

"You got any mean little animals keeping you company, Joaquin?"

A long pause. "I wish I will die and all of you go free," he replied with such misery that I felt grieved for him. Then the explanation gushed from him. "Gomez said he would not kill you if I did not tell what I heard him say about Jack Powers. He promised. That day I shot at you, it was because he pointed up and said, 'Look quick, boy! There is the bandido Powers coming, shoot him quick!' And then I shot, and he slapped me. Later he said if I tell you, he will slit your throat in the night. But now we are tied like hogs and left for the ants to eat when the sun gets hot. I pray that I will suffer more. I pray that I will die and you all will get free before the day grows warm and the ants come awake! May God send His angels to set you free!" he cried.

I will admit that there are few things that make me more angry than a grown man who will threaten and bully a help-less animal, a woman, or a youngun. Gomez had not only shot at my dog, he had threatened and bullied a boy I had taken as my own. How many days and miles had young Joaquin carried the burden of terror that we would be massacred in our sleep if he spoke up about what he knew? And now, on top of it, he had the weight of a guilt that was too heavy for his young soul. This was more brutal than the sting of a whip for a child.

Most younguns don't know that there's a big difference between a mistake in judgment and sin.

Tor spoke up a bit too cheerful for our situation. "Well, it
ain't no mortal sin that you tried to keep us from gettin' our
fool throats slit, boy. I ain't dead yet, and neither are you. I
don't aim to be the main course in no red ant picnic, neither.
How 'bout you, Andrew?"

"Nope." Then I added, "Don't let it trouble you, Joaquin.
I'd of done the same." This last was true. I remembered
clearly how at the age of twelve I had been bullied by a brig-
and who threatened the lives of those I loved most in the
world. If we got free from this mess, I would tell Joaquin of
my own experience at his age, and how a man had died because of my mistake. "Gomez won't get away with this. And
you know I don't make idle promises."

No matter how brave I sounded, the thought came to me
that maybe Gomez had gotten away with it and maybe I was
making idle promises, after all. The sun rose higher, and the
little mound of sand came alive with parades of red-worker
ants, heading off to search for food.

My feet and calves were numb, and so I watched with a sort
of detached horror as the first insect crawled out from between my big toe and my second toe. A horde followed,
climbing the bottom of my foot and swarming through my
toes like warriors breaching the top of a fortress wall. Tiny
pinpricks of pain penetrated the numbness, and right before
my eyes, my feet and ankles became a mass of bright red
welts.

Moments after the first assault, John shouted that the ants
near him were moving his way. James gave a sharp cry of
pain, and we knew that he had been stung. The knoll, carefully chosen to provide a painful death for us, was coming
alive.

I closed my eyes and prayed for some miracle—some
avenging angel to fly our way and set us free!

No avenging angel came with flaming sword to slice our
bonds. Most times the Lord does not work that way. Miracles
come as ordinary messengers. Ours came that day in the form

of my half-coyote dog who trotted up the knoll and whined and wagged and licked my face. Behind him followed a stiff, cold breeze, and on the wind floated the first dark tide of rain clouds.

I cannot say what understanding the grinning stock dog had of our predicament, but he licked a row of ants off my right foot and then tugged at the rawhide reata that held my ankles.

"Yes!" I cried. "Good dog!" My praise disrupted him, and he stood and wagged and wandered up to lick my face. I inwardly upbraided myself, closed my eyes, and ignored him. Some other voice was speaking to his critter mind, and I knew I must not interfere with its instructions!

Another whine came as Dog sat down to consider me. With my hands bound behind my back and the reata encircling me and the tree, I was a curious sight in his yellow eyes. He licked my arm again, and then as his tongue rubbed over the rope, he paused, bumped against me, and then began to gnaw at the braided leather in earnest.

The sky darkened with the troop of storm clouds.

I heard Tor give a whoop of delight. "I felt a drop! By gum, Andrew! A raindrop!"

I dared not reply, for fear of breaking the intense concentration of Dog. He was tugging and chewing the leather with the same enjoyment he might have gotten from a T-bone steak.

"Rain!" cried James.

"I felt it on my face!" shouted John. "Look there! The ants!"

No word came from Joaquin as those few light drops were joined by more and still more. I opened my eyes as the dry leaves rattled in the oak limbs above me. With pleasure I saw drops splash down on the frantic red horde as they scurried back toward the gravel hill like an army in retreat!

My red, swollen feet and ankles were washed clean of my tormentors! Thunder erupted, and lightning flashed just behind the mountain. Dog paused a moment, looked up, and then returned to his work as though his only aim in life was to chew through that tough hide rope!

"Andrew?" Tor called to me. "Andrew!" He demanded an answer.

"Shut up!" I shouted. Dog smiled at me and crunched his teeth, tugging as the leather frayed and weakened.

He seemed to be wondering why I did not help him? Could I not fight against the loop and break free? his look asked me. My arms were bloodless, dead. It would take me a while to move, I knew, even when I was loose from this hold.

I leaned my head back against the rough trunk of my prison and squeezed my eyes tight. I prayed as I had not prayed before in my life! The raindrops broke with the thunder into a downpour, clattering through the branches, drenching me and my fur-covered angel. The rawhide dampened. Dog tugged harder, chewed more fervently, pulled back in a tug of war until the reata yielded at last with a sharp snap.

With a cry, I toppled over in the mud. My hands and ankles were still bound with leather strips. Dog stood over me, nosing me as if to ask why I did not stand.

"Tor!" I shouted after another thunderclap. "Dog has chewed away the reata! I can't move. Got no feeling in my arms or legs."

Another crash of thunder drowned out his exultant reply. I lay on my side and eyed a small rain puddle forming as my arms and legs began the excruciating ache of rushing blood. And now the fire of the ant bites took hold. I gasped and groaned. Dog patiently licked my wounds and waited.

The heaviness of my limbs dissipated, and I suddenly felt the soothing coldness of the rain and the roughness of Dog's tongue. I moved my legs and scooted toward the mud puddle. Thrusting my hands and wrists into the mire, I began to work the leather. It stretched, it swelled with moisture, at last it yielded, and my hands slipped free!

With fumbling fingers I worked the knots of rawhide at my ankles. Then I grasped the trunk of the oak and managed to pull myself erect on unsteady legs. A moment more of agony broke as the full force of sensation flooded back. Then I raised my eyes gratefully heavenward and knew that what was just a sudden squall for another man was my miracle! What might be a hungry dog chewing through leather, to someone else's thinking, was for me the mighty hand of the Lord!

I stumbled down to unloose Tor. Then I raced to free Joaquin, who was bound with my black bullwhip! James and John half-crawled, half-stumbled to us. We all embraced. We cheered Dog and thanked heaven for the rain, and then we helped one another to the mint patch by the creek bed to doctor our ant bites.

21

COLD WATER FROM the stream and crushed mint leaves did something to soothe the searing sting of our bites. But there was no remedy to cool the burning anger we each felt toward the men who had deceived us and left us to die.

Still, I felt the obligation for the safety of the Reed brothers and for young Joaquin. We were without weapons and on foot. What chance would two men and three boys have against five armed vaqueros with a talent for ruthless cruelty?

The settlement called Tuleberg was several days' hike from where we were stranded. We would take the boys there for safety, and then Tor and I could set out alone to track Gomez. I laid out this plan to the boys as we rigged makeshift moccasins out of a discarded cowhide and a torn saddle blanket left behind by the gang.

James Reed raised his chin proudly, and I saw the determination of his father burning in his eyes. "If we go to Tuleberg, we will lose the herd."

"'Peers to me we already lost the herd, boy," Tor said, sucking on a mint leaf and rubbing his legs.

James turned on Tor angrily. "They killed Peter. Stole my father's cattle. Left us to die! By some miracle we are not only alive, but well and strong—"

"And angry," added young John. "I could not look Father in the eye again if we let them get away with this!"

"You youngsters don't understand, it seems to me—" Tor began, only to be savagely interrupted by the fury of James Reed.

"No! It is you who do not understand! We can beat them!"

"They have our guns," I tried to calm the boy. "Our horses."

"We have more than they would have if they were an army with cannons!" James cried with clenched fists.

Tor and I exchanged doubtful looks. "James—"

"We are stronger than they!" said Joaquin, joining against our better judgment.

"Yes! Stronger!" John leapt to his feet. "They cannot win! Will not win!"

"We are unarmed," Tor argued. "I don't aim to take you boys home to your mama in a sack, and that's final."

James narrowed his eyes and considered Tor for a moment. "You are a coward, Tor Fowler!" he said in a level voice. This was a foolish thing to say to Tor. I have known the mountain man to knock the teeth out of a man for a lot less than those words.

"Whoa up there, James," I said.

Then the boy turned on me. "And you are a coward, Andrew Sinnickson! And you spit in the eye of God if we do not go after Gomez and the others!"

"Spit in the eye!" Tor declared, puffing up like a bullfrog. "Why you little whelp pup! I ought to—"

"He is right, Señor Tor," Joaquin leapt into the fray. "Angels bring the rain to save us! Dog, who is a smart dog, but all the same he is still a dog . . . he chews through the rope! We are free. It is a miracle. Any priest will say it is so. Now you want to run away."

"Not run," I fumed. "Get you boys safe, that's all."

"It is our fight as much . . . no . . . more than yours!" James insisted. "It is my brother who lies buried in Mariposa." He fished a rumpled paper from his pocket and unfolded it to reveal a page from my Bible. "I found this," James held the page up. "I took it for a sign. For a promise." He began to read the words from the fragment. " 'Who hath any strength, except our God? It is God, that girdeth me with strength of war.' " He looked up. "It's torn there, but see the rest of it." He gave it to me to read.

I studied the ragged slip a moment and then read aloud what remained. " 'He teacheth my hands to fight: and my arms shall break even a bow of steel. Thou hast given me the defense of thy salvation: thy right hand shall hold me up. Thou shalt make room enough under me for to go: that my footsteps shall not slide.' " I swallowed hard and then finished the verse. " 'I will follow upon my enemies, and overtake them: neither will I turn again till I have destroyed them.' "

It was here that the page was torn away. I passed the fragment to Tor, who reread the words silently as James Reed stared me down like the shepherd boy David must have shamed the men who said no one could beat Goliath.

"Well, then." Tor blinked at me and then looked at James in a new light. "I'll be . . ."

"They're just men," James replied firmly. "And dark sinners at that. What hope do they have when they're in the wrong? And how can we turn away when we're in the right? I got to tell you. If I strike out from this place alone, I'm going to do it! There it is . . . *the word*. Isn't it? You think it's just an accident I found that? The rain and the dog? Just coincidence? Right is right and wrong is wrong. And there's a God who knows the difference. Father always taught us boys that this was true."

"That's right," agreed John.

"So you go to Tuleberg if you want," James said, putting his arms around the shoulders of Joaquin and John. "We three are striking out to take back what's ours. If we do not, then no honest man in all of California will be safe! We stop it here, or there will be no stopping it!"

It would have been easy enough I suppose for Tor and me to wallop the lot of them, tie them up, and drag them to safety, but the truth was that we two grown men were shamed and instructed by what they said. Two unarmed men and three boys taking back eight hundred head of cattle from an armed gang would be some sort of warning to others who might try murdering and stealing over honest employment . . . if we did indeed succeed in such a desperate gamble. Could I now discount what I had considered a miracle when I was set free?

Could I doubt that some kind force was watching over us? Helping us when we were helpless, yet expecting us to also do our part in the drama?

These were matters far beyond my understanding and my ability to wholly believe. And yet I knew that what James said was true. Right was right and wrong was wrong. Deep down I felt that the battle of Good and Evil was an ancient war fought in the fields of men's eternal souls. Many times evil triumphed simply because good men backed down or turned away or gave up in the face of difficult odds. James Reed did not say all these things out loud, and yet I heard them as clearly as if the boy had preached a sermon. He, like a young shepherd boy named David, was willing to face what I perceived to be a Goliath simply because he believed unshakably that Good must prevail over Evil.

James retrieved the thin leaf of paper from Tor and returned it to his breast pocket. "If I am killed, Señor Andrew," he leveled his green eyes on me, "take this to my father. Tell him I died believing this. Tell him I fought like a man." He turned his gaze to the hills. "I could never go home and tell him I ran away from the men who killed Peter."

22

THE OWL HOOT was low and mournful sounding. Its aching tone brought to my mind a hollowed-out old snag of an oak that stood on the bluff above the Cherokee camp where I grew up. There had been a great horned owl who lived in that snag. Its call had been a beacon from far across the prairie.

The difference was, this night owl I knew by name. It was Tor Fowler, and the signal meant that he was in position.

That we had caught up to the rustlers in one day and half a night had more to do with good fortune and Divine Providence than how fleet-footed we were. Truth to tell, our feet were sore, and only periodic stops to reline our improvised moccasins with moss and crushed mint leaves kept us going.

When I had spotted the herd from the tall pinnacle, I had not only seen the box canyon, but had located another feature of interest as well. This second observation I had not shared with anyone until after the theft of the herd.

It seems that the wandering course of the stream bed and the track by which the cattle would be moved curved around the range of hills. By hard hiking and climbing, we five were able to across the narrow range and traverse in three miles what the herd would cover in ten.

That still left us miles behind, but we never slackened our pace. We knew that with only five vaqueros to handle eight hundred head, they would not be moving any too fast.

We were right. By midnight we were close enough to see the glow of their campfire. At three in the morning by the set of the stars, we were almost ready.

The biggest worry in our plan was right at the beginning. A loud yell or a gunshot fired by either of the two sentries would bring the other three boiling out of their camp. Their pistols would be too much for our fists unless we could even the score some first. "The problem," as Tor phrased it as we had hiked and plotted, "is how to separate two snakes from their fangs without waking up the rest of a nest of vipers."

On the far side of the grassy plain, Tor, James Reed, and Dog were watching the movements of a night herder. Even though I could not see what was happening with Tor, I watched it unfold in my mind's eye. A hand signal from Tor sent Dog across in front of the guard, close enough to be momentarily in sight, but not so close that the vaquero could be sure of what he had seen.

If it worked, the sentry's attention would be focused on the place where a gray spotted shape had appeared and disappeared. Tor would be creeping up behind, readying himself for what came next.

I motioned for John and Joaquin to stop the moment I picked up the outline of the vaquero on our side of the herd. He was less than thirty yards away; and what was more, from the white patches that stood out against the shadow, he had drawn Shawnee from the string as his mount.

I gave a deep owl call of reply that meant we were also ready. Now it was up to our prayers and the resolve to not draw back once it started.

Shawnee's ears had no doubt been pricking back and forth ever since the first owl hoot. As an old Indian fighter herself, she would know what was afoot.

I moved up so as to keep a sleepy black steer between me and the guard. When the animal moved closer, so did I. Just when I was congratulating myself on how well things were going, the wayward critter abruptly turned off the wrong way, leaving me hanging out like a shirt on a clothesline.

I dropped flat on my belly behind a clump of brush. After a moment, I started to inch my way forward, but a bunch of dead weeds crackled under me. The vaquero turned his head at the sound, and I ducked my face so there could be no reflection off my eyes.

The sweat broke out on my forehead, despite the coolness of the night and the damp grass. One shout, one shot, and all would be lost. If we were caught this time, there would be no second chance—not even an anthill—just five dead bodies left for the buzzards.

Another steer ambled by, actually stepping over me as it grazed. As I held my breath, fearful that it would tread right on me, it too broke through the brush with a rattle and a snap.

No gunshot came and no call of alarm. The vaquero must have decided that the steer had made both noises. When I chanced a peek again, he was facing away from me into the dark.

I thought I heard a muffled thud and the sound of hooves from away off on the other side of the drove, but it could not matter now. It was time to get this show on the road.

Slowly and quietly, making no noise, I stood up. I shook out the coil of my whip. If Shawnee knew I was there, she gave no sign, giving me the only chance I would have. My first cast would have to be perfect.

In the dark it was hard to judge distances. I slipped a little closer, then a little closer yet.

Now! The whip flicked out, but instead of slashing the vaquero's back, it knotted around his throat. It is human nature that when something grabs you by the neck, your hands instinctively fly upward to try to clear the stranglehold away.

That is exactly what the night herder did. As his grip left the reins to reach for what was choking him, I gave a sudden yank, and Shawnee spurted forward. Remember, he was riding bareback with just a blanket under him. The guard slid off backward like a watermelon seed squirting between your fingers.

By the time he hit the ground, I was on top of him. It was Sanchez. He was dazed from the impact and still trying to uncoil the lash from around his gullet. His eyes went wide when he saw me, but the right I threw at his chin from two feet away laid him out cold.

A low "hist" from me brought the boys to my side. We stuffed Sanchez's mouth with rags, then trussed him up with my whip. The pistol had been knocked from his belt by the fall, but John and Joaquin scoured the clumps of grass until they located it.

Another crackle in the brush made me whirl around, pistol in hand, but it was only Tor with James and Dog. They were leading a lineback dun.

"How'd it go?" I whispered.

"Like a charm!" Tor's hoarse reply was all smiles. "It was Garcia. Dog got his attention, and I give the Paiute rush. I taken him clean off the horse while it was between one mouthful of grass and the next. He hit the ground without never havin' a chance to draw, nor call out. 'Course," he said without remorse, "I think his neck is broke. Anyways, he ain't movin'."

Tor and I sat our mounts and waited in the chilly dark. I was grateful that the serape I had taken from Sanchez was both disguising and warming. We were waiting for the stars to swing round. Too early and Gomez would know something was wrong.

When it was time, I grasped Fowler by the hand. "I'm glad to have you," I said.

Tor's reply was grimly humorous. "Thunderation, Andrew! I wouldn't miss this show for all the gold in the Calaveras."

We separated then, one to either end of the camp. We left the three boys and Dog to guard Sanchez.

I held the pistol low across my chest behind the serape and moved Shawnee into a slow walk, directly toward the fire. I needed a chance to locate all three men if I could. These bandidos weren't dumb; even if they did not expect to be attacked, they still slept back in the shadows and not up close where the firelight would pinpoint their whereabouts.

I saw Gomez first. He was the one closest to the warmth, which seemed right in character to me. Over on the right, underneath the low-hanging branches of a fir tree was another, but whether Ortiz or Ramos, I could not tell.

Gomez stirred and rolled over. I knew that as he came awake he would be thinking, "What time is it?" and "Is it the end of the watch?" I adjusted Sanchez's sombrero lower to shield my face and cocked the hammer of the pistol.

Sitting up and rubbing sleep from his eyes, Gomez heard the sound of Shawnee's hooves and reached for his gun. Catching sight of the familiar serape relaxed him, and he called out, "Hola, Sanchez? Qué hora es? What is the time?"

Where was the third man? In just a few seconds the ball would open and the location of the missing dance partner was important.

"Qué ocurre? What is it, Sanchez? Is anything wrong?"

It was time. I could only hope that Fowler had been able to pick up the last outlaw's location from his different vantage point.

I drew the pistol and tipped back the sombrero. "Freeze, Gomez!" I ordered.

His hand started to move toward the weapon, and then he stopped. A momentary anger was replaced by a grin as he sized up the situation. "You have made a losing bet, señor," he said. "You are here alone and we are three."

"I don't think this wager was so bad," I said calmly. "Listen carefully, Gomez. Raise your hands over your head. Then tell your friends in the brush to do the same."

The familiar smirk was back. "Why would I do that, gringo? Right now you are surrounded."

"Because whatever happens, you are going to die," I replied. "Do you really think I won't blow your head off from this distance? It doesn't matter who shoots first, because you'll be just as dead."

I was near enough to see his throat work as he thought this over, and then he said, "Ortiz, don't do anything stupid."

Clearly he was hoping that the remaining unseen gunman would circle and get the drop on me. Was he right?

Out of the dark and off to my left came a familiar throaty chuckle. "It's okay, Andrew," Tor's voice called. "I got Ramos. Caught him with his pants down, so to speak."

That's when Ortiz decided to make his play. I caught a movement out of the corner of my eye, and the pistol bucked in my hand as I snapped a shot into the thickest shadow under the fir branches.

I heard Ortiz yell, and then Gomez was going for his gun. The muzzle was turning my way, the barrel pivoting up as I whipped my sights back around and fired.

Gomez was overeager. He shot before he aimed, and his bullet went through the broad brim of the sombrero I wore. I don't know where my slug caught him, but he fired only the one time.

I slid off Shawnee and divided my attention between Gomez and the brush where Ortiz lay. Tor marched Ramos into camp and roughly ordered him to sprawl on his face by the fire. With me covering, Fowler checked the other two and announced that they were both dead.

"Well, pard," he said, "looks like we got us a herd again."

23

THREE MORE GRAVES beside the trail greeted the dawn below Sierran skies. Sanchez had his hands tied behind his back, and I had my whip coiled and hanging again at my side.

Tor and I had a serious discussion with Ramos. He seemed the least hardened of all the outlaws, and we surely needed help with the herd. In the end we compromised. We gave him his parole in order to gain a sixth drover to our band, but we kept his gun and knife.

The dewdrops sparkled on the milkweed, and the morning brightened into what we hoped would be one of the last few days on the trail. "Head 'em out, James," I called. The boys, who had done the work of men and seen trouble and shown courage and resolve beyond their years, set the herd on the move.

We made Sanchez walk. Aside from being a rough kind of justice, it gave us little need to watch him. Besides, he had the most watchful of all possible guards. We set Dog to keep an eye on him, and you can believe that a meaningful growl and the flash of white teeth gave the outlaw plenty of mind to keep up and not stray.

The day passed without incident. We moved the cattle slowly, keeping them bunched so as to not make more work for ourselves. The herd had been pushed into a narrow place between two low ranges of hills. The trail followed the watershed and curved around to the north about a half mile ahead of where I rode the drag spot.

I was thinking that even eating trail dust felt good after all we'd been through, and even better since it would soon be done. Up ahead the steers were starting to bunch up and mill around. The leaders had stopped for some unknown reason, as though they had run into a wall just around the bend.

I kicked Shawnee into her ground-eating canter. I had been woolgathering for so long that I'd lost track of Tor and James, who should have been just ahead of me and on either side.

It was too early to halt for the night. Through my mind went thoughts of high water across the trail or an encounter with a grizzly, but there was no serious concern in me.

So I was completely unprepared when Shawnee and I loped around the corner and ran smack spraddle into Jack Powers. Flanking him were Ed and Patrick Dunn.

My move to draw Sanchez's pistol was stopped when I saw that Patrick Dunn was holding Joaquin off the ground under one arm. Ed held a rifle on Tor, Ramos, and the Reed brothers, while a grinning Sanchez collected our pistols. Dog had run off again.

I yanked Shawnee to a savage halt, setting her haunches down. "Let him go," I growled at Pat.

It was Powers who answered. "Not so fast, Sinnickson. Tell me, who is holding all the cards this time?"

"I've got ten men with rifles coming up pronto," I bluffed. "If you know what's good for you, you better light out quick and not mess with us."

Powers laughed until his eyes ran a stream of tears past the red bulb of his nose. And what could I do, while Dunn held on to Joaquin?

"Ten men with rifles, you say? That's rich! I say this sorry band of dog meat is everybody. What you've got is a broken-down mountain goat, a traitor, and three cubs that should have been drowned at birth. Rodriguez has been watching you since noon—we just didn't want to scatter the herd, so we waited until now to collect you."

He was so sure of himself it made my blood boil. From behind a boulder rode Rodriguez, the vaquero who had disappeared after the snake episode long before. He also had a rifle across the withers of the palomino. "Greetings, señor!" he said with mocking cheerfulness. "How pleasant to see you again. Where is my good friend Gomez and the others? I thought to meet *them*, but we were not expecting *you*."

"Gomez is dead," I said coldly. "So are Garcia and Ortiz. You sure you're on the winning side, Rodriguez?"

"Enough of this pointless jabber," Powers interrupted. "Drop your gun and get over with the others. Pat, throw down the kid. That's the lot of them, except the dog."

We six, since they intended to kill Ramos along with us, were herded into a small group. Facing us were four men with rifles in their hands and greed and murder in their hearts. "Gold on the hoof," Powers said, marveling at the size of the drove. "All right, let's get on with it."

A rifle shot from the ridge line back of me split the afternoon stillness. The slug hit the ground right between the front feet of Powers' buckskin. The animal jerked and danced, bumping into the other mounts while the outlaws nervously tried to regain control. Patrick raised his rifle to meet the unexpected threat and was cautioned by these words. "Stand easy, boys," said a nasally, Yankeefied voice. "That was just to get your attention."

It was Ames. Beside him with a smoking Allen rifle stood Alzado. Hulking nearby was the grizzly bear figure of Boki, and as if this weren't enough, Dog was wagging among two hundred Angel's Camp miners.

"There's your beef, boys," Ames said. "Just like I promised."

Whooping and hollering so that I thought the herd might turn and hightail it back to southern California, the troop of hungry prospectors charged down the hillside, surrounding both us and Powers' men.

Tor went up to Powers and demanded that the outlaw chief get off his horse. Tor proceeded to explain exactly what was going to happen to the bandit when he did so.

Powers shook his head and waved the rifle. "What's the matter, mountain man? Can't you take a joke? Why, all we did was ride out to meet you same as these others. I wanted to make an offer to buy your herd, not knowing it was already spoken for."

"Why you . . ."

I thought for an instant that Tor would do his Paiute trick right there on Powers, but the would-be rustler and murderer spoke quickly. "Easy there, mountain man. If you want to start a war, remember we've still got our rifles. Besides, a whole lot of innocent people might get hurt."

"He's right, Tor," I said reluctantly. "Let him go."

"But he . . . this . . . lowdown . . ."

Words failed my friend, and I have to admit that I didn't like it either, but for once, Powers was right. The cheering, celebrating miners scarcely noticed when a sullen file of riders, led by Jack Powers, exited up the canyon and out of sight.

24

NEVER TRY TO tell me that the Almighty does not have a sense of humor. After all the tragedy and triumph of weeks on the drive, you would think that a period of rest and relaxation would follow.

Rest, yes. Relaxation, ha!

Three days after we got to Angel's Camp, we had tidied up the details of the sale. All tolled, the cattle brought in some eighty thousand dollars worth of dust, nuggets, and the three-ounce gold slugs called "adobes." And then I got sick.

Not anything life-threatening, like cholera, or dramatic, like pneumonia. No sir, I couldn't even get sympathy. I came down with the mumps.

The doctor gave me a mess of willow bark tea and a bandage to wrap around my swollen jaws. When I asked him what else to do, he scratched his head and said, "Ache some, I guess. You'll be better in a week or two."

He was right, but the trouble was, the rest of my party couldn't wait. You see, Powers was still a force to be reckoned with, especially with so much gold at stake. So we had gratefully accepted the offer to journey south with a company of United States infantry.

The lieutenant of that detail, a young man with the imposing name of William Tecumsah Sherman, set the departure date. When it was time to leave, I was still a week or so from being well enough to travel.

Tor, Joaquin, and the Reeds had come to tell me goodbye. It was not a tearful farewell. Truth to tell, they mostly stood way back and laughed at my cheeks.

"I'm powerful sorry, Andrew," Tor said. (He didn't look sorry.) "We'll see your share safe to Santa Barbara and meet up with you there in another ten days or so."

"Just you leave me a thousand of my share," I instructed, "and you won't see me for a month. I've a mind to see San Francisco before I head south. You can start the next roundup, and then I'll join you."

So, a few days after that parting, Dog, Shawnee, and I were finally on the trail. I was headed down the same Calaveras path I had ridden up a few months before. It seemed both a short while and long ages since I had seen it last.

The road had been widened and improved some to accommodate Ames's supply wagons and the tracks of some thousand eager miners who had come after us. I could still recognize the original landmarks though, like the creek bottom where the Indians had been attacked and the precipice where Ames had almost been killed.

When my casual inspection took in the top of the cliff where the rock slide had started, I almost dropped my teeth. I thought I saw the glint of light on metal in the same spot as we were ambushed before. Just a quick flash and nothing to follow, but it took me aback enough that I called Dog to me and looked things over in earnest. I even pulled my brand-new Colt repeating rifle from its boot.

Well, after watching a while, and not remarking another sign, I put it down to the aftereffects of my sickness and nudged Shawnee forward. We were well on down the trail when some distance ahead I saw a mounted man blocking the road with rifle in hand.

It was too far to say if it really was Patrick Dunn. But when I halted and looked over my shoulder, I saw a similarly armed rider closing in behind me. This second fellow looked like Pat's brother Ed.

You know, I hate coincidences. I turned Shawnee to the side, dashed down a short slope and splashed across the creek. Once on the other side, I set her up the incline at a dead run. I had just reached a clump of rocks at the summit when a gunshot from the *far* side of the hill told me that I had ridden right into their trap. I pulled up by the rocks, flung myself down and settled in to watch a bit.

I did not have long to wait. A second bullet smashed into a boulder near my head and scattered rock fragments all around. I fired a blast to make him keep his head down for a second and was gratified to hear a yelp of pain. I yanked the saddlebags off Shawnee and slapped her into a run across the grade. Dog and I ducked back under cover.

Three riders crossed the creek below me. It was the two Dunns and a dark-complected, rough-looking character. This last man shouted, "There's his horse!"

Patrick Dunn yelled back, "Let it go! It's Sinnickson we want!"

I snapped off a quick shot and rolled to a new position as the return fire came in. I heard Pat shouting, "Ed! Ed!"

So I'd accounted for Ed Dunn. But how many more were there, and what was their plan? Another shot splintered the tree bark just back of me and reminded me just how bad things were.

"Sinnickson!" a bellowing voice raged. "Sinnickson, do you hear me?" Patrick Dunn screamed at me again, "Sinnickson, I'm going to butcher you! You killed Ed, and I'm going to cut out your heart and feed it to you!"

I knew better than to make any reply, since any sound would draw a shot. All I could do now was wait for one of them to make a false move. By keeping still, I was able to wing the dark-complected killer, but then things settled into a stalemate of sorts. I kept wishing that someone from the Angel's Camp road might come to see what the shooting was about, but in those lawless times, I knew this to be a vain hope.

Sundown would finish me. If a ricochet had not struck me first, the cover of darkness would let them move up close enough to fire directly into my hiding place.

"Sinnickson!" Jack Powers' voice this time, trying to work on my nerves. "Johns here says he's going to skin your dog. Says he owes the dog one from last summer!"

I don't know why, but that was the point at which I gave up despair and began to hope again. Somehow, the humorous idea of that Johns fellow holding a grudge against Dog for ripping the seat out of his britches; well, it just struck me funny, and I knew everything would work out, some way.

It wasn't full dark in the west, but the stars were filling up the eastern sky. I figured the rush was coming most any time, and I needlessly checked the load of the rifle again.

One star directly east of me seemed especially bright. In fact, it appeared much brighter than usual. As I studied it for a while, it looked to be growing larger and larger.

I was so fascinated, I almost forgot to duck when the bullets started flying. Dog and I ducked back successfully again, and I squeezed off a few rounds to let them know I wasn't done yet.

When I glanced eastward again, the star had visibly grown. It was now plainly a fireball in the sky, and it was headed straight for me! There was a fearful roaring noise overhead; then the sky all around blazed with sudden light. A rushing hot wind that accompanied the shooting star blasted through the trees, and the tops of several pines burst into flames. A second later there was a fearsome impact, as if two buffalo the size of mountain peaks had collided head-on.

The whole hillside shook with force. Boulders bounced around me, one clipping Dog with a glancing blow. Trees toppled like matchsticks, and a jumble of them exploded into a fire that swept the bottom of the hill on the wings of that strange, unnatural wind.

Through the dancing flames I could see my enemies jumping and running toward the creek to escape the conflagration. One of them shook his fist in my direction, but whether the gesture was meant for me or Almighty God, I could not say.

A few minutes later, Dog and I crossed the bare peak and descended the reverse slope. The body of the man I had shot earlier lay where he had fallen, unmindful of the inferno raging just on the other side of the hill. I whistled up Shawnee, and we rode out of the River of the Skulls.

EPILOGUE

IT WAS SOME six months later that I returned to the Calaveras country. After the winter snows had melted and the river crossings had become manageable, Tor and I pushed another herd of a thousand head up to the hungry miners.

If the second drive lacked the adventure of the first, it was also minus the tragedy. Will Reed's vaqueros had returned from trying their hand at prospecting, and there was no shortage of reliable help. By the way, Will and Francesca's child arrived—a red-haired boy that they named Simon.

The charred remains of a whole hillside made locating the spot of the ambush easy. There was even a pattern to the way the oaks and firs had tumbled down that sort of pointed me back to the meteor's impact.

I had a real worshipful feeling as I walked Shawnee slowly over the ground. I went there with the intention of saying a few words of thanks, and this I did.

The crater on the muddy hillside had already started to erode from the runoff of the melting snow. Shawnee was headed back toward Angel's Camp road when something caught my eye.

Washed clean of the clay and standing out against the backdrop of a quartz ledge was a black, fist-shaped chunk of rock. I knew it immediately for what it was: a piece of a shooting star.

But it was more. This misshapen lump of iron was a flaming messenger with a fiery sword sent by the hand of God. I have kept it with me ever since.